Survive at Midnight

Rituals of the Night Series
Book Three

Kayla Krantz

This is a work of fiction. All of the characters and events portrayed in this novel are either products of the author's imagination or are used fictitiously.

Survive at Midnight

Cover by James Price
Edited by Hillary Crawford

ISBN: 978-1-9505300-0-7
Library of Congress Control Number: 2016920434
Third Edition April 2019

https://authorkaylakrantz.com/

To anyone who has ever lost sight of who they are.

Acknowledgements

For my friends and family, for the many Chance jokes I've endured.

For my readers, without whom, I would be nothing, and who have continued to inspire me since book one.

Chance salutes you!

Rituals of the Night Series

Book One: Dead by Morning
Book Two: Alive at Sunset
Book Three: Survive at Midnight

PROLOGUE

THE VERY FIRST night after Chance's death, Amy slept on her own, without her usual cocktail of pills the nurses gave her to help her sleep through the night. Though she had been at ease when she went to sleep, her anxiety came back as soon as she woke up to DreamWorld.

A rumble in her chest announced that she wasn't alone. The Voices never made physical appearances; they existed in thoughts alone and passed information in a variety of sensations.

Today, it came as a chill down her spine. *We need you,* it told her.

Then her masquerade Keeper mask appeared at her feet, and she stared at it. The elegant white and black piece of fabric, nestled into the grass, took her back to another time. The last time she had laid her eyes on it, her partner had still been alive. Amy's eyes narrowed to slits. She had always hated her responsibilities as a Keeper, even before the incident with Chance, but now, regaining the role, she realized she had been running from *herself.*

She reached down and scooped up the mask, placing it firmly over her eyes with the soft click that connected it to her magic. Just like that, she was a Keeper again.

CHAPTER ONE

Four Months Later...

THE NEWSPAPER IN Cody's hands was heavier than it should be, as he read the front-page story for the umpteenth time. It was months old, but it still pissed him off, as much as it had when it was brand new. Most of the people in the compound felt the same, giving the newspaper ashamed glances every time they passed it. What Chance had done *had* been betrayal, after all. Taking his own life was the *last* thing Cody had guessed he'd do. How could Chance do something so brash, so *unpredictable,* without letting Cody in on some idea of what he was planning next?

Cody's nose twitched in aggravation as he threw the ugly paper back onto the dust-covered table it lived on, and swung open his bedroom door with a creak. Early in the morning, the compound was quiet as everyone slept. But Cody couldn't sleep. Not today. There was an impossibly loud voice in his brain that reminded him that he had issues, which were currently going unresolved, and he had no idea how to fix them.

One way or another, Chance would find his way back. He always did. Chance and his antics were just one thought in Cody's mind. The other was the girl who Chance continually risked life and limb for, the girl who had so much power and absolutely no idea what to do with it. The girl who was now only a couple months away from having their baby, and even though he had never met her, that thought made him even angrier. He wished the baby would disappear, wished *she* would disappear, so he could have his friend back—his brother in blood.

As long as the girl was in the picture, Cody knew that was impossible. Sure, Chance was dead for the time being, but Cody had a feeling it was part of a new elaborate plan between him and that ex-Keeper he had put so much faith in. He would be back, and when he was, he would gravitate toward the girl, just as he always did.

Only time would tell what plan Chance would pull out of a hat, but there was no one to tell Cody he couldn't form his own, to help nudge Chance's mind back in the right direction, to bring him home. Cody pulled the short knife out of his pocket. It was polished impossibly bright, the shine interrupted in the tiny gouge of the gut hook. He turned it over in his hands, the slight bite of the blade slicing across his flesh.

Luna may be imbibed with otherworldly power, but she herself was still mortal, and without the proper knowledge, he could rip it away in a heartbeat.

***

THE LEATHER COUCH Luna Ketz rested on did little to relieve the ache in her spine. She adjusted, groaning to herself when the pain intensified, and slumped farther down the fabric, flicking through the channels on the television slowly. One show blended into another with nothing really piquing her interest. She came to a rest on the news and swallowed, trying to urge her finger to keep surfing, but it didn't comply. Helpless, she watched the familiar story.

Lima's tragedy, the title read, and Luna blanched. Chance's suicide had been a *tragedy*—an unheard of destruction of her hometown's youth. Despite everything Chance had done, he was *marveled, admired* even.

"An attractive, intelligent young man in the prime of his life with everything going for him—," a news anchor was saying, before Luna tuned her out.

The cops knew he was responsible for Sarah's *and* Amanda's deaths. For his *parents'* deaths. Yet, he was *mourned*. Instead of being shown in the light for the monster he was, he became the face of undiagnosed mental illnesses in her county.

"Such a waste," the news anchor continued.

Luna laughed out loud, watching the story with a mind too stunned to think properly. She flicked through the channels more rapidly, as her hand rubbed across her swollen belly. Even in death, Chance was everywhere. Luna flicked to a different channel to see another version of the Chance story, how "blindsided" the town had been by his "sudden violence."

She watched, mouth open, as video footage showed him standing at the top of a building, his face pale and calm, as if the next minute of his life wouldn't prove traumatic. If he felt anything then, he certainly hadn't shown it. Luna's heart rate increased as she watched him bay at the edge.

They aren't really going to show him die … are they?

In the next second, Chance took a breath and stepped over the edge. Luna closed her eyes as the television sounded the thump of his body. He hadn't even uttered a final word, only glanced toward the sky, as if he was sending out a silent prayer. The memories of May came to her—the sight of his golden hair in the sun as he walked away—and she wondered if she had been the last person he talked to.

Why would someone record that? she thought in disgust.

Despite how much she had hated him, she never wished to watch him die. It should have been enough to concrete the idea he was gone, but instead, it left an odd feeling in the pit of her stomach like something was missing.

It was a strange time to focus on old news. It was Halloween. Chance's death was supposed to be a reminder that death wasn't a joke, that horror was real, and people should never take tomorrow for granted, because it wasn't promised.

4

It was a great message, but their approach was wrong, plain and simple.

They're taking it too far. Why does the FCC allow this to play on TV? Luna thought. *He really died ... this isn't a movie.*

Luna heard two careful footsteps as her mother, Rose, walked into the living room, catching sight of the expression on her face. "Oh, honey," she said, scooping the remote out of her daughter's hand to turn off the television. "You don't need to watch that."

Rose was a woman who, a few years ago, had been strong, until life beat it out of her. Ever since the death of Rose's husband, David—Luna's father—she changed. She quit her job, no longer having the energy for the work she once loved more than her family, and prepared to stay in Ohio for the rest of her life, working a part-time job at a restaurant, as a means of socializing.

"All day they've shown it. What do they think it's going to accomplish?" Luna asked, staring at the black television screen.

"They want people to be careful today," Rose said.

"They're immortalizing him, making it seem like his death was an accident," Luna pointed out, her head moving to glance up at her mother. "He *chose* to do it, because of everything he did to those girls. Why pretend anything else?"

"People handle things differently. The town is still reeling from it all. It's terrible to see someone so young choose to go down that path in life."

Luna sighed. It had been three months since Chance's death, and it seemed as if the news found every opportunity they could to remind everyone of what he had done—the suicide part—not the real tragedies, the girls who had died at his hand. Why was there no focus on the crimes he had committed? Or the people who had lost their lives to him? Why were people so quick to forget that he wasn't a *victim*?

They don't want to remember him that way.

Luna was sure the culprits of the stories were old friends of his who had chosen to be reporters. It was still hard for her to believe Chance wasn't alive anymore, to grasp the fact he had ended his own

5

life. The thought that she was free was one of the hardest concepts to come to terms with.

Luna glanced at the deep purple scar on her arm and thought of the matching one on her stomach. They were the remainder of his rage, his hatred, and his desperation. Of all the people he had killed, she was the only one who had ever made him think twice, because of his twisted need to *own* her. He had wanted her the way insect collectors want butterflies—something beautiful to capture and admire.

Luna rubbed a hand over her pregnant stomach again. At twenty-one years old, she wasn't ready for a baby, but she didn't have a choice in the matter either—Chance had made the decision for her. She frowned down at her stomach, hating that thoughts of her baby came packaged with those of its monstrous father—an unavoidable punch in the chest.

All she wanted to do was forget and move on with what was left of her life, but it couldn't be done. *I should know better than that by now.* When the bad memories began to bite, she took a deep breath, counted to ten, and forced herself to remember a happy memory instead.

It rarely worked.

When Chance was on her mind, *nothing* worked.

"Why don't you go for a walk, dear?" Rose asked, sitting in the armchair across the room.

Luna nodded, turning to study her mother, with the hijab that held her black hair from her eyes. *Paradise lies beneath the feet of mothers,* she mused. "I guess, Mom."

"When you get back, dinner will be ready."

Her baby stirred with hunger, but Luna herself had no desire to eat. She got up without a word and went outside, avoiding the sympathetic look Rose passed her on the way. Trick-or-treaters jogged past her, and Luna paused to let them go ahead, avoiding looking at them directly. She had seen enough gore in her lifetime to keep her from ever taking part in Halloween again.

A kid in a skeleton costume darted into the street, giggling as he ran from his friends. She shuddered at the thought. Skeletons were all that was left of most of her friends now. She glanced at the decorations on the nearest lawn—fake tombstones and coffins—and sighed, dropping into a steady level of depression. What most of the town saw as fun, she saw as a constant gaping reminder that she was alone.

Her stomach gnawed at her, reminding her that for as dead as she felt inside, she was still technically alive. She decided to comply with her mother's wishes to go home and eat, before the flashbacks started again. As Rose had promised, dinner was ready by the time Luna walked through the door, but she picked at it, eating only a bite or two, before she began to push her food around the plate to make it seem as if she had eaten more than she had. Her long, black hair created a veil on either side of her face, and she was grateful for the pseudo-shield.

"How are you feeling?" Rose asked after she swallowed the bite she had taken.

Luna shrugged and set her fork down. "Today is … hard. Why do people think it's fun to celebrate death?"

Rose frowned at her question. "Honestly, I don't know. At one time, you were one of them. You can't blame them for being naïve. They're just kids, sweetheart."

Luna tilted her head to the side, but didn't say a word. Memories of her old, normal life seemed like a faraway dream or a snapshot of someone else's life. What was it like to not have a care in the world?

"Are you thinking of Amanda?"

Luna felt the color run from her face. Halloween brought to mind the deaths of *all* her friends, not just the most recent one. "Her *and* Dad, really. This is our first Halloween without him."

A shadow fell across Rose's eyes. "The living room seems so quiet now," she remarked with a small smile, before she looked at the table, obviously regretting the turn the conversation had taken. "Things will get easier with time."

"Will they?" Luna asked, slamming her palm on the table with a frown on her face. "We've been saying 'it'll get easier' for months, and so far, nothing has."

"Do you want to go visit them later?" Rose asked, glancing up from her plate.

7

"No. I just want the memories to go away," Luna said and stood from the table, her chair scraping loudly across the floor. She then lumbered to her room, in the hope of escaping the vicious trap of her mind.

***

ROSE SIGHED, SETTING her fork on the plate with a clatter when she heard Luna's door slam down the hall.

Most of the time, Rose didn't know what to say to her. They had a horrible mother-daughter relationship that was so strained, it was visible. It was awkward at times, and ever since Luna had moved back home, that feeling had only intensified. Abuse victims had to be handled carefully, that seemed especially true of Luna, and Rose didn't know enough about her daughter to properly navigate the landmine she had become.

Rose had never thought of herself in terms of being a grandmother—maybe because her own child's experience had been so taxing. Part of her had believed her daughter wouldn't make the same mistakes she had, so when Luna had announced the news to her, she was more or less emotionless.

Did that make her a failure as a mother? She certainly didn't feel as if it did, but no one would *want* to admit otherwise. She had always been proud of how strong-willed Luna had become, how *determined* she was. Her future had looked brighter than Rose had ever dreamed, but now, it was different.

She didn't know when Luna had derailed, but her daughter was dead inside—she could see it in her eyes. No matter how much she tried to hide it, Rose recognized the look well. When she had been Luna's age, she had been in the same position.

CHAPTER TWO

THE NEWSTATIONS WEREN'T the only media form that had picked up on the Chance story—the newspapers spread their share as well. When the black and white paper was passed to Amy through the gap in the door, and she once again saw that Chance was on the front page, she dropped it to the floor. In the confined space of her asylum cell, newspapers were the primary way she received her information of the outside world, but today, she wished she didn't know a thing about it.

He was all she could think of for the rest of the day, despite not picking the newspaper up from where she had dropped it. It stayed in a scattered pile of pages in the middle of the room, and she glared at it from her place on her stiff white bed. It had been a long time since she had allowed herself to think of him, to think of *anything* outside of her world, and she hated the intrusion now.

Part of her still found it so hard to believe that he was really gone, that after all the damage he had done, he was snuffed out like a match. She held her breath, knowing there was a way she could *verify* the information, but that was another thought that made her skin crawl. What if he wasn't as dead as he seemed? Amy hated her gift, but she had to admit that at times, it had its benefits. Reading the newspaper would not bring her the comfort that it did to countless others. No, if she was to ever feel resolved, she would have to see for herself.

That night, she did just that. Cheeking the medication the nurses fed to her daily, she stuffed the red pills into her mattress when she was alone, and drifted off to sleep of her own doing. When she opened her eyes on the other side, she felt disoriented. It had been a long time since she had last crossed the boundary between worlds and her body was very aware of that fact.

When her eyes cleared, the room around her was a vast experience of white nothingness. The walls, ceiling and floor were all white. There was no window and no door. It was like a room at the asylum had been designed with the intention that the resident inside would never see the light of day again.

Then it came to her, the Voice.

"Amy," it said simply.

She stiffened, glancing up at the pure white ceiling, as if a face would appear if she stared hard enough. "Yes, sir?"

"Things have changed since your last visit."

Amy's mouth hung open as she struggled to find her words. "Yes, sir, I was—"

"Reasons are not important," the Voice cut her off. "You have been tasked a mission you cannot continue to ignore."

Amy nodded, wide-eyed like a scolded child.

"In your time away, your primary target departed the mortal world."

Amy bobbed her head, the faintest hint of a smile on her face. That was good news. It would *always* be good news … no matter how many times she heard it.

"There is, however, a catch," it continued.

Amy hardly repressed a sigh. When *wasn't* there a catch when it came to Chance?

"He has bonded with your previous surveillance target, Luna Ketz."

Amy pursed her lips. She already knew that much, and tried to keep a poker face in the following silence. A twinge of guilt and regret rattled her heart when she thought back to a couple months prior, when the girl had literally *begged* her for her help, and she had declined without a beat of hesitation.

Part of her was tired of Luna. They had been through too much together, to the point that Luna and trouble had become synonymous in her mind.

"Find her, warn her, and above all, keep her safe," the Voice commanded.

"If she needs help so desperately, why don't you go to her directly?" Amy quibbled and gestured to her hospital attire. "Clearly, I'm not good for this job."

"With the bond in her only growing stronger, I do not dare approach, for fear of contamination."

Amy wrinkled her nose. "Is that something I should be worried about?"

Although Amy was sure the answer was "yes," the Voice remained silent.

CHAPTER THREE

L UNA GLADLY HID in her room for the rest of Halloween. Rose was an avid neighborhood figure, which meant spending her evening dressed in a random costume she bought on impulse, to dish out candy to the kids who decided to knock on their door. Rose used to pick out elaborate outfits for Luna to wear, too … when she was home, of course, and Luna had never minded it when she had been little.

Before everything went to hell.

After the past four years of her life, Luna wanted no part of it. She probably never would again. A holiday that brought joy to others, would forever be stained with the horrors of her memories. As the evening progressed, she felt worse and worse, until she was finally able to fall asleep, to dream of things she'd rather forget.

The next morning, Luna's mood improved, despite herself. She went through her morning routine without a nagging thought, and lay down in her room, reading a book. It was a big day, but she couldn't muster the excitement needed for it. With Halloween finally behind her for another year, she faced the first day of November with an important appointment—her first ultrasound.

She googled the experience, reading the excitement of other women in positions similar to hers. She didn't even know them, but she could *feel* their happiness through the typed words on the screen, and wondered how they did it. She couldn't even create that much emotion in person.

When did I stop feeling human? she wondered, staring blankly at the book in front of her.

She wasn't sure when she had stopped reading it, but it held no interest for her anymore, with the worry weighing her down. What if they found something wrong with her baby or something wrong with *her*? Would they be able to tell its gender for sure, or would she be forced to wait four more months to see for herself?

Rose knocked hesitantly on her door, and Luna was yanked from her spiral of thoughts. "Are you ready to go, sweetheart?"

Luna nodded and sat up, studying her mom's neat bun. It was odd for Luna to see her mom like that. The hijab Rose had worn for years was nowhere in sight today, and Luna knew why—she struggled with her faith after David's death. It hurt Luna to come to that conclusion, to acknowledge that was the truth. As long as she could remember, Luna had wanted to get away from Islam, from the religion her father had followed like life or death. Rose had turned to it in times of hardship for comfort, so to imagine that she now had the same nothingness Luna did to pull her from the darkness, left Luna cold.

"You seem hesitant, is everything okay?" Rose asked as Luna glanced down at her stomach.

"I'm hoping it'll go well," Luna said quickly, passing Rose to go into the hallway with the hope her mother hadn't seen the emotion on her face.

Luna was quick to lead the way out to the car and sat awkwardly in the passenger's seat, twining her fingers, before she set a hand to her stomach, feeling the roundness of it beneath her fingers. After five months of being pregnant, it was still strange to think she was growing someone inside of her.

"Nervous?" Rose asked and climbed into the driver's seat.

Luna quickly tucked a strand of dark hair behind her ear, knowing the gesture was an answer in itself. "Of course."

"Do you want me to come in with you?" she asked.

Luna looked at her for a long time thinking, *Treat your mother with the best companionship and then your father.* She would love to have her mother see her child at the same time she did, but she didn't know if she could handle it. Finding out the gender was the most important point of the meeting to her. If it was a boy, she didn't know how she would respond, and that was the last thing she wanted Rose to see.

"I think I'll be okay, Mom, thanks. I'm sure they'll give me pictures to show off."

Rose smiled. "Well, I want to be the first to see them," she said as she pulled up by the hospital doors.

Luna smiled back and climbed out, before checking herself in with the receptionist to wait in the stiff waiting room. She tapped her foot impatiently until the nurse came to fetch her, leading her into a small, dimly lit room filled with equipment.

"My name is Rosalie," the nurse said. "Go ahead and lie down on the table."

Luna obeyed, taking a deep breath as she lay on the table, staring up at the white ceiling. A sickening feeling rioted in her stomach, as she remembered staring at a similar ceiling after her car accident. The nurse picked up a nearby tube and pulled up Luna's shirt, oblivious to the thoughts running through her mind. Luna held her breath, wondering if the nurse would notice the ugly scar Chance had left, knowing it would be impossible for her *not* to.

"It's gonna be cold," Rosalie said, squirting clear gel onto Luna's skin.

Luna let out the breath she had been holding, as Rosalie picked up her sensor. "Ready?"

Luna nodded, and Rosalie began to move the sensor on her belly. Luna's eyes stayed on the monitor beside her head. The heartbeat of her baby filled the room, the only sound that mattered.

"Your baby looks healthy," Rosalie said, before turning to Luna. "Would you like to know the gender?"

Luna's interest was instantly piqued. "Yes, please."

"It's a boy."

Luna stared at the monitor. Did that mean her baby would look like his father? Would he be *like* him in any aspect? Her baby was a positive thing to look forward to, she knew, but she was living in her past. She could see the faces of everyone who had died—people who, at one time, had meant something to her—and her therapy was useless.

Dizziness overcame her.

"Are you okay?" Rosalie asked.

"I'm excited," she said quickly, hoping to hide the horrified expression on her face.

"Well, I hope you can handle just a little bit more, because here … is your baby."

The wand on Luna's stomach stopped moving, as the image on the screen focused. It was hard for Luna to make it out, until Rosalie clarified. Then, an unusual trill of joy pierced through her when she caught sight of her baby.

"Th-that's him?" she asked softly. "He's so small."

Rosalie nodded. "Handsome little guy," she said, as the baby on the screen twitched and stretched. She smiled at Luna. "Do you feel that?"

"Yeah, I do," she said in amazement.

"Motherhood's beautiful," Rosalie commented, joining Luna in watching the black and white image.

Luna let the smile stay on her face. The baby on the screen twitched, and a tiny kick landed against her stomach once again, almost like her baby knew when she was upset, knew when she was thinking about his father.

"Here, let me get you cleaned up," Rosalie said, snapping Luna out of her trance.

Luna swallowed back her thoughts and shot Rosalie a smile, as the girl moved to rip some brown paper towels off of a nearby roll. She wiped away the gel on Luna's stomach, before helping Luna to her feet.

"It was nice to meet you," Rosalie said, holding her hand out.

Luna returned the handshake. "You as well."

The woman looked away sharply, and Luna's eyes widened in

concern, as Rosalie bent over beside the ultrasound machine. She picked something up, cramming it into an envelope that she then handed to Luna. "Here's a few pictures of your beautiful baby," Rosalie said.

Luna took it with shaking hands, looking at the floor rather than the nurse. For some reason, the woman reminded her of Amanda, and the thought was too much. "Thanks," she muttered and rushed from the room.

Holding a hand to her stomach, Luna made her way down the hallway, forcing her depressing thoughts back into the box they had overflowed from. Rose sat in a chair in the waiting room, and as Luna approached, she looked up from the magazine she had been reading.

"Well?" she asked. "Do you know?"

"It's a boy!" Luna chimed with that same odd surge of joy that had come from seeing her baby.

"Aww, congratulations, honey!" Rose said, pulling her daughter into a hug that Luna wasn't used to.

"Here's some pictures," she said, handing Rose the envelope, with the hope that she would let go and give Luna the only comfort she had left—her personal space.

Rose took it, instantly flipping through the photographs, until she beamed at Luna once she reached the end. "He's so beautiful!"

"Yeah, he is," Luna replied. *Just like his father.*

The cheer died out then and silence rolled in. The trip to the parking lot was awkward, with Luna clutching the envelope to her chest, but she couldn't decipher why. Inside the car, she stared out the window without a word, as Rose drove them home. She pushed away the familiar feeling Rosalie had given her, and for once, she let herself revel in the bit of joy she had felt earlier that day.

It was rare for Luna to feel happiness at all, so in the fleeting moments it was possible, she tried to capture it and hold onto it as long as she could, before reality could rear its ugly head and make the sensation shatter like glass against rock. She was having a baby—despite his conception and the possible problems in the future—it was a magical time in her life. One that she would have to recall to tell her son later on. For all her trying, the joy didn't last long.

Later that night, it left, and all she could think of was the fact that she was having a boy—*Chance's* boy.

***

LUNA WAS SMILING, yet Rose had an inkling that she wasn't truly happy. The picture her daughter had handed her showed the promise of a beautiful human, her grandson. The event brought back memories of when she had first learned about her pregnancy with Luna ... and the pregnancy before that. Thinking of Cassandra made the joy drain from every inch of her body, as she handed the envelope back to Luna.

During the walk across the parking lot, she hoped Luna hadn't sensed her change in mood, but at the same time, it was hard to focus on her. Rose didn't allow herself to think of Cassandra much, but occasionally, her mind would bring it up.

As if she could ever truly forget.

When they got home, Luna rushed inside, but Rose held back, looking through the pictures of the baby boy Luna had decided to name Asher. Even though it had been almost thirty years, she still felt Cassandra's loss, and was glad that despite Luna's seeming reluctance to have a baby, she had decided to keep it.

CHAPTER FOUR

6 Weeks Later...

LUNA SAT AT the kitchen table, picking at the food in front of her. She had been "eating" it for over an hour. She was hungry, but the meal had no taste. Eating had become simply mechanical, like everything else in her life. She set her hand to her stomach—swollen now with her seven months of pregnancy—feeling for the life inside. A small kick greeted her, and she glanced at her stomach with mixed emotions. She loved her son, but the thought of creating another version of Chance made her sick.

The memory of the video she had seen on Halloween, thinking again of the day she had found out what Chance had done to her, turned her stomach. *Asher, please have none of your father's personality,* she thought, her fingers clutching into her belly.

Luna wondered a lot about her future. Now that she had the freedom to live her life without an eye over her shoulder, she didn't know what to do with it. For the longest time, she had dreamed of an Ivy League school and a career as a doctor, but that seemed like another life now. Day by day, that dream had begun to fall apart, starting with the year she had skipped college completely.

While the rest of her classmates had set out to begin their own journeys after high school, she had stayed home with PTSD and a stab wound. After having to drop out of the college she had finally managed to enroll in, she looked ahead with a bleakness in her heart. As a young, single mother—with too many psychological problems—she was bound to have a difficult life trying to support her child.

She glanced out the window, at the snow falling outside. In Lima, Ohio, it snowed a lot in December, especially as it grew closer to the holiday season. Luna studied each flake carefully. Even though they all looked the same from a distance, no two flakes were alike … or so they said. Luna had always had a hard time believing it. If it *was* true, she wished that principle could've been applied to her life. If it had, so many of her friends might not have succumbed to the same fate.

Sure that Asher got his fill of food, Luna yawned and pushed her plate away, desire to finish eating gone. The phone on the wall rang, and Luna made a move to answer it. Rose rushed in from the living room to intercept.

"Sit down, you," she ordered her daughter, before scooping the phone off the receiver, eyeing her sideways to make sure she actually obeyed.

Luna didn't argue, plopping back into her chair with her hands on her stomach.

"Yes? Oh … huh. I see. Yes, she's here," Rose said, looking at her.

Luna crinkled her forehead as she listened. When Rose held it out to her, Luna's face turned in surprise, as she took the phone and held it to her ear. Since all her friends were dead, it was odd for her to have any phone calls. "Hello?"

"Hi, is this Miss Luna Ketz?" the male voice asked.

"Yes, this is she," Luna replied, pursing her lips. "Who's this?"

"I'm Bryan Lebeau, an attorney dealing with the Harris case," he began.

Luna was all ears. When he said "Harris," her eyes grew wide, and she almost dropped the phone. Harris was "Chance's" real last name.

"Okay," she brought herself to say, her fingers clutching tighter into the phone, with the urge to hang up barely resisted.

"We found some last right documentation recently, and your name has been mentioned in one of them," he said.

"It has?" Luna asked and her mouth gaped open as she tried to process that fact. *Why in the world would Chance have mentioned me in his will?*

"Yes. We need you to make a trip out here if you can," he said, "to go over some things and sign some paperwork."

"You want us to go to Illinois?" Luna asked, unable to recall the actual name of Chance's hometown.

"Yes. We're aware you live in Ohio, so if you can't make it, we understand," he said. "We could just—"

"No, no, I can be there," she said, not wanting to hear any possible alternatives.

"I'll give you the address, got a pen and paper?"

"Hold on a minute," Luna said, glancing around her for something to write with. She looked at Rose. *Paper and pencil?* she mouthed to her mom.

Rose nodded, before she pulled a small notebook and pen out of a nearby drawer and passed them to her.

"I'm ready," Luna said, propping the phone between her ear and shoulder.

"I need you to meet me at 430 Elida Road in Alto Pass, Illinois, tomorrow, promptly at eight in the morning, and we'll discuss these documents," he said.

"I'll be there," Luna said.

"We look forward to seeing you," he said. "I'm sorry, however, about the circumstances we're meeting under."

Luna couldn't press the end button fast enough.

Rose looked at her curiously. "Who was that?"

"Do you remember that boy, Chance, from my high school?" Luna asked, wincing as she said his name. It had been months since she had mentioned him out loud, and the sound hung in the air.

"The one who killed your friends?" she asked, eyeing the ugly scar running down her daughter's arm.

"Yes, that's the one," Luna said, swallowing at her mother's stiff tone, and set her hand on her arm in a too-late attempt to hide her scar. "That was his attorney. Apparently they found papers of his with my name on it, and they need me to sign something."

Rose looked as shocked as Luna felt. "Why involve yourself in this mess?" she asked, sitting down slowly in the chair beside Luna. "Do you really want to keep something of his?"

I kept his baby ... doesn't that count? "No. I don't, but I have to *know*, Mom. I have to know why I'm in his *will*, of all places."

Rose sighed, tapping her fingers on the table. "You're sure this is what you want to do?"

Luna shrugged and stubbornly repeated, "I have to know."

Rose could see there was no winning that fight. "If you feel up to it, we can go."

"It's in Alto Pass," Luna warned, "that's in Illinois."

Rose breathed in through her teeth. "That's about an eight-hour drive; what time are you supposed to be there?"

"Eight tomorrow morning," Luna said, pushing the notebook with the address toward her.

Rose looked at it, before she glanced at the clock and back at her daughter. "It's getting pretty late," she said and held a finger to her lips. "Do you really want to go?"

Rose was stalling, her stance apparent in her actions, and Luna knew how the situation looked to her mother. Luna didn't understand what Chance would have to say about her in his will, but if he left her something, she had to know what it was.

"I do," she said finally.

"All right, well, we'll have to leave now," Rose said. "I'll grab a bag with some snacks and clothes. Are you ready to go?"

"As ready as ever," Luna replied.

"Let me get my purse, and then we'll be on our way," Rose said, standing up from the table.

Luna put her coat on, carefully covering her swollen belly so Asher wouldn't be exposed to the cold. She and Rose dashed out into the winter afternoon, Rose climbing into the driver's seat, and Luna in the passenger's. She settled into the seat, trying her best to get comfortable with her awkward stomach, as Rose started the car. The trip ahead of them would be long, and the seat wouldn't get any more comfortable, once her joints began to stiffen. Luna sighed, setting her hand gently to her stomach. She wanted to ease her mind, but could imagine no way of pulling that off.

"Are you comfortable?" Rose asked.

"Of course, Mom," Luna lied, knowing there was no reason for Rose to make a fuss over nothing.

They didn't speak again, as they drove down the highway that would take them out of Lima. Luna leaned against the glass, grateful for the cool surface beneath her cheek. For all her attempts, Chance was all she could think of. They had a long past, even though they had never been close, had never been friends or acquaintances, only sworn enemies. He had wanted her, but her honesty and outspoken attitude had drawn his violence instead.

Even after his death, the battle seemed to continue.

Why would Chance write her name in *anything*? Especially something that might've been the last thing he ever wrote. Images from last May flashed through her mind, before she had the chance to think of something else. She remembered the fire that burned down her apartment.

The strongest memory of that night was not the sight of her old roommate murdered, or the feeling of Chance's dagger as he planned to kill her. No, her strongest memory was also her strangest. That night was the first time she had thought about him in terms of being human. Chance never showed a wink of emotion if he could help it, but on that night, he had broken, which left Luna wondering if he had really been the monster he always tried to be.

"Luna, honey, you're shaking. Are you okay?" Rose asked.

Luna snapped out of the memory, not realizing that the thought had caused her to cry. She wiped it away, hoping Rose hadn't noticed the tears, before she looked at her. "Yeah, Mom, I'm fine. Just cold."

She nodded and turned the heater on high. "It'll be a long drive, so if you feel like you need something, let me know, and I'll pull over."

"Okay."

Rose didn't push the topic further, but peeked at Luna from the corner of her eye.

Luna wouldn't ask her mom to stop for anything. She wanted to get to the town and get out, as soon as possible.

***

LUNA DOZED IN and out of sleep the entire drive, trying to turn over every few minutes, only to find that her stomach and the seatbelt made it impossible to do so. Before she knew it, they were in unfamiliar territory. With grogginess still wearing her down, she snuggled against the door, keeping her eyes open as she looked out the window.

"You're awake," Rose noted.

Luna stifled a yawn. "Where are we now, Mom?"

"Almost there. I'd say about a half an hour away from the edge of the town," Rose replied.

A ball knotted in her stomach at her mother's words. She didn't know why she felt so anxious to see the place Chance had grown up, but she was. There were a lot of questions she would be faced with as soon as Rose stopped the car, but Luna felt as if seeing the place where Chance was born would allow her to visit a chapter of his life that would otherwise be unknown to her.

She didn't quite know what to expect of Alto Pass or its inhabitants, but Chance's statement about his old home didn't leave her with a good feeling. Did Chance have any relatives still living in town? If so, would she have to meet any of them?

Luna turned her focus back out the window, to the abundance of trees beyond. It was no wonder Chance was so comfortable in them. As a kid, he had probably spent most of his time in the woods, away from the parents he had apparently scorned. Snow dumped from the sky, falling so heavily that Luna almost wondered if it was a sign they should turn around and go back home. She shivered again, unsure if it was from the cold or the thought of where they were going.

23

"Here we are, Alto Pass," Rose announced, bringing Luna back to focus.

She concentrated on the scenery that passed her and noticed how *small* the town was. It surprised her for a reason she didn't know. The way Chance had been so heavily accepted in Lima, led her to believe he had grown up somewhere big, somewhere more … populated. She would've assumed this town was long abandoned if she hadn't been called to meet someone here.

Luna hadn't even noticed when the sun set, but the sky was already purple, beginning to turn black, as stars made their appearance for the night. The town looked even stranger in the darkness.

"It certainly is small," Rose noted as she looked around. Obviously, she hadn't expected it either.

Luna bobbed her head in agreement. "It shouldn't be too hard to find the office tomorrow. I think this town only has one major road."

Rose smiled. "I think so, too. Plus, it'll be daylight when we look, so we don't have to worry about getting lost in all this snow."

"We're here early," Luna said disconcerted. "Where are we going to spend the night?"

"I'm gonna find us a nice hotel so we can get breakfast before your meeting tomorrow," Rose said. Then she glanced at Luna worriedly, as if she suddenly remembered her daughter was pregnant. "Are you uncomfortable? Are you hungry? Do you need to use the restroom?"

"No, Mom, I'm all right, really," Luna assured her. "I just want to get to the hotel and rest."

Rose nodded and continued to drive through the heavy, white snow. Even though Rose was silent, Luna noticed she began to drive a little bit faster. Luna sighed. She hated when people worried about her. Fidgeting in her seat, she tried to find a way to sit so her numb hip could find some relief. The seatbelt restricted her—it definitely had not been designed with pregnant women in mind. She couldn't wait to get out of the car and stretch her legs.

"There's so much land here," Rose said, as she observed the dirt road that lie under a layer of snow in her headlights. Lima wasn't a particularly big town either, but compared to this, anything would be.

"I don't think they get very many visitors," Luna said, watching the houses creep past. She was yet to see any businesses, and she wondered if it was because they hadn't made it into the heart of the town yet.

Or if this village even had such a thing.

"There's nothing here to visit," Rose pointed out.

"I hope they *have* a hotel," Luna said.

"We'll find one," Rose promised, "even if we have to go the next town over. Don't worry about it."

Luna blinked at her, wondering why she was being so optimistic. Then she remembered that not everyone had had to go through the things she had. Being happy was easy—and natural—for them. There was a time she used to be like that, though she barely remembered it now.

When they were about to give up their search—and Luna was ready to suggest sleeping in the car, despite the possibility of freezing to death—they found a small bed and breakfast. There were only two cars in the parking lot, which Rose assumed belonged to the people who worked there. Based on the size of the town, it seemed right.

Rose shut off the engine and hurried to help her daughter climb out of the car. The blast of cold air hit Luna hard, and she shivered, pulling her coat closer around her small frame. Rose walked behind her, as if she was worried about Luna slipping on black ice. Not a farfetched fear, with so much snow dusting the ground.

Luna looked at the nearby houses again, wondering which of one of them had belonged to Chance's family when he was growing up. Luna had so many questions, but the only person who could answer them was buried in the town cemetery.

CHAPTER FIVE

DESPITE SLIGHT CRAMPING in her legs and back from the eight-hour drive, Luna felt fine. That was the problem as she lay in the stiff bed, staring at the shadows on the ceiling. Sleep was next to impossible to come by, when all she could do was think about things she'd rather leave in the past. The whole place reminded her of Chance, and why wouldn't it? He was the reason she was here, after all.

Luna frowned, remembering the description of his parents' deaths. With the vast forests that surrounded the town, she wondered which tree had held their remains. Luna's breath was hard to draw in, and she knew she was on the verge of a panic attack.

Rose's deep snoring filled the room. She was already asleep on the small couch, had been for at least an hour now, and Luna envied her peace … in more ways than one. Her eyes were heavy, and her body yearned to sleep, but her mind would never let it happen.

That was the last thing she needed.

Luna sat up on the bed, careful of jostling her rounded stomach, and sighed with disheartened sadness. There was no point trying something fruitless. Quietly, she stood to her feet. Light from the tiny window glinted off of the screen of her mother's phone, and Luna stared at it, thinking, while the snores of her mother continued undisturbed. Luna hesitated a second longer, before she picked up the phone and hurried back to her bed. She turned it on, narrowing her eyes against the bright light.

She turned on the Internet and searched for cemeteries in Alto Pass. The Alto Pass Cemetery was less than a mile away from the bed and breakfast. She could go there and come back, before Rose ever realized she was gone. Luna memorized the map, got dressed quickly, and returned Rose's phone to the table. Luna put her shoes on, before she grabbed the keys and shoved them in her pocket.

Outside, the moon was at its peak, radiant in the clear black sky. The chilly night air was blistering; it had dropped at least ten degrees since they had arrived a few hours ago, but it had stopped snowing. Luna shivered slightly and drew her coat closer around her, making sure to tuck her long hair into the collar, and bowed her head to the wind.

As she neared the cemetery, all she could think of was the bitter cold that ate at her ears and fingers. She held a hand to her stomach, hoping her baby was warm, as she hurried to the cemetery. Her feet were beginning to hurt, and she wondered idly if her nighttime adventure would turn out to be worth it.

Inside the small gate, she searched the name on each gravestone. The only light in the cemetery came from a street light that sat about ten yards away from the cemetery, making it hard to distinguish one tombstone from the next. She was beginning to near the back of the cemetery and saw Chance's name on none of them. Toward the back of the field, stood a cross unlike the other grave markers—it was carefully polished, made out of an expensive kind of marble. On the stone base was the name "Stephen Harris."

Luna only stared.

Chance's grave, proof he was actually gone. Proof he had *died*. Until then, part of her had believed he was fine, believed he was planning something sinister, and his "death" had been a ploy to avoid suspicion and start over with a new identity. There was no denying it now.

"It's tragic really," a voice said softly from behind her.

She turned to see the speaker. Sapphire blue eyes shone at her from under bright silver-blond hair. For a heart-stopping second, she thought it was Chance. Her heart began to hammer again in that unpleasant, yet familiar, trill. Then, she realized the face was gentler, the features a bit plainer than they had been on Chance. The boy came to a rest beside her, glancing at her stomach. Even though her coat was thick, it couldn't hide her pregnancy.

"You knew him?" the boy asked.

Luna nodded, glancing back at the name engraved in the stone. It was the simplest answer she could muster.

"You were special to him?" he guessed, gesturing to her stomach.

Luna nodded again. She looked at the boy, wondering what he was doing out so late—in a *cemetery* of all places—and why he seemed so interested in striking up a conversation with her.

"You could say that," she said finally.

"The baby's his, I take it," he observed.

Luna sniffled. "How did you know that?"

"Anyone who visits a grave in the middle of the night must be thinking of the person buried there," he said, clasping his hands together behind his back.

"Good guess," Luna replied. "Is that the reason you're here?"

The boy sighed, and a smile crept onto his lips. "Yeah, it is." He gestured to a house she hadn't noticed during her frantic search. There was a light on in the upstairs window. "I saw you come up. Thought it might be worth the time to say hi."

"So, you knew him, too," Luna surmised.

"What's your name?"

"I'm Luna," she replied, barely able to look at the Chance lookalike. "What about you?"

"I'm Brendan. I was Stephen's cousin," he replied.

Luna looked at him, unable to believe she was looking at one of Chance's relatives. Coming into the town, she knew it had been a possibility, but she didn't expect to run into one who looked so much like him … and in a cemetery, of all places.

"Not biological, of course," he added suddenly, as if he could see the way she was scrutinizing him.

Luna drew her eyebrows together. "You look a lot like him."

"I didn't think so," Brendan said, shrugging.

"You both had blond hair and blue eyes," Luna pointed out. "He even wore his hair a lot like yours."

Brendan shook his head. "Stephen had brown hair."

Luna wondered if she was at the wrong grave.

"It's the same person," he said, as if he was reading Luna's mind. "He was adopted, you know. He always tried to run away from that, tried to hide who he was, like it would make that fact go away."

"Ch-Stephen was *adopted*?" Luna asked, not able to hide her surprise.

"Not a lot of people knew that." Brendan looked down as his boot scuffed the snow at his feet, kicking up a bit of dust. "He was always so shy; he kept everything to himself."

Luna could hardly digest what he said with a straight face. "Is that right? The Stephen I knew wasn't shy. He was the most popular boy at our school."

"I met him when we were just toddlers. I grew up with him. He was so small and quiet … I just wanted to protect him," Brendan said.

"Poor Chance," Luna said, despite herself.

"Chance?" Brendan questioned, pulling his eyebrows together.

"At home, I knew him as Chance," Luna explained. "I didn't know his real name until I read it in the paper."

"Where are you from again?" Brendan asked, glancing at her from the corner of his eye.

"Ohio," she answered, not pointing out the fact that she hadn't told him in the first place.

"So that's where he went," Brendan said, staring at the grave at his feet.

"He didn't tell you?"

"He didn't tell anyone, just disappeared."

Luna was silent; it was her opportunity to ask, but it took her a minute to find the nerve to do so. "He killed his parents, didn't he?"

"His adopted ones, yes," Brendan answered.

Luna frowned. That hadn't been the answer she was expecting. She could understand him killing his biological parents and ending up adopted, but why kill his adopted parents? Where was the logic? Remembering back to a conversation she had with him before he died, he had talked about his parents pushing him until he cracked. If that was true, she was left with another question: What happened to his biological parents?

"He left, because he did it." Brendan's voice was a silky whisper.

Luna's lips parted, and she wondered if Brendan had really said that or not. "You knew?"

Brendan nodded. "I knew everything."

"That was your aunt and uncle, right? Your *family*. Did you call the police?" Luna was perplexed. How had Chance managed to get out of Illinois for all those years, with witnesses placing him at the scene?

"He never knew how to handle people; it was only a matter of time, before he hurt somebody. I knew that, but I also figured he left anyways, so why bother calling the police? We thought he'd make a life for himself somewhere else. The one he had here was so hard, he deserved a second chance," Brendan said.

"We?" Luna echoed. When he didn't answer that, Luna asked a different question. "He had a hard life?"

"He had the hardest life of anyone I knew," he replied. "This might be wrong to say, but it feels almost right to see his grave, like he's finally at peace."

Luna studied the gravestone, as she said, "What happened?"

Brendan looked at her with a quirked eyebrow. "He committed suicide. You didn't know that?"

Luna shook her head. "No, I meant ... what happened to him when he was little? Why do you keep saying he had a hard life?" *What made him a killer?*

"My aunt and uncle adopted him when he was five. All they were told of his real family was that they abandoned him. I found out the truth later—his mother had tried to kill him," Brendan said.

Luna narrowed her eyes, picturing Chance as a helpless infant. *Innocent.* "She did?"

"Yep. Held a knife to his throat, I believe. Whatever the case, whatever she did, has always affected him."

Everything that had happened to her, thanks to Chance, suddenly seemed to make sense.

"I can only imagine," Luna replied, staring at Chance's tombstone with a new surge of pity.

CHAPTER SIX

THE TWO OF them talked for quite some time. When the feeling disappeared completely from Luna's hands and feet, it was time to go back. She bid Brendan farewell, and headed out of the cemetery, oddly uplifted for the chat, though the entire walk back to the inn, it filled her mind with thoughts.

Brendan's words were branded in her mind, playing over and over like a terrible lullaby.

She couldn't believe Chance's own mother tried to kill him. *What an awful way to start your life.* Things that had confused her for years, suddenly made sense, as pieces moved into place. Chance hated himself so much, he had run from everything that made him Stephen Harris. Luna frowned, as she realized he must've dyed his hair blond ... maybe in an attempt to mirror the look of his cousin, the one person who actually cared about him. People going through things change what they can—their hair, their clothes. He had done that.

The only thing he *couldn't* control was how cold he was inside.

Brendan's story explained Chance's distaste for people ... especially women. Deep down, he must've targeted them, killed them, before they had the chance to hurt him like his mother. It was why he craved love; he wanted the only thing he couldn't have, the only thing he was never offered by anyone. Despite Luna's hate, it saddened her to think he never had a real family. Hers was far from perfect, but at least her parents had been there for her … in their own way.

It was no wonder why Chance had fixated on Luna after her rejection. It reminded him of the truth—who he really was, and the fact that no matter how far he ran, his past would be right there with him. In his mind, he must've assumed he was saving her, by killing everyone around her, keeping away everyone who could ever hurt her in the way he had been hurt so many times. She didn't understand why he had chosen her to "save," but she made peace with the fact that she'd probably never get an answer for that question.

She used to assume Chance's suicide had been dramatic, because he was an egotistical, narcissistic jerk, but maybe he did it because, for once in his life, he wanted someone to care.

***

WHEN LUNA GOT back to the room, the sound woke Rose, who instantly worried about her daughter's disappearance. She played her usual game of twenty questions, trying to figure out where Luna had been in the middle of the night. Luna usually would've been annoyed, but she shrugged it off, her mind still mostly on Brendan, and let her mom tuck her into bed, as if she was five years old again. Luna was too cold and distracted to pay much attention anyway.

In the morning, Rose rushed to get everything ready to head to the lawyer's office, before Luna woke up. The second she began to stir, Rose rushed downstairs and came back with a large breakfast. Luna ate what she could, which was little for a heavily pregnant girl. Rose frowned once, but didn't comment, as she ate silently beside her. When they finished, Luna went to get a fresh change of clothes on from the bag Rose had insisted on bringing, and Rose checked them out of the inn.

Outside, it was snowing again, though the temperature was warmer than it had been last night. Luna didn't bother to buckle her seatbelt as Rose frantically began to search for Bryan Lebeau's office. All of Luna's thoughts were once again focused on Brendan and Chance. What she had learned last night was revolutionary. It made her rethink everything she thought she knew about him, and it unsettled her that she still couldn't decide how she felt—that this information helped her to see him as a *human*.

A few minutes later, they stopped in front of a small concrete building. Rose studied the slip of paper Luna had written the address on and Luna watched with her eyebrows raised.

"This is the right place," Rose said at last.

They didn't waste a minute climbing out of the car. Luna, once again determined to figure out what Chance had written about her, led the way inside. The building opened into a lobby with a few chairs, a desk and a receptionist.

"Hi, we're here to see Mr. Lebeau," Rose said to her while Luna held back, studying the plant by the door.

"Yes, you're Miss Ketz, right? He was expecting you. Go right on in," the woman replied, typing something into the computer.

Rose dipped her head thankfully. The woman caught sight of Luna's stomach and cast a smile full of pity at her, but Luna ignored it, along with the prickles of irritation under her skin.

The office was small, adorned with many delicate figurines and valuables. Luna's skin crawled as they entered. It was much too fancy for her. Rose's and her boots were wet from the snow, and they trekked the substance all over the hardwood floor, causing her to feel even worse, though she wasn't sure why. A small man with short, well-trimmed brown hair stood up to greet them, taking no notice of the mess they made.

"Hi, I'm Bryan," he said as he shook Rose's hand.

"I'm Rose Ketz, and this is my daughter, Luna," Rose said, pushing Luna ahead of her.

Bryan gave her a small smile as he shook her hand. "Hello, Luna."

She nodded, not meeting his gaze, because she caught sight of pity in his eyes as well.

"I'm so sorry we had to meet under these circumstances," he continued and moved past a mahogany desk to sit on the soft red seat beyond. Rose and Luna sat in identical chairs on the other side.

"As are we," Rose said.

Luna was silent as they exchanged small talk. With her head bowed, she twirled her thumbs, trying to be polite, but their conversation seemed to have no end. "You said Stephen mentioned me in something?" she blurted out.

Bryan turned to look at her, surprised at the sound of her voice. "Oh, yes, Miss Ketz." He sifted through the papers on his desk. "This will was found among a variety of belongings."

What does it say? Luna thought, sitting up in her seat, though she kept the question to herself.

If she asked it out loud, Rose and Bryan would only assume she was in a hurry to know what she got, but she didn't want anything from him … except maybe answers. He had been thinking of his death while writing it, yet she hadn't left his thoughts. Why? Why had she been on his mind during such a critical moment? Had he killed himself because of *her*?

"Would you like me to read the entire piece, or read only the piece you're mentioned in?" he asked.

"Read the whole thing," Luna replied without missing a beat.

Bryan cleared his throat and held the paper up as he began to read. "I haven't had the best life. There are things I should've done better; people I shouldn't have wronged. But nobody's perfect, especially me. I had more problems than anyone. Deep down, I knew that, but tried my best to ignore it. I know I'm supposed to write this to entitle my belongings to someone after I've passed, but I don't have anyone or anything, so it'll be quick.

"Just in case, in the very likely event that I shall perish—either by my hand or someone else's—in the near future, I'd like to leave my earthly belongings to Miss Luna Ketz. She'll need them more than me now. Signed, Stephen Harris, a.k.a. Chance Welfrey."

Luna was stunned and was glad she wasn't too far on the edge of her seat, or she might've fallen right out of her chair. The dagger and truck were the most important things he owned, and he had left them to her. He didn't mention a single other person in his will, acknowledging how alone he was as he wrote those final words.

"I have the dagger here," Bryan said opening one of the drawers to pull out a small wrapped bundle. "If you'd like it."

He pushed it across the table, but Luna didn't move. She couldn't. She only stared at it—the knife that had caused so much anguish. It used to be Chance's best friend, a dark reminder that her past was real. Ever since her little black book had been destroyed in the fire that claimed her previous home, she had no proof she wasn't insane. The knife was concrete. She glanced at the scar on her arm. It was a match.

"And here are the keys to his truck. It's parked a few buildings down," Bryan said, setting the keys down beside the knife.

Luna's mind went blank. The truck did the same thing as the knife, and she hated it, but at least the truck was practical. Haunting or not, it was a vehicle, and she needed it. As long as she ignored the dents and scratches that marred the inside from Chance's victims, she could imagine it was somebody else's used car.

"Thank you," Luna said to him.

"You're welcome," he replied.

"Is that all?" Rose asked.

"Yes," he replied, standing to his feet.

Rose stood up as well, and Luna struggled to do the same. She scooped up her things, and Rose shook Bryan's hand in farewell. As they neared the door, he spoke again. "Oh, and Luna?"

She turned to look at him.

"Congratulations about your baby."

A cold knife sliced its way into her heart. She got the same awkward feeling every time someone congratulated her. And like always, she had nothing to say in response.

CHAPTER SEVEN

"IT WAS NICE of Stephen to leave you his things," Rose said as they stepped outside of the office.

Luna could hear the tension in Rose's voice as she said those words. She didn't mean them, it was a passive-aggressive statement, an attempt to pry into Luna's real emotions without acting as if she was doing so. Rather than think of a response, she glanced at the dagger and keys in her hand. Chance's actions seemed kind on the surface, but there was something sinister behind the gesture, even if she couldn't quite put her finger on *what* was so sinister.

"Yeah, it was," she said finally.

Her hands shook as she clutched the objects that had caused her so much torture over the years. She hated touching them. It was hard for her to take her eyes off of the blade of the dagger, remembering when Chance had embedded it in her stomach. She shivered slightly as the memory washed fresh fear over her.

"Cold again?" Rose asked.

"Yeah," Luna said flatly.

She wouldn't tell Rose about that awful memory from four years ago, just like she wouldn't tell her about the one from earlier that year. Luna had the sudden urge to cough, and when she did, she brought the knife up by her face again. Chance had written that she would need it.

37

But for what? All Luna wanted to do was throw them in the nearest river when she thought of what Brendan had told her. Had Chance left her his most prominent things, because he wanted her to have something to remember him by?

As if our son isn't enough.

"You seem upset," Rose commented as she studied her daughter's face. "Are you all right?"

Luna looked at her mother carefully. Her concern was genuine, but Luna didn't know how to respond. She wanted to be honest, but was that possible at this point? There was no way to explain what she was thinking without telling her everything Chance had done.

"I'm just … thinking," Luna said simply.

"About what, dear?" she asked.

Luna tucked her lip in her teeth. This was her chance, but she took her time answering. Asher kicked as if he sensed her anxieties. "About Stephen," Luna replied finally. At least that was the truth.

"He hurt you, Luna. It's perfectly normal to think about it in this difficult time."

Luna smiled, but it was bitter and full of irony. "You don't understand."

"You can't let the stress get too high. It's not good for Asher. You've already been through so much, with what happened to Amanda, not to mention your father."

Luna looked at her, brain racing through thoughts again. She couldn't help but flinch at the word "father." For good reason. Rose didn't know who the father of Luna's baby was, she had never told her, though it wasn't for lack of trying on Rose's part.

"Chance was-was …" Luna began, mentally preparing herself in case Rose decided to overreact.

"Oh?"

"He was the father of my baby," she forced herself to say, squeezing her eyes shut to miss whatever expression would flicker across Rose's face.

Rose froze before turning on her daughter. "Did I hear you right?"

Luna nodded, flinching in anticipation.

"How did this happen, Luna? He didn't … I mean … did he …?" She bit her lip, and her eyes filled with desperation as her hand hovered above Luna's shoulder.

Luna knew exactly what her mother was thinking and wished "No" was the truth. But it wasn't. Seeing that pain in Rose's eyes proved to be too much for Luna to let the truth slip.

"No, Mom, he didn't," she said, somehow maintaining eye contact without giving away the pain in her own eyes.

"Why didn't you tell me who he really was?"

"I haven't told anyone," Luna admitted. It was the truth; she hadn't even told Amanda who fathered her child, pretending her friend Max had instead.

"I hate to pry, but, Luna, you never did tell me how exactly you wound up pregnant," she said. "If he didn't … do *that*, then how did you go from a relationship to what happened?" She pointed to the scar on Luna's arm.

Luna peeked up at her. "I don't want to talk about this right now, Mom."

Rose's eyebrows drew together, and her mouth parted, but no sound came out.

"I'm a little tired," Luna admitted before she could say anything else.

"Do you want to check back into the B & B to get some rest before we drive back?" Rose offered.

"Can we just go home?" Luna asked, eyes on the nearest snowflake.

Rose nodded, looking oddly surprised at how firm her daughter's tone was. "Of course. You'll have to drive Stephen's truck behind me, unless you wanna call a tow truck to bring it back for us?"

Luna stared at the hulking shape, before at last she said, "I can handle it."

"Okay. If you're sure," Rose said and headed toward her small car, stopping once to watch Luna.

Luna wandered halfway down the snowy block, hoping she wouldn't slip. Memories of Chance filled her from head to toe as Luna thought about how many things that truck had witnessed, the unaccountable horrors it had taken part in.

Luna tried to use her passive therapy technique, thinking of her old friend, Violet, which proved to be a mistake when she remembered how Chance had brutally murdered her. She shook her head to clear it, and through the snow, saw Rose's car drive away. She forced herself to open the door of the truck and sit in the driver's seat, the same seat that had once held a murderer. As she closed the door, she remembered being locked inside, wondering where Chance was going to take her and hoping against hope that she would live. Then he had stabbed her in the backseat.

Luna sighed and tossed the dagger into the passenger seat, disgusted with holding it, and considered throwing it out the window instead. Looking at the road ahead, she couldn't see Rose anymore. Not wanting to be left behind, she slipped the key into the ignition. Even though the truck hadn't been driven in months, it came to life effortlessly. Luna carefully followed Rose's small, light-colored car. Driving the truck was awkward. She instantly hated it and regretted accepting the gifts.

Through the shadows of the snowstorm, Luna could see the lurking shape of a cross in the distance. It towered over everything—an omen—and she tried not to think about it, about the irony of it, as she drove.

Yet, it was perfect. A dash of irony and confusion added onto everything else. Chance was all she thought of as they left Alto Pass a few minutes later and Chance's final resting place with it.

***

ROSE WAS GLAD Luna wouldn't be driving back with her. The alone time would be good for both of them. Rose had managed to keep her face composed, but the truth was, Luna's words stung. It was hard to grasp the idea of just how many secrets Luna held, but Rose would bet money that none of them were good. Tears stung the corners of her eyes as she remembered Luna telling her the truth of the nasty scar down her arm—that she had been assaulted by the same man who had killed her roommate.

Luna was quick to deny being harmed beyond that, but it was exactly that, which made Rose believe it had happened. She couldn't see Luna getting pregnant by that monster any other way. Rose wanted to get mad at Luna for not telling her all her secrets when she swallowed it back. There were things Luna didn't know about her either.

***

JUST BECAUSE LUNA was out of Alto Pass didn't mean a thing. The snow mesmerized her, and before she knew it, she was going through her memories again. She went all the way back to the day she met Chance, about a decade before.

The amount of snow on the day they had met rivaled what she drove through. Her windshield wipers made quick work of clearing the flakes that had gathered, but she could imagine them filling her brain and overflowing.

Luna and Violet fought valiantly to claim the monkey bars for recess. Today, they won. Luna victoriously sat on top, and Violet climbed along the slippery bars at the bottom, as she struggled to join her best friend. Even there she had been a slip away from falling. Shivering, they talked, waiting patiently for recess to be over, so they could return to the warmth the classroom provided. After a little while, Violet gave up on trying to climb and circled the base inside. The girls contented themselves with simple conversation as they watched their classmates bundle through the snow, remarking on the ones who slid on the ice.

The girls' conversation was broken by a tremendous amount of noise from a group of boys engaged in a snowball fight. A few were in Luna's class and the others were in Violet's. Chance was on the outnumbered side of the fight, but he fought like a true victor, wearing only simple jeans and a thick red coat, unlike his competition, geared in multiple layers of thermals. Chance's long blond hair had been short and spiky then. Even in the coldest of weather, he didn't bother to wear a hat. His eyes glowed their usual piercing shade of blue.

He had only been at the school for two or three days, so short that Luna had never noticed him, and Chance had never noticed her. After the snow stopped flying, things changed. Chance wiped what had crusted to his coat off and turned to walk away, stopping in his tracks as he caught sight of the monkey bars, and the tiny girl perched on top.

When Luna pushed the thoughts of the snowball fight away, a clump of powdery cold substance hit her square in the cheek. Gasping, she turned to look at who had thrown it. Chance smiled warmly at her in response, and she knew from that moment on that he would be trouble.

Her first impression had been completely right.

CHAPTER EIGHT

WHEN LUNA GOT home, she was beyond exhausted and craved an energy drink that she couldn't have. She stayed in Chance's truck, contemplating whether or not to bring his knife into the house. She didn't want to be forced to look at it on a daily basis, but she had already accepted it, and that meant accepting *everything* that came with it.

In the end, she decided to bring it in so Rose wouldn't question why she left it outside. Never before had she thought she would walk into her own house holding Chance's dagger, but she did it and she hated it. Luna shrugged off her coat and hurried to her room as Rose worked on hanging their jackets up.

Luna was glad to have a little while to herself to let everything from that morning sink in. In her room, she collapsed to her bed. It was only a little after two, but she felt as if the whole day had already come and gone. She tossed the knife onto her desk and rolled over on the bed, staring at the ceiling as she tried to get her feelings under control.

"Luna?" Rose's voice called to her from the doorway. "I heard a noise."

Luna forced herself to sit up, partially amused with her mother's sharp sense of hearing. "Yeah, Mom, I'm fine."

"Okay. I'm heading off to work," Rose said.

43

"Okay, Mom."

Rose passed her her cellphone, holding her gaze as she did so. "Hold onto this. If you need anything, don't hesitate to call me."

Luna nodded and took it from her mother's grip.

"Promise me," Rose said.

Luna looked her full in the face. Her mother knew her well enough to realize Luna wouldn't call for just anything. "I promise."

After a few more cautious remarks, Rose disappeared from the room, and a moment later, Luna heard the front door close. She was alone again.

Alone.

The word floated through her mind though she barely registered it. She was used to it. It was the way she spent her days in high school and her time afterwards. Chance had made sure of it.

Luna closed her eyes, rubbing tenderly at her temples. The beginning of a headache came over her, but despite her trying, she couldn't calm the anxiety in time to stop it. Luna missed her friends, Max and Violet. She hadn't seen either of them in months, and she would never see them again. Images from their funerals flashed through her mind, reminding her only of what they looked like in death. It broke her heart that she couldn't remember the good times, because any thoughts of them instantly took her back to the memory of seeing them in their coffins.

In an attempt to stay awake, she wandered into Asher's room. It was pale blue with a crib in one corner and a changing table in the next. A handful of toys were scattered about the inside of his tiny bed. It was odd for her to think that in a few months she would be using it to care for her son. He would sleep there, waiting for her to come and take care of him day to day. Despite his origin, she looked forward to Asher's birth. He would be someone who would love her ... he would give her life *meaning* ... the opposite of what his father had done.

She left the room, and took a catnap on the couch. When she woke, it was past dark. Despite it, she considered going for a walk to clear her mind, to try and escape herself, if only for a little while. She pulled on her big coat and heavy boots in the living room, before stepping outside into the crisp December evening. The briskness of the cold air brought her back to her senses, so much so that just staying on the porch made her second guess her idea of a walk.

The hairs on the back of her neck froze in a familiar sensation—the feeling of being watched. It was the same feeling she had had in Alto Pass, before Brendon had revealed himself. Before she could process it, the sound of footsteps on the packed snow hit her ears, and she looked up in time to catch a glimpse of a shadowy figure and the glint of a knife stretched before them.

Luna was caught knowing she should run, but also finding it particularly impossible to do so. Then, all at once, she regained control of her body and rushed inside the house, slamming the door behind her and sliding both locks into place. Her heart felt ready to give out as she tried to think about what had just happened.

Then the door clanged behind her with the thudding of heavy hands on the wood, and Luna couldn't breathe. She backed away slowly, tears welling in the corners of her eyes. She wished it would stop, that the this would end, and she would be free.

"Come out, bitch!" a voice threatened on the other side of the door. A voice she didn't recognize and had no desire to know.

Luna made a choked sob in response and held a hand over her mouth as she continued to back away. The banging resumed before she got her wish, and it stopped entirely. Tears streaked down her face, but Luna didn't move, just counted the seconds into minutes. Then she approached the door on tiptoes, making absolutely no sound. When she reached the door, she set her hands tentatively to the wood, cautious of a blade shoving through the surface at any time, and peered through the peephole. There was no one on the porch.

Whoever it had been, they were gone now.

LUNA STAYED LOCKED in her room for the next few hours, Chance's dagger nearby and her eyes searching out the window for any sign of whoever it had been. She saw no sign of life outside, but she couldn't imagine that they had left just like that. Her heart hurt at the memory and the way it blended into her past, into her memories of Chance. She considered calling the police, but brushed the thought off when she remembered how unhelpful they had been in the past.

Luna had no idea who the assailant could've been; who else would have a vengeance against her, besides Chance? So, she stayed in her room with the knife until her mother returned home. Only after she went to bed, did Luna venture from her room to check the locks on the doors and windows. Luna didn't tell her what happened, but like a child, she crawled into bed beside her mother and went to sleep.

So long ago, Max had told Luna that DreamWorld was capable of giving people *anything* that they wished for, even people who didn't have her ability. She could only marvel at the idea of what she could garner from the place. There was only one thing in the world she truly wanted, so that night, when she went to sleep, she let herself have it—a bliss so naïve and carefree that it took a considerable amount of effort for her to achieve.

She imagined herself in a life where she didn't have anything to fear, a life where she was in control. Every second of it was worth the work, until she woke up to the coldness of reality, and hated herself for ever having the idea.

***

CODY WASN'T USED to being pulled into other people's dream cycles, so when he felt the tug of one upon going to sleep that night, he didn't fight it. When he opened his eyes, he was miles from the compound, in the woods outside of town. Chance stood before him, arms folded across his chest.

Cody's eyes were alight as he scoffed, looking the figure from head to foot. "You finally dare show your face to me?"

"Yeah, and you should be damn well grateful. I have things to do, you know."

Cody sneered. "Is this about the girl? Again? After she already caused you to sacrifice so much, to turn your back on your brothers?"

Chance smirked and dropped his arms. "I'm a grown ass man,

Cody. She's never *made* me do anything. And don't you get it? She's not just some girl, she's the key to *everything*."

Cody laughed at that. "You really believe that, don't you? The girl is a hindrance to me, to you … to *everything* we stand for!"

"If you weren't such a jealous bitch, you would see what I mean to do. I don't just act on impulse, I plan. *Carefully*."

"Me too," Cody said, snapping out the tiny blade in his pocket.

Chance's eyes darted to it, then back to Cody, before understanding dawned on his face. His beautiful human features morphed into something animalistic, primal, as he lunged forward, pulling the blade out of Cody's hand before he knocked him to the ground with a palm to the face.

"It was *you*! You tried to *kill* her? What the hell were you thinking?"

Cody gnashed his teeth, blood from his nose running over his lips and into his mouth. "You're so much better without her. She's dead weight."

Chance growled, even more furious for the comment, and slammed Cody's head to the ground. "Is she? Or are you?"

"You ungrateful piece of shit!" Cody spat his blood onto Chance's face. "I taught you everything you know! Who would you be without me?"

"I'm quite proud of who I am without you," Chance assured him, and smashed Cody's head to the ground again for good measure, before he dropped him and wiped away the bloody saliva from his cheek.

Cody didn't show any pain from his previous wounds as he sat up. "You'll regret this."

Disgusted with his old alliance, Chance turned to walk away.

"You'll be back," Cody called, almost in a singsong voice. "You'll be *back*!"

CHAPTER NINE

W HEN LUNA AWOKE, Rose was gone, once again at work for an early shift, and Luna was sick for the solitude. She checked the house and locks, and satisfied that she was safe, felt suddenly filthy and cold. She yearned to take a bath and hopefully lose her mind to the comfort the water would present her. Grabbing Rose's phone, which her mother had left on her end table for Luna, along with a detailed note reminding Luna to call if something happened, she made her way to the bathroom.

Luna closed the bathroom door and set the phone on the sink as she turned on the water, carefully beginning to fill the tub. She stripped off her clothes and looked at her rounded stomach before she climbed in. She stretched out, dipping her head backward to let the warm water rinse through her black hair.

Luna sat back up, settling herself in place as she scrubbed her bronze skin. Like a bolt from the blue, the worst pain of her life erupted through her as her stomach shifted, then twisted, causing itself another spasm of pain. She sat up quickly, even though the action gave her another jolt of pain, and held her hands to her swollen stomach, fingers clenching at her skin, as a trickle of blood tainted the clear water.

Luna turned off the faucet, convinced she was merely hallucinating as she had done before. She blinked and tried to clear her eyes, but when she opened them again, there was only more blood. The water parted upon her touch, but the blood was still there, smearing onto her fingers as she skimmed through it.

Another pain scorched her stomach, and her eyes screwed up. She whimpered as the agony began to grow unbearable. It seemed that every year she experienced a pain in her stomach that was worse than the last, and this one topped everything she had ever felt. It beat when Chance stabbed her, when he had created the voodoo doll of her, and when he had taken her virginity.

Luna looked up at the cellphone on the sink and reached for it desperately, struggling to pull her heavy stomach over the edge of the tub. Her fingers were bloody as they reached for the phone. The substance smeared all over the edge of the white tub and dripped to the floor as she cried, and her stomach shifted once more. With her last bit of energy, she heaved herself over the edge and finally managed to grab the phone.

Luna sank back into the bloody water in relief, as she quickly moved to call Rose. As she looked through the contacts, she found the number to her midwife, Kylie. Even though she seemed quite knowledgeable, Luna had only seen the woman twice in the past. She had been advised to call her if anything seemed off, but Luna never called *anyone*.

Luna dialed it without conscious thought of doing so. "Hey! I need help!" she said desperately, as soon as someone answered on the other line.

"Who is this?" the voice asked warily.

"It's Luna Ketz! Something's wrong!" Luna screeched, fingers digging painfully in her stomach with the wish Kylie would understand the severity of the situation.

"What's the matter?" she asked, her tone rising to meet Luna's panic.

"I-I think I'm going into labor, but something's not right … there's blood everywhere," Luna said, suddenly faint as she realized more of the maroon substance had slipped out into the water.

"The baby is two months early."

"What do I do?" Luna asked, tears running down her face. She ignored Kylie's comment, since she was in no situation to point out that she already knew.

"You're at home?" she asked quickly.

"Yes," Luna replied.

"Stay there! I'll be there as soon as possible!"

The phone went dead in her hand, and Luna tossed it to the floor. Her hands gripped the edge of the bathtub, as the pain threatened to overcome her, and she began to pant, trying anything to keep herself from passing out. She had no strength to climb out of the tub. If she passed out, the water could prove treacherous.

Luna managed to keep herself conscious using breathing exercises she had learned in Lamaze class, and waited as patiently as she could for Kylie to arrive. Five minutes passed, then ten. Luna cried harder than she had ever done before, as the pain made its way lower in her abdomen. Her fingertips lost feeling from gripping the tub so hard, but the absence went unnoticed.

Twenty minutes passed, and Luna twitched as another painful spasm took her body over. She gritted her teeth, trying her best to repress a scream. The pain deepened as her baby found its way free from her womb in an attempt to make it to the outside world. Everlasting tearing pain made her sure she'd need stitches as she passed the baby's shoulders.

Finally, it was over, yet her baby never uttered a cry. She bent forward to scoop the tiny creature up. When she cradled him to her chest, she realized he wasn't breathing. She bowed her head as more tears fell from her eyes. Sitting in the tub full of blood brought Luna a cataclysmic mess of emotions. Tears streamed down her face and, though the ripping pain in her had stomach dulled, the trauma of her birth was still very real. Her gift was already going to work, healing the worst of her damage, but the progress was slow. With the corpse of her dead child still cradled in her arms, she hardly even noticed.

She looked at the time and noticed Kylie still hadn't arrived. Blood boiling, Luna stared desperately at her son's face. He was covered in her blood, eyes closed and tiny body still with his eternal rest. Luna wished more than anything her baby was asleep, but she was no fool; she had seen that look on many faces before.

"Our poor child," a shockingly familiar voice whispered.

Luna gasped at the voice and looked around, panicked that someone had broken in, but like usual, she was all alone. Another tear streaked Luna's face, as she turned her attention back to her still child. She stroked the side of his face, cuddling him close to her, as she planted a kiss gently to his forehead.

"Someone has to pay for this," the voice spoke again, louder this time.

Luna looked up at a figure in the doorway. Cloaked in all black with shockingly blond hair, was none other than Chance Welfrey. Luna hurried to cover herself, unable to tear her eyes away. She blinked, hoping her eyes were deceiving her, but when she opened them, he was still there. Just like the blood in the tub, it was no illusion.

She couldn't help the thought that escaped her lips. "Y-you're dead," she whispered finally.

He didn't respond, merely frowned, as his eyes caught sight of the small baby in her arms. "Our child is dead."

Luna looked at the precious bundle in her arms, and the pain came back. She didn't know why she was seeing Chance, but the death of her child was more real, more important. She'd worry about her sanity later.

"You can't let this go," Chance said, crouching beside the tub as he looked Luna in the face.

She shook her head, staring him in the eyes. He looked so real, so *alive*. "How are you here?"

"You called me, remember?" a female voice responded, and the image of Chance vanished, replaced by Kylie. "What happened, Luna?"

Luna blinked, staring at the woman as she tried to decipher what had happened. Kylie's eyes were wide, a few strands of her brown hair tumbled from the loose bun she had failed to gather her hair in. Her eyes strayed to Asher as she waited for Luna to speak. Even though

Kylie's voice sounded worried, Luna noted the lack of emotions in her face.

As soon as her shock was gone, Luna's rage built. "What happened?" she asked Kylie calmly, shielding Asher from her sight. "You want to know what happened?"

Kylie bit her lip as if she was unsure if she should answer or not. "Yes, Luna, tell me!" she demanded, her fingers clutching helplessly at the side of the tub.

"My baby is dead!" Luna roared, unable to contain the rage she suddenly felt at the tiny woman beside her.

"I'm so sorry … are-are you okay?" she stuttered. "Do you want me to call you an ambulance?"

"What the hell took you so long?" Luna asked, shaking in her rage as she held Asher stubbornly to her chest.

Kylie didn't say a word, her brown eyes growing wider as she stumbled away from the tub. "I-I," she stuttered helplessly.

"You could've helped him," Luna whispered teary-eyed, as she ran a hand gently across the side of Asher's face.

"Use that anger," Luna heard Chance whisper.

She flinched, looking for him before she wondered what exactly she was looking for. The sound of Kylie's words brought her back to focus.

"There was nothing I could do," she whispered, horrified. "Th-the traffic was too thick to get here in time."

Luna looked down at the bloody child in her arms once again. It was another death she would have to deal with, more sorrow that would be piled onto the rest. Gently, she kissed him on the forehead and set him down onto a towel on the floor. She grabbed her robe and wrapped it around herself before she stood to her feet. Kylie uncertainly did the same.

Luna stepped out of the tub and pushed Kylie backward, smearing blood onto her white coat. Kylie's hip caught on the sink, and she knocked Rose's cellphone to the floor in the process. Neither of the women noticed as Kylie winced from the impact.

"You didn't care to try," Luna hissed, tears staining her cheeks.

"There's never traffic in Lima. You could've been here ten minutes after I called you. Instead, you took your time, and now Asher's dead!"

"Let's be reasonable here," Kylie said holding her hands out, as she tried to pacify the distraught woman before her. "I tried, I really did, but the bus ran late."

Luna took a breath trying her best to calm herself like Kylie suggested. From the corner of her eye, she could still see the blood-filled tub, and knew her anger wasn't leaving anytime soon.

"Fuck you. You killed my baby," Luna growled and grabbed Kylie by the hair to slam her head onto the hard tiles on the wall. The sound of her skull on impact, gave Luna great satisfaction. Red splattered onto the white as Kylie groaned in pain. Luna released her hair, and the woman fell limply to her side on the floor. It wasn't enough.

"You have to finish this," Chance's voice said, and she realized he was standing beside her, with a wicked look in his eyes.

"How?" Luna asked, looking around frantically as the midwife began climbing to her feet.

"My knife," he said simply. "It'll end your fight in a heartbeat."

Kylie struggled to stand, and Luna knocked her down with ease, afraid the woman would run before she had a chance to grab the dagger out of her bedroom. Once Kylie hit the ground again, Luna was out the door of the bathroom. She hurried to her room and pulled the dagger off of the nightstand, arriving back in the bathroom at the same time Kylie picked Rose's cellphone up off the floor.

"Uh-uh," Luna said, stomping over to her.

The thought that the woman was trying to save her life, that she actually believed she *deserved* to live, angered Luna more than she thought possible. She stepped onto Kylie's wrist as hard as she could, listening to the grotesque cracking as she put all her weight onto it. The woman let out a shriek and released the phone to cradle the new fracture in her wrist. Luna took the opportunity to kick the phone away, and it skittered across the bathroom tiles, hitting the wall with a thump— Kylie's eyes on it the entire time.

Tears bubbled in them, and she glanced at Luna, perhaps

searching for pity. Luna looked back down at her, feeling nothing but hatred. With the bloody tub—and her dead baby—once again in sight, it was her best move.

At the sight of the knife in Luna's hand, Kylie let out an eerie high-pitched squeal that hurt Luna's ears. "Please, don't do this, Luna."

"You have to," Chance's voice lilted in her mind like an eerie reminder.

With her two options laid out before her, Luna found that she agreed with the father of her deceased child. If she didn't kill Kylie, the woman would report what had happened. The last thing Luna needed, was to be sent to prison for attempted murder.

"Why not? You did this to Asher," Luna said and slipped to her knees beside Kylie.

The woman was on her back, trying to pull herself away from Luna with the one good hand she had left. When her back hit the bathtub, panic filled her eyes, and Luna stared at her, drawing in her fear.

Luna drew back the dagger, carefully deciding where she would aim first, and launched it forward, stabbing Kylie over and over. First, she aimed for her stomach—hoping she would feel as much pain as Luna had when Asher was prematurely birthed—and then she aimed for her chest and neck. Kylie held her hands up, trying as hard as she could to deflect the blows. With one wrist already hurting, Kylie only had the strength to hold up her good hand.

Luna didn't slow down, despite the obstacle. Whenever her hand got in the way, she cut it, too. The knife was sharp; it didn't matter what Kylie tried to do, the dagger squelched its way through her flesh, releasing her blood. It sprayed all over the knife and eventually Luna, to add to her own, as her stabs got more vicious, more full of rage, the longer she worked.

Finally, Kylie stopped fighting. Her head slumped weakly against her shoulders, and her eyes went blank as her chest stilled. Luna's chest heaved from her frenzy as she stared down at the bloody body—the murder she had committed—and her shaking hand dropped Chance's bloody knife beside her.

Her logic and reason came back in time for her to be horrified at what she had done. Her attack had been so brutal that she had nearly succeeded in cutting the woman in half, yet the pulse of adrenaline made her feel more alive than ever before.

"How do you feel?" Chance's voice asked from the shadows.

She glanced up at him, vaguely alert of the warmth on her face where a few drops of blood had splattered. She wiped it away on her white sleeve, and replied, "Great."

CHAPTER TEN

LUNA WAS FACED with a new worry. Rose would be home soon, and Luna had a freshly slain woman to hide. Her shaking hand clenched into a fist as if she was trying to account for the sudden absence of the knife.

"Oh, my God," Luna said, staring at the corpse in front of her. It was hard to believe she had been alive only minutes before. Luna reached out to the dead woman as if she were about to touch her, to try to save her from the fate that had already been decided.

"Don't touch her!" Chance warned.

The sound of him stopped her in mid-movement, and Luna's head whipped to the sound of his voice. "This is all your fault!"

His golden eyebrows shot upward. "*Mine?*"

"Yes, yours!" she insisted. She stood cautiously to her feet, trying her best to ignore her toes sliding in the blood.

"Don't blame me. She did it to herself! She let our child *die*. She didn't *care*, Luna. Why should you care about her?"

Luna was torn between screaming and crying. "I don't understand what's happening! How are you here, Chance? You *died*!"

"In the Real World," he replied with a shrug, his tone emotionless, as if his words made sense.

Luna had a flashback, remembering Max's words nearly four years before. When he told her about DreamWorld, he had mentioned seeing dead people in it. At the time, his words held no significance, but she remembered he specially said that it was a bad situation—one to be avoided at all costs. Luna didn't know what it meant to see dead people when you *weren't* dreaming.

"Do you need help with that?" Chance asked, pulling Luna from the memory, as he pointed at the dead midwife Luna had all but forgotten about in the heat of the moment.

"What do I do?" she asked, mind split between challenging him and covering up her crime.

"Take her out to the back of my truck, drive to the woods, and bury her by the temple," he instructed.

"I won't have time," Luna fretted, running through the list of things she'd have to accomplish in the short amount of time available.

"Don't doubt me," he said.

"But I'm not dressed for it! It's fifteen degrees outside and my stomach—I'm ..." She swallowed and pressed her hand to her stomach. "I'll have to get dressed and then drive for at least ten minutes. Rose is due home soon! I can't leave this bloody mess in the bathroom!" Luna said, staring at him through wide eyes.

Chance's eyes glazed as his gaze dropped to her stomach. "If your gift could heal you through a stab wound, it can take care of this."

"But—"

"Hey! Do you want to get away with this?" he asked, cocking an eyebrow.

She swallowed and nodded slowly.

"You have to trust me. As you've said before, I am a monster," he said with an amused smile. "I know what I'm doing."

Luna blinked. "W-what do I do?"

"First of all, be grateful she didn't drive here. A car is a lot harder to get rid of than a body."

Luna had to acknowledge the truth in those words, even if she didn't want to.

"Pick her up," Chance ordered.

Luna glanced at Kylie's body, shuddering at the idea of touching her. Rigor mortis would be soon to set in, and she wondered how long it would take before she was stiff as a board.

"Won't she get blood on me?" Luna asked quietly.

"Yes, but with so much of your own all over you, no one will question why you decided to buy a new robe," he said, folding his arms over his chest.

"Right."

Luna swallowed away all her disgust and crouched beside the body. She hoisted the corpse up into her arms, feeling her legs buckle and the pain in her abdomen made a new appearance, but she forced herself to ignore it. Blood soaked through her robe to her skin, and she grimaced at the warm, sticky substance mushing with her own, but didn't stop on her way toward the door. She was in too deep to stop. If she did, she would leave a trail of blood that would eventually connect her to her crime.

Luna carried the body outside. It was dark and the thin layer of snow against her bare feet burned like an icy hell, but that didn't stop her as she hauled Kylie into the back of Chance's truck. The body landed with a heavy thump that made Luna wince.

"The sheet is in the backseat," Chance said suddenly.

She flung open the door and pulled out a long white cloth. With a shudder, she mentally compared it to the cloths used in a morgue. She hurried to the back of the truck again and threw the cloth over the bloody body, before climbing into the driver's seat, praying Kylie's blood wouldn't soak through the lightly colored cloth, in case someone got suspicious.

She listened to Chance's instructions to go to the same woods where Chance's cabin was—the place everything bad seemed to happen. In ten minutes, she was at the edge of the trees. Luna climbed out of the truck, and her feet sunk into the bitter cold snow once again. She bit back a cry of pain and looked at the white sheet. Tiny spots had soaked through it. Wrapping the sheet around the bloody carcass, she quickly hauled out the body. Groaning under the weight, she balanced the woman with one hand, and grabbed a shovel from the back with the other.

Pain already picked at the frozen skin on her feet, as she hurried through the woods. The midwife's blood continued to soak through the robe to her skin, though it was freezing now. Finally, she dropped the body to the ground and began to dig. Shivering uncontrollably, sweat accumulated on the sides of Luna's face, and her fingers froze to the wooden handle of the shovel. Luna wiped at the sweat, leaving a grimy line of dirt on her face in its place.

The ground was frozen solid, which made digging next to impossible, and she wanted to stop, but every time she tried, Chance urged her onward. He stood beside her, his gaze sharpened and serious the entire time. She worked the shovel through the multiple layers of dirt until she had blisters forming on her palms.

With the adrenaline all but gone, the effects of her blood loss were more apparent. Weakened, she struggled to keep her balance as she moved shovel-full after shovel-full of dirt aside to finish the grave. Her forehead was burning up, and her vision blurred. Every time she stumbled, Chance caught her and encouraged her to keep going.

"That looks good enough," Chance said.

Straining, Luna rolled Kylie's bloody, broken body into the hole with the sheet still wrapped carefully around her. She hurried to push the bloody snow on top of her, when Chance's voice made her freeze.

"Stop. What are you forgetting?"

Luna looked at him quizzically.

"Burn her, so it's harder to ID her," Chance said.

Luna winced, thinking back to the sight and smell of Susan's burning body four years ago, but pushed it away as quickly as it had come. She had no time to argue. Leaving the shovel beside the open grave, Luna dashed through the snow toward the truck.

The feeling in her feet was long gone, which made her footsteps wobbly and uncertain, as she made her way out of the forest. When she reached the truck, she rummaged through the small toolbox in the back. With the matches in hand, she turned to go back to the open grave and struck one, watching as the tiny flame flickered before her eyes. Her fingers were so numb, they didn't register the heat, before she dropped it into the pit, catching the body on fire, as if the blood was gasoline.

Luna gagged on the smell, not liking the déjà vu, as once again, she was reminded of the first time she had smelled it. She waited a few minutes for the flame to rip away the top layer of Kylie's skin. Even in the darkness, the fire allowed Luna to see how charred the body at her feet already was.

"Cover it up," Chance ordered, seeming bored by Luna's current dark deed.

Obediently, she began shoveling dirt and snow onto the flames, putting them out in the process. She kept working until Kylie was hidden by the mixture. Carefully, she smoothed out a layer of snow over the grave and looked at Chance.

"Now, get home before Rose does," he ordered, "and be glad you didn't get your robe muddy."

She nodded. "Thank you," she said, before the pain in her feet and fingers had her racing for the warmth of the truck.

She tossed the shovel into the backseat and hurried home to dash to the bathroom. She cleaned off the dirt on her hands and face in the sink. As quick as she could, she mopped up the blood that had collected on the floor with toilet paper. The substance weighed it down, smearing across the tiles and ultimately causing more work. Luna was determined not to give up. She wiped and wiped until the most noticeable stains were cleaned up. She tossed all of the soiled paper into the open toilet before she flushed it twice to make sure the evidence was gone.

When she was sure the bathroom was in order, she stripped off her robe and came back to the reality of her life. Her heart was once more filled with sadness as she admired the small form she had abandoned in the towel. She had to force herself to sit back down in the bloody tub. The warmth of the water sparked feeling in the worst of her frozen skin, and Luna bit back the urge to cry as she picked up Asher to cradle him against her chest. A minute later, she heard the door open.

"Mom," Luna said as loudly as she could and sniffled, letting the tears flow naturally down her cold face.

"Luna, is everyth—" Rose stopped midsentence as she caught

sight of the bloody scene of the bathroom.

Luna turned to look at her. "He's not breathing!" she sobbed, holding up her lifeless baby for Rose to see.

CHAPTER ELEVEN

ROSE RUSHED TO Luna and dropped to her knees beside the tub. "Oh, my God! What happened?"

"Go on, tell her," Chance's voice urged.

Luna noticed him standing in the corner from her peripheral vision and did her best to ignore him. He stood with his arms folded across his chest, though his sapphire blue eyes were locked on hers, as if he sensed her trying to pretend he didn't exist.

"About a half hour ago. I was taking a bath, and I got these pains, and it happened," Luna said, tears streaming down her face as she glanced up at her mother.

"Why didn't you call me?" Rose demanded.

"I-I was scared!" Luna admitted.

"I'm calling 911." Rose scooped her phone up from its resting place on the floor.

Luna nodded and stood carefully from her bloody bath, as Rose rushed out to the front room. The crimson substance beneath Luna's feet made the tub dangerously sleek, and she clutched her baby tight in her arms—part of her wary of dropping him—as she pulled her robe on for the second time that night. She continued to cry as she closed the lid of the toilet and sat down on it, cradling the corpse of her baby. She looked down into his face. A few drops of blood ran from his closed eyes to make it look as if he were crying.

The sight made her heart twist in a brand new kind of agony. Chance stood beside her as she brushed the bloody tears away. He set his hand gently to the other side of Asher's face, his large hand only briefly brushing against hers, but he didn't speak. Luna dared to glance up into his face, wishing he would say something, so the intensity of the moment would be broken. His eyes locked on hers, and she could see the pain reflected back there.

"They're on their way," Rose said suddenly as she re-entered the room.

Chance vanished instantly.

Luna dropped her gaze back to Asher as Rose crouched beside her daughter. Luna couldn't bring herself to look at her. The look on Chance's face had been enough; she couldn't imagine seeing the same emotion from her mother.

"How did this happen, Luna?" Rose asked, brushing the wet, tangled hair out of Luna's face.

"I don't know, Mom," Luna said, not taking her eyes off of Asher.

Rose didn't say anything else, instead she hugged her daughter a bit closer. In the chunk of time until help arrived, they stayed huddled together, crying and trying to grasp what bit of comfort they could manage. Both of them were too shocked to be able to think of anything else.

There was a knock on the door, and Rose rushed to open it. She let three men come in, and they hurried into the bathroom. Luna was numb as they moved about the room, observing the scene. At first, none of them seemed to notice her. When they did, one of them gently pried open her arms and took her baby. The other two swarmed the bathtub, documenting the blood that streaked the insides.

All Luna could hope was that they wouldn't stumble across any of Kylie's. She was so lost in her thoughts; she didn't hear the man who stood only two feet beside her. It was the man who had taken her baby away, but in her delusion, she didn't piece the two together.

"Are you all right, miss?" he asked and touched her shoulder gently to get her attention.

She jumped; the contact brought her mind slamming back into reality. Slowly, she turned to look at him. She could hear, but his words were muffled and hard to distinguish, like her head had been submerged in water.

"She's in shock," she heard him say to someone, though she wasn't sure who.

"Get her to the ambulance."

"Come on," he said to Luna.

Very gently, he helped her to her feet. She stumbled as her numb toes hit the floor, but allowed him to lead her outside. When the cold once again greeted her, she realized she didn't know where he was taking her. In her current state of mind, she hadn't heard the man mention "ambulance," and panic ran through her mind. She prayed he wasn't taking her to jail.

"Stay calm," Chance said. "They suspect nothing. All you need to worry about now is recovering."

Luna searched for him, but he was nowhere in sight.

The man beside her glanced at her curiously, noticing her reaction, and she turned her attention to him. "Where are you taking me?"

"The hospital. Your pregnancy had a bad complication. We need to know what's wrong," he said.

Luna nodded and allowed two men to strap her onto a bed in the back of an ambulance. Usually the restraints would've sent her into a panic attack, as her mind remembered back to her day in the cabin, but her emotions were too shot to react.

"Hi, my name is Stan," the EMT said as he sat beside her. "Don't mind me; I'm here to write down your information."

Luna stayed silent. She clutched her hands into fists at her sides and stared straight ahead at the night, through the windows of the ambulance doors. Why wasn't she allowed to have any time alone to grieve? Her tears hardened into the corners of her eyes at the thought, though she knew she was far from feeling better.

"I'm so sorry this happened to you," Stan said suddenly.

Luna heard him, but said nothing. His words seemed so pointless to her—they didn't make the situation any better, and they didn't make *her* feel better either. Closing her eyes, she relaxed against the bed. The next time she opened them, she was being unloaded at the hospital.

The last time she had been through a similar situation, had been after a serious car accident. When she had noticed Chance was employed at the same hospital, and was in charge of helping her, she had assumed he was going to end her life that night.

Instead, he had helped to save it.

It was almost ironic that, on this night, she was being shipped to the same place. Luna tried not to think while the doctors picked at her with needles of all shapes and sizes, trying their best to figure out what had been the cause of her premature labor. Luna was there for hours, and they still had no explanation to offer her. She wondered if there *was* a real reason. In her lifetime, she had been forced to learn that many bizarre things were possible.

They wheeled her bed into an ER cubicle to wait for the results of her tests. Luna didn't know where Rose was, but she hated that she was suddenly alone. In the ambulance, Luna had wished for it, but once she had actually gotten it, she wished her mom was with her. *Be careful what you wish for.* The walls of the cubicle seemed to close in on her, as her sobs threatened to rise again.

She curled up on the bed, a hand to her loose stomach; the knowledge that her seven months of pregnancy were over just like that weighed in her mind. She kept her hospital gown over her abdomen, not wanting to look at herself, and wished more than anything that she could go to sleep and never wake up.

A half an hour later, a doctor came in to see her.

Luna forced herself to sit up when she heard the curtain around her cubicle swish open. "What's wrong with me, doctor? Why did I lose my baby?"

"You seem to have suffered from a placental abruption," he said.

Luna blinked at him; her mind blurred, as she tried to process his words. "What does that mean?"

"A placental abruption is when the placenta is, for whatever reason, disconnected from the uterine wall," he explained.

Luna frowned at him. "If that was the case, wouldn't Asher have been born? Why did he die?"

The doctor bit his lip as if he were unsure of speaking.

"Tell me the truth, please, doctor," Luna said.

He sighed before he caught her eyes. "Your baby was alive when you went into labor, but he was breech. Without the proper medical assistance, he suffocated in the birth canal," the doctor explained and gave her a moment to process his words, before he added, "I'm sorry."

Luna's heart was heavy as she collapsed against the bed. She felt as if someone had stabbed her directly through her heart. There had been a chance to save her baby, but because of Kylie, she had lost him.

"Why did the placental abruption happen?" Luna asked, her voice weak as she stared at the ceiling. She gave up on eye contact.

"It's hard to tell sometimes with these things. The biggest contributors are usually stress and abuse."

Luna knew exactly what caused her stress. The conception of her baby alone hadn't been under ideal conditions, and the past few months had been riddled with nightmares and flashbacks of her past. Living every day with survivor's guilt, had been the hardest thing to cope with of all.

"In your case, it's most likely caused by a pre-existing medical condition. During your exam, I noticed a scar on your uterus. I would say that old injury caused it to fail in properly holding the placenta as your baby grew to full size," he said.

Luna wished he would stop talking. She would've been able to handle the situation better without knowing the details. With her eyes open to the truth, she was once again faced with the irony that threatened to suffocate her.

In high school, Chance had stabbed her so she wouldn't be able to fight him while he kidnapped her. She hadn't gotten medical help for the wound, because at the time, she had been too scared of the attention it would receive. She even declined an invitation from her first choice college, just to stay home and heal. She had no rational way to explain to her mom and dad how she had gotten wounded, so it seemed easier not to. Looking back, she regretted it, but she had been a kid then, doing what she thought she needed to in order to survive.

She never thought this would be the result.

Luna thought she'd be happy once Chance was dead. Instead, she felt unresolved. No matter what she did, she couldn't escape the lingering effects he had had on her life. The father of her baby was the one to kill him.

"I'm sorry this happened to you," the doctor said.

Luna wished—more than anything—that someone would shoot her.

***

ROSE SAT IN the parking lot, head slammed to the steering wheel with tears streaming down her cheeks. She was doing everything in her power to work up the nerve to go inside, to comfort her daughter, who no doubt needed her, but it was hard.

Almost impossible.

Besides the aching pain of Asher's loss, lots of old feelings stirred inside her, and she didn't know how to cope. She thought of paying a visit to her therapist, but knew she couldn't spare the time. Rose was perhaps the only one who understood the pain washing over her daughter, but at the same time, she was the most clueless person as to how to make it go away.

CHAPTER TWELVE

WHILE THE DOCTORS wrote up her discharge papers, Luna remained in the ER cubicle, alone. She stayed on her side, staring at the wall for longer than she even knew. At the swish of the curtain, she sat up to see a small nurse peering in cautiously. She had a pixie-like face with spiky, shoulder-length hair and offered Luna a smile when she finally worked up the nerve to make eye contact.

"Hi, I wanted to check in on you," she said. "How are you feeling? Any pain or discomfort?"

Luna shook her head once, before she settled back down onto her pillow. "I suppose emotional doesn't count?"

The nurse simpered and just like that, the urge for communication was gone. "You're beautiful, you know," the nurse said suddenly, as if she sensed what Luna was thinking. "You seem so strong."

Luna blinked, wishing she would go away. The woman had no idea what kind of mess Luna really was.

"I'm sorry this happened to you," she continued, simpering again, and patted Luna's foot nicely, before she turned to leave the cubicle.

Luna smiled sardonically at her words. She didn't feel beautiful; she didn't even feel *human*. No one looked at her as if she was; they hadn't in a long time. Ever since she had gotten pregnant, she had gotten looks she didn't like—eyes glazed over in an awkward mix of pity, made even worse now that she had lost her baby.

Lima was a small town; it wouldn't be long, before everyone heard what had happened to her. People who could never understand her would sympathize, pretending they knew what she was going through when they didn't have a clue. She hated them, hating being pitied, hated being the center of an awkward conversation every time she tried to reach out to somebody.

She hated it all.

When Rose finally did return, Luna said nothing. She didn't bother to ask where she had been, because a voice in her warned that maybe it was better to not know.

Luna's mood slipped into depression when they released her two hours later. By the time Rose led her out to the car, she was ready to explode. She settled into the passenger seat, pretending she didn't notice the look on Rose's face, and changed her attention to the window. The tension in the car was enough for Luna to know that Rose wanted to say something, but she didn't, and Luna certainly wasn't going to press the matter. The evening had been too long, too surreal. She was glad her mom gave her time to grieve, instead of prying, but how long would it last?

After bouncing back and forth between wanting comfort and alone time, Luna decided she needed to be left alone. Upon reaching their home, Luna wandered into her room and closed the door. She stood in the middle of her room, unsure of what to do next. It was hard for her to keep a straight face, a solid composure.

The people who wanted her to talk, simply didn't understand that talking about it didn't help her any. People of a sound mind were just sounding boards, walls for her voice to bounce off of. They didn't have the capability to imagine what she felt, and she didn't want to watch anyone bother to try. Luna wondered how she would feel just having someone in a similar position listen to her. It would be easier, she was sure. She could imagine her own questions.

What do you think about when you're home alone? Do you ever get flashbacks? What about panic attacks?

She closed her eyes, almost wishing she could trade places with one of Chance's many victims. As horrible as their lives had ended, at least she wouldn't have to live with the memories anymore.

Or would she?

Luna struggled to figure out how Chance had appeared to her. That was the one thing about her evening that made her almost positive the whole thing was just another one of her terrible dreams. Her nightmares were worse than what normal people experienced, because they weren't just dreams … they were flashbacks—flashbacks to when she had been stabbed, looked down the barrel of a gun, and raped. She was lucky to be alive, or so people told her. Most people in her situation didn't live to tell the tale.

This was one of the times in which she desperately missed Max. Of all the deaths she had witnessed, his had been the one that rocked her the most. If he was still alive, he would be able to comfort her; he knew all the right things to say. He had been her closest friend, her confidant. He was the only person who had ever been able to fully understand her. In her crazy, upside down world, she needed someone like that—a rock to keep her going, an anchor to keep her from drifting away.

Instead, she was alone.

Growing up, she had always heard the phrase, "You get what you deserve," but do you really? Did she deserve everything she had gone through? She wouldn't wish her life on her worst enemy.

In her head, she replayed the images of earlier that evening, wondering if she had really killed her midwife, if she had actually spilled her blood, or if the entire thing had been a figment of her imagination. The fact she had seen Chance, seemed to indicate the latter. She put her hand over her flat stomach. Had she really lost her baby, lost the one thing that could've turned her life around?

Despite her denial, the absence of life beneath her fingers was her answer. Tears tried to bubble in the brim of Luna's eyes, and she blinked them back, glancing at the table she had leaned against for balance. That was when she noticed Chance's dagger sitting there. She picked it up slowly, cautious of the blade that had caused so many years of unfixable pain.

At one time, Chance's hands had molded to fit the pattern of the delicate markings in the handle. The weapon had an extensive history, and in the short time she had owned it, she only managed to update it. The bloodshed from earlier was stained in her mind, lighted with new horror, as she remembered the ecstasy that had rushed through her. She hated herself for it … she was *becoming* what she hated.

Luna clutched the handle of the dagger tightly and ran to the bathroom, before she turned on the radio, blasting the rock music from the CD she had put in days before. She stared at the mirror, the knife between herself and her reflection. The girl she saw looked so worn down, cold, and sad at the same time, her face so hollow of emotion or life that she hardly recognized herself.

That made her next move much easier.

She flicked her eyes away as fast as she could, not wanting to look at the girl who stared back at her. Instead, her eyes traveled to the sharp edge of the blade as she held it up to the light, and lifted up her shirt to reveal the flabby skin on her stomach. The heavy purple scar across her abdomen was a ghastly reminder of what the blade was capable of.

If she was dreaming, would the pain wake her up?

Her hand shook, and her fingers flexed. It didn't feel right to be on the other side of the blade, the side that could *control* it. Without thinking, she moved over to the toilet and sat down. Her mind didn't process any thoughts beside those about the knife in her hand. As she held it dangerously close to herself, she glanced at the line on her arm.

She pulled down the waistband of her pants to reveal the caramel skin on her thigh. She lowered the blade. Would she even feel it in the state she was in? The cold metal rested against her flesh and part of her almost reconsidered it, but she easily dismissed it as thoughts of Asher filled her mind. With a quick slash, she opened the skin beneath the blade and gasped at the pain, at how *real* it was, as the endorphins flooded her system.

The pain sharpened and blood welled on the surface of the new laceration. She watched it streak down her skin and onto the toilet beneath her. The music from the CD player barely registered in her mind, and she found herself somehow calmer than she had been in her "stable" state of mind.

Luna stood up, watching as drops of blood streaked down her leg. Without meaning to, she left a trail from the toilet to the sink. She ignored it and set the blade on the counter, more of her own blood dripping down to stain the inside of the white sink.

She didn't move. She *couldn't* move.

A thought stitched itself in her mind; if this was real, why had she seen Chance?

CHAPTER THIRTEEN

REESE BARELY GLANCED at the graded exam as it was placed on his desk. He didn't have to in order to see the giant "F" written across the top. Growling in his throat, he wadded it up and threw it into his backpack, not caring who would see, before he stormed out of the classroom despite his professor's protests. He hated college, and the way it always made him feel so stupid. That was part of what had drawn him toward being a drama major—acting was something he was good at. People smarts were easy, book smarts weren't.

No one followed him or even tried to stop him, as he stormed down the hallway, only stopping once he bounded down the stairs to catch his breath. His fingers gripped around the railing, and for a moment, just a fraction of a second, he caught sight of the bracelet on his wrist. It was the one woven from thread that Amanda had made him years before, back when they'd been dating.

He forced his eyes away. Like the test, the memory hurt him and left him feeling inadequate. Amanda hadn't wanted a thing to do with him, then she had died. Yet, he couldn't bring himself to stop wearing her gift. Reese's heart twanged in guilt and regret, as he remembered that he *was* partly to blame for her fate. Her murderer had gotten the idea to

73

act as he had on *Reese's* behalf. Reese alternated days where he felt righteous for what he had done, and days where he felt sorry. Unfortunately, today was the latter of the two.

The universe has a way of kicking me when I'm down, he thought, and laughed into the empty hallway.

It didn't matter. Nothing really did, not when the Other Realm existed with the seemingly sole purpose of morphing this world, of manipulating all the painful details. Except for death—that was something that couldn't be changed.

Not completely *true,* he thought and sat down on the steps outside of the campus building he had just emerged from.

Chance Welfrey was a man who Reese should hate. He *had,* after all, murdered Amanda, but Reese could never imagine finding any negative emotion to associate with him. Chance was something more than a man. He was a God in a way, manipulating the Other Realm to the point where he was beginning to learn the secrets of life and death and manipulate those as well.

It had been a long time since the last time Chance had appeared to him in DreamWorld, and idly, Reese began to wonder if the plan was a failure after all. Several times, he had found himself skimming through the notes he still had from his apprenticeship, but he had done and instructed as they said. It should work.

So, where was Chance?

CHAPTER FOURTEEN

L UNA WAS EXHAUSTED, her eyes and face raw as she lay in bed, the skin worn away by hours of crying. She held a hand to her flat stomach, acknowledging the fact she had lost her baby, even though it pained her to do so. Every time that line registered in her mind, fresh salty tears scored the raw flesh on her face.

Her baby was as dead as his father, and she lost herself in thoughts of her loneliness, how she was secluded from the rest of the world without the tiny ray of happiness Asher had offered. Most of the night she cried about him, but occasionally, her mind would present memories of Kylie's murder. That, of course, didn't make her sad, but it *did* give her yet another thing to stress over.

Luna curled into a tight ball, trying her best to get to sleep, but it was a luxury she couldn't come by. Her body rattled with her small cries until her chest ached once again. When her face started to sting like sandpaper scratching away at her skin, she tried to get herself to calm down enough to drift off to unconsciousness.

A gentle breeze stirring over her face woke her up. She sat up, rubbing her sore swollen eyes, and realized she was lying on the ground. Trees and lush foliage surrounded her, and she swallowed nervously as she stood to her feet. She had an idea where she was, but hoped it wasn't true.

Years had passed since the last time she had been here. The breeze blew again, billowing her clothing about her slight frame and causing her to shiver. It wasn't cold that caused it, but uncertainty. Glancing at herself, she noticed the loose black dress she wore. It was knee length, a gentle V-neck with sleeves curling down to her hands. She didn't recognize it, but that didn't stop her from not liking it.

Luna took a wary step forward, and a twig snapped beneath her foot, causing her to jump, then she chastised herself for her own skittishness. She expected trouble to somehow find its way to her, since it always did. When she realized she was alone, she looked up toward the sky. The canopy of branches left little room for sunlight to filter through, and she had the feeling she was in DreamWorld, in the same woods where her late best friend, Violet, had lost her life, and Luna herself had been kidnapped.

The memories were heavy, but she pushed herself onward through the forest. A tingling in her spine warned her the path that lay ahead was dangerous, but her curiosity placated her, driving her onward against her instincts. After years of being freed from the curse of her nightmares, she wondered what would bring her back now. Did it have something to do with Asher? Eventually, she reached an ashen path and familiar terror shot up her spine. What demon urged her this way, she didn't know, but she found herself following it just the same.

When the path emptied into a clearing, Luna stood on the end, staring at the open ground ahead of her. There it was, the cabin. In the Real World, the cabin before her was a broken down mess, overgrown with foliage from lack of use, before Chance had burned it down to the ground after Sarah's murder. In DreamWorld, however, it held together as if it had never been destroyed.

She set her fingertips to the wood of the door. It felt so real, so sturdy beneath her fingers that she still couldn't believe it wasn't. Her heart hammered in her chest as she pondered going inside. Her body was on autopilot as she prepared to push the door open, when it opened from the inside instead, knocking the wind from her lungs. She stood face to face with Chance, and he stared at her, his amused blue eyes wide, as he studied her with a hand on the doorknob.

"Luna," was all he managed to say.

She didn't know why she suddenly felt ashamed, but she did. After everything he had done to her, she had sought him out, and now she wasn't sure why.

"Hi," she said, bowing her head to study the grass that lined the cabin. She didn't want to meet his eyes.

"What are you doing here?" he asked, his tone even and emotionless—no way to guess what he was thinking.

"I woke up here," Luna said, her voice wavering.

His blond eyebrows pulled together. "D-did you *want* to come here?"

"Maybe," she ventured, keeping her eyes on the ground, though they squinted in anticipation of his answer.

"Oh?" he asked, all traces of his cocky attitude lost to his surprise.

She swallowed hard, convincing herself to look at him. He eagerly met her gaze. "You're the only one who understands how I feel." Saying those words was like trying to throw up glass.

"I knew you'd come to me eventually," he said smirking, which crumpled the scar on his left cheek.

Luna narrowed her eyes at the sucker punch of his words. Fresh tears started to streak down her face, and she knew they mostly came from embarrassment. What had she been thinking to come to *him*, of all people? Chance had been out to ruin her life. Why had she thought for an instant that he would suddenly decide to help her?

"I'm a *killer*, Chance," she whispered, wishing he would understand the depth of her pain, wishing *someone* would, even if he would just use it as fodder to gloat over.

"Me and you both," he said shrugging, as he lifted his hand to observe his fingernails casually.

Her eyes welled with more tears, and she was ready to admit defeat, to turn and head back into the woods to curl up and die, positive he would be no help to her, when he set a hand on her shoulder, freezing her in place. The smile was gone now.

"Come in," he invited, as if he could sense her thought.

As he stepped aside to give her room, she hesitated. Was this really a smart move? Memories of her stay in the cabin flashed through her mind, reminding her of the painful laceration in her abdomen, as clearly as the day it had happened. When he crossed his arms over his chest, her eyes were drawn to him. The sapphire blue pits made her shudder as she remembered how Asher had been conceived, and she unconsciously held a hand over the scar on her stomach.

"Well?" he asked. "Are you coming in or not?"

She steeled her nerves, deciding there was nothing more he could do to her that he hadn't already done. If he killed her, he'd only put her out of her misery. She threw her fear aside, nodded, and went to sit on one of the two chairs inside. Never in a million years would she have actually done that, before the untimely death of her baby, but since it had happened, she almost felt like a different person.

She was.

Chance situated himself into the other chair across from her. The windows were covered over in black, allowing no sunlight to leak inside. One lit candle sat on top of the table, casting eerie shadows over Chance's pale skin. He looked at her cautiously, waiting for her to speak. His eyes sparkled as they focused on her face, searching for some sign of thought.

"What did you need to talk about?" he asked. "It must be pretty bad for you to come to me."

"I-I keep thinking about last night. I can't stop myself from crying," she admitted and wiped away a tear in demonstration.

"You're upset about losing our baby. It's perfectly understandable," he said gently, resting his elbow on his side of the table. "You know as well as I do that it wasn't your fault."

The way he said "our baby" sent chills down Luna's spine, but she ignored them. "Sometimes it feels like it was."

"How?" he asked skeptically.

"I should've driven myself to the hospital when I first got the pains."

He narrowed his eyes at her. "You're smarter than that. How

could you have driven anywhere in as much pain as you were in? Were you looking to get in another wreck?"

Luna clamped her lips together.

"Exactly my point," he said and sat back in his seat.

"Even if Asher's death wasn't my fault, Kylie's was," Luna said quietly.

Chance raised a pale eyebrow yet again. "Really?" he asked, setting a hand on the table to drum his thumb on the surface. "You're still going on about that bitch? You can't honestly tell me you give a damn about that whore who costed us our son."

Luna watched the fiery glint in his eyes. It was a look she had seen a number of times in the past. She wiped at the corner of her eye to dry the tears that had collected there, considering she *didn't* care about the midwife, only the crime she had committed; she worried about getting caught.

"You're right," she said at last, but said it to the table rather than him.

He nodded briskly, a hint of a smile on his face again. "I know you better than that."

Luna simpered. From anyone else, that might've been a comforting statement, but not from him. "How do you keep yourself from caring about what you've done to other people? I mean it's—"

He cut her off. "I don't let it show. That doesn't mean I don't feel it," he replied, catching, and holding, her gaze.

Luna allowed herself to look into his eyes again, and caught the haunted look that hung there.

She shivered and dared herself to ask, "Do you regret what you've done?"

"To all those people? No," he said. "Most of them, like Kylie, deserved it for some reason or another."

"What about me? Did I deserve to get stabbed and raped?" she asked, unsure where the sudden surge of fury came from.

His jaw clenched. "No," he said softly, and it sounded as if it was *his* turn to throw up glass.

"Then why did you do it? To take your pain out on me?"

He looked down at his hands without a word. It was one of the only times Luna had ever seen him speechless.

Luna, dangerously close to progress, decided to change her approach. "Was I the girl you were talking about back in the apartment?"

Chance looked up to show the contemplation in his eyes, before he stood to his feet. Luna scooted backward in her chair, tilting her face upward to watch him. Every footstep seemed to happen in slow motion, and then he reached her. He cupped her face gently in his hand, and she went rigid in his grip.

He could snap her neck so easily. After everything, she wondered if he would do just that. Instead, his thumb gently stroked her jawbone as if he were admiring her. He judged her movements before he bent down to push his lips to hers. Stunned at the contact, she pushed him away, heart fluttering with its usual twitch of panic.

"What are you doing?" she demanded.

"You asked. I answered," he replied, his face hovering an inch away from hers.

Luna stared back at him. "Why me?"

"I've told you that before," he replied and dragged his hand from her. "You were always different from the rest of them. The only girl I ever met who was true to herself. Who didn't just cave to peer pressure, but held her own."

A tear dripped free from Luna's eye, and he wiped it away gently. The girl he described had existed at some point, but she didn't anymore. Inside, she was hollow; outside, she was a shell. With his confession hanging in the air, all Luna could do was stare.

She could remember the Rosebone, the thing that bonded her to him, and the fact that for all her trying, she had no idea how to break that connection. Now, it was all too easy to shrug away the thoughts. Things had changed so radically between her and Chance, in a way that no one could repair, and it was becoming even harder for her to know if she cared or not.

"You don't have to be alone anymore, Luna," Chance said, timing perfect to her thoughts, as if their minds were synchronized. "I can be your family now."

"I've underestimated you so much," Luna whispered, looking up at him through glazed eyes.

"What do you think of me now?" he asked, his voice sounding a bit rougher, as if he was trying too hard to control the tone of his voice.

Her answer was critical, and she knew it. "I don't know."

"That's better than how you used to feel," he said small bitter smile on his face.

Luna blinked, and when she opened her eyes again, it was morning.

CHAPTER FIFTEEN

"*THAT'S BETTER THAN how you used to feel.*" Chance's words rang in Luna's mind as she lay in bed.

Luna stared blankly at the ceiling of her room, numb all over. His words had been so straightforward, so honest; the emotions in his face had been the most truthful ones she had ever seen. It hit her hard to realize her opinion of him had *changed* over the past week…the past twelve hours especially. Her mind was so rattled by that discovery that she wasn't sure what she felt of anything.

It was as if she was living in a surreal version of reality, another dimension that fell somewhere between DreamWorld and reality as she knew it. Last night, she hadn't consciously decided to seek Chance out, but once she had woken up in the familiar strips of woods in DreamWorld, she had shrugged off her feelings and decided it was her best option. The fact she had so freely decided something so heavy scared her. It was like she hadn't been controlled by herself but instead someone inside her like a zip-up costume.

Last night had shown her there was a new part of her, a part that actually *sympathized* with Chance, maybe even *agreed* with him. It was a terrible thing to do after what he had done to her family and friends…after what he had done to *her*. She should hate him, should be glad for the fact he no longer breathed the same air as her and yet she couldn't muster the energy to feel that way, the energy that used to come easily.

The new part of her scared her more than anything. It was the girl Chance had wished for since high school, the one she had refused to be, the one shaped by a lifetime of agony came out to play. Luna was on the verge of a depression she would never escape from, and she didn't know what she could do to stop it...if she even could.

Luna heard a knock on her door suddenly, glad for the distraction from her biting thoughts and sat up, gathering her blankets around her as Rose entered the room. She smiled gently at her daughter before sitting down on the edge of the bed. Luna bit her lip, waiting for her to say something that would only manage to further upset her.

"Feeling any better this morning?" Rose asked.

"Since yesterday?" Luna asked, chewing on her cheek skeptically.

"You've been sleeping an entire day, Dear."

Luna wiped her hair from her eyes, trying to pretend the information wasn't news to her. "Is that all? If anything, it's worse."

Rose sighed and set her hand to the side of her daughter's face. "I didn't think so."

"Do I have to get up this morning?" Luna asked, looking at her mother through wide, sad eyes crumpling from the simple gesture.

Rose nodded slowly. "Of course you have to. I know it's hard, but you have to be able to go on with your life."

Luna pursed her lips and wished she had the power to make time hurry forward and her mother go away. "You have no idea what I'm going through, Mom."

"You're right. I can't imagine that pain," Rose said, twitching her nose, "but I can't stand to lose *my* child over it...you understand?"

Luna blinked and avoided eye contact. "What's your point?"

"I worry about you...even before this. It's a terrible thing, the death of something so innocent."

Terrible didn't seem a strong enough word for it.

"But, that doesn't mean you have to shut down and completely give up on life," Rose continued.

Luna shook her head. "I'm not giving up on life just because I wanna take it easy for a day."

"I know perfectly well what you're doing, Luna," Rose said. "You're blaming yourself, making yourself suffer worse than you have to. This is what you did after Violet died. You put off going to college for a *year* because of it. Don't you know that sitting alone in your room will only make you think about it? You're going to torture yourself."

"What else am I supposed to do?" Luna snapped, all her defenses spring back to life at once.

"Anything but that. This isn't healthy. I don't want you to shut down again. It's okay to grieve, but you go about it the wrong way. You need to learn how to talk it out with someone. Either me or a therapist, as long as you let out what you're thinking once in a while. You'll be fine. It's okay to let me know what you're feeling, you know," she said and let go of Luna's face. "I am capable of understanding."

Luna blinked at her. Conversations weren't her strong suit especially ones about her emotions. What would she tell her mom? So many years of abuse weighed on her that she was honestly for a loss as to what was normal and what wasn't. She couldn't talk to her mother about it; she couldn't talk to *anyone* about it.

At the same time, she wouldn't be able to hold her strong charade against Rose for long. Out of her parents, Luna had always preferred her mother, but now, she missed her father and his distant carelessness. She didn't want to talk about her feelings, didn't want to have to worry about her own life. She wanted someone to control it for her. Clearly, she was unable to do it on her own.

"Why did this happen to me?" she asked, sobbing loudly to punctuate the end of her question. Rose would assume she meant Asher when she meant *everything*.

Rose shook her head and continued to pet her daughter's hair. "Sometimes bad things happen to good people."

"Bad things *always* happen to me. They have ever since senior year. When will it be time for me to have something good happen?"

Rose's face scrunched up at Luna's words, and Luna realized her mistake. Rose had no idea of her senior year terrors; no one did besides

Max and Chance.

"What happened senior year?"

"Just all the fighting with Dad, and then Violet…" Luna said, waving her hand to distract Rose's gaze from her face. While that wasn't the depth of her issues, it was another series of memories she wished would disappear.

"Good things have to be on the horizon," Rose said finally.

"I thought my baby would be the good that came from all the bad," she admitted, twining her thumbs, "but even he got taken from me."

Rose was silent as she leaned in to hug her daughter close. Luna could tell she was out of comforting things to say, but she was glad for it; words would never make her feel better anyway.

"What did they do with him? With my baby?" Luna asked quietly when they pulled apart.

"He's in the morgue right now," Rose said. "They still need to perform an autopsy on him."

Luna frowned at the idea of her baby on a cold gurney with his tiny organs in a bowl beside him. It was enough to make her want to curl up and die as well. Leave it to Rose to be direct in situations that could use subtly.

"We'll have a proper ceremony for him in a few days," Rose tacked on as if the thought had left a bad taste in her mouth as well.

Luna only slightly felt better. "I'd like that."

"He's with your father now," she said with a tearful smile on her face.

Luna smiled at the irony and had to bite her tongue to keep from saying it out loud. Asher was with *his* father as well. Her son would be buried in the same cemetery Luna's father had been, the same place as Violet, Max, and Amanda. Chance's cemetery as she liked to call it. Now, a piece of Chance himself would rest there forever.

"Try to feel better today. It *is* Christmas after all." She offered her daughter another gentle smile and squeezed her leg gently.

"It's Christmas?" Luna whispered looking up at Rose as if her mother had just informed her she was going to check her into Brentwood with Amy.

Rose nodded. "I thought you knew that."

Luna shook her head. "I had no idea."

"Well, when you're ready, I got you a present. I'm gonna make some breakfast, okay?" Rose said.

Luna was silent but grateful for Rose's departure. With everything that had happened the day before, she had forgotten the holidays were so near. Nothing in the hospital had suggested it, and she had managed to sleep through the entire day of Christmas Eve. Luna frowned, hugging herself tightly.

No matter what, the day didn't feel like Christmas to her.

She remembered years ago when she had been just a little kid and the word alone had been enough to make her happy. Nothing stirred in her now. Her childhood felt like it had been another life. As she sat alone in her room with tears drying to her face, she resolved that no matter what the calendar said, it wasn't Christmas.

If it was, she'd be happy, not depressed.

***

CHRISTMAS IN A psychiatric asylum was just as festively depressing as it could be. There was a wreath on the door to the rec room and a pre-lit tree without any ornaments for fear Amy or her friends would use them destructively. The staff tried to make things cheery by singing Christmas carols and handing out cheap gifts that Amy imagined had picked up from the nearest pharmacy on their way to work. She wished it would be over. She had never been a fan of Christmas, but she had also never hated it to the extent that she did inside the walls of Brentwood.

She went to bed early that night, grateful to put three-hundred and sixty-four days between herself and the next Christmas. Then she realized her mistake, horrified when she woke up in the unescapable white room in DreamWorld.

"I will not allow you to shrug off your responsibilities this time. To refuse will earn you consequences."

Amy clenched her jaw. Michelle's illness had been the last price she was forced to pay. What would it cost her this time? "The bond … it's forged from black magic. I don't … my old partner … he never taught me. I don't know what I can do to help," she admitted.

"Then you must learn."

Amy's face was stoic.

"You underestimate yourself," the Voice chastised.

Amy looked up with wide eyes.

"The answer is simple. You just need to find the source of the magic."

Amy frowned. That didn't sound simple at all. She thought about every interaction with Chance she had ever had, eventually forcing her mind to run through the memories of the cabin and the temple. He had had plenty of evil things there, hadn't he?

If I was a psychopath, she mused.

Then, like a bolt from the blue, the answer came to her—the bone and the flower. It had been sitting on the table when Chance had taken her into the cabin to force her to change her clothes before the ceremony. At the time, she hadn't thought anything about it, but thinking of it now, it certainly fit the part. Amy let out a slow breath of air as the ah-ha moment sparkled in her blood.

There were always many aspects of the case that worried Amy more and more, but if the Voice assigned her to break the bond, it was something she would have to do. If Luna followed the same path Chance had, it was very possible her potential, her wonderful ability, would be wasted, and then Amy would be forced to kill her friend.

All she could think of was how Luna had selflessly saved her life in the cabin. Could Amy really kill her in cold blood? She closed her eyes. *I'll do whatever I have to do to end this,* she vowed.

CHAPTER SIXTEEN

I T TOOK A while for Luna to convince herself to get out of bed. She wanted to turn over and resume sleeping, but knew Rose wouldn't allow that. There was some part of her dignity that didn't want to be shattered by having her mother literally *drag* her out of the bed. With a heavy sigh, Luna trudged to the bathroom and washed her face in the sink. She stripped off her nightgown to pull on a loose T-shirt and pants, eyes lingering on the ugly red scar—the reminder—she had left on her thigh. Even though it had stopped bleeding, it looked deep enough to crack open again at any second, and part of her hoped it would. She swallowed in disgust and dropped her shirt to cover it, before she looked at her reflection in the mirror, at the redness of her eyes and hollow pockets in her cheeks.

She looked as bad as she felt. It chilled her to see herself in that state, and she wished the piece of glass didn't exist, that mirrors had never been invented and the world wasn't full of vanity. She picked up her nightgown off of the floor and tossed it into her room from the hallway. Slowly, she found her way to the living room, feet sliding against the carpet as she trudged in a zombie-like fashion through the house.

The second she left the hallway, she noticed the Christmas tree Rose had set up in the corner of the room. Lights stretched around the branches, sparkling in rainbow colors that suggested a radiance of happiness.

Luna didn't feel anything like it.

A glint of anger sparked in the back of her mind, for a reason she couldn't determine, as if the tree was mocking her. Luna rushed toward it, her hand hovering above one of the branches, when she decided to spare it. It took all of her energy to not knock it over. Luna looked away from the tree, stalking toward the couch to sit down, and muttered a string of curses under her breath as she did so. She put her hand to her face and took in a shuddering breath, trying to compose herself. Rose heard the sound from the kitchen, though Luna was unsure how, and came into the living room as cautiously as she had stepped into Luna's room.

"I set up the old tree," Rose announced.

Luna nodded numbly, refusing to look at it again. "I noticed."

Rose frowned at the tone of her voice. She glanced at the Christmas tree, before she bent down beside the tree to pick up a small, white box wrapped in a delicate ribbon. Luna already decided she didn't want it. Rose pondered something for a minute, before she handed it to Luna.

"What is it?"

"Open it," Rose urged.

Luna sighed, deciding against the urge to argue. Her hands shook as she reached out to take the box from her, and Rose sat down beside her, watching her every movement. Luna slid the ribbon off and dropped it on her lap.

A small, black notebook sat neatly inside.

"Do you like it?" Rose asked as Luna pulled it out of the box.

She didn't respond, her eyes studying its every detail. It looked so much like the one that had been destroyed in the fire that she found herself looking through it for her handwriting, only too late remembering that she wasn't alone.

"You used to keep a diary. I thought it might help you to try that again," Rose said. "That way, you have a safe place to vent when you don't wanna talk."

Luna smiled, but it wasn't out of joy. The notebook she had kept before had been a collection of all of Chance's crimes. Newspaper clippings, drawings and notes had lined the pages—a dark scrapbook, and her only way of proving her past was real. How could she explain that to someone who was normal like her mother?

"Thank you," Luna tried to say, but the words didn't want to leave her lips. She absolutely hated it. She didn't want to record details of her terrible life, to know her past was real. Sometimes, it was nice just clinging to the fantasy that she was okay.

"I'm glad you like it," Rose said with a gentle smile on her face, squeezing Luna's knee, before she got up to go back into the kitchen.

The second she disappeared through the arch, Luna set the book back in the box and closed the lid. She wanted to chuck it across the room, but she had enough sense to know it would be rude of her. She hated reminders … especially the ones that marred her arm and stomach, and now her leg to match.

She stood up and left the box, coming face to face with the Christmas tree again. It seemed like no matter where she turned, there were things that reminded her, plagued her, with the emotions she tried to keep hidden inside.

Not too long after that, Luna wanted to go for a walk—it would be the only way she could possibly escape … if only for a little while. Rose heard her movement from her place in the kitchen and peeked her face around the bend to glance at her.

"Are you okay?" she asked.

"I want to go for a walk," Luna said simply.

The frown that crossed Rose's face immediately let Luna know she wasn't finished fussing over her yet. "I don't think you should do that," Rose said, wiping her hands on a dishtowel as she stepped into the room.

"Why not?"

"The doctors said you needed to rest," Rose reminded her.

"I've gotten enough."

"I think you need to lie down for a little bit," Rose insisted.

Luna had no intention of doing that. "Rest" merely brought her more stress. Last night had proved that. She didn't know why she had wanted to go back to sleep when she had first woken up, but she was glad she hadn't. "Rest" meant visiting the land—and person—who had begun all of her nightmares.

"For just a few minutes?" Luna asked, and hated that she was on the verge of pleading for her freedom. Who was Rose to say what she could and could not do?

"I don't think it's a good idea," Rose said.

"I need to have some time to clear my thoughts. Please."

Rose sighed. "Okay, if you come back in ten minutes, you can go. But you should rest when you get back."

Luna didn't like the idea of being on a leash—especially one so short—but she would let Rose fuss over her. She knew it was a kind of healing process for her mother. As long as Rose was willing to let Luna cope, she could do the same for her mother. Luna may be obligated to rest when she returned, but ten minutes of a walk would be ten minutes of freedom that would allow her time to try to run from herself. Who knew how far she could get in that time.

Luna grabbed her coat and hurried out the door, before Rose could change her mind. As she stepped onto the porch, a small pain in her abdomen appeared, and she knew Rose was right, that she shouldn't exert herself, but she couldn't help it. She bolted from the porch and only when Luna was out of range of her house did she slow down. The gentle snowflakes brushed her raw cheeks and brought her a small sense of relief.

"What are you doing?" a familiar voice asked from behind her, making her skin crawl.

She turned to look at Chance. He stood on the sidewalk a few steps away, staring at her like he thought she might be the craziest person he had ever seen. He looked so real that even the snowflakes acknowledged his presence enough to part where he stood.

"Going for a walk," Luna replied, innocently enough.

"You know damn well you're too frail for that right now," he said and folded his arms across his chest.

"I'm fine," Luna insisted.

"Is this another one of those things where you push yourself to physical pain to ignore the emotional?" he asked, curling his lip with each word.

Luna didn't answer him. She didn't meet his eyes either.

"You need to find a better way to cope with Asher's death," he said pointedly.

She frowned at him before she took a few steps away. The point of her walk was to *forget,* and instead, it was becoming harder to do so.

"Stop," he ordered, setting a hand on her arm.

She looked up into his face, eyes glittering with grief. She was on the verge of crying again, and this time, she didn't care who saw it. "Why?" she snapped.

He flinched but didn't let go. "This isn't good for you."

"What *is* good for me? Do you know? Is there even such a thing anymore?"

Chance licked his lips, and she could tell he was trying to keep himself from getting angry, to hold his temper until he could get his under control. "I don't know. Anything but this."

"I'm tired of trying. We're both miserable people with a lot of emotional problems, *Stephen,*" Luna said, tears beginning to catch in the crooks of her mouth.

Chance stood petrified to the sidewalk, his grip on her arm tightening. "What did you call me?"

"Stephen," Luna replied. "Stephen Harris. That's who you are ... or at least, used to be."

"Good to see you read the newspaper at least," Chance said, scratching the back of his head. "I forgot you knew that."

"I know a lot more than that," Luna replied, chin high and thoughts full of Brendan's words. Tearing him down brought her great joy, even if she wasn't sure the situation was real or not.

Chance looked so confused that Luna continued.

"Your cousin told me about you."

Chance's face hardened. "Brendan? You talked to Brendan?"

Luna nodded.

"What did he tell you about me?" Chance demanded and took a step closer to her.

"Why didn't you ever tell me who you really were? Why didn't you tell *anyone?*" she asked in response.

"I *was* a nobody. Here? I made a life for myself. People liked me. What was the point of talking about who I used to be?"

"People *liked* Chance, because you never gave them the opportunity to meet Stephen."

"Oh, they adored Chance all right, just not in the way I had hoped," he said, looking down at the ground before glancing back at her. "I've had a hard life," Chance admitted, the anger dissolving away. "That, I won't lie about, but you were better off than I was. Always have been. At the very least, you had parents who cared and a best friend to watch your back."

"Yeah, they cared so much that you were able to twist them against me in what ... a month? Less than that?"

Chance shrugged. "Maybe, but Max was always there for you."

Luna narrowed her eyes. "How do you know that?"

He shook his head and ran a hand over his face. "Does it matter? My point is," he said slowly, "if I can handle what happened last night, then you can as well."

Luna closed her eyes before opening them to glare at him. "Yeah, looks like you handled it perfectly. That's why you're dead, right?"

She whisked away from him without waiting for a response, and a few seconds later, she realized he had disappeared.

CHAPTER SEVENTEEN

"THANK GOD YOU'RE all right!" Rose exclaimed when Luna returned home ten minutes later.

"Of course I am, Mom," Luna said, laughing more out of awkwardness than anything. What had Rose assumed would happen in the short amount of time she had been allowed to be free?

Rose frowned, catching the lack of emotions on her daughter's face. "What's the matter? I thought going for a walk was supposed to help you cheer up."

"It was *supposed* to, but I guess the cold wind gave me a migraine." Luna lied and shrugged, feigning a sudden throb in her head as an excuse to look away. "I'd better go lie down."

Rose looked at Luna through narrowed eyes, and she knew instantly her mother suspected something. "Did something happen out there?"

"No, I just don't want to push myself."

Rose didn't seem to believe her daughter, but she didn't question it further. "Good."

Luna turned away to head down the hallway before Rose could say another word. Luna was quick to move to her room, rushing to her bed, as if the floor was made of lava. She curled up on her sheets and used her thick blanket to block out every sliver of light that bounced around her walls. She tried to do it in a way that would avoid touching her stomach, but she couldn't manage it. Every time she accidentally nudged it, it made her want to cry. It was so flat, so lifeless, so *wrong*.

Luna closed her eyes, praying desperately for sleep. The thought of cutting herself again had entered her mind, and she didn't like it. She didn't want to be like that, didn't want to be that girl. She could nearly hear Chance's voice floating through her head. Luna remembered the ugly wound she had already inflicted and didn't want to do it again, but part of her seemed to crave it. It was Luna's drug, something to help her escape from herself, if only for a few hours. She ran a hand through her long ebony locks as she tried her best to get comfortable, and slipped into a deep sleep not too long after that.

When she opened her eyes, she was in DreamWorld again. Instead of waking up in the middle of the woods, she was beside the cabin. Luna blinked, knowing full well Chance was somewhere inside. What was he thinking … what he was doing? It was weird she would care, but for some reason, it was the only thought that consumed her mind.

Before she knew it, her feet led her to the front door. *Traitors.* Remembering their conversation from earlier, she wasn't sure if she wanted to see him or not.

Her thoughts were disconnected from her body. In her mind, she wanted to head into the woods to avoid the situation before her, but her body betrayed her. She watched herself knock on the hardwood door, the little person in the zip-up costume at work again, and before she could register what she had done, it opened. Chance stood there, his blond hair a mess about his head, staring at Luna as she bayed at his doorstep like a stray cat.

"I-I'm sorry about earlier," she said before she knew why.

"It's fine," he said, turning away to head back into the shadows inside the cabin.

Luna could tell he wasn't in the mood to talk, so she didn't understand why she decided to follow him anyway. "I don't feel like it is."

"Did you want something?" he asked, setting a hand on the chair beside him, still refusing to look at her.

"I have to know … why did you help me … w-with Kylie? I thought you hated me."

He glanced at her over his shoulder with a carefully guarded look. "Things change." He was almost calm, except for one twitching finger that betrayed his façade.

"All those years … that was an act, wasn't it? You never wanted to hurt me, did you?"

He turned completely at that and looked back at her through eyes pleading for forgiveness, for love. The strength of the look from usually so hateful eyes surprised her. "Of course not," he murmured and swiped his shaggy hair from his face.

"Then why did you do everything you did?"

"I wanted you to *accept* me," he said, running his tongue along his teeth. "After everything that happened with Max, I felt so betrayed. I didn't know how else I could get your attention."

"Max?" She tipped her head to the side. "What happened with Max?"

Chance laughed and looked down at his feet. "Maybe you should just go."

"No, I wanna know why!" she said, taking a step toward him and paused with her hand just above the crook of his elbow, uncertain if she really wanted to touch him or not.

"Then why interrupt me when I try to pour my heart out to you?" he asked, a twisted smile on his face.

She didn't know why, but her heart twanged at his words. "Fine … but you *tortured* me, Chance. Did you really expect me to want anything to do with you after everything you did?"

He shrugged and looked away. "I thought I was protecting you."

"Protecting me from what?" Luna asked.

He narrowed his blue eyes. "Even if I told you, you wouldn't understand."

"There's a lot of things I don't understand about you."

He laughed again. It sounded so light and hollow, almost as if he meant it. "I don't understand you either," he said, then swallowed, seeming to forget what he was about to say next.

"What is it?" Luna asked. "What about me don't you understand? I was terrified of you, scared you'd kill me. Do I need to remind you of the way you strangled me? Come on, Chance … you admitted to killing all those people. What else could I think?" Luna bit her lip. "Why are you talking about this?"

"You'll laugh, I'm sure, but I feel bad for everything I've done to you," he admitted and tucked his bottom lip between his teeth, looking up at her through his lashes. "Is it too late to say I'm sorry?"

Luna smiled—he was right; she *did* want to laugh. "I suppose not, but 'sorry' is just a Band-Aid. It does nothing to heal the wounds you caused."

The expression on Chance's face didn't change, though his eyes fell to the scar on her arm. "You're not the same as you used to be."

"How can I be? I-I'm a *monster*."

"Anyone can be a monster when they have to be," Chance said stiffly.

Luna scoffed, though she was unsure of why his haughtiness surprised her. It was who he was. "How do you just … just *shrug* it *off?*"

"My apology should've suggested otherwise," he said.

"Well, it didn't." She paused to stare at him, breathing in to calm her nerves. "Riddle me this—why did you kill yourself?"

He smiled at her diffidently, caught off guard by the question. "Isn't it obvious? I didn't want to go to jail."

"Asher had nothing to do with it?" Luna asked sheepishly, raising her eyebrows.

"Fuck. You really don't know when to quit, do you?"

"And you do?"

Chance glared, but the emotion softened as he began to speak. "I wouldn't have been a good father. Besides, with the cops on my trail, I never would've had the chance to try."

"So it turns out I was the bad guy after all," Luna said, laughing.

"It's a fucked up situation all around. It's like they say, 'No one's perfect.'"

97

"Maybe, but I never imagined I'd fall this far either." Chance laughed, but she wasn't joking. In desperation, she grabbed his hand. "I don't want to be a killer."

"I didn't want to be either," Chance said, "but I had to."

***

ACROSS TOWN, AMY lay alone on her white bed, a newspaper held up as she learned of the world outside her walls. Despite the Voice's pleas for her to keep Luna safe, she remained in the confines of her room, indecision keeping her life virtually unchanged. She skimmed the pages, looking for any news of her sister, or anyone she knew, when a headline caught her attention.

Midwife Missing

Local police are baffled after the disappearance of Miss Kylie Gordan, a well-known midwife in the town of Lima, Ohio. She was reported missing this morning after she never returned from a house call the night before. Her patient, Luna Ketz, was rushed to the hospital after the birth of her stillborn child. Miss Ketz reported that Miss Gordan never made it to her home.

If anyone has any information about her disappearance, please contact the Lima Police Department.

The girl's eyes went wide, and she dropped the newspaper.

"Luna," she whispered, jumping to her feet.

She paced the room, wondering how her friend was doing, and if she was okay. Amy frowned and looked up at the camera perched in the corner of her room.

"Hey! I want to make a phone call!" she said, hoping the people surveying her room would respond.

Nobody did.

Her frown deepened as she sunk to her bed, her indecision finally gone and a mission in mind. She needed to find her sister and see that the few people she called "friends" were okay, or if the Voice had made good on its threats.

IT SEEMED AS if no time at all had passed until Amy was in DreamWorld again, staring at the horrendous mask in her hands. Her thumb stroked the cheek gently, but all she wanted to do was throw it on the ground and stomp on it until just dust remained. When she finally forced it onto her face, the mesh material gripped her in a way that her skin was no longer accustomed to.

In the back of her mind was her mission, but the way her body moved, it seemed as if she didn't have a care in the world. She hated herself for the conflict that she really had no control over. A rustle sounded from the trees nearby, and she jumped, hurrying onward with fresh fear in her blood. It was all too easy to imagine that she was being hunted like a weak baby deer.

She reached up to touch her mask again, reminding herself of the power that came with it. In this place, she was not *weak,* she was not *helpless.*

So stop acting like it, she scolded herself.

She felt no better.

In her head, she could picture the library on the edge of town so clearly. In the Real World, it was the place she and Max would meet in person to discuss vital issues. It didn't happen often, so rare, in fact, that Amy had gone a long time without knowing who Max really was, apart from just her "partner."

She went to the library anyway, finding comfort in the shadows of the overhanging trees near the entrance. He wasn't there, of course he wasn't, but Amy couldn't help the disappointment that came. When Max had been alive, they had had a special connection that always let the other know when they needed them. She guessed now that was a thing of the past.

Amy crept up to the building, setting her hand on the bricks on the edge of the building, in the place where Max would wait for her. Her hand curled into a fist, and she rested her forehead to the bricks, the slightest prick digging into her skin as tears ran down her cheeks.

"Howdy, stranger," a voice called behind her.

Amy froze instantly, slowly turning to look over her shoulder. "Max? What are you doing here?"

"Just because I'm dead, doesn't mean our Keeper connection is broken … when you're here anyway."

"You could *hear* me?"

He nodded, his face looking uncertain. "Did you not want me to?"

Amy took a step closer to him, clenching her hand into a fist over her heart. "I just didn't know it was possible."

"You look pale as a ghost. How've you been?" Max asked, shoving his hands in his pockets, as if this was just another day in Hell.

"The Voice brought me back to the job."

He nodded again, his eyes on the mask. "You never should've left."

Amy couldn't look at him, feeling the way his gaze scorched her. Both of them were aware of the thing that neither of them were willing to point out—if Amy had never gone into hiding, Max might still be alive.

"You're right," she murmured and looked up, meaning to look him directly in the eyes, but chickened out at the last moment and stared at his chin instead. "I should've been there for you and Luna. We could've beat him. He was weak after everything, but … but I only thought about myself."

"Yeah, you did, but it's not too late to make it up to me," Max said, setting his fingers under her chin.

Amy looked up at him through her lashes.

"If you really are sorry, then *prove* it. Take that bastard down once and for all. For me, for you, for Luna, and for every poor soul he's ever damned."

CHAPTER EIGHTEEN

LUNA'S EYES FLUTTERED open, and once again, she was in her room. She sighed and sat up as she ran a hand through her hair, mechanically coming to rest on her stomach, before she remembered the pain of losing her baby, and dropped it away as if her skin burned. The desire to get up was gone and replaced with depression. In an attempt to distract herself, she thought about the conversation she had had with Chance, though it didn't do much to make her feel better.

The emotion he had showed her, the emotions she shared with him, didn't seem real. They couldn't be. It scared her to think the entire time that she feared him, she was *becoming* him. How many times had they looked at each other and wondered the same things?

It was hard for Luna to grasp. As she lay in bed, her brain drove on a three-sixty trip back to senior year of high school, to the first date she had been on with Chance, and the way he had looked at her through calm, sapphire eyes and told her she would enjoy killing.

Luna had gone away from that night disgusted with his assumption, and positive he was sick in the head. Little had she known, it was *her,* who was sick. All the time of trying to glue together her fragile sanity had been for nothing. Her breakdown had been a long time coming, whether she had realized it or not.

Footsteps in the hallway jolted her from her thoughts. "Luna, are you awake?" Rose called from the hallway.

"Yeah."

When Rose entered her room, Luna looked up wondering what her mother had to talk about this time. "Luna, I need to ask you a question," Rose said.

Luna could sense the hint of urgency in her voice. Something was wrong. "What's wrong, Mom?" she asked, forcing herself to sit up.

"Kylie's gone missing," Rose said, not breaking her gaze from her daughter's. "There's a police officer here to question you."

Luna's heart sunk in her chest, and she was glad Rose couldn't read the thoughts running through her mind. An extra weight joined the bed as Chance sat down beside her, his arm draped over her shoulders.

"Just stay strong," he whispered in her ear.

On reflex, she visibly tensed.

"Are you all right?" Rose asked, setting her hand gently on Luna's knee.

Luna nodded and nervously licked her dry lips, torn between taking comfort from her mother or her enemy. "I just woke up, Mom," she said in the way of an excuse.

"Before he comes in, I need to make sure ... .she really never showed up last night?" Rose asked.

Luna looked deep into her mother's face, not liking the glint of suspicion she found there. Luna's throat felt dry, and she had to force herself to swallow, to keep her face neutral, but her heart pounded so hard, all she could focus on was the sound of blood in her ears. She had never fainted before, and she hoped this wouldn't be her chance to experience it.

"What are you implying?" she asked, trying her best to talk with an even voice.

"I just needed to know," Rose said, dodging Luna's question.

"I'm positive, Mom," she managed to say, hoping her mother wouldn't question her again. Luna didn't trust herself to not say the truth.

"I believe you," Rose said, squeezing Luna's leg gently.

For a minute, Luna was hurt by the accusation. Her mother had no idea what her daughter had done, like she had no idea what her daughter had been through. In reality, Luna had no right to feel upset. Her mom was *right,* after all. It wasn't Rose's fault she could see the monster that lie within her own daughter.

Rose was silent as she got up to lead the police officer into Luna's room. As he approached her bed, Luna studied every detail of him, searching out his weaknesses. He was a small man—even the big police uniform couldn't cover that fact up. He seemed nervous, though Luna wasn't sure why. She briefly remembered him from her trip to the police station, and wondered if he remembered her as well.

Chance scoffed, and Luna jumped slightly, but resisted the urge to look at him. She had all but forgotten he was there. "I remember Officer Smith. He talked to me about Kate's death." He laughed slightly. "He hated me. Probably got his jollies when I died."

Luna felt oddly better for his weird statement. Chance had never been brought into custody for that murder … for *any* of his murders. Luna wondered if it was because the cop was easy to trick, or if Chance was that smooth of a talker.

Officer Smith looked back at her, and it was hard for her to read the thoughts that ran through his mind. Did he suspect she had done anything to her midwife? Or did he pity her like half of Lima did?

"Relax, you'll do fine," Chance said, rubbing his hand over the spot in her back that held the most tension. "I'll help you."

"Good afternoon, Miss Ketz," Officer Smith said, tipping his hat to her.

She nodded in response.

"First, I'd like to say I'm sorry about what happened to you," he said. "I know you must be going through a lot right now."

Luna forced herself to show no emotion from the line that pained her, not even a hint of aggravation. *You have no idea.*

"I have just a few questions for you," he said, flipping through a small notebook. "You called Miss Gordan last night? When was that?"

She couldn't help but glance at Chance, but he was silent, offering none of the help he had promised. He glanced back at her, sapphire blue eyes wondering as he studied her.

"This morning. I-I made a house call when I went into labor. My mom had her number in her cellphone, just in case of emergencies. I waited at least a half an hour for her before I gave birth, but she never arrived to help me," Luna said, tears trailing down her face. She didn't know when she started crying, but she was sure she wouldn't be able to stop it.

Officer Smith offered her a sympathetic look, and Luna noticed a small smile appear on Chance's face. She wasn't sure which one made her feel worse.

"I'm terribly sorry to keep you, but I need a little bit more information," he said and wrote something down. "When you called her, did she answer?"

Luna bobbed her head, but even she knew the gesture would look lifeless. It did.

"How did she seem?"

"Lie," Chance said before she could even think. "Don't let them know she was fine or else you look bad."

"She seemed frantic and distracted," Luna said saying the first thing that came to mind. "She hurried to hang up on me."

Chance bobbed his head, and Officer Smith wrote down her words in his notebook. "Did she mention anyone she had to see, or something she had to do? Do you think she had someplace else to go?"

Luna shrugged. "I don't know, but it seemed like it. She barely took the time to hear me out."

He nodded, jotting down another note. "Anything else you'd like to tell us?"

Luna shook her head. "No … just … I hope she's all right, you know?"

"Thank you for your cooperation, Miss Ketz. I'll be in touch. Make sure you get your rest," Officer Smith said, before he left the room.

"You did great," Chance said to her, and Luna's shoulders

drooped.

"I'm worried they'll be back," she admitted.

"If they didn't take you into custody now, then they never will," Chance said confidently. "They cleaned up their only clue of her disappearance when they took care of your labor mess, and they'll never be any the wiser. You don't have to worry about a thing."

Luna should have been relieved, but her heart was heavy.

***

FAR AWAY IN Alto Pass, Brendan stared at the phone on his table. He needed to make a call, but it would be no easy conversation. His eyes drifted out the window to the snow gleaming back at him from his adopted cousin's grave. He couldn't stop thinking about the pregnant girl he had encountered in the cemetery, and the knowledge of her baby still rang in his mind, along with the tragedy of his cousin's loss. It was such a waste.

Finally, he swallowed his hesitation and picked up the phone.

On the third ring, a woman's voice replied, "Hello?"

"Hey, it's me," Brendan said.

"Brendan, how've you been, angel?" she asked, sounding happier.

"I've been all right." Brendan stuck his tongue in his cheek. How would she sound *after* he dropped his news? "You remember that girl I told you I met in the cemetery ... Luna?"

"Uh-huh?"

"I read the paper today, and well, she had a miscarriage."

The woman gasped. "That's terrible! I bet she's devastated!"

Brendan was silent for a minute. "You're not thinking what I am? I mean, she was pregnant with *Stephen's* baby. She probably knew about his ... urges ... I just hope she isn't like him. The newspaper said her midwife went missing the same night," Brendan said.

"Oh, Lord, that's a red flag," the woman said. "If she wasn't crazy, she might be now."

"That's what I'm worried about," Brendan admitted, tapping his finger against his lips.

"I'll pay her a visit and see how she's doing. She might appreciate the company."

"Will you tell her who you are?" Brendan asked.

The woman was silent. "Yes, I believe I will. I have nothing else to lose."

"Thank you, Layanna," Brendan said.

"Anything for Stephen," she replied and hung up, leaving Brendan to listen to the dial tone.

CHAPTER NINETEEN

ROSE SAT IN the armchair her husband used to adore, with a cup of tea held to her lips. Straining her ears to hear down the hall, she fidgeted with uncertainty. Rose had known Kylie a lot better than Luna did—they had been classmates back in grade school—yet the officers weren't nearly as interested in her as Luna.

All of their focus was reserved for her daughter—that was never a good sign.

Her lip twitched in irritation. Her daughter had been through enough; couldn't they see that? As quickly as the anger had appeared, it vanished. As much as she hated to admit it, Kylie's disappearance *was* odd, and Luna was the last to speak to her alive. Rose didn't think Luna would have any reason to lie about the horrible night she had endured, but what if she did? What if the reason Luna had been involved with the demon who impregnated her was because she was nowhere near the angel people believed her to be?

***

AN HOUR AFTER Officer Smith left, Luna hadn't left her room. She stayed curled on the bed, looking at the knife on her nightstand, drained, tired … and so guilty and had no desire to get out of bed ever again. She

107

hated the lies she was telling—the karma she was building wasn't going to be good. Chance had gone, and she felt worse for his absence. Rose came into her room suddenly, and Luna's mind plummeted. *I didn't know it was possible to feel any worse.*

"Luna, honey, how are you feeling today?"

"The same," she said, not bothering to sit up.

"You're starting to worry me," Rose said, tilting her head. "I know the doctor said to rest, but this is overdoing it."

"You're the one who said I needed it," Luna pointed out.

"You know this isn't what I meant," she said.

Luna sighed and pressed the heels of her hands against her eyes. "I'm fine, Mom."

"You need to eat something," Rose said. "I don't remember the last time you have."

"I'm not hungry," Luna replied, her eyes still closed as she dropped her hands to her blanket.

"I know you're sad, but you have to take care of yourself," Rose insisted, taking just one step closer.

"I need time to *grieve*, Mom."

"That's what you said after Violet died, and it got out of hand."

Luna opened her eyes, but didn't look at Rose. Her sight was lost in her memories. After Violet's funeral, Luna had locked herself in her room every day until graduation, only leaving for school. She skipped a number of meals, and her body had been dangerously underweight, as she fought off the infected wound in her stomach. The guilt that she had gotten her best friend killed, had almost taken her out as well. She had gotten better a few months after graduation, through Max's careful coaching, but Max wouldn't be around to help her this time. If she was going to recover, it was up to her and her alone.

"I could've handled it better," Luna admitted, avoiding eye contact, "but I promise this isn't like that."

"I hope not," Rose said, tucking her chin to her chest.

"It's not," Luna assured her, looking at her mother through bitter eyes.

"I'm worried about you," Rose said.

"Don't be."

"I have to go into work for a few hours. I want you to come," Rose said.

Luna groaned. "I'd rather stay here, Mom."

"I know, and that's exactly why I'm insisting you come with me. It'll do you some good to get a good meal in your stomach and some fresh air in your lungs."

"You know how ironic that statement is, right?" Luna asked. "When I wanted to leave, you told me to stay. Now that I want to stay, you want me to leave?"

"That's right, sweetheart, just for today."

Luna shivered at the pet name—that was one of Chance's favorites for her. That thought broke through her stubbornness. "All right, fine."

Rose smiled, visibly pleased with her daughter's decision. "I'll be waiting in the car."

When she left the room, Luna took her time getting ready. She found a thick comfortable pair of pants and a sweater that she was convinced were pajamas, before she sought out her jacket and boots, and then met Rose in the car. She could survive a few hours with pure fakeness, she had plenty of times before.

Luna kept her head down when they made it to the restaurant, glad it wasn't during a rush. Rose sat her down on a bar stool by the front counter while she went to clock in. Catherine, Rose's boss, was the only one who noticed her presence.

"Hi, sweetpea," she said in her voice a few octaves too deep from decades of smoking. "How are you doing today?"

Luna propped her chin on her hand. "Surviving."

"Hmm, aren't we all?" she replied, and for a fraction of a second, a genuine smile found its way to Luna's face. If there was one thing she appreciated about her mother's boss, it was that she wasn't comfortable in emotional situations either. "Can I get you something to eat?"

"I'm really not that hungry, ma'am."

"Nonsense," she said, walking away, before Luna had the chance to argue again.

Luna sighed and relaxed, shrugging off her coat. She glanced around the café, and her heart slid to her stomach when her eyes locked onto a familiar pair—Drew. Months ago, Amanda had set him up with Luna for a double date ... they hadn't spoken since.

Neither of them moved, until Luna blinked. Drew took the moment of broken eye contact to jump up and rush out the door. Luna watched him go, feeling her shoulders slump. He was the closest thing to a normal social outlet she had, and he clearly had no interest in her.

"Here you go, dear. Pecan pie, your favorite," Catherine's voice cut into her thoughts as the woman set a plate with a giant piece of pie on the counter. "And I don't want to hear any excuses—everyone likes pie!"

CATHERINE WAS RIGHT—Luna had no protests to the pie, but she took her time eating. By the time Rose clocked out, she had only managed to get down half of it. Catherine wrapped up the rest for her, but Luna doubted she would eat it. When they got home, Rose seemed pleased for her daughter's cooperation, even if it was reluctant.

"Maybe you can come with me again tomorrow," she said, smiling at her daughter, before going to her room to change out of her work clothes.

"You don't need her stressing you out like that," Chance said from beside her.

Luna jumped at the sound of his voice. "What other choice does she have? She suspects what I did," she said, her voice trailing off. "This is her way of babysitting."

"She suspects nothing."

Luna turned to look at him. "Yeah. You keep saying that, but how do you know?"

"I recognized that look in her face—it's worry. She doesn't blame you for a thing, but after what happened, she's still in shock. Give her time to adjust," Chance said. "Not everyone is a fake human like us."

"I hope that's all she needs," Luna said, tilting her head to the side. "I don't know how much of this stress I'll be able to handle."

The phone rang in the kitchen, and she turned toward the sound. When she looked back, Chance was gone. Luna was relieved for the solitude as she sank down onto the couch, listening to Rose talking on the phone. Before she knew it, she was asleep.

In DreamWorld, she opened her eyes to the sound of her name. The voice that said it was small and soft, and if it weren't for the repetition, it would've been easy to ignore.

"Luna?" it prompted again.

She turned and saw the speaker. It was Amy.

"*Amy?*"

Luna hadn't spoken to her since her last visit to Brentwood Psychiatric a few months before. The girl had been volatile, angry, and the memories made Luna visibly cringe as she faced her.

"I'm sorry to come to you in this form, but I ... I think we need to talk. Can you come visit me?"

Luna's instant response was to say "no," but she could see the sincerity in Amy's eyes, *hear* it in her voice.

But why now? They hadn't talked in months, and before that, it had been *years*. When Luna had needed Amy to listen to her, she wouldn't do it. Luna frowned and pressed her hand to one of her eyes in frustration. Despite what had happened in the past, Luna wasn't the type to turn her back to a friend in need.

"I'll be there as soon as I can," she promised.

***

LUNA DROVE CAREFULLY through the snow-covered roads. She wasn't used to driving a vehicle as large as Chance's truck, and it didn't help that she didn't exactly remember where she was going. Her stress was short-lived when she found the building and parked the truck, before trudging through the snow to the front door, the entire time wondering what she would face once she saw her old friend.

"I'm here to see Amy Jimenez," she said to the nurses at the front counter.

111

"Put your belongings in here," one replied and passed her a small bucket without looking up from the paper she was reading. Luna put her keys and wallet in it, then followed the nurse down a long white hallway, looking at the heavy steel doors along the way. She could only guess what kinds of people were kept behind each one. Amy was kept in the most secured part of the sanitarium; she wasn't a threat, but they didn't know that. Luna herself wasn't even one-hundred percent sure anymore.

"You got twenty minutes," the nurse said, pushing Luna inside Amy's room, as if she was feeding her to a lion.

Luna was prepared to face the run-down look Amy had held during Luna's past visits, so she was shocked at the girl in front of her. Amy was healthy and plump, her hair, once brittle, was flowing, luminous and shiny. Color radiated from her full cheeks and a small smile hung on her lips at the sight of her old friend.

"Amy, you look a lot better," Luna blurted out, then decided after the fact that it was a rude thing to say.

Amy nodded. "I'm sad I can't say the same for you."

"I've had better days," Luna admitted, ruffling her hair. "Now, what did you want to talk about?"

"I read in the newspaper a few months ago that Chance *died*. Is it true?" she asked, holding her breath.

Luna bobbed her head, feeling faint. Of course she'd want to talk about Chance. Why had Luna let herself believe it could've been about anything else?

Amy noticed the sickly look and offered Luna a seat on her bed, which Luna graciously accepted.

"How'd it happen?" Amy asked.

"He killed himself," Luna said, locking her gaze on the small girl. "Just like the paper said."

Amy glanced away from Luna, before she mumbled, "He got what he deserved."

Luna shrugged, and for a reason she didn't understand, she actually felt sad.

Amy must've sensed it. "Are you okay?"

Luna gave her a small smile. "I don't know, honestly." She

112

swallowed heavily and let the smile fall. "It's been so long; I don't remember what 'okay' feels like. Can I tell you something?"

Amy pursed her lips. "Is it something I want to know?"

Luna registered the look on Amy's face as disinterest, which made her want to change her mind.

"Wait," Amy said, holding a slender hand up. "Was *Chance* the father of your baby?"

Luna looked up at her, her soul bared in the emotion in her eyes. "How'd you guess?"

Amy's eyes widened. "Y-your reaction when I brought up his death," she said. "How did that happen?"

"Long story," Luna answered simply.

Amy screwed up her face. "Well, I *am* sorry for your loss. Both of them."

"It's okay." Luna wiped at her face. "I think I'm just hormonal from the whole pregnancy thing still."

Amy shot Luna with the look of pity she hated the most.

"Why did you want me to come?" Luna asked, slightly irritated. Amy had called her here, yet all they had done was discuss the things Luna would rather forget. She hadn't needed to leave the comfort of her home for a reminder.

"I … I've been looking into your bond with Chance," she admitted at last.

Luna moved her eyes around to look at anything besides the tiny Keeper before her, the corners of her eyes burning with unshed tears. "I thought you said it was magic you couldn't handle."

"There's a lesson to be learned in everything." Luna blinked, but couldn't muster up a response, so she waited for Amy to continue. "Have you ever seen a contraption of Chance's that consists of a rose and a bone?"

Luna licked her teeth. "Yeah, I have. He used it to bond with me. Why does it matter?"

"We need to destroy it," Amy said. "Then you'll be free of him."

Luna gathered her hands into fists. Did she know that Chance wasn't gone like his death promised? Did she suspect that he was still alive, using Luna as a source of energy? "Could it really be that simple?"

Amy stared into her eyes and caught sight of something she wasn't used to seeing on Luna's face—hope. She didn't know for sure if she could bring herself to lie.

"Maybe. Maybe not. Before that, I need to get out of here."

Luna shrugged. "Call Michelle."

"You don't understand," Amy said, frowning as she clutched Luna's forearm. "They won't let me. That's why I had to come to you on the other side. This place, it's a prison."

"Even prison gets phone calls," Luna said, cutting her a sideways glance.

"Luna, I'm serious! They think I'm here for a reason and that calling someone might bother them," Amy said. "All the phones here are on lockdown."

"That's not right," Luna said with the same frown Amy wore. "You're a *human*; they can't deny you the right to talk to your family."

"Try telling *them* that," Amy said, folding her arms across her chest. "They won't listen to a word I say."

"How can *I* possibly help?"

"I need you to talk to Michelle for me. Tell her what's going on. Get her to come and sign my release papers," Amy said. "I want to go home."

Luna could understand the pain in her voice. Chance's death was the reason behind her recovery—she felt safe again, no longer seeking safety in the solitude of her padded cell. Yet she was stuck, held from everything she loves, in a prison of her own comforts.

Luna stood carefully to her feet. "Of course I will. I'll talk to the nurses and see what else I can do in the meantime."

"Thank you," Amy said with glittering eyes, before she pulled Luna into a hug.

"It's no problem," Luna said, patting the girl's back awkwardly before she pulled away. She hated physical contact and moved away, ready to leave the room when Amy's voice stopped her.

"Hey."

Luna turned uncertainly.

"For the record, I'm sorry about how I was a few months back when you came to talk to me," she said. "I was out of my mind. I know you needed me, and I let you down. But ... just know that wasn't me. I was going through so much stress and everything, I hope you understand."

After everything Chance had done to her, Luna didn't blame her for reacting as strongly as she had.

"Can you apologize to Sarah for me, too, if you see her?"

Luna cringed at her name and failed in doing so subtly.

"What's wrong?" Amy asked, face scrunching in desperation.

"Sarah is dead."

Amy was silent, and Luna took her opportunity to slip out of the room. Even though she considered Amy a friend, she blamed her for Sarah's death, as much as she blamed herself. Luna pushed the thought away and went back to the front counter. She gathered her belongings and looked at the nurse, finding the words to speak.

"I don't think she needs to even be here anymore. Would there be any way for me to sign her out?" Luna asked.

The nurse shook her head. "Only the person who signed her in can. In this case it's a Michelle Jimenez."

"There's no other option?" Luna asked.

The nurse shook her head. "I'm sorry. She can check herself out if Miss Michelle was unable to for some reason."

"Thanks for your time," Luna said, disheartened. She turned to leave and gasped as she crashed into Chance.

"You can't give up that easily," he said, locking his sapphire blue eyes onto hers.

"What do you mean?" she whispered.

"You can get Amy out of here," he said, chin raised high. "All you have to do is kill Michelle."

CHAPTER TWENTY

"**W**HAT?" SHE SCREECHED, perhaps a bit too loudly. Of all the things he could've said, she hadn't expected that to be the one he decided on.

"Are you okay?" a nurse called to her.

Luna swallowed unevenly. When Chance had appeared, she had forgotten the nurses were there. She turned nervously. "Yeah, I'm fine."

"Are you sure?" she asked, raising an eyebrow.

"Mm-hmm," Luna said flashing her a fake smile. The last thing she needed was to be admitted into the hospital with Amy. She turned back to look at Chance, as soon as the nurse looked away. "What did you say?" she whispered to him.

"You heard me."

"Chance, she's a Keeper. She'll *know* if I do it."

He shrugged and waved a dismissive hand at her. "Maybe. Maybe not."

"Miss?" the nurse asked again.

"I said I'm fine," Luna snapped without looking at her. She blinked, trying to compose herself, and when she opened her eyes again, Chance was gone.

Good, she thought to herself. She looked for him casually for a minute, before she made her way out to the parking lot, the entire time, her mind ablaze with thoughts. Did he really expect her to kill Michelle for no reason?

Kylie had been an accident, the result of a fit of rage. Luna could never kill someone who hadn't provoked her, someone who was her *friend* nonetheless. She wasn't a monster, or maybe she was just fooling herself. It was hard to trust herself anymore.

Luna sighed and drove home. After she parked, she sat in the truck, thinking about the events her day had presented her with. She couldn't shake the thought of the look on Chance's face, so calm and *serious,* as he talked about taking Michelle's life.

Where does he get off? she thought crossly.

The creak of the front door broke Luna from her thoughts, and she turned to see Rose standing in the doorway, staring at the truck with wondering eyes, arms crossed tight against her chest to guard from the cold. If Luna waited long enough, Rose wouldn't hesitate dragging her out.

"Come on inside, honey!" she called, hovering on the edge of the porch.

Luna sighed and pushed her troubles to the reserve at the back of her mind before she complied.

"Are you okay?" was the first thing Rose asked her daughter as she crossed the threshold.

"Yes, Mom, I'm fine," Luna said automatically. She thought about recording the statement to reduce the number of times she would actually have to say it.

"You ran out like your pants were on fire. How did it go?" Rose wondered, closing the door.

Luna shrugged off her jacket. *Good question.* "Better than I expected. Amy's getting better."

"That's good to hear," Rose said as Luna sat down on the couch. "Will they be sending her home soon?"

"That's the thing she wanted to talk to me about," Luna said, reaching up to scratch her ear. "They won't let her leave."

Rose's face screwed up. "Why not?"

117

"She didn't check herself in, her sister did, so she's the only one who can sign for Amy's release," Luna said, "and the doctors won't let her get a hold of her."

Rose shook her head. "Those places are simply trouble. I would never trust them with a person I love."

Luna was unsure how to reply. If Rose knew what her daughter was actually capable of, she might be quick to change her mind.

"She was pretty upset then, huh?" Rose prompted.

"Yeah, she was. She tried to talk to me about Asher, for sympathy points I think."

Rose sighed. "You know you're gonna need to talk about it sometime, right?"

Luna looked up at her, torn between pain and irritation. "Now isn't the time for this, Mom. I don't think Amy cared about *me*; she just wanted to see if she could use me to talk to Michelle for her. I'm a glorified gopher. Pretending to be interested in me was her way of going about asking me to do her dirty work."

"Oh, why can't you tell when people are being nice?"

"People have their reasons for being 'nice.' There's no such thing as a selfless good deed."

"You're so stubborn," Rose said, putting her hands on her hips.

"Just like my mother," Luna replied, with a hint of a smile.

Rose sighed and rubbed at her temples. "Well, I see there's no changing your mind, so what are you going to do? Are you going to help her?"

Luna shrugged and stared at the lines in the floorboards. "Maybe."

"What's stopping you?"

Luna bit her lip as she thought of what she could say in response. "When Amy was checked into that place, she was in bad shape. She was still pretty bad off when I visited her a few months ago. She's messed up in the head. Whatever happened to her, changed her. When I went to visit her today, she seemed so calm, like the past couple of years never happened. I don't think it's healthy, or possible, for someone to actually recover that quickly."

"What happened to her that troubles her so badly?" Rose asked.

There was no way she could tell Rose what had happened to Amy, without telling her what had happened to herself as well. "I don't know, honestly, but the rumor around town is that it was something bad," Luna lied, hoping Rose would accept it.

"You think she's just *pretending* to be better?"

Luna nodded. "Exactly. Besides, I don't think getting her signed out of there is any of my business, Mom."

"Maybe not, but Amy's your friend, isn't she?"

"Yeah, but it should be up to Michelle to decide," Luna argued. "That's her family, after all. And if Michelle hasn't checked her out, I'm sure she has her reasons."

"I think you should at least *try* to talk to her. What could it hurt? Part of having friends is being there for them when they need you."

You have no idea what I've already done for her, Luna thought darkly to herself.

"The last time I visited her, she didn't act like I was her friend," Luna pointed out.

"You also said she's mentally unstable," Rose said, looking at Luna as if she was ashamed of her.

She has no idea what kind of things were running through my mind at the time. Luna frowned at the thought. Her parents had a way of supporting everyone, but her, it seemed. "All I'm saying, is she wasn't there for me when I needed her, so I don't see why I should jump through hoops to help her. I'm tired of helping people who are never around when I need them."

"Luna, I thought I taught you better than that."

Luna blinked. "After everything I've been through, do you blame me for not wanting to reach out anymore? Asher died less than a week ago, Mom. I'm sorry my manners went out the window."

The hardened look on Rose's face melted away. "No, that's not what I meant, honey. I meant, I thought it would be good for you to try and reconnect with Amy. You two used to be close in high school."

Luna made a face. Rose had been gone most of Luna's high school years—she had no idea who Luna was and wasn't close to. "We weren't *that* close, Mom. Besides, I did what I could. She wants me to help her out of that institution and then she probably won't talk to me again anyways."

"You don't know that for sure."

"I can guess."

Rose's shoulders drooped, and her fight went out. "I'm gonna start dinner. Do you want me to make anything specific?"

Luna shook her head; the thought of food made her stomach churn as it usually did.

Rose raised an eyebrow. "You're going to eat, right?"

"Yeah, I'll eat," Luna replied, though she knew she wasn't telling the truth. She just wanted Rose to drop the conversation and go away. To her, what was one more lie? Thoughts of Kylie's murder reminded her there were worse things in the world.

Rose eyed her strangely, but didn't say a word as she left the room. Luna was relieved, but couldn't stop the afterthought of the conversation from burdening her mind. Was Rose right? *Should* she have more of a desire to help Amy than she did?

Luna was losing touch with herself—so much so that she couldn't decide what the best course of action was. Amy had been locked up in solitary confinement for a long time with only her thoughts for company. According to her, it had been a while since even Michelle had decided to visit. Sure, Amy seemed fine, but maybe the stress of being back in reality would cause her to crack under the pressure. If that happened, she might end up worse than when she was first admitted.

Would it be best for Amy to remain in Brentwood?

Luna wanted to say yes, just so the whole situation would be behind her, but there was a small part of her mind that tried to turn her attention to the positive side of helping her friend. Even if Amy was unstable when she got out, she would be someone Luna could talk to. Someone who would *understand* what ailed her. Chance had scarred a lot of people during his lifetime, but most of his victims, with the exception of Luna and Amy, were dead.

"Just going to ignore me now?" Chance's voice said from beside her.

She jumped at the sound, holding a hand to her heart. "Would you stop *doing* that? How long have you been there?"

"Long enough for me to know you're worried about what I told you," he replied. "Which is good, in a way. It means you've at least thought about it."

Luna stood painfully to her feet. "I don't want to have this conversation right now."

"I think you need to," he argued as she turned her back to him.

"Yeah, well, you're not me."

"Where are you going?" he asked, holding his hands out to either side of himself.

"To lie down," she replied, holding a hand to her forehead.

Couldn't anyone understand that the thing she wanted the most was just to be left *alone*? She didn't wait for him to speak again. Instead, she hurried past the kitchen to the hall that led to her room. There would be quite a few benefits to getting a nap in. The rest would allow her a break from the insane reality she called her life, not to mention the fact that Rose wouldn't be able to force her to eat if she was unconscious.

Luna hoped Rose hadn't noticed her as she slipped inside her room, letting her sheets offer her the little bit of comfort she was still able to feel.

CHAPTER TWENTY-ONE

LUNA'S BRAIN WAS scrambled when she woke up from her nap. Her subconscious had sent her through a complicated maze of her memories and thoughts, making her wonder what reality she was in when her eyes opened that final time. Her mind spun, with different possibilities of what her future could hold. One of these considered the possibility that Chance was right.

She had come a long way from herself to ever think murder could be an answer.

Distant knocking sounded from the front door suddenly, but Luna didn't move, fearing the police had come back to question her again.

"Hold on, I'll get her for you," Luna heard Rose say to their visitor, before she appeared in Luna's doorway.

"There's someone here to see you, honey."

Luna looked up through her lashes. "Who is it?"

"Not the police this time," Rose replied and headed back to the living room.

Luna got up slowly to follow her, her heart like a jackhammer pounding against her ribs. If it wasn't the cops knocking on their door, who could it be?

"Luna, this is Layanna," Rose said, gesturing to the armchair in the corner of the living room. Luna almost didn't see the human seated on it, she was so thin.

The woman dipped her head in greeting, with a warm smile, as she watched Luna sit down on the couch across from her. Rose left the room, and Luna was glad. Who was this woman and why did she want to talk to *her* of all people? Was she a detective? Had she tied her to Kylie's murder?

"Luna, it's nice to meet you," she said, smiling wide enough to show her teeth.

Luna had no patience for small talk. "How do you know me?"

"My name is Layanna. You don't know me, but I know a little bit about you. I'm Stephen's sister."

Luna's mouth hung open, and she waited for her to speak again, to say it was a joke, but the silence stretched on and she said nothing. Luna's eyes ran over her long brown hair that curled around her shoulders and landed on her eyes as green as emeralds. The resemblance to Chance was obvious in her features.

Layanna wasn't a healthy type of skinny—it showed in the spots where her bones bulged under the skin. She lifted a rail-thin arm to scratch at the back of her neck, and Luna could see the ugly scars—track marks—in the crook of her elbow.

"At least I know I'm in the right place," she said as she observed Luna's reaction.

"Why are you here? Stephen's dead," Luna said coldly.

Layanna blinked her large green eyes closed for a minute before she opened them again. "I know," she said. "I just wanted the chance to meet you. Brendan said he met you, back home, in the cemetery?"

Luna tilted her head to the side. "You know Brendan?"

Layanna nodded. "We're practically family. When Stephen and I were separated, Brendan was the only one who tried to keep in touch with me."

Separated, Luna pondered the word, and in the back of her mind she could almost hear his voice saying *"I'm emancipated."* Maybe in some way, he had felt that was the truth.

"H-how old were you when you were separated?" Luna asked as she came back to focus and saw that Layanna was staring at her.

"I was ten. I remember it so vividly. You know, I was the one who took Stephen away from our mom. As a baby, I thought his chances were better out in the world, away from our parents, so he'd have a chance to make something out of himself before he grew old enough to learn the truth."

"You didn't go with him?" Luna asked.

Layanna's bottom lip jutted out. "No, I chose to stay with her."

"Why?" Luna asked, widening her eyes.

"It's easy to demonize my mother, based on the part of the story Brendan may have told you, but she couldn't help what she did. She was *sick*, and despite everything, she was my mother," Layanna said. "I loved her as much as I do Stephen. It was hard, managing both sides, but I did everything I could to make sure Stephen was okay—that he got what he needed. Once I knew he was okay, I made it my goal to look after our mother, because *someone* had to take care of her. After she lost Stephen, she was never the same again. Think what you will, but losing him was devastating to her."

"She tried to kill him!" Luna pointed out.

Layanna sighed, looking frustrated. "This isn't a black and white case, Luna."

"Look, my heart goes out to you … really, it does … but I don't think you've said what you're doing here," Luna said.

Layanna breathed out slowly, flaring her nostrils. "I read in the paper about your miscarriage."

"How did you even find me?" Luna asked, folding her arms across her chest.

"In this day and age, it's not hard to find anyone," she replied with a shrug.

"Then what do you want?" Luna asked.

"Straight to the point, I like that." Layanna quirked her lips into a half-smirk that reminded Luna so much of Chance. "Look, I knew about Stephen's 'secret' side. He had the same issues *before* he … well, did what he did. They found a lot of dead cats in that last year. Brendan tried to take the fall for a few, but Stephen didn't even make an attempt to hide them toward the end."

"You knew?" Luna asked in a breathy whisper. She could hardly believe it. In high school, no one would ever even consider the possibility that he could do anything wrong. *Family knows best.*

Layanna nodded. "Your tone tells me you know that side of him quite well."

Luna bit her lip to keep from crying, as memories flooded her mind. It was the only side of him she knew, and it was hard to believe her life would've been completely different if she *didn't* know about it.

"The baby was his, wasn't it?" Layanna asked, before Luna could brace herself for the blow.

Luna clamped her eyes shut as tears threatened to flow. "Yeah."

Layanna frowned. "Did you care about him at all?"

"I used to hate his guts, but now—" Luna said, breaking eye contact.

"What changed how you felt?"

Luna looked at her, confused. "What do you mean?"

"You said you *used* to hate his guts ... what changed?"

"My son died ... the son I shared with him," Luna replied quietly. "Ever since then, I don't know what I've been feeling. What I *should* feel. All I know is ... I'm not myself anymore."

"You're talking the same way he did before he snapped," Layanna mused as if she were talking to herself.

A flair of anger ignited inside Luna's chest. "Excuse me?"

"I-I just ... okay, you don't have to tell me if you've succumbed to those ... darker urges. I'm here to convince you to not do it again," Layanna said, holding out her hands.

Luna cringed. Layanna assumed Luna was going down the same path as her brother ... and she was right.

"Why do you care if I do?" Luna snapped.

"Even if you hated Stephen, he obviously cared for you. He'd want you to be safe, well taken care of," Layanna replied. "That'll never happen in prison."

Luna stiffened, not wanting Layanna to find out how bad of an effect her words had. "I can take care of myself."

"You're unstable, Luna. Postpartum depression can warp you into someone you won't even recognize, if you're not careful," Layanna cautioned.

Luna glared at her; she had crossed the line. "Get out." The words were easy to say and as Luna quickly discovered, *pleasurable.*

"Okay, I won't argue with you," Layanna said, standing to her feet. "Just whatever you do, be careful." A pause. "It was nice to meet you."

Luna glared, not feeling the same.

With that, Layanna left the house without another word, letting the door slam closed behind her. Luna stared after her with a whirlwind of emotions flowing through her. Every time she thought Chance's story couldn't get any more complicated, someone new waltzed into her life long enough to inform her she was wrong.

Rose peeked into the room at the sound of the door. "Everything all right?"

Luna shook her head. "Yeah. Another person passing along her condolences for Asher."

Rose threaded her fingers together and murmured, "I'm sorry, dear."

Luna's eyes trailed the edge of the coffee table as a long minute of silence dominated the conversation. "When's his funeral?" she asked softly without lifting her eyes.

"A few days," Rose said, then tacked on, "Do you think you'll be okay enough to attend?"

"Doesn't matter if I am or not. I'm going."

"Okay, honey," Rose said, kissing Luna on the forehead before she left the room.

Luna was glad for the room to breathe; she needed it more than anything.

***

LAYANNA STAYED ON the porch, just staring out into the darkness of the early morning. She didn't want to leave, not with the feeling in her gut, but Luna hadn't given her any other choice. *I messed up.* She sighed, ruffling her brown hair and thinking of how attached to the girl her brother must've been to do all that he had.

With another glance up at the sky, she took a step off the porch, and stopped when she caught a glint of light in the darkness across the street. Layanna froze, but not with fear, with *anger.* She knew what could create such a glint—a knife. Streaking forward, she headed toward the culprit without an ounce of hesitation and shoved him backward.

"What are you *doing* here, Cody?" she demanded.

Cody squinted up at her through the shadows before his eyes stretched wide, as if he hadn't expected to see her here. "This has nothing to do with you."

"If you're planning, even *thinking,* of hurting that girl, it does."

Cody scoffed. "Why? She means nothing to you just, as the Order doesn't."

"Your *Order* is nonsense. All you did was drive Stephen into devil worship, and he's no better off for it. He knows that, that's why he's fallen out of your favor."

Cody didn't even bother to look at her. "You have no business here."

"Neither do you," she countered. "You really think this is going to win him back? All you're doing is making him hate you. If you interfere, you'll come to regret it one way or another … that's for sure."

Cody snarled as if he hated her to her very soul and peered past her, through the shadows and into the lit-up windows of the house. Cody breathed out silently and just like that, his anger went out with it. "Fine," he said at last.

No emotion spread across Layanna's face as she watched him, taking in every second of his internal debate. "Thank you," she said finally.

"I don't understand why you'd side with her. Don't you want your brother back?"

Layanna folded her arms across her chest. "Of course I do, but I have faith that he's got a plan."

"And if he doesn't?"

"Then you'll find a way to save him, I'm sure."

***

LUNA SAT SILENTLY in the living room for a long time after Layanna left. Every time she began to cope with the horror story that was her life, the realization came that she wasn't strong enough to deal with all of it. How would she deal with Asher's funeral, or the days leading up to it? It would be harder than all the other funerals she had been to.

"I haven't seen her in years. She's grown," Chance observed.

Luna jumped at the sound of his voice and looked to see him seated beside her. "Why didn't you tell anyone you had a sister?"

"It was painful to think about," he replied.

"Why? She cared about you. All this time you led me to believe you had *no one*, but that's not true. I wonder just how much of what you've told me *is*."

He sighed and put a bitter smile on his face. "You've found all the other skeletons in my closet, I might as well tell you everything."

Luna shuddered at the metaphor, knowing perfectly well the "skeletons" in Chance's closet were both literal and metaphoric.

"When Layanna was a kid, and I was a baby, she saw our father beat our mother. She told me it didn't happen much, but I don't know if I believe her. She didn't want to see our mom hurt anymore, and she— she—"

Luna leaned forward, eyes wide in anticipation.

"She slit our father's throat in his sleep."

Luna gaped at him. Layanna might've worn her scars on the surface, but she hadn't seemed capable of murder.

"I had the same reaction at first. I couldn't believe what my own sister was capable of … that she was a monster," Chance said, his voice cold. "That dagger I gave you, it was hers originally."

"So … why did the police never search for you after Layanna gave you away? Didn't anyone notice you went missing?"

"From what I understand, my father's body was never found. I always guessed that they just assumed he kidnapped me and ran away. They got so caught up in their false lead that they never looked for the truth. Never thought there *could* be another truth."

"I don't think that explains why you killed your foster parents."

"Need to know it all, huh?"

"I think it's time, Chance."

He sighed and swiped his blond hair back. "Fair enough. A few days after Layanna told me what she had done, I began to figure out why she had done it. My foster parents … weren't bad people, I guess, they just pushed me until I cracked. After I killed them, I felt guilty … for my adopted father anyway."

"Not your mother?"

Chance scoffed. "Are you kidding? That bitch deserved it."

Luna thought of Kylie, thought of how she had stabbed her with the knife that had taken the lives of so many others. "Put the emotions you feel for both of your parents together, and it's exactly how I felt when I killed Kylie."

Chance smiled, but the look was painful. "You've got the right idea."

"How did you deal with it?" she whispered. "There has to be something I can do."

"You think so? Hell, I ran away. Away from my hometown, away from Layanna and Brendan, away from it all."

"That didn't stop the pain though, did it?" Luna asked.

A tear ran down Chance's face, though the bitter smile didn't leave his lips. "No, nothing did."

CHAPTER TWENTY-TWO

THAT NIGHT, LUNA'S mind was clogged with thoughts ranging from Michelle and Amy, to Layanna, to Asher's approaching funeral, and finally to the look on Chance's devastated face. Had that really all happened in just *one* day?

She turned over, staring at the blackness corroding the wall. Would she ever regain herself? The question felt like a trap. Finding herself, left her faced with a new complicated question: Who *was* she? She wasn't the same Luna, she *couldn't* be. The moment she had trusted Chance, had *confided* in him, was the moment she lost sight of who she was. Was he still the bitter enemy she had hated for as long as she could remember? Or was he her friend?

What did *he* consider himself to be?

She closed her eyes and tried her best to fall asleep, wanting nothing more than to relax for a little while. The thoughts that swarmed her brain, hurt her in ways she never would've guessed. When she began to slide into a deep sleep, she let a smile spread across her face. The sweetness of unconsciousness was alluring and she wished she could feel that peaceful all the time.

Just as she began to slip away, knocking sounded, loud and obnoxious. Luna groaned at the thought of company, especially company so *late*. The knocking annoyed her—jolting her away from the promise of peace—and she wished more than anything that it would stop.

But it didn't, and Rose wasn't home to play doorman. Finally, Luna rolled out of bed with a curse, dragging her feet toward the irritating noise. She planned to give the culprit a sound piece of her mind for waking her up, but when she opened the door, her malice dissolved and she froze like a deer in the headlights. She blinked once, twice, three times ... but he was still there.

With his long, greasy hair and standoffish attitude, Drew wasn't the type of guy girls would look at twice, but he wasn't unattractive either. Luna had only met him once, during the forced double-date Amanda had set up. Thinking of it now brought tears to Luna's eyes.

"Hi, Luna, how are you?" he asked.

A tear ran down her cheek. She let that serve as her answer.

"Can I come in?"

Luna nodded weakly, but had no conscious thought of doing so.

"I'm sorry about the other day—about running off like that. I honestly never expected to see you again, and when I did ... I don't know. I guess I panicked."

"It's fine," Luna said, thinking just how close to the same reaction she had had.

"I never got the chance to tell you how sorry I am about Amanda," he said and slunk into the armchair in the corner of the room. "She was a good person."

Luna swallowed, unsure of how to respond, as she plodded to the couch, sinking down into the fabric with the wish that it would swallow her whole. *Ironic choice of words.*

"Yeah."

"I still can't believe it was that boyfriend of hers. He seemed like an all right guy. I guess you never know. You always hear this type of stuff on the news, but I don't know ... when it happens to someone you *know*, it's so jarring." He tilted his head to the side, shaking his long, greasy hair, and Luna was tempted to grab a handful and pull as hard as she could.

131

She didn't need his account to come to that conclusion, and found herself wondering why she had answered the door, or better yet, why she had let him in after she *had*. "Drew, don't think I'm not happy to see you …" That was exactly what she wanted him to think. To *know*. "… but why have you come today? These are fresh wounds I just can't pick open right now."

"I know. I debated coming here today. I really did. But … I just can't stop thinking about Amanda. Or dreaming about her anyway."

That caught Luna's attention. "You've been … *dreaming* about her? Does she say anything? What does she say?"

"Yeah, er …" He paused to scratch the back of his head, and Luna hated the hesitation. "She just tells me she worries about you."

Luna drew her eyebrows together. "About *me*?"

Drew nodded. "Yeah, with everything going on … I guess that's just my conscience's fucked up way of telling me to come visit, to check up on you."

Luna licked her bottom lip, her mouth suddenly too dry. Drew didn't understand the weight his words carried, but she couldn't ignore it. "I appreciate your company … I do … but I just …"

Drew eyed her like he was torn between his attempts at being friendly and a desire to leave and never look back. "It's hard, I get it. I'll be on my way. It was nice to see you again," he said, hopping to his feet.

Luna appreciated his understanding. It was almost a shame that she never got to know him. *Almost*. "We should do this again sometime," she said, hoping it wouldn't be anytime soon.

"Agreed," Drew said, offering a smile that came off pitiful.

Luna moved to stand up—to guide him out of the house—when he reached a hand out, the smile that didn't match the rest of his appearance was still on his face.

"I can let myself out."

Luna relaxed her tensed shoulders, watching him go in a swish of black clothes and hair.

"He's still sniffing around, huh?" Chance's voice filled the room.

Luna turned, just in time to see the corner of his lip twitch up into a smirk. "He isn't 'sniffing' anything. He just wanted to see if I was okay."

"Right," Chance said with an amused shake of his head. "When I was alive, I wanted to see if a lot of girls were 'all right' after tough times, too."

"It doesn't matter what his intentions were … are … whatever," Luna said, gesturing wildly with her hands. "Did you hear what he said about Amanda?"

Chance nodded, amusement blending with fascination. "Matter of fact, I did."

"So what does it mean? She's never come to my dreams before. I've looked."

Chance ran his tongue along his teeth. "I don't know, but if she's making a point to stay hidden from you, then there's a reason."

***

THAT NIGHT, LUNA was in DreamWorld once again. She sighed in relief at the familiarity of her surroundings, and on instinct, wandered toward the cabin. It was dark and closed up like it had been abandoned for quite some time. Where was Chance, and why wasn't he here to greet her? She pushed her way inside the cabin to confirm his absence.

Sorrow yawned in her stomach. Was he avoiding her, or was he angry at her for kicking Layanna out of her house? Frowning heavily, she backed out of the cabin and the frown deepened as she dared herself to glance at the stone temple a few feet away. It was falling apart; chunks of stone that had once contributed to the structure, were piled around it like rubble as ivy wove through the holes like a 3D wallpaper.

She wondered if he was in *there*—the one place she refused to go, and he knew it. Memories clogging her mind, she took a clumsy step backward. Why had he chosen to go in there if he had? He hated it, too; it had been the place he had lost his memory in.

He's avoiding me. She didn't want to admit it, but she felt lost without Chance. He had become her guide, ironically—the light she followed when he used to be her darkness.

133

"Where are you?" she whispered under her breath.

She received no response.

In disappointment, she turned away from the cabin and bowed her head in defeat as she began to make her way to the surrounding woods. If he was determined to avoid her, then she wouldn't make herself a burden on him. It tugged at her heart to think that even her dreams couldn't bring her happiness anymore. *They've never brought me much.*

She trudged through the trees and bumped into Chance suddenly, both of them caught off guard by the other's appearance. She gasped before she took a step backward to observe him and the layer of mud that covered him.

With eyes shining exhaustion, he wiped a hand over his mouth, and Luna found herself wondering what he had been up to.

"Looking for me?" he asked, raising an eyebrow.

She nodded. "Yeah, I thought you were avoiding me."

"No," he said simply and ran his tongue along his teeth. He didn't want to talk—she could tell that from his tone alone.

"What happened to you?" she asked, eyes drawing in every rugged feature.

He shook his head. "It doesn't matter. Why are *you* here?"

That hadn't been the greeting she had expected. She didn't think he'd roll out the red carpet by any means, but the deadpanned expression on his face unnerved her. "It *does* matter," she said softly.

He closed his eyes. "Why are you here?" he asked again, slower this time.

He wants me to go away. "I just—I wanted to talk about Amy ... what you said," she said to him, trying to meet his gaze.

It was hard for her to look him in the eyes, and even harder for her to keep them there. She remembered those sapphire eyes seeing her through the worst of her times, always with a hint of amusement. There was none now. His eyes were glassy and dull. The years had not been kind to him either.

At the mention of Amy's name, a glint of interest appeared. "Come on," he said, leading her gently inside the cabin.

134

They traveled through the lopsided doorframe and sat down in the unsteady wooden chairs, staring at each other. In the back of Luna's mind, she remembered her senior year of high school, when he had nearly killed her in the building she now willingly ventured into.

"I think I know what you want to say—you're upset about my idea, right?" he guessed.

Luna blinked, his voice snapping her back to reality, back to the reason she was there. "Of course I am! How do you think I could *kill* Michelle? She's a nice person, and my friend at that. Have you forgotten I still have feelings?"

He smiled bitterly. "No, I haven't forgotten. Is this the only reason you came? We've had this conversation already."

"Yes, but ..."

Chance held up a hand to stop her. "I've said my opinion, and for the record, I'm very aware that you are indeed human. I saw the cut on your leg. Self-inflicted, right? That's about as human as it gets."

She frowned at him.

"Don't look at me like that," he said, a light chuckle falling from his lips.

"Why not? You're judging me," she said. "And it's unnecessary. This is about Amy and Michelle, not me."

"I'm not judging you ...," he groaned and ran a hand through his dirty blond hair. "Okay, let me ask you something. The last time you saw Michelle, did she look happy? Did she look well? You say she's a nice person, but is she really? I mean, look at what she did to Amy, her own sister! She locked her away in that place like a feral animal and never listened to her. Never called just to make sure that she was still alive. Would you want to be there? I sure as hell wouldn't. Amy was in shock, but instead of helping her get through it, or finding her a counselor, Michelle had her *committed* and then had the audacity to forget about her!"

Luna was silent. He had a point. Amy had been beyond help; refusing to speak a word and barely eating enough to sustain her. Michelle had probably exhausted all of her options before making the choice the she had.

"No, she hasn't. Amy's forbidden to call her."

"Don't you think that makes Michelle just a little bit wicked?" Chance asked.

Luna tilted her head slightly to avoid his gaze. She didn't like that every word he said held a hint of truth. Out of the corner of her eye, she saw him frown.

"Look, all I'm saying is you like to see the good in people, but I have some news for you, Luna. Not everyone *is* a good person. Some people have hidden motives and secret ideals."

Luna shivered at the sound of her name coming from his mouth. All the times he had said it before hadn't been under good conditions. "Like you?" Luna retorted, trying to hide the shiver that ran down her spine.

"I'm being serious."

Luna shook her head slowly. "I'm sorry … I know you're right."

"Then stop being stubborn and listen to me. Amy deserves better than to be locked away like an animal for the rest of her life," Chance said.

Luna narrowed her eyes. "Why are you acting like you suddenly care?"

He lifted his eyebrows in surprise. "What do you mean?"

"You. You hate Amy. You tried to kill her for crying out loud. You keep saying she 'deserves better' than what's happening to her, but what does it matter to you? Why are you trying to help her now?"

"The only reason I didn't like her, was because she was set to destroy me. As a Keeper, it was her *job*. Besides, I know that you feel for her," Chance said shrugging. "I hate to remind you, doll, but she's the last friend you have left."

"Because. Of. You," Luna growled, stabbing her finger into his chest with each word.

He licked his teeth and looked down at her, smiling sarcastically. "Get it out of your system?"

She sighed, loosening her hold on her anger. "I *do* care about her. Especially since it's your fault she got locked up."

Chance shrugged again. "I can take that shot. I've made a lot of mistakes in my time."

Luna's jaw set before she asked, "How do I know helping Amy get out won't be a mistake?"

"I know you don't believe helping your friends can ever be a bad thing," Chance said.

"She's mentally unstable," Luna replied.

"So are you."

"My point exactly," Luna said. "Look at the things I've done over the past few weeks. I shouldn't be out on the streets either."

"I don't think you're worried about Amy's mental health. I think no matter what the subject is, you still don't trust *me*. I'm telling you one thing, and by instinct, you want to do the complete opposite, but you can't keep doing that. We're on the same side now. Stop fighting me, love," he said softly.

Her chest heaved under the pressure of the breath she was holding. "How can I trust you after everything you've done?"

"I didn't say I blamed you for not."

Luna sighed. "It's not *you* that detours me, believe it or not, but …," she trailed off.

"The thought of taking another life sickens you," Chance finished.

Luna nodded, looking up at him through helpless eyes.

Chance breathed in deep through his nose, before he looked at the tiny girl before him carefully. "Think of it this way … Michelle has *cancer*. Can you think of a worse disease to have to endure? She's dying anyways, suffering, too. All you'd be doing is speeding up the inevitable, ending her pain as well. If you killed her, you wouldn't just be helping Amy, you'd be helping Michelle as well."

"I never thought of it like that before."

"You're too kind to think like that," Chance said with a bitter half-smile on his face.

"I'm not kind," Luna argued. "I'm twisted."

"If you *are* twisted, it's not because of you, but because of me … because of every single terrible thing I've ever done to you."

"You've been through your own list of terrible things," Luna said, lifting her nose in the air pointedly. "If you're a bad person now, it's because you've been through hell and back yourself."

Chance turned his back to her, purposefully making sure she couldn't see his face, as he busied himself with moving a candle across the room. "It's not an excuse."

"It's as good as any," she said gently.

"You have a friend to help," he said dismissively, "and when you get weak, remember, *she's suffering.*"

CHAPTER TWENTY-THREE

IT WAS HARD for Rose to rouse her daughter from sleep the morning of Asher's funeral. Luna's brain was already ninety percent shut down from the dream with Chance, and the idea of what her day would bring, pushed her over the top. Despite the tension between her and Chance, she hadn't wanted to wake up. Their conversation wasn't over yet, but she had been given no opportunity to argue. When Luna's eyes filled with morning sunshine, tears brewed in the corners of her vision, and she wanted to rip her eyes out of her skull. Her previous night of crying made them sting worse than anything she had felt before.

Rose had to talk her daughter through waking up. Luna took the fancy black clothes from her mom and went to the bathroom to change, glad for the solitude it offered her. She didn't know how much more of Rose's "comfort" she would be able to take. She stared at herself in the mirror, picking out every detail of her face that disgusted her.

She hardly recognized herself anymore. Her eyes, which had once held determination, were blanketed with sorrow and regret. Red marks scored the skin around her eyes from her constant flow of tears. Her caramel face looked unhealthy and emotionless. She wanted to break the mirror, except the thought of spilling more of her own blood made her sick, too.

Luna turned away from the mirror at that thought and worked on

139

getting dressed. The silk black shirt and black knee skirt didn't feel right to her, but they brought back memories. It was the same outfit she had worn to all the funerals she had attended. She used it so much, it was almost becoming eveningwear—a macabre ball gown. Luna glared at herself one more time in the mirror before she left the bathroom. She made her way to the living room and froze as she wiped at her face. If Rose saw the tears, she would tear into her like a pack of coyotes.

Rose turned at the sound of Luna's footsteps. "Are you okay?"

Luna was at a loss for words. How could she even *try* to answer that question? "No," she said finally, as a dry sob overcame her. She could picture her baby in his coffin and would give anything to skip the real view. How many ways were there to say she'd never be okay again?

Rose rushed to Luna's side and set a hand uncertainly on her shoulder. "Honey, I know this is hard."

Luna looked at her through eyes bleary with her tears. Why did people offer peace for a pain they would never experience? "No, Mom, you don't. You have no idea what it's like."

Rose took a breath, considering Luna's words. "You're right, I don't. I wish I had some way to help you get through this."

"If you wanted to help me, then you wouldn't make me go," Luna said, her usually soft voice rough from crying.

"I'm sorry, but that's the one thing I have to make you do."

Luna shrugged her mom's arm off of her as bitterness bit at her. "Why? Why do this to me?"

"Because he was your *child*, Luna. If you're not there to see him put to rest, it'll only make you feel worse inside," Rose said. "If you think this is hard, imagine how much worse the regret for not going will be a year from now."

Luna narrowed her eyes at her. "How do you know? How do you know *going* won't be a mistake?"

Rose swallowed, glancing behind Luna, as if she were looking for some excuse to change the subject. "I'm assuming what I think would be best for your situation. I realize it'll be hard, but you have to move on eventually. Giving him a nice burial will help you do that."

"You shouldn't assume things you don't know," Luna muttered

bitterly.

"I'm your mother. Mothers always know best," Rose said, and then hesitantly added, "as should you."

Luna glared at her before the expression dropped. Maintaining it cost her too much energy that she just didn't have. "Okay, I'll go. Just don't ever call me that again."

Rose was silent as she brushed a dark lock of Luna's hair from her eyes. She opened her mouth like she had something else to add, but Luna was quick to look away, disinterested in even the *idea* of continuing that conversation. Rose gave up on what she had been about to say and turned to lead the way outside. Luna plucked her black jacket off of the coat rack, glad Rose had taken the hint.

That was the first time anyone had called her a mother. It didn't sound right ... or *feel* right. She couldn't be a mother—the major defining characteristic of one was a fierce desire to protect their child from harm. She had failed to do that for Asher, and because of it, she would never know her son, never find out what kind of a person he would've been.

"I really think—" Rose began to say as they stepped outside into the cold.

Luna glanced up at her with a frown on her face, and once again, Rose changed her mind. Luna craved a freedom she would never have—there was always something, or someone, that reminded her of her misfortunes. She had no choice about that, but she could choose whether or not to talk about it—which she wouldn't do.

Rose got into the driver's seat and urged Luna to climb into the passenger's seat. Luna gave her a long meaningful look before she slipped into the backseat. It was safer. If she sat in the front, Rose would keep urging her to talk. Luna wanted to be left alone—which her mother didn't seem to understand—and was past the point of subtleties. Rose casted a disgruntled look over her shoulder as she turned on the engine, but kept her venom to herself. Luna shrugged it off, positive she would get over it before they arrived, and if not, it wasn't the end of the world.

Luna pulled her knees up to her chest, trying her best to curl up into her thick jacket. Maybe if she curled up tight enough, she would disappear. She didn't care enough about her safety to fuss with the seatbelt. Relaxing against the seat, she propped her head enough to stare out the window. Even though the only real sight outside was snow, she didn't want to look at it. She could imagine herself being curled up asleep in the warm solitude of her bed. Instead, she was awake in the nightmare that wouldn't end.

"Gloomy day, chica," a familiar voice said from beside her.

Luna opened her eyes and craned her neck to see Chance sitting beside her. He wrapped an arm over her stomach as he cuddled beside her. She didn't know how long he had been there, but she was relieved to see him. Luna blinked at him, but didn't speak as she returned her gaze to the window. She didn't know why his presence made her feel better, but it did. Besides his greeting, he said nothing. He understood the need for silence and that was a very precious gift. Rose parked the car and proceeded to climb out. Luna stayed in the backseat, still in her catharsis.

"Hey," Chance said, trying to rouse her from her trance.

She turned to look at him over her shoulder, not saying a word as their eyes locked. He offered her a sorrowful look back, but it was oddly comforting. He *understood* the pain she was going through, not assuming it like Rose, and he didn't expect her to magically get over it. Instead, he *allowed* her to feel it. Luna absorbed that look, absorbed the knowledge that for once, she *wasn't* alone.

"Luna, what are you doing? You don't want to be late," Rose's voice called from outside.

Chance blinked, and his blue eyes flicked in the direction her call had come from. Luna could see the distaste clearly in his features as his lip curled slightly into a snarl before he looked back at Luna. The look softened as he whispered, "She's right."

Luna broke eye contact with him as Rose opened the door to pull her daughter out of the car, toward the cemetery. That line from him was like a stab in the heart. He was the one who was supposed to understand her, not argue with her. Luna began to shiver again, her breath fanning out into the air around her. Why had her mother insisted she wear the flimsy skirt of her funeral attire instead of pants? She frowned to herself; it was one more thing she had to be upset about.

Chance walked beside Luna the entire time, his hand set on her tiny back to support her, as her boots stumbled over the snow and ice that had collected on the ground.

"Now that you're here, it's not so bad, is it?" Rose asked, smiling gently at her daughter.

Luna's throat felt dry as she replied, "Of course it's bad. It's my newborn son's funeral." She shook her head in disgust and pushed herself to walk a bit faster.

"Your mother didn't really say that, did she?" Chance asked, with a hateful glare trained on Rose that made Luna wonder if he wished he had killed her, rather than David.

Luna glanced at him, her answer apparent in her look.

Rose pursued her lips as they continued to walk. Luna hoped more than anything she would stay silent the rest of the day, but knew that was asking for too much. When they approached the group of mourners, Rose gave her daughter a long look.

"I'm gonna go talk to my brother for a few minutes. Will you be okay by yourself?" she asked.

Luna nodded, oddly elated at the information.

"Okay," she said and walked away.

Luna watched her with relief. "That's the first time she's left me alone in too long to count."

Chance sighed, his eyes focused in the distance. "I would agree with you, but you're too unstable to be left alone for long."

"Traitor," she scoffed and wrapped her arms across her chest, before storming over to the rows of metal folding chairs. She plopped down, her eyes focused on Asher's coffin a few feet away. The chair was freezing, the cold sinking right through her clothes, but she barely noticed through her rage and sorrow. She hung her head to tear her gaze away when a hand gripped hers comfortingly.

She looked up into Chance's face once again. "Why are you here?"

"Asher was my son, too," he said, his chin jutted out defiantly, as if he wanted her to challenge him.

Luna had no urge to argue. She was glad he was here, glad he was mourning their son, and even happier he could bring her comfort she no longer thought was possible.

"I'm glad you're here," she admitted and glanced at the white snowflakes that had gathered on her black boots.

"Are you?"

She looked up at him. His face didn't look smug, only sincere. "Yeah."

He offered her a small smile and clutched her hand tighter. "Thank *you* for coming. I know it was a hard morning for you."

Luna was glad when the pastor began to speak, because she had nothing to say in response. The mourners gathered around the tiny coffin, shivering from the cold, but none of them seemed as sad she did. She frowned to herself, knowing perfectly well Asher's death didn't matter to them; they were only present, because they felt it was an obligation as her family. Luna wondered why Rose hadn't made her way back over to her, but cherished the silence. Luna let herself believe that maybe, for once, she had realized what she had said was wrong.

Luna could only hope.

Her baby's funeral was so similar to the many funerals she had attended in the past, and yet, it was different. At the other funerals, the thought of Chance only brought more sorrow, more pain, but now he was the only comforting thing around. Everyone else made her sad. Not because they had done anything wrong, but because they simply didn't understand the complicated web of emotions that made up her brain.

Chance did.

The entire duration of the funeral, he stood beside her, hand in hers, as they observed the funeral of their only child. A tear dripped from the corner of her eye, but she didn't wipe it away. Chance noticed it, but he didn't say a word.

Tears ran from his eyes, too.

CHAPTER TWENTY-FOUR

THE FUNERAL WAS rough on them both. Luna's legs were numb as Rose herded her back to the car. They drove back home in silence, and Luna was sure to plop down on the couch the second they made it home. As Rose wandered away into the depths of the house, Chance appeared once again and just gathered Luna into his arms. She was too out of it to react.

She dozed off into a very light sleep, with him whispering comforting words in her ear.

During Luna's brief time in DreamWorld, Amy appeared to her again.

Luna raised an eyebrow as she stared the girl down. "How do you know the moment I fall asleep?"

Amy shrugged and looked up sheepishly through her lashes. "Keeper gift."

Luna blinked and looked away, wondering what it would be like to have that kind of connection to somebody.

"Have you thought any more about what I've asked?" Amy asked, and Luna could nearly *hear* her desperation.

Luna hesitated, looking down at her hands as if they were a separate entity that could answer for her, and she suddenly regretted her decision to fall asleep.

"Look, you don't have to answer, but I'm just … *worried* about you, Luna, and I can't do anything here."

"It's your own fault," Luna said pointedly, before she could stop herself. There was something about the concern in Amy's voice now, after everything annoyed her more than anything. Thankfully, the aggravation helped her wake up, and the second she realized she was back in her living room, she hopped to her feet, desperate to not fall asleep again anytime soon.

"Get enough rest there, Sleeping Beauty?" Chance asked, quirking an eyebrow as he watched her strange fit.

She casted a sideways glance at him, positive he wouldn't be joking if he knew the truth of the dream she had just had.

"What? Don't look at me like that."

She shook her head slightly. "Why are you staring at me?"

"You have work to do," he reminded her. "Or have you forgotten?"

Luna wanted to argue, but the numbness had seeped to her very emotions. "I'm not going to do it," she said. "I'm not going to kill Michelle. I want to see what she has to say for herself. That's it."

Chance sighed. "Baby, you really are just a simple creature."

She curled her lip at him before she made her way outside to the truck. What did he know? *She's just suffering,* Chance's voice radiated through her mind once again.

You're wrong, she thought back. Luna found herself solemn as she walked up to Michelle's porch, knife in her pocket. She watched herself as if the entity in the zip-up costume was in control once again.

Luna slid her hand into her pocket, feeling the handle of Chance's snake-handle dagger. Her finger traced the edge of the sharp blade, remembering the pain it was capable of inflicting with a single swipe— the power it had to destroy lives. She wondered how much of a history Layanna had given it before passing it onto her brother … and where the blade had been before that.

Luna swallowed nervously and looked around to make sure no one was paying attention to her as she stood on Michelle's porch, skin burning with anxiety so sharp that the cold seemed non-existent. To Luna, eyes watched her from every angle, even though there wasn't a single person around.

When Michelle opened the door a minute later, Luna hardly recognized her. Her long dark brown hair had been cut to hang loosely around her small face, and her eyes had a bit of light that had been absent during Luna's last visit. When she smiled, her cheeks were so full, it was hard to believe she had ever been sick.

She's suffering, Chance's voice floated through her mind.

Luna couldn't force the surprise away.

"Luna! This is a surprise!" Michelle greeted her.

Luna swallowed again as the sound of her voice pulled her back to focus. *Yeah, it is.* "Hey, Michelle, it's been a while."

"Yes, it has. What are you doing here?" Michelle asked, turning her head to the side.

"I wanted to see how you've been," Luna lied, though in her mind, she wasn't sure why. She could've just as easily said the truth about Amy, right then and there, and went on her way. If she hadn't been so caught off guard, she would've done just that.

"Come in," Michelle offered, stepping aside to leave an opening for Luna.

"Thank you," Luna said politely and moved to sit on the couch. "You look like you've been doing well."

Michelle nodded, closing the door. "I've been great, actually. Well, as great as a cancer patient can be."

"Good to see you're recovering," Luna said, tucking her hands together in her lap.

"Yeah, things have been great for me—but ..."

Luna raised her eyebrows.

"How's Amy? Is she better? Have you visited her?"

Luna flinched at the arsenal of questions. If Michelle was so curious, why had she not gone for herself? "Yeah, I did, but it didn't go well."

Her mind flashed back to months ago—when Chance had still

147

been alive, had still been hunting her. When she had tried to get Amy's help, the girl had been belligerent, violent and wild. Signs of recovery were far on the horizon. She didn't know why that memory was the one to come to her mind, over their most recent encounter, but her brain had been conditioned to do that—absorb every ounce of negativity she encountered.

"What happened?" Michelle asked with a frown, as she sat down in the armchair across from Luna.

"She was …" Luna paused to pick her words carefully, "… *hostile*. She didn't want to see anyone."

"It's a shame, really," Michelle said, shaking her head. "I was hoping she would've recovered by now. It's been so long. I miss my little sister … I was thinking of visiting her and bringing her home."

"This isn't a meeting to catch up," Chance growled suddenly from his place on the couch beside Luna.

Pretending to be bothered by a fly, she swatted at him, her hand oddly warmed as it passed through the place he sat. The distortion caused his image to flicker, but he didn't disappear. She looked back to Michelle. Her words were all that mattered.

"Were you really?"

"Yeah, it's lonely here without her. I've finally felt well enough to travel, so I was going to head over there sometime this week, but if she's still that bad off …"

Guilt stabbed through Luna like nothing she had ever felt before. Chance had twisted her mind, convinced her Michelle was a bad person, but *circumstances* had kept her away—not a personal debate. Luna knew *she* was the bad person—the knife that rested gently in her pocket was as good of a reminder as any.

"Luna, you're drawing it out," Chance warned.

She glanced at him, anger barbed in her words as she whispered, "Why do I have to kill her? She's going to help Amy on her own!"

"What? I'm sorry, I didn't catch that," Michelle said, with a quizzical eyebrow raised.

Luna jumped at the sound of her voice, wondering how much she had heard. "I said she'd probably be happy to see you. She called me yesterday, and I went to visit her. She's doing a lot better now," Luna said quickly. "I hardly recognized her."

"That's fantastic!" Then her face dropped. "Why hasn't she called?"

"She told me they won't let her."

"That's ... I can't say I'm surprised. I'm going to check her out of that place," Michelle said, shaking her head as she stood up. "If she's not better by now, then they're no good for her anyway."

"End it!" Chance nearly yelled at her.

Luna took a deep breath through her nostrils and gritted her teeth, but managed to keep her eyes on Michelle. She was determined to ignore him, determined to do what she felt in her heart was right. No amount of anger would change that. She was losing who she was and crossing that line would make sure she could not return. She put her mind at peace for what she had done to Kylie, by resolving it as the outcome of a fit of rage. If she killed Michelle, it would be pre-meditated.

It would be the final transition into a full-blown murderer.

"I'm so glad to hear it," Luna said, standing up as well. Mentally, she prepared herself to run from the house with the speed and mindlessness of a cockroach.

"Do it," Chance ordered. "Now."

Luna looked at him relaxed against the couch, eyes hostile. His blond hair hung menacingly around his pale face, casting a shadow that further intensified the emotion. He expected her to obey him, so her refusal both infuriated and confused him.

"She's going to let her go on her own," Luna hissed.

"She's *lying*," he said through his teeth. "She just wants you out of her house."

Michelle watched Luna, confused. "Luna, who are you talking to?"

"Kill her!" Chance growled, sitting up so quickly that Luna flinched with the assumption he would strike her.

Luna turned to Michelle, and her knife fell out of her pocket, before it was thrust across the room, sticking blade first in the wall.

Luna and Michelle locked eyes on it. Neither of them could think of a thing to say.

"Is that ... *yours?*" Michelle asked, her eyes as wide as saucers, with the obvious assumption that *she* had thrown it.

"Y-yeah," Luna said hesitantly.

"Why ..." Michelle began to ask and then she trailed off, standing petrified as if realization came over her. "*You* killed Kylie ... didn't you?"

"Move now!" Chance ordered.

The voices were becoming overwhelming, with panic gripping at her heart.

The time for choices was over. Michelle had seen something, a side of her that Luna wished would forever disappear—the same monster Luna had seen in Chance. She ripped the knife out of the wall and approached Michelle, who raised her hands in a submissive gesture, taking slow, careful steps backward. Luna raised the dagger at the same time Michelle fell into her chair.

She looked up at her through wide eyes. "What are you doing with that, Luna?"

"I'm sorry, Michelle," she whispered and swung the knife toward Michelle, stabbing once.

The tip slipped easily through Michelle's windpipe and blood flowed out to welcome it. Luna didn't move—she couldn't. Her hand stayed clutched on the dagger, as she watched Michelle try to swipe feebly at it. Her arms barely lifted before they slumped back to the chair. A horrible strangled sound made its way up her chest, as Michelle struggled against her destroyed windpipe to breathe, her dark eyes staring up at Luna. The resemblance to Amy made her heart ache. Luna kept her eyes on Michelle's wound, watching every second of her death. When Michelle took her last breath, her eyes locked on Luna and the hint of betrayal was unmistakable.

"Atta girl," Chance consoled from the couch. "Messy one, but at least you got the job done."

Luna merely stared at the blood that soaked Michelle's shirt and seeped into the fabric of the chair she rested on. A stream had already begun to flow over Luna's fingers, but she didn't feel it. In her head, she was miles away, thinking about Layanna's visit. The woman's words were as clear as if she were speaking right there, instead of in her memory.

Luna had killed a friend, someone she had no intention of ever harming. She had crossed the line.

"Don't go weak in the stomach now," Chance's voice called, snapping her back to reality.

"Wh-what do I do?" Luna asked, as she watched blood seep from the gaping hole in Michelle's neck.

"Get my knife back first," he said crossly.

Luna nodded and swallowed heavily as she regained the feeling in her hand. The warmth of the blood on her skin made her sick. Slowly, she pulled the knife from the carcass, hating the resistance Michelle's body offered, the squelching sound when the knife finally slid free. Swallowing back her disgust, she wiped the blood onto Michelle's clothes. With the blade clean, she set it back into her pocket and clutched her hands into fists at her sides, in a weak attempt to hold herself together, and looked back at Chance for guidance.

"Now, you do to her what you did to the baby murderer," Chance said.

"It's still light out though," Luna pointed out nervously, and wondered if Chance knew what she was feeling. Did he care?

"It'll be dark in an hour; wait 'til then," he said.

Luna casted another glance at Michelle's body, thoughts of burning it made her want to disappear. She couldn't imagine spending the next hour in the same house as the corpse of her friend, *staring* at it.

It would be the most agonizing hour of her life.

"Why did you make me kill her?" Her voice was so weak, so faint, that at first she wasn't sure if she had really spoken.

"What do you mean?"

"You threw the knife. She thought *I* did it and … why did you do that to me? She was *cooperating,* about to go get Amy *on her own.* We didn't need to kill her."

Silence greeted her question.

Luna turned to look at where he had been sitting to see he had disappeared.

"But you already knew that," she whispered solemnly.

She never felt more alone.

CHAPTER TWENTY-FIVE

L
UNA RETURNED HOME, exhausted, and haunted with the memories of her day. No matter how hard she tried, she couldn't get the image of Michelle's final resting place out of her mind. She wished the cold that numbed her fingers would work its magic on her mind as she stepped through the door of her house.

She glanced around the living room hesitantly for any signs of her mother, but she didn't appear. Luna was glad Rose wasn't home to greet her. Mud streaked her arms and smeared across her forehead, and blood had soaked through her clothes. It was almost obvious where she had been.

She was lucky … if that was the right word for it.

Chance had reappeared an hour before, guiding her through each step in disposing of Michelle's body. She had taken an oath to hold her silence as she moved through the process. It was a silent vigil to the life she had taken. The guilt welled in her mind already, and she didn't know how she was going to bear it for the rest of the day, let alone the rest of her life.

Chance sensed the beginning of her spiral. He talked her to the bathroom, where she washed up and got a fresh change of clothes. His eyes watched her with concern, as she soaked them in bleach before tossing them in the garbage. Luna didn't know why she cared, but she waited for Chance to vanish before she found herself sitting in the bathroom, once again, with Chance's dagger in her hands. She flashed back to earlier, when the silver had been bathed in Michelle's blood; she couldn't believe how much there had been … how much she had taken from Michelle.

The thought made her sick to her stomach. She was disgusted in her actions, disgusted in herself. She ran her fingers down the blade, imagining the blood that had coated it, before she inserted it into the flesh on her thigh and gasped at the pain, her mind focused on the fact she had committed another murder.

She watched the blood flow freely from the new cut. There were two lacerations and two lives ended, thanks to her. Her thigh was a gory scoreboard. Luna felt like a madman as she let out a short burst of raspy laughter, just as the first drop of blood fell to the floor. As quickly as it started, the laughter ended and turned to a vicious sobbing. Luna cleaned herself up and wandered into the kitchen, trying to put as much distance between herself and her thoughts as possible.

She didn't know what had compelled her to go into the kitchen, but she stood at the entrance, not feeling good about what she had done. When she had killed Kylie, she hadn't felt *that* guilty.

She had done a terrible thing, made worse by the fact that she knew there was no redeeming herself from it. It was murder … cold-blooded murder. Michelle hadn't *looked* like she was suffering … she had looked like she was recovering. Now, she would never be healthy again. Luna questioned everything about herself. Why had she even gone to Michelle's? Because Chance had said so? If she hadn't, the whole situation could've been avoided.

Michelle could still be alive.

Luna took a step forward and nearly toppled over her own feet, as her exhaustion threatened to bring her down. Part of her looked forward to the cold of the wooden boards, so she was surprised when she didn't hit the floor. She opened her eyes to see Chance helping keep her steady. He tried his best to hold her up as her body threatened to shut down. He whispered to her, trying everything he knew to console her, but she didn't feel better about the words he said.

He had forced her to kill her friend, and then left her alone to clean up the crime without a reason to his madness. He didn't care to help Amy; it had been for himself. He had wanted Michelle dead, but had no way to accomplish it.

He had used her.

"You lied to me," she said softly, suddenly aware of how close his body was to hers.

"I told you to do what was right," he said.

"Murder is wrong," she said, her voice small. She couldn't bring herself to look at his face, into his eyes. She didn't know what she would see there, but she didn't want to know.

"When you see Amy tomorrow, and she gets to leave her cell, you'll see you did the right thing," he assured her.

"But Michelle was going to let her out," Luna said, her mind swirling with guilt once again. "She was going to help her sister, and things would've been fine."

Chance frowned and wiped a lock of black hair from her eyes. "You don't know that. She might've just been saying that."

"We didn't give her a chance to find out."

He shook his head. "Don't think of it like that."

"But I *murdered* her in cold blood."

"You did what I asked," he said.

Luna frowned as she looked at him through eyes glazed with sorrow. "Does that really make it better?" When he didn't reply, she tacked on, "Why did you make me do it?"

"I know it's hard for you to understand, but one day, you'll see it was the right thing to do. Like I said, when you see Amy, you'll know."

"How can I face her, knowing her sister is gone, because of me?" she asked softly. "How can I console her when she cries, knowing it's my fault she feels that way?"

"Just remember, she gets to live her life, because of you," Chance said.

"Maybe," Luna said, "but I know once she finds out her sister is dead, she'll be devastated."

"Luna, you need to sleep. You're not doing yourself any favors by being like this."

"I'm not tired."

"At least lie down."

Her knees wobbled, threatening to buckle, and really, she had no reason to argue anymore; sleep, after all, would offer her relief that consciousness would not. She let him lead the way to her room and she fell onto her bed, looking up at Chance. Her heart pounded in her chest as she finally brought herself to look into his eyes.

"You'll be okay," he promised.

Luna stared at him, wishing he was as dead as she had been promised.

"Get some sleep," he whispered, planting a kiss on her forehead, before Luna closed her eyes to submit to the darkness.

WHEN LUNA OPENED her eyes, her heart sunk to her stomach. It seemed her troubles followed her, even when she was asleep. She was standing on a step in front of glass doors and senior year memories hit her like a truck, as she studied the halls of her old high school.

She took a few cautious steps inside, glancing down the abandoned walkways. It was eerily quiet with shadows dotting the walls, watching her progress. When the sounds of the footsteps died in the distance, the doors behind her swung shut. She jumped and hurried to pull them open. Despite her best efforts, they wouldn't budge. Swallowing heavily, she turned back toward the hall, aware of the fact that she had woken up in a nightmare.

"Hello?" she called.

The lights above her head burst as she spoke, showering her in an array of sparks. Slowly, she began to walk, her footsteps deafening with the blood pounding in her ears. In high school, she had walked this route every day, but in the dream, it seemed foreign, strange.

"Chance?" she called.

Silence greeted her.

Luna was beginning to panic. She had never been brought back to this place, to this *hell*. There had to be a reason for it. She passed a classroom and glanced inside, desperate for answers. There was a body lying on the table that caused Luna to freeze in the doorframe. Her eyes widened as the corpse slowly sat up and she looked into the eyes of Kate Red.

Luna didn't have a thing to say. She had been aware of Kate's death—the first murder she had suspected Chance of—but she had never *seen* her dead. The ghastly puncture in her chest leaked fresh blood and made Luna's stomach turn.

"Luna," the girl rasped.

Luna gasped and backed away. When she turned, she met Susan's gaze. Multiple wounds oozed blood from every inch of her skin. She walked awkwardly as she slowly approached Luna with an extended hand like a zombie in an '80's horror movie. Luna swallowed, closing her eyes to block out images of her corpse.

"Luna," she joined in with Kate's chant.

Panicked, Luna hurried to walk away, to find a way out of the school. There had to be one, even if it was hard to see at the moment. That was when Luna bumped directly into Michelle. She could see all the muscles in her neck as the ugly wound sagged open.

"Look what you did," she whispered. "Why would you do this to me?"

"I-I'm sorry!" Luna shrieked, taking a quick step backwards. She bumped into Susan, and when she made a move to run down the hall, she realized her path was blocked by Kate.

"Luna … Luna …," they chanted as they closed in on her.

"No!" she yelled as they circled her. "What do you want!?"

Before the ghostly fingers touched her, a voice halted them, "Back off!" it demanded.

The girls parted, to reveal Chance standing a few feet away. He reached a hand out to Luna as she stared at him, petrified.

"Come on," he said.

Luna's eyes were wide, but she grabbed his hand and hurried from her spot. When she opened her eyes, she was once again in her room. A deep gasping breath filled her lungs, relieved that the school around her was gone. She sat bolt upright in her bed before running a hand through her long raven hair.

"Are you okay?" Chance asked her.

She swallowed once to compose herself before she looked at him. "Y-yeah. I think so. What was that place?"

Chance shook his head. "Part of DreamWorld."

"Michelle was there," she said softly, her throat tightening at the thought.

He nodded. "I know, I saw her, too."

"I didn't think I'd *ever* see her again," Luna said.

Chance sighed and wrapped his arm around her shoulders comfortingly. "It's okay, you'll never see her again after this."

"How can you be sure?" she asked, pulling away from him to curl her lip at his lack of concern.

"I'll make sure of it," he promised with a face that left no room for "buts."

"If I could see her, doesn't that mean *Amy* can as well? What if she gets summoned to that … *place*? I'll be done for."

"That place is not where good people go," Chance said at last. "That being said, Amy wouldn't search there first. She'll go somewhere else, because she won't want to believe her sister might actually *belong* there."

"But she doesn't, does she? She's there, because of *me*," Luna said with a frown.

"Not true."

Luna sighed. "How long will she avoid the place before she decides to check it anyway? Whenever she does, I *will* be done for. It'll *all* be over. She's a *Keeper*, Chance. The fact that she hasn't already figured it out, is nothing short of a miracle. I mean, she has power over life and death."

Chance grinned, and Luna wanted to punch him in the face for even being capable of twisting his face in such a way. "I have that power, too, and I've never been a Keeper."

"True," Luna mused, tapping her fingers. "Are *all* the dead people there?"

Chance nodded. "Somewhere they are."

"What about Asher?" she whispered, unable to look into his eyes.

Chance's smile faltered. "He is, but I haven't been able to see him."

"Why not?" Luna asked.

"It would take a long time to explain," he said softly. She opened her mouth to ask a question, but he cut her off. "I know it'll be hard, but try to get some more sleep. You need it."

She sighed and laid her head back on the pillow. If there was a chance she could see Asher again, she wanted to take it. "I guess so."

Chance smiled at her until she closed her eyes. When she did, he let it drop. There were some parts of DreamWorld she was never meant to travel.

***

WHEN AMY'S BLEARY eyes opened in the nothingness of DreamWorld, she instantly sunk to the ground, too out of it to do much else. In her head came the horrible memories of the officers informing her of Michelle's disappearance, and the lack of a lead they had in the case. Amy had an idea, of course, and she was sick with the knowledge that it didn't matter, that her sister's current state could be her own fault. Leaning against the nearest tree, she closed her eyes, wondering if she could fall asleep inside of a dream, and also finding it weird that the thought had never crossed her mind before.

"I thought … if I did what you said, then nothing else bad would happen to Michelle," Amy whispered.

She waited, hoping the Voice would hear her, that it would offer her some kind of solution, or at the very least, some form of comfort, but after two minutes of complete silence, Amy knew that that *was* its answer.

"You promised!" she screamed in a dry voice, devoid of any real emotion. As her fist struck the earth, bits of dirt clung to the side of her hand.

Silence still.

"You promised," she said again, her voice much softer this time.

Her own sobs were the only thing she could hear. The bark on the tree, though it had hurt the first minute she rested her face against it, was nonexistent the longer she stayed. Amy sobbed and then the sound stuck in her throat, as someone's hand wrapped around her upper arm, ripping her upward with a force that sent pain all the way into her back.

In automatic shock, her eyes flew open, landing on the sneering blue pits of Chance's own eyes. "I've promised you nothing," he said coldly.

Amy's surprise quickly turned to a fear that sharpened into anger when everything came into perspective. She held up her hand, and it began to glow, an unearthly bright light that launched directly into Chance's feet, sending him yards away from her. She landed roughly on her tailbone, but hardly felt the pain. As she watched Chance land on the ground, she *heard* the sound of his bones and muscles jostling upon impact.

He groaned and sat up slowly, his eyes narrowed to slits in order to glare at her. For the first time, she didn't look away, didn't run. She stared right back.

When Amy came out of the dream, she immediately looked at her arm, and there was the proof that the encounter had been real—based on a ring of fingerprint bruises. The smell of his cologne still hung in the back of her nostrils, haunting her. Even though he was dead, things were no different from how they had always been. Amy had no idea why the thought of his physical demise had brought her so much comfort. The entire time he had been lurking in the background of her thoughts, waiting for the time to strike in DreamWorld.

Tonight had been her proof. She had *seen* him.

So close to Michelle's disappearance ... it can't be a coincidence.

***

WHEN LUNA CAME back to consciousness, she was in DreamWorld

again, but she thanked the heavens she wasn't in the high school anymore. Lush forest surrounded her, but she wasn't near the clearing that housed the cabin. She got up, looking around carefully to try to decide where she was. She wandered slowly through the nearest group of trees, worry in her heart. Why was she out here, instead of the usual place she woke up at? Had Chance sent her away, because even he wanted nothing to do with her?

"Chance?" she called faintly, hoping he would appear at any minute to console her.

"He doesn't come to this part of the woods," a familiar voice said from behind her.

Luna turned to see Sarah. The girl watched her through familiar blue eyes, eyes that Luna hadn't seen in years. The thought made her knees weak, and she feared she'd collapse as she stared at her.

"Sarah," she whispered.

"You and I both know why you're here," Sarah said.

"We've come to try and stop you," another familiar voice said.

Luna turned to see Amanda. She had forgotten how pretty she used to be. Even in death, with the ragged wound that had killed her, gaping open her neck, she was beautiful.

"All of us are here, trapped in Purgatory, because of our deaths," she said.

"But *your* killer died," Luna whispered. "You should be free."

"He condemned us to this," Sarah said. "Forever."

"Our deaths are unsolved, cold, and given up on by the mortals," Amanda said, swiping a lock of her long blonde hair over her shoulder. "We'll never be free from this fate."

"He lives on in you," Sarah said.

Luna's eyes volleyed between her dead friends. She knew where this conversation was going, didn't she? "W-what do you mean?"

"You can't continue on the path he's trying to lead you down," Sarah said.

"You've become the very thing that destroyed us," Max said, stepping into view from the foliage.

161

Luna's heart felt like it was going to burst at the sight.

"Look at you, Luna," he said, setting a hand to the side of her face. "You used to be so sweet, so kind. You did what was *right*, regardless of what you felt. What happened to you? Chance used to be our *enemy*," he said, pulling his hand back as if she disgusted him. "In high school, he *tortured* you. I know you haven't forgotten that."

"I-I haven't, but—"

"But nothing."

"Where have you been?" she asked, barely able to stifle her emotions. "You abandoned me."

"Even if you feel alone, you're not. We're here, we always have been. You don't have to listen to him."

Sarah nodded in agreement. "We never abandoned you. We're *weak*. Chance takes our energy away so only he has enough strength to be able to get to you."

Luna monitored the emotion on Sarah's face and realized Max and Amanda had the same looks. They looked at her with caution and concern, not love. They were *judging* her, not consoling. Her heart fell to pieces at the thought. How could they pretend to care, when their looks said otherwise? For all of the terrible things Chance had done, he had never looked at her like she was a monster.

"I'm not a bad person, and neither is he," Luna said, taking a small step backward. "He's misunderstood."

Max closed his eyes and looked sadder than Luna had ever seen before. "Did they ever tell you how I died?"

"No."

"I'll show you."

He grabbed Luna's hand before she could protest, and suddenly the scenery changed. They were in a basement. Luna shivered at the cold that radiated off of the gray stone walls and floor. It was nighttime, and the single tiny window perched toward the top of the stone provided no light to see.

"Why are we here?" she asked.

Max didn't say a word as a bolt of brightness flooded the room. Luna's eyes flicked to the large body that lay sprawled on the floor. It was Max lying at the base of the stairs, his neck twisted at an angle, while his blank eyes fixed on nothing through the darkness. Blood pooled under his unmoving figure from the knife embedded somewhere in his back.

"He came into my house in the middle of the night to do this," Max said from beside her. "Do you still feel as if he's a good guy?"

Luna studied the remains of her best friend. The last memory she had had of him was how peaceful he had looked in his coffin on the day of his funeral. The sight before her would replace that one forever. Sobs escaped her. "Oh, my God, Max," she said, collapsing into him. "I had no idea."

Max closed his eyes and a smile crossed his lips. Luna knew he was trying to keep himself from showing his true emotions, but he was failing.

Who was she kidding? They were right to judge her—she *was* becoming a monster. "I was wrong," she whispered. "I know that now."

"Remember this, if you get the urge to kill again. Remember the way Chance *used* you. Remember the way he ended our lives and doomed us to Purgatory forever," he said, opening his eyes to show the true sadness that lived there.

"I won't forget," Luna promised, then her eyes turned to observe his body as another flash of lightning lit up the scene. "I'll never forget."

CHAPTER TWENTY-SIX

"WON'T FORGET WHAT?" a voice asked Luna softly as she slowly found her way back to reality.

Luna opened her eyes the rest of the way to see Chance sitting on the edge of her bed. His hand was to the side of her face, and he stroked her hair, his blue eyes full of concern. Luna sat up stiffly and backed away from him until she hit the wall. She curled her legs up to her chest and stared at him through wild eyes. How could she have let herself see him as anything besides the demon he was?

"Are you okay?" he asked, holding out his hand.

"You killed my friends," Luna whispered, still seeing Max's dead body.

"Yeah, but I thought we were past this," Chance said, recoiling in hurt from her topic of choice.

"You killed them in *cold blood*," Luna said. "Just like you had me do to Michelle. How could you ever expect me to get over that?"

Chance was silent as his hand dropped back to the mattress.

"Why did you kill them?"

Chance continued his silence, looking down at his hands.

"I-I can't look at you for a while," she said, holding out a hand to block him from her sight. "I need some time alone."

Chance didn't look up as Luna buried her face in her lap and began to cry. What had she been thinking? Luna had been a strong-willed girl only a few years ago, but lately, she was easily pushed around, manipulated. Like Max had said, before his untimely death, she was *weak*.

Chance knew she wasn't capable of defending herself anymore, and he was right ... he *was* winning, after all. Her mind was empty of thoughts, like a drone waiting to act upon the next order given. Chance had somehow infected her mind, and now, he knew how to control her.

What was wrong with her? Normality had turned its back on her. Rationality and sanity were going the same way. Who she used to be, what she used to stand for, she didn't know. This was exactly what Layanna had been warning her of—the moment she would completely fall apart.

Chance had won.

His all-consuming reason for life was to tear Luna down for refusing him. Things were different now, but did he still feel that urge to drag her down? To see her ruined? The incident with Michelle certainly made her think so. *How did I change so much?* Luna wondered, thinking back to when she had been ready to give up her life for Amy, rather than kill her. How had she gone from martyr to murderer?

Luna sighed and stood clumsily to her feet. According to her alarm clock, it was already one in the afternoon. Her body protested her progress, willing her back to the comfort of her bed. Her stomach argued back, rumbling with hunger. Swiping her black hair out of her eyes, she wandered to the kitchen, not caring to change out of her nightgown. Rose wasn't home, so Luna decided to busy herself by making a salad for lunch.

She rummaged through the fridge for ingredients and set them on the counter to grab a knife, finding the smallest one she could. One any larger would only inspire her mind to focus on things she would rather forget. She picked up a carrot and began to work on cutting it up, but her hands shook at the sound of the knife hitting the sink, and she tried her best to dull it. Despite her busy hands, all she could think of was Max's broken body at the foot of the stairs, and Amanda's and Sarah's shockingly real corpses in DreamWorld.

As if those memories weren't enough, she would remember that single gash across Michelle's throat. That one gash that resembled the mark on Amanda's throat. The only difference; *she* had made Michelle's mark … not Chance.

Murderer, a tiny voice in the back of her mind said.

Luna squeezed her eyes shut, trying to tune out her thoughts and will her mind to silence. It didn't work. When she closed her eyes, the visions came to light much more vividly. In her mind, she was back at Michelle's house, holding the blade to her throat, blood streaming down her hands.

She would give anything to take it all back.

"Luna," Chance's voice said suddenly.

She jumped, and in the process, the knife came down, slicing the skin open on her thumb. She yelped in pain and threw the blade to the counter, and put her bloody thumb to her mouth. The skin throbbed, and idly, she wondered how much worse Michelle's wound had hurt.

"Damn it," she muttered, trying her best to soothe the pain by wrapping her hand in a dishtowel.

Chance watched her helplessly. "Are you okay?"

She glanced up at him. "I'll be fine. What are you doing back here? I told you I can't see you for a while."

He pursed his lips. "This isn't about what I did in the past, is it? You feel guilty for what *you* did."

Luna wished she still had the knife to throw. "Of course I feel *guilty*! I killed Michelle *for* Amy, but I don't know if I can even face her."

"You feel guilty, because you still don't think it was her time to go," Chance said.

Luna glared at him. "It *wasn't* her time to go. I don't know how you could overlook the fact that she was *recovering*. You used me."

"I didn't use you, Luna, I was trying to help you," Chance said.

"Why do you keep trying to sugarcoat it?" she asked. "You might've been able to manipulate Amanda and all those bimbos with that little act, but not me. I can see the truth. I *killed* her in cold blood. Just like you did to Violet, Max and Amanda. Even you don't have reasons for it, because you know deep, deep down, it was *wrong*."

"Violet and Amanda, I'll admit I didn't need to kill, but Max, I did."

That caught Luna's attention. What a way to kick her when she was down. "How could you say that? Are you just trying to hurt me?"

"Our past is long and complicated," Chance explained, raising his hand to study his fingernails.

Luna frowned. "So is ours, but I've known Max forever. I would've known if he had anything to do with you."

Chance smiled, looking so smug that Luna's heart sunk right into her stomach.

"What are you keeping from me?" she asked, wondering if she really wanted to know.

"Let's just say, you're not the only one who's killed for me."

"Max would never do that!"

"You didn't know him too well," Chance said, shrugging as he dropped his hand to his side. "Oh, well."

"How dare you accuse him of that?" Luna snarled, narrowing her eyes to slits. "You *killed* him, remember? You can say whatever you want about him, because he's not here to defend himself anymore, thanks to you."

Chance flared his nostrils. "We're off topic. My point was, you killed your midwife and haven't felt guilty about it once. Do you want to know why that is? *You felt you had a legitimate reason.* She killed Asher, so when you killed her, it seemed justified."

His words stunned her and for all her trying, Luna couldn't seem to react. Even when she thought back to the grisly murder, guilt didn't accompany her. "That can't be."

Light filled Chance's blue eyes at the sound of hesitation in her voice. "You feel like I tricked you with Michelle. You assumed she would fight her cancer off and have a long life. Did you ever think about the fact that it could and probably *would* come back? She was dying. You were weak. All I did was give you a push, help you do what you needed to do."

"I can't get over the look on her face. It was the worst look of betrayal I've ever seen."

"Stop regretting what you did, and accept that it's over," Chance said. "There's nothing you can do to change the past."

Luna sighed. "You're right," she said, removing the towel to look at her cut. "What other choice do I have?"

He bobbed his head. "How's your thumb?"

Luna ignored the question and slammed her hand to the sink. "I can't go tell Amy today."

"Why not?" he asked, folding his arms over his chest.

"I don't think it's a good idea," she said. "I mean, won't people find it funny if I try to check Amy out, before her sister was reported as missing?"

"Perhaps, if they decide to look into her family."

"The police are already suspicious of me," she said. "I don't want to do anything else to make them look my way."

"You have a good point," Chance replied, scratching the stubble on his chin thoughtfully.

"Maybe if I wait, someone else will do it," Luna said.

He frowned at her. "You can't always wait on someone else to do your work for you. She's your friend, Luna. Remember when you risked your life to save her?"

How could I not? she thought sourly, with that same feeling of loss. The old Luna would've rather died than take a human life.

"It's the same idea now," he countered.

"When did I lose sight of myself?" she asked quietly.

His forehead crinkled. "What?"

"When did I *change*?" she asked, looking up at him through eyes glazed with sorrow. "You … I used to hate you, and you wanted to kill me. What happened to us that made us change our opinions of each other?"

"Life happened," he said with a less than empathetic shrug. "We're all we have now."

Luna looked up at him through eyes resembling a doe's. "It's too bad you're dead."

CHAPTER TWENTY-SEVEN

AFTER LUNA FINISHED eating her sparse lunch, she went in the living room to watch television with, the hope of numbing her mind for a bit and calming her tattered nerves. No matter what she tried, nothing seemed to work … television included. All she could think of were Chance's solemn words, and his accusations against Max.

Even after he killed him, he's still trying to turn me away from him.

As she channel surfed, she noted television was more violent than she remembered as a child. Then, she remembered she never watched television as a kid—her mother had been too afraid of rotting her mind. Luna flicked it off and threw the remote onto the couch beside her.

Chance had disappeared a while ago, and Luna appreciated the solitude. Lately, she needed some time where she didn't question herself, didn't question everything she thought she knew. Unfortunately, when she was awake, that was a luxury she couldn't afford. She cuddled into the couch, and when she opened her eyes again, she was in DreamWorld, in the woods where Max had confronted her.

"Max!" she called out desperately, her throat irrationally dry. Only a second passed, but to her, it felt like eternity. She wanted answers … answers he had denied her in the time he had been alive. "Answer me!" she demanded, and her voice was a weak rasp, very unlike her.

169

Silence surrounded her again.

She sighed, ready to force herself to wake up, when she heard nearby footsteps and turned to see Max waddling toward her. "What's wrong, Luna?"

"I want the truth, Max," she said, her arms folded over her chest. "Before it's too late."

Max sighed and glanced around, as if he expected Sarah or Amanda to appear and bail him out. "I suppose that's fair, but this may be the last time we see each other, if you react the way I think you will."

Luna huffed, trying to keep the emotion out of her eyes and voice. "What is it, Max? What have you been so afraid to tell me for all these years?"

"Chance ... he's telling you the truth ... about me. Me and him were friends, Luna. I have the ability ... *your* ability. He came for me first, before he ever really noticed you."

Luna stared at him wide-eyed and open-mouthed. "No. That can't be, Max."

Max smiled bitterly at the hurt in her voice. "It was years ago, back in freshman year of high school. We were best friends, had been ever since I met him in elementary school. He taught me everything I know about DreamWorld."

"Why don't I remember any of this?" she whispered. "*We've* been friends since elementary school, too! I've been by your side all these years ... how—this whole time I thought you hated him."

"And I do now. He hurt you, Luna. I don't know what he did to you, but he hurt you ... because of me. He-he didn't like my focus on you. He hinted a few times for me to do it, but I wouldn't. That's *why* I hate him. I had no choice, but to wipe your memory. When I did it, I didn't know how much of an effect it would have, or if you would even have your memory at all when it was done, but I thought it was for the best. I-I didn't realize it was only going to put you in more danger."

"Is that why you went to juvie? You *helped* him do whatever it is he did to me?"

"No, Luna, God, no. I tried to stop him, but I was too late. We got charged for the fire he set, but we couldn't convince the cops to connect him to what he did to you, because you weren't able to press charges."

"Why erase my memory? I would've been prepared for everything that happened!"

"I thought if I wasn't around anymore, he'd have no reason to hurt you again. I-I didn't think he'd pin all of his frustrations on you."

"No one ever told me what happened," she whispered. "My parents never even told me."

"I-I did what I could to make *everyone* forget. It was the only way you would never find out the truth. It would've destroyed you."

"Wait … it was you who took the gun the day Violet died, wasn't it?" she asked.

Max sighed and looked away. "Yes, it was me."

"H-how? Your leg was *cut off* from that bear trap," she whispered.

"It wasn't easy," he admitted, reaching up to scratch at the back of his neck. "In fact, it was one of the most painful things I've ever done. But our gift? We can heal."

"Then why do it, Max? That was the only evidence we had against Chance. Why would you take it?" she asked, feeling as if there were a gaping hole growing in her heart.

"If Chance were to go down for his crimes, I would as well."

"You—*killed* for him?" she asked, hearing the echo of Chance's words telling her the information she wished was a joke.

Max nodded. "He took the bodies away. All of them, as insurance if I ever turned on him. If he ever got caught, he planned to use me as a scapegoat."

"H-how many bodies were there?"

Max looked away. "He thinks of himself as a God, you know. He was so jealous of you, expected me to be at his every beck and call. He practically wanted me to worship him for showing me this place. When I picked you over him, he set out to destroy you, in the hopes of hurting me for abandoning him, but somewhere down the line, things changed."

He paused to stare at her, and she stared back.

"The relationship he tried to force on you was so *twisted*, it was sick. Somehow, he lost sight of his goals to hurt me, and he changed to trying to possess you—what he thought would forge an intimate relationship. His hate turned to passion, his determination to desire, and there was no changing it back."

"And you just stood by and watched." Luna exhaled slowly, staring at him. "You watched and pretended you had no idea why it was happening."

"I didn't think he would go as far as he did, Luna," Max admitted. "I thought if I came back into the picture, he would turn his sights back to me, to finish what we started."

"How could you do this, Max? You were everything we fought against. This whole time … I-I thought I *loved* you, but you were just as bad as Chance. No, actually, you're worse, because you actually managed to gain my trust."

"Luna, wait," he said. "I didn't tell you, because my biggest fear was losing you. I wanted so badly to stop him … but it can't be done. Trust me. He's too strong."

"Is that why you want me to kill myself … because I'm the only link left?"

"You broke the chain, Luna. Of all his victims, you were the only one who ever walked away, and he hasn't forgotten."

Luna closed her eyes, tears trailing from the corners. "I don't want to hear anymore, Max," she said. "When I wake up, I never want to think about you again."

***

IT WAS KNOCKING that pulled Luna from sleep, and she opened her eyes, tempted to ignore whoever it was. The pain in her heart from Max's words was all that mattered.

"Open up, police!" a voice boomed out.

The exhaustion was gone, as Luna's eyes opened the rest of the way. She could imagine four or five officers waiting outside in full uniform to handcuff her and throw her into the police car for all the neighbors to see. As panic overtook her, she began to sweat and had to force herself not to cry.

"Open up!" he insisted.

Luna bit her lip; she couldn't stall any longer. Wiping the sweat away, she tried to relax her racing heart and opened the door. Officers were trained to detect the slightest hint of a lie. They would probably be able to *smell* it on her.

"Hi, officer, can I help you?" she asked, surprised at how calm her voice sounded.

"Luna," Officer Sterrling said and tipped his hat to her. "It's been a while. How are you?"

"I'm doing okay," she said cautiously. "You?"

"I've been doing great. Sorry to meet under these circumstances again, but I need to ask you a few questions," the man said, looking at her through deep blue eyes. "May I come in?"

"Of course," Luna said in a friendly voice, though she felt on the urge of passing out as she led him to the couch. "What is it regarding?"

"There's been another missing woman," he said.

Luna blinked, looking at him through wide eyes.

He continued without waiting for her response. "It's still early, but Miss Michelle Jimenez has been reported missing."

Luna did her best to try and appear surprised. How had anyone noticed? It didn't seem as if Michelle left her house much, and the only real family she had was Amy. Who knew she was missing so quickly?

"Michelle went *missing*? When?"

"We're not exactly sure, but we believe sometime yesterday afternoon," he said.

"Have you had any luck finding her?" Luna asked.

He shook his head. "We had a few possible leads, but they all had dead ends."

"That's terrible!"

He nodded as he observed Luna. "I thought I would investigate people in town who knew both Michelle and Kylie. When was the last time you saw Miss Jimenez?"

Luna swallowed heavily despite herself. His eyes bored into hers as he waited for her to speak. She fidgeted, feeling as if they were trying to probe directly into her soul. "It's been a while, so I'm not exactly sure," Luna replied hastily, hoping he wouldn't notice the fresh bead of sweat trailing down her face. "If it helps any, I talked to her sister the other day."

"A Miss Amy Jimenez?" he guessed.

"Yes."

"What was the conversation regarding?" he asked.

"Amy said she wanted to call her sister, but the people who watched her wouldn't let her. She wanted me to see if there was a way I could check her out," she replied.

The officer raised a quizzical eyebrow.

"She lives in Brentwood Psychiatric," Luna explained.

"Ah," he said, jotting something down on a tiny notebook. "Do you remember about what time this conversation was?"

"Between three and four," Luna replied.

"Did you go and see Michelle after visiting her sister?"

"No," she said quickly, perhaps too sharply, the force of air made her voice come out louder than she had intended. If he hadn't known she was lying before, it had to be obvious now.

"Mm-hmm."

"Is something wrong?" Luna asked nervously.

"No, but I have a feeling I'll be seeing you around, Miss Ketz," he said, before standing to his feet.

"I hope everything works out with Michelle," Luna said, trying her best to sound innocent.

He peered at her through half-narrowed eyes, and Luna recognized the suspicion that plagued them. Her act wasn't nearly as good as Chance's, and he could see something wrong. The only thing that saved her was that he didn't know *what*. "Well, I have some questions I need to ask your friend, so I'll be heading out. Thanks for your cooperation," he said, smiling politely, and left without another word.

Luna followed him to the door, standing in the frame, as she watched him get into his car. He sat in it without even bothering to turn the engine on. Was he radioing the information he had learned into the office? Was he suspicious of her, or had the look in his eyes been a figment of her imagination? More importantly, what questions was he going to ask Amy?

Me, she thought. *He's going to ask her about me.*

The look he had given her told her that.

Luna waited for him to drive away, before a nervous laugh slipped from her lips as she watched his police car disappear down the street. She closed the door, more thankful than ever that Rose wasn't home. The fact that another police officer had been by, surely would've drawn suspicion.

Luna's insane laughter would've screamed for it. As suddenly as her fit of hysterics had begun, it stopped. Her legs gave out, and she collapsed against the couch, her body shaking with a hint of the laughter she had channeled seconds before. It was a solemn thought to realize she hadn't laughed like that in a long time, and she still wasn't sure what had sparked it. What would Amy tell the police about her? Would she tell them the truth about senior year?

I'm gonna get caught, she thought to herself.

Her head swam with so many thoughts, she might as well have been drowning. At first, she thought time would lessen the burden of guilt, but she realized it only made it harder to carry. She didn't know how much longer she could go on—the struggle was tearing her in half.

How had Chance been so comfortable with this life, when he had been living with the same risk of being whisked off to jail? How could he live with the skeletons in his closet? She thought back to high school, to his carefree charisma. Everybody who ever met him, loved him. Nobody would've believed murder was his hobby. And even with the evidence, no one did.

He didn't feel guilty for what he did, she reminded herself, *he was* proud *of it.* Luna bit her lip. *Apparently Max was, too.*

No matter what Chance told her, she had a feeling he would never tell her the truth about his final day on Earth. Could guilt and shame have been the true motivation behind his suicide, and he didn't want to admit it? Or maybe he finally wanted to be caught for what he had done. Maybe he wanted the families of all of his victims to feel some sense of justice, and he didn't want to have to go to jail to achieve it.

Luna remembered the hint of suspicion in Sterrling's eyes once again. She didn't know what she would've done if he had called her out on Michelle's murder. She would've been stupefied into silence, and that silence would've been her ticket to jail. The thought of the humiliation and shame, of being connected with her ghastly crimes, made her shiver, as she pictured the disgusted looks of horror and disapproval from the people who had once accepted and loved her.

It was easy to picture her mother sitting in the court room, listening to the twisted testimony of her only child. Not only had she lost her beloved husband, but she would lose the monster she had come to call her daughter as well.

The thought made Luna laugh in another string of hysterics. When it died down, Luna wondered, once again, if she was generally losing her mind and whether or not she should care.

CHAPTER TWENTY-EIGHT

"YOU HANDLED THAT better than I would've thought," Chance said a few minutes later.

At the sound of his voice, she blinked. Her eyes stung a bit, and she wondered how much time had passed, when she noticed him standing a few feet away. Usually, she would've gotten angry that he had been spying on her, but she was too upset to have anything light her fire. The fear that had bundled in her heart was beginning to fade, but the feeling lingered enough to make her uncomfortable.

Luna's vision was blurry with tears that caused the scene around her to move eerily slow. While she hated showing emotion in front of him, lately, it was nearly impossible not to. Even though he had been her enemy at one time, he was something different now; the shoulder she leaned on—a much-needed piece of her life.

"H … how did you do it?" she asked softly, blinking to clear the water from her eyes as she studied his face.

He raised an eyebrow quizzically and sat beside her, his sapphire eyes locked on her face the entire time.

"How did you not freak out when a cop came to the house to question you? How were you not burdened by all the horrible things you did? How did you not worry about spending the rest of your life in prison?" she asked, her voice trailing off in a sob.

177

"First of all, you know me, Luna. I don't *care* what other people think of me, and I didn't, even back in high school. That's probably what saved me from worrying about what I did. If I didn't worry, people wouldn't see it on me. I didn't have a family to frown on me for what I did. I had Layanna and Brendan, that's it. As you know, Layanna has done a lot worse than me," Chance said.

Luna shivered slightly with the bloody story of Chance's dagger in mind. "So … you never worried about going to jail? Even when you first started … killing?"

He shrugged. "Not really. When I was little, I knew to clean up my tracks. Every time I killed someone, I knew what I was doing, and even if I did leave something behind, I could charm my way out of any cop's suspicion. Not to mention DreamWorld's amazing ability to change my fingerprints. Remember Kate and Susan? Those cops knew it was me who killed them, but there was no evidence for them to link me to the crime anyway. People around here only thought positive things about me … until you got Sarah pinned to me, of course."

"People around here never liked me," Luna said, sidestepping his comment. "They've judged me for every little detail, for as long as I can remember. That's the weight of being an outcast, I guess. I liked Sterrling when he helped me with you … but it seemed as if he knew I had something to do with these murders. If I messed up some little detail, I can't charm my way out of suspicion like you used to. If I messed up, I'm finished. What if I did something wrong, Chance?" She glanced up at him, staring at him through wide eyes, pleading for an answer.

Chance stared at her through emotionless sapphire eyes in return. "You did everything I told you to."

Luna looked away, not certain.

"You did everything I told you to," he repeated tensely, "right?"

Luna nodded.

"You'll be fine."

"But there's so many perspectives in this case that could point to me," she said desperately. "I mean, what if Amy tells the cops I was supposed to go talk to Michelle the day she went missing?"

Chance shrugged. "So what if she does? There's no proof you went. Besides, you killed her a few days *after* you promised Amy you'd visit, remember?"

Luna was silent for a minute, considering his words. "You really think I'll be okay?" she asked, glancing up at him again.

He smiled slightly. "I don't see why not. If she did mention it, then right now it's a 'he said, she said,' kind of thing."

Luna sighed, feeling the weight of her heavy heart. "Maybe I should go talk to her about it and find out what she said. Wondering about it just stresses me out."

"That'd be smart."

She smiled with a twinge of irony and looked up at the ceiling, before standing carefully to her feet. She paused, turning to look at him. He was relaxed against the couch, his arms draped over the back.

"I'm gonna go get it over with then," Luna said.

Without moving his arm off of the couch, he made a gesture with his hand, his face hard to read. "What are you waiting for?"

Luna blinked, wasting no time searching for her keys, before pulling her coat on to rush out to the big truck. It had snowed again during the night. A blanket of the fluffy white substance covered the street. Her feet slid helplessly on a hidden patch of ice, and she prayed she wouldn't fall before she got in and turned on the engine. Luna drove slowly, with thoughts of last year's car accident fresh in her mind.

Finally, she made it to Brentwood Psychiatric and parked the truck, preparing herself the best she could. Nerves strengthened to the best of her ability, she climbed out of the truck, glancing around to catch sight of familiar brown hair. Layanna locked eyes with Luna before she tried to duck into the nearby line of trees, out of Luna's sight. Luna's rage bubbled inside her at the thought, her nerves already on end. How long had she been following her?

Did she know about Michelle?

Luna slammed the door of the truck before storming up to her. "I thought I told you to leave me alone."

Layanna sighed and stepped out of her hiding place. "Yes, but I don't trust how unstable you are. I wanted to keep an eye on you."

"How long have you been following me?" Luna demanded.

"Does it matter?"

"Yes, it will when I try to file for my restraining order."

"You don't have to do anything *that* drastic," Layanna said, tucking a strand of brown hair behind her ear. "I wanted to make sure you were okay … unless, of course, you have something to hide?"

Luna silently let out a breath of relief, content she hadn't seen anything of importance. "I told you before, I'm fine."

Layanna held her hands out. "I'm not trying to pick a fight. I just want to let you know, I think you're doing the right thing." She glanced at the building once. "These people can help you, I promise."

Luna groaned. "Look, just stop following me."

Layanna blinked her huge green eyes, looking oddly sad. "Just be careful, okay? Stephen had alliances," she said and turned away.

Luna was dumbstruck as she watched the retreating figure. "Wait, what?"

Layanna casted a sad glance at her over her shoulder, but kept going, remaining silent. *Like brother, like sister.* Luna tried to shake off what Layanna had said, but she couldn't. What had she meant by alliances? Was it possible that the man who had tried to attack her had done so, because he knew Chance, and knew that she was trying to break their bond?

She bit her lip as she walked the path to enter Brentwood. With thoughts of Layanna still stubbornly bound to her mind, Luna followed the routine procedure of emptying her pockets and followed the large nurse down the hall to Amy's solitary cell. She wasn't surprised to see Amy sitting in the chair in front of the window with her back to the door.

"Hi," Luna ventured.

Amy got up, turning to face her, as if the sound of her voice had been her cue to move. "Luna."

Luna was relieved to hear the lack of hostility in her voice, though the small girl's stature made the butterflies in her stomach flutter harder. "Are you okay?"

"No," Amy said, plopping down on the edge of her bed. "Michelle's missing."

"I know," Luna said. When Amy looked up at her surprised, she added, "An officer came to talk to me earlier. I'm so sorry, Amy."

Amy shook her head. "It's so hard to believe."

Luna went to sit beside her tiny friend. "I know what you mean. When I ... when I saw Violet get *killed*, I couldn't believe it really happened ... no matter how long I stared into her eyes."

Amy turned to look at her hesitantly. "The other day ... did you talk to her for me?"

Luna swallowed, panicked sweat clamming her forehead and hands. "I wanted to," she began uncertainly, "but I didn't feel too well, so I went home instead. I'm sorry, Amy, if I would've known ..."

Amy put up a hand to stop her midsentence. "It's okay, Luna, I understand. I mean you just lost your baby; things are hard for you, too. I only wish you could've talked to her, and let her know I missed her before ... before ..." She smiled and wiped her nose on the back of her hand. "Can I ask you something?"

Luna looked at her, but the expression on her face didn't change.

"Have you ... seen Chance, since he died?"

Luna was violently startled by the question and fought a visible reaction as she decided the best way to respond. "No," she choked out at last, feeling sick.

Amy's brow furrowed and then, for the first time in four years, Amy broke down crying. Real tears stained her cheeks and the sound nearly broke Luna's heart. *She* had caused it, knowing exactly what pain Amy would go through.

"Do you want me to go?" Luna asked, praying she'd say "yes."

Amy shook her head. "I want you to do me a favor."

Luna paused—the last favor had been taxing. "What is it?"

"Can you ask the nurses what my future is, taking the situation with Michelle into account?" she asked weakly.

"Of course, but you're coming with me."

Amy blinked back tears. "Why?"

"So they can see you're not some crazy animal," Luna replied, gesturing to her tears. "I think if they see you grieving, they'll realize you're a human being with feelings."

"Maybe."

Luna stood up, gently grasping Amy's hand. Together they walked back down the hall, Amy's steps small and uncertain, as her bare feet padded against the cold white floor.

"Hey, she's not allowed out here!" one of the nurses exclaimed, jumping to her feet as if she had spotted a mouse.

"Why not?" Luna asked calmly as she and Amy neared the desk.

"She's a patient," the nurse said crossly.

"Not anymore, I'm not. My sister's gone missing," Amy said, holding strength in her words and her gaze that caught Luna by surprise.

The nurse looked surprised, too, and turned her attention to a clipboard in front of her. She was silent as she shuffled through the papers, as if she were waiting for the situation around her to disappear.

"Your sister was Michelle Jimenez?" she asked finally.

Amy nodded. "I'm sure the cop told you about it when he came to tell me."

The nurse pursed her lips and stared at Amy like she thought agreeing with a mental patient might convert her into one. "He did."

Amy blinked, waiting for the nurse to continue.

"Since she's unable to sign for you, and you're over eighteen, legally you're allowed to sign yourself out, if that's what you'd like."

Amy's face lit up instantly with a smile, the weight of the burden of her imprisonment finally lifted. "Yes, it is. Thank you."

Luna smiled despite herself. Maybe Chance was right when he said it'd be worth it in the end. In the back of her mind, pictures of Michelle's final minutes flashed like a disco ball, and the smile dropped.

She pushed it away and asked, "Want me to wait for you while you fill out the paperwork?"

Amy looked at her through eyes carefully guarded of emotion. "No, that's not necessary. You've been a great friend. Go ahead and get some rest. I'll be all right on my own."

CHAPTER TWENTY-NINE

AMY FELT STRANGE wearing street clothes again. As she walked through the front doors of Brentwood and out into the parking lot, her discomfort turned to desperation. She was lost—a feeling she hadn't expected. It had been years since she had walked across pavement, the sound beneath her shoes odd, foreign, and she thought hard about Michelle.

The world was even stranger, knowing her sister was no longer a part of it.

Amy didn't know where to begin rebuilding her life. She thought about going to Luna's old house, but pushed the thought away. She was trying to get as far from her as possible, wasn't she? She had options to exhaust before she'd resort to asking Luna for another favor.

Amy tucked her hands into her pockets as she walked down the street, and out of the corner of her eye, she spotted a cab. She waved it down, creating a plan, one step at a time.

ABOUT TWENTY MINUTES later, the cab pulled up in front of a small apartment building. It was downtown, in a part of the city that made Amy look over her shoulder multiple times a minute. She gave a handful of money to the driver, before hopping out into the cold. Shivering as the breeze hit her, she ran up to the door, the warm light

183

from the window bathing her as she rang the doorbell. A girl with messy brown hair hurried to open the door and took a quick drag of her cigarette, as she stared at Amy with a surprised smile on her face.

"Long time no see, girl," she said. "How's it feel to be free?"

"It has its ups and downs," Amy said quickly.

"Great! Doing better, buttercup?"

Amy smiled warmly. "Yes-I-I … I really am. Can I ask for a favor, Heather?"

Heather blew out a puff of smoke as she held the cigarette by her face. "Need a place to crash?"

"Just for a night? To get my things sorted out?"

Heather glanced into the apartment before looking back at her. "Yeah, that should be fine. Come on in."

Amy nodded gratefully and stepped inside, swiping the smoke out of her face as she did so.

WITHOUT HER USUAL medication, Amy was subjected to a horrific night of nightmares, flashbacks to her time with Chance, and she felt sick, sure that it was Chance's way of indirectly torturing her. She missed the blackouts that her meds had provided and knew that it was what her freedom would cost her. He could find her again as he had already proven.

Amy's eyes flew open and sweat clung to her forehead. Sighing, she lifted her hand and peeled her strands of dark hair from her forehead. At the other side of the bed, her friend was fast asleep. Amy smiled at her and sat up. It was nice to sleep in a bed that didn't feel like concrete for once, even if she did have to share it. Amy searched for her bag, quickly gathering her things, and stood up to do a final survey, to make sure she didn't forget anything.

Her gaze came to rest on Heather. "Thank you," she said, planting a kiss on her forehead, before she left the apartment.

When she stepped outside, the sun shone bright, sending pain through her eyes and straight to her brain. She ignored it and walked down the sidewalk, searching for another cab. She waved one down and as Amy climbed into the cab, she found herself almost grateful for the night of nightmares. They gave her a renewed sense of purpose, and she had a feeling that DreamWorld was preparing her for the mission she could not ignore. Hate it or not, she had to admit it worked.

Amy ruffled her hair with both hands, as the cab came to a halt in front of a small convenience store on the edge of town. The cab pulled beside the curb, and Amy paid the driver before climbing out.

"Are you sure you wanna be here, kid?" he asked.

She swallowed heavily and glanced at him. "Yeah."

"Okay," he said, offering her a gentle smile, and drove off without another word.

She glanced around, careful to look for any interested eyes who might notice her, before she plunged into the woods with confidence that she would not be missed. Memories hit her in the face, and she found that for all her trying, they were impossible to push away.

Amy didn't know Chance well, but she knew Luna. The girl had a penchant for the same woods that he had, during the creation of his hell. It was that information that gave her certainty. If Chance *had* to hide the Rosebone anywhere, Amy would guess he'd pick somewhere he treasured, a place in which he spent a lot of time. The cabin was the place she was willing to put all her money, so it was the first place she would check. When she made it to the clearing, however, she froze with the realization that it was *gone*.

It burned to the ground, Luna told you that.

As Amy studied the burnt rubble on the forest floor, all she could think of was Sarah. The girl had died here, if not from her injuries, then from the inferno that destroyed every shred of evidence that she had ever existed. Amy forced a glance to the building still standing a few feet away. It was the temple. Being made out of brick and stone had ensured that the fire hadn't spread there. She wished it *had,* so she wouldn't have to step inside, so she would be free from her demons for just a little longer.

Lord, why does it have to be the temple? she thought, cursing the sky as she took one step closer.

Then, all at once, she began to run, and hurdled into the darkness inside, knowing that if she didn't, she would've run the other way. There was no fire, but she would swear she could *smell* the smoke that been so thick when she had been bound and gagged in its depths. Holding her hand over her mouth, she pushed onward, despite the memories telling her to stop, to turn around, to save herself. She found the Rosebone sitting on the floor in the same place she had been four years prior.

She didn't know whether to laugh in relief, or cry with the irony.

AMY HAD ONE last place to go before she submitted herself to Luna's mercy. And it was the place she had grown up in. She stared at her old childhood home, at the police tape surrounding the yard she had once played in.

You shouldn't be here, a voice whispered in her head.

She knew it was true, but she couldn't help her nagging curiosity. She passed the tape and wandered inside, knowing it wouldn't matter if she did or not. Police had already scavenged whatever evidence they would find.

Amy held her breath as she crossed the threshold and saw the rips on the armchair, the bloodstains on the carpet. She forced herself to walk past it and to the room that had once been hers. It was in disarray, too, but it was a chaos of her own doing. Swallowing back her feelings, she reached under her bed, probing for the loose piece of carpet, and peeled it back. There was a moveable board, and she was quick to shove the Rosebone into it, before hiding it from sight beneath the protective measures.

She didn't look over her shoulder again as she made her way back to the living room, to see the extent of the crime scene once again, with the urgency of her DreamWorld mission pushed to the back of her mind. Whatever had happened to Michelle, she would bet money that Chance was involved.

CHAPTER THIRTY

DAYS BLENDED INTO one another, so much so that Luna barely knew where one had ended and the next began. Luna hadn't heard a word from Amy since the day she checked out. It was like she had walked out of Brentwood and simply vanished from the face of the Earth, further cementing the idea in Luna's mind that Amy had used her.

Luna sighed, pushing the thought to the back of her mind with the reminder that it was over and done with now … that all the wishing in the world wouldn't bring Michelle back. Holed up in the pit of her dark room, it all seemed endless to Luna. Chance talked to her sometimes, and on occasion, she would think of Drew.

Beyond that, she was alone.

Rose brought plates of food that more often than not, went abandoned on Luna's dresser. It was like Luna's little bubble was suspended in time and place, while the world continued to spin around her. Life hardly seemed worth living anymore, but Rose seemed determined not to give up. After a week of Luna's hibernation, she turned the light on, and Luna groaned, her eyes so accustomed to the dark that the brightness literally *hurt*.

"Luna, you need to get up for a bit," Rose said.

"No, Mom, I—"

"It's been *days* since you've left your room," Rose said, her tone caught somewhere between harshness and tenderness. "You need to stretch your legs."

Luna frowned. The peace of her time alone had blinded her as to how annoying other people could be.

"I ordered a pizza—your favorite," Rose said, clasping her hands together, as if she was praying that news would be enough to get Luna up.

She considered the offer, not for the pizza, but for the fact that Rose would leave her alone if she complied. On shaky legs, she forced herself out of bed. Rose set a hand on her shoulder as Luna passed into the hall, but she hardly noticed. A cautious smile hung on Rose's lips as they walked out to the living room, and Luna sat down on the couch, pretending she hadn't seen it.

Rose watched every bite that Luna forced herself to take, before she pulled out a board game. Luna had just the slightest wave of nostalgia wash over her, but it wasn't happiness that accompanied it. When Luna was a kid, Rose would come home with a new game between every business trip. Luna used to wait all night for her mom to come home, too jittery to even attempt to sleep. Rose would be gone so much that the few days a month she *was* home—if that—had seemed spectacular.

The idea of a board game now, after everything, didn't seem right. It physically hurt Luna to think that something that at one time had brought her so much joy, no longer even caused a flicker of warmth.

All her tricks of forgetting couldn't wash away that disappointment.

***

REESE PLOPPED DOWN in the sand, his feet dangling in the water that was such a beautiful shade of blue, it could only exist in dreams. He sat and waited until he heard footsteps behind him, and got up to see Chance. Reese couldn't help the smile that broke out across his face.

There was something about the infamous Chance Welfrey that excited him to the bone. It was still hard for Reese to believe that such a legend would listen to *his* plan, that he would ever depend on *him* for his next course of action, but he supposed crazier things had happened.

"It worked!" Reese said, clapping as the blond rolled his eyes.

"*What* worked, exactly? You haven't done anything for me yet."

"Yeah, uh … I mean, it's cool that you're alive *and* dead." Reese hated how awkward he could really be in these situations, but it was one of those things he'd just have to learn to live with.

Chance stayed silent, so Reese continued to chatter, hoping against hope to draw some kind of emotion from the steel of Chance's face.

"It'll work. I just need the Rosebone, and things will be right back on track."

Chance scoffed slightly, as if they weren't discussing a plan to bring him back from the dead, but arguing about an order at a restaurant. "I have it."

"Yes, yes, of course," Reese said, clapping with both anticipation and awkwardness. He knew what Chance saw when he looked at him, or at least he could guess—a failure, just as everyone else saw him. In a way, it was true. He failed school, his apprenticeship as a Keeper, and even his relationship with Amanda. He was tired of that, tired of losing to the monster that was himself. He wished so badly for confidence, the kind that Chance had, the kind that told the world, "Fuck you," but he had a feeling it would take time. "Let's go."

Chance didn't agree or argue. He was a shadow clinging to Reese, as the boy began to travel down the long stretch of sand. When they made it to the trees on the edge of town, Chance walked into the clearing and then before Reese knew it, they were in the temple.

"Wait here," Chance said, leaving Reese in the entrance as he disappeared into the depths.

Reese waited through the sounds of slamming objects and frustrated groans. When Chance came back, his eyes were stretched wide and his face was paper white.

"What's wrong?" Reese asked before Chance blurted out, "It's gone!"

That was the last thing either of them wanted to hear, but Reese couldn't decide how it made him feel. Then, he decided he wanted to cry, so trapped in the well of his emotions that he called himself every negative name he could think of. How stupid he felt for not helping Chance keep it hidden, how ashamed he was to feel Chance's disappointment.

"I have an idea of where to look," Chance said, scratching his chin, and left before Reese could ask any questions.

Reese was almost glad for it. He would do the best he could to do his own search with the knowledge he had. He was sure Chance was aware of the different Realms within DreamWorld, but he didn't know if he could maneuver them or not. Chance's two places to go were the Real World or the woods, where he had painstakingly crafted his cabin.

Reese, being an ex-Keeper, had access to more. He could get to the Realm of the dead … or more specifically, the part that housed all the people who had been unfortunate enough to meet the demon inside of Chance. While they could leave, many of them had no idea how to make it back to the main level of DreamWorld, so they stayed there, trapped in their own misery.

Reese supposed it was possible for one of them to get out long enough to steal the Rosebone and return without being noticed. If they took it, there was no telling what they could do with it. One person in particular came to his mind.

Amanda.

He was shaking with excitement at the thought, as he picked out the line between Realms. It wasn't visible to non-Keepers, but he could remember how to make himself *feel* the energy.

She's in there somewhere, Reese thought, and that was enough to get him to move onward. He gasped once he walked through the invisible boundary. The air was heavier here, making movement more difficult than it should be, but he wouldn't be detoured.

"Amanda!" he called.

Silence. *Just like when she was alive,* Reese thought darkly.

190

"Amanda!"

Cracking branches told him he wasn't alone. He whipped on his heels and caught a glimpse of blonde hair through the trees. She was here.

"What are you doing here?" she asked, sounding exhausted.

Reese frowned. "Come out so I can see you!"

"Just tell me what you want," her voice shot back.

Reese gritted his teeth. He knew she didn't want to see him, but to not even let him see *her*, hurt him in a new way.

"Did you take it?" he forced himself to ask.

Silence.

"Did you take it?" Reese asked again slowly.

"I've taken nothing," she replied.

"You're the one with the biggest motive," Reese said and rushed over to her hiding place. Was she refusing to see him, because she had it *on* her? He refused to be played for a fool by her anymore. "Come out!" he demanded and rounded the bend in the trees.

"Reese, please," she squealed.

He gaped down at her, surprise waving everything away. She was curled up on the forest floor, but she didn't have the Rosebone, she had a baby.

CHAPTER THIRTY-ONE

T HE NEXT DAY faced Luna with a new trial—New Year's Eve. She lay on the couch, staring at the festival taking place on the television. Though her eyes watched the screen, she didn't see a thing happening on it. Where would Amy go on her own? Was she okay? Or had something bad happened to her?

"*Have you … seen Chance since he died?*" her tiny question floated through her mind.

Luna's heart clenched—*why* had she asked the question?

Sighing, Luna laid her head down on the couch. Supporting the weight of her head suddenly seemed like too much work. The angle she had assumed made the images on the screen appear sideways.

Luna watched the confetti on the television fall against the snow with sad eyes. Every flash of teeth from the smiles on the excited faces of the people in Times Square made her feel worse. She had no excitement for the New Year ahead. To her, the confetti fell to the snow like her tears to the floor, and she wished her world would be over when the year was. *Only the good die young.* Then she thought of Chance and frowned. *Do they really?*

Luna sighed and cuddled deeper into the couch, curling her body up loosely. Her hair slid across her face in the process, and she brushed a black lock out of her eyes. No matter what she did, her sorrow masked everything.

Even though Rose got on her nerves more often than not, she felt her absence when she wasn't around. She had gone out with a few work buddies, but not without insisting Luna come along. Luna refused, not wanting to leave the comfort of her dip in the couch. The situation felt too familiar, too inescapable. Even Rose had friends and company to turn to, while Luna's friends were dead like she was doomed to be alone forever.

"Feeling lonely tonight?" Chance's husky voice whispered.

Luna opened her eyes slowly to see him standing beside the couch. He looked back at her with a mask of calm on his face, no indication of the thoughts that ran through his mind, and she wondered how he did it.

She shuffled herself to sit up. "Yeah, holidays are always hard."

"I know what you mean," Chance said, sitting beside her. "You look lost in thought."

"I was thinking about Amy, and why I haven't heard from her since yesterday. She … asked about you, you know. Wanted to know if I've seen you."

Chance's eyebrows raised in an expression that Luna could best describe as surprise. "And what'd you say?"

"No, of course. I couldn't let her know, could I?" she asked.

"I might have had the slightest of encounters with her on the other side."

Luna's eyes squinted involuntarily. "What does that mean?"

Chance chuckled at the look on her face. "You always see the worst in me, don't you? I just wanted to let her know that I'm still around. She took the Rosebone. Did you know that?"

Luna could feel the color drain from her face in the same way it had when Amy had asked her about Chance.

"No," she forced herself to say.

Chance blinked and narrowed his eyes to slits, as if he couldn't tell whether to believe her or not. "So you … *want* to stay bonded to me?"

The tone of his voice was one she had never heard from him before, and the question felt like a trap—a test to see exactly where her loyalties lie.

Luna shuffled a bit in her spot, uncertain as to whether she wanted to move closer or farther away. "Ten minutes to the new year, and I haven't thought of a thing for my New Year's resolution," she said, forcing out a laugh, in the hopes of changing the conversation.

Chance shook his head, his face looking the slightest bit crestfallen. "I don't have one either."

Luna glanced at him. "It wouldn't make sense for you to."

Chance frowned, then that careful mask of calm once again enveloped his features.

Luna caught the second of emotion and dipped her head. "I-I'm sorry ... that was rude."

He shook his head. "No, you're right. I'm kind of in a place where that stuff doesn't matter anymore."

Luna ran her tongue along her teeth. "New Year's resolutions and wishes seem too much alike ... at least for me."

Chance sighed and looked down at his fingers. He seemed so out of character that Luna wasn't sure how to approach the situation. Was he still thinking about the unanswered question?

His careful mask had disappeared, and the hurt wore clearly on his face. "Hey, um ... I really am sorry about what I said, I—" Luna began helplessly.

Chance held up a hand. "It wasn't that big of a deal."

Luna gauged his emotions. "Are you okay?"

He looked at her and gave her a bitter half-smile. "Honestly, no."

Luna looked at him. "What's wrong?"

"You ever do something and then wonder why you did it? You think and think, but you never seem to find an explanation?"

Luna simpered. "Yeah, I can relate. Is there something you regret?"

"Yeah," he said glancing up at her, "ending my life."

Luna's eyes widened. "Then why did you do it?"

"At the time, it seemed like the only option I had." He stared at the floor, looking as if he had nothing else to say.

"You were young ... you had a life ahead of you," Luna said.

Chance laughed, the sound rough and hoarse. "No. With the police closing in, I didn't stand a chance. Something in me broke—the day of your car accident and I ..." he trailed off. "I couldn't get over you trying to kill yourself, because of me."

Luna was glad he wasn't making an effort at eye contact.

"In high school, I was going through a lot. I don't know what was wrong with me, but after getting out of juvie, I felt like I had something to prove. I dug a hole too deep to escape from. I don't know why I've done every terrible thing I've done to you. I just wanted you to feel like I was always there for you, which in a way, I guess I was, but ... instead of comforting you, I scarred you for life."

"I don't understand you, you know that," Luna said, shaking her head. All her psychology classes had come nowhere close to helping her understand a full-blown psychopath like Chance. "If you wanted my affection, then why were you never like this when you were alive? Why did you want to *kill* me?" she asked, her voice dropping to a whisper.

"I had a lot of problems, I told you that," he said, looking into her eyes. He dropped the gaze first. "I think I was jealous."

"What were you jealous of?"

"Max, he-he always seemed to be that person you depended on ... that person I wanted to be. Every time I saw him, it drove me crazy. Me and him were exactly the same yet you wanted nothing to do with me. I felt like no one could ever be that for you, as long as he was still alive. Even bonding us didn't change that."

Luna frowned. The thought that he and Max had been friends still made her head hurt.

"I was also jealous of you," he said.

"Of *me*?" Luna asked, holding her hands to her chest.

"You always had everything perfect. Good grades, a family who loved you, and long-lasting friends. I didn't have any of that."

"My parents weren't so great. Mom wasn't there for me for most of my life, and I'm pretty sure my dad loved his TV more than me."

Chance smirked at her comment.

Luna looked at him. "I never apologized to you for the other day. You … you were right about Max."

Chance looked at her through interested blue eyes.

"He came to me in a dream and told me everything. I never knew … who he really was. He wouldn't tell me any of it when he was alive, and I don't think he ever would've, if you hadn't told me first."

Chance scoffed. "Of course not. I know you don't want to hear it, but he was as shady as I am."

"I see it now and feel like a complete idiot, because this whole time, I had such a wrong view of him."

"That's because he erased your memory."

Luna looked at him. "Yeah … but *why*? That's the one thing he wouldn't explain. What did you do to me that day?"

Chance sighed. "It was another stupid chapter of my life. I could tell you, if you really want to know, but Max is right on this one. You're better off not remembering."

Luna frowned, hating the fact that Max and Chance had both acknowledged the other as being "right." With the amount of stress she already suffered through at his hands, she decided to listen.

"Did he say anything to you? About the Rosebone?" Chance asked.

Luna frowned and pushed her eyebrows together. "No, why would he?"

"No reason," Chance said quickly.

Luna shrugged it off. "Can I ask you one question about that day?"

Chance nodded, though he looked at the floor with uncertain eyes.

"Were you going to kill me?"

Chance breathed in through his teeth, before he looked at her like a child stealing cookies. "Yes."

Luna shook her head slowly. Despite her new feelings for Max, there was no way to ignore the fact he had saved her life. "I hope you don't think my question is distasteful, but why is it I can still see you?

Sleeping or awake, I can see you as clear as day, even though you're ... you know, *dead*, yet I haven't seen any of my friends or family like this ... Max and Sarah, and all of them, say they can't even come to me in DreamWorld, because it's too hard. Why is that?"

"Your Teardrop of Knowledge ... it connects you to DreamWorld," he said, shrugging. "All these years later, it's only gotten stronger. As for you and me? It's the bond that brings us together like this."

"I guess that makes sense," she said, though she wondered again if he knew how badly she wished that bond was broken.

"One minute until New Year's!" a preppy girl on the television screeched.

Chance smiled sardonically as he watched the TV. "Ready to bring in the New Year?" he asked with fake cheer.

Luna shook her head. "I don't even have anyone to kiss at midnight. Forget New Year's."

"Five ... four ... three ... two ... one ... Happy New Year's!" the people roared.

Chance leaned over suddenly and kissed Luna on the lips. She froze at the contact, but it wore off as she blended into the moment. There was emotion in it for both of them. In the times he had kissed her before, the feeling was rough and forced, no emotion, merely mechanical. There was no trace of that now. She set a hand to the side of his face as he deepened the kiss. As suddenly as he had started it, he pulled away and looked at her through wide eyes, as if he were suddenly frightened of her.

"I ... I'm sorry about that," he said.

Luna shook her head. "Don't be."

CHAPTER THIRTY-TWO

AMY SIGHED, SITTING underneath the overpass, wrapped in an old scraggly blanket she had snagged from her home, without a clue as to what her future held. Her hope had fallen on residing in her old home. Police had instantly dashed it—if she lived in a crime scene, she might contaminate any evidence that could be important to finding her sister, though she was sure the kind of evidence she needed would never be found. Not in this Realm, anyway.

Amy wrapped her arms around her knees, holding herself tightly in a desperate attempt to warm up. Grungy and unkempt, her hair was matted about her head and a foul taste filled her mouth. She wished for nothing more than a shower and a decent meal, but she couldn't even scrounge up enough money to buy a measly burger.

Wiping sleep from her eyes, she looked around. She couldn't stay here another night—between the cold and the people, it was too dangerous.

I don't know what else to do.

Amy briefly considered going back to Heather's place, but shot it down. She didn't fit in with Heather's crowd—they were as dangerous as the people who frequented the overpass. Staring at her numb fingers, she realized she only had one option left—Luna. The time had come. Frowning to herself, she slowly climbed to her feet, numb both inside and out. As she gathered her stuff back into her tiny bag, she had one question on her mind.

After everything, would Luna accept her?

I'll have to find out.

***

LUNA WAS COMFORTABLE as she slept in the first morning of the New Year in peace. Even though the cold from the snowstorm outside had leaked into her room, the warmth of her blanket created a feeling of bliss she never felt when she was awake. She cuddled deeper into her pillows; she could sleep forever. A rare smile lined her face and she tossed and turned in her light stage of sleep.

When a knock sounded at the front door, she was jolted awake, and the bliss vanished. Luna rolled over to look at her clock, careful of letting out any of the warmth that enveloped her, and saw it read nine in the morning. Groaning again, she closed her eyes as the morning sun hit her. She wasn't ready to get up, despite their waiting company.

"Mom! Someone's at the door!" she called, hoping Rose was awake to answer it.

She looked up at the ceiling and waited for a response. To her relief, she could hear Rose heading down the hall. Luna let out a content sigh, as the sound of knocking stopped, and snuggled into her pillow, prepared to go back to sleep. Through the wall, she heard Rose and their guest talking, and she began to doze off once again.

When the conversation continued past a minute or two, she realized the company must be important. Was it another officer coming to question her about Michelle's death? The thought made her heart race with anxiety, and she knew it would be impossible to regain her comfort until she got answers. Straining a bit harder, she heard Rose say, "Amy."

Luna climbed out of bed instantly. Her feet brushed against the frozen floorboards as she carefully crept closer to the door. The sound of voices echoed better down the hallway, and she listened, waiting until Amy's name came up once again. Were her ears deceiving her? Was

199

Amy here after being MIA for nearly a week?

If she was, what could it possibly be for? Had she found the Rosebone?

Luna brushed a clump of black hair out of her eyes and straightened her nightgown. The only way to get answers would be to face Amy head on. Taking a deep breath in preparation, she made her way to the living room, to where Rose and Amy stood, engrossed in their conversation.

Luna stared at Amy, thinking how strange she looked in street clothes. For the past year, all she had seen Amy in was the white hospital gown she had been forced into. The closer she observed Amy, the more she realized her clothes looked dirty and ragged, as if she had worn them for a *while*. Where had Amy gone in the days after her release from Brentwood?

Did he say anything about the Rosebone? Chance's voice echoed dully in her mind.

"Hey, Amy," Luna said, breaking the conversation between her and Rose.

Amy noticed her suddenly, and her face lit up a bit. "Hi, Luna."

Rose turned to look at her as well. "Sweetheart, I thought you were sleeping."

"I was," Luna said before turning to Amy. "What're you doing here?"

"It's a long story," Amy said, "but I'm going to let you know before I ask that I have no other places to go."

Rose glanced at Luna quizzically.

Luna shrugged. She never thought she was going to see Amy again, especially at her doorstep. Amy was full of surprises.

"What is it?" Rose asked.

Luna stayed silent, as a lump grew in her throat. The last time she had done Amy a favor, it had been morally wrong. Luna glanced around, hoping to catch a glimpse of Chance in the room, but a quick look was enough for her to know she was alone.

"My house is under police investigation. I tried going to my friend's house, but she didn't have extra space for me. I feel uncomfortable asking this, but I have no other options," Amy said, and she paused before asking, "Can I stay here, please?"

Rose and Luna were startled at the question. Luna never thought Amy would be out on the street without Brentwood. Even though Michelle was missing, she didn't know Amy would be turned away from her *home* because of it.

I should've known. While Luna was deep in the land of her thoughts, Rose recovered from her surprise.

"We have one extra room," she said hesitantly. "I don't see why you can't."

Luna's head snapped in her direction and she looked at her mother through eyes clouded with sorrow. Suddenly, Amy wasn't in the room anymore. "B-but that's Asher's room."

Rose looked at her through sympathetic eyes. "Honey, it's the New Year. I think you need to consider moving on."

"He's only been gone a couple weeks, Mom," Luna said in disbelief.

"Keeping his things won't make you feel better, they'll only force you to hold onto how sad you feel. Asher doesn't need a room anymore, honey, but Amy does."

Luna closed her eyes, hoping to hold in the tears trying to flow. Did Rose realize how cruel her words actually were? *The Curse of Allah is on the one who causes difficulty to his mother,* Luna thought and frowned. *What happens when your mother causes difficulty for* you? Luna opened her eyes slowly and turned to look at Amy.

The girl had already taken so much from Luna and really, she had no clue exactly how much. "Are you sure you wanna stay here?"

Amy nodded. "I know I haven't always been the nicest I could be, Luna, but you've always been good to me. We're both going through the same thing, me with Michelle, and you with your baby. This is hard for you, I get it, but I gotta say thank you for everything you've done for me. Staying here will give us an opportunity to be friends again … like when we were in high school."

A painful twinge stabbed in Luna's heart at Amy's words. High school had been the worst time of her life. If she had her choice, she wished she could forget about it entirely, but life wasn't that kind.

"Yeah …," Luna said softly, at a loss for how else to respond. There was a twinkle in her eye when she said *high school* that made Luna sure there was more to her words.

"Let me show you to the room," Rose said, her eyebrows drawn together, before she led Amy out of sight.

Luna watched them go on shaky legs. They chatted as they left the room, neither of them apparently aware of the feelings running through Luna. As soon as they disappeared into the hallway, she suddenly felt unstable, as if she was going to fall over. She moved over to the couch and sat down, putting a hand over her face, as the world around her began to spin.

"You okay?" Chance's voice called.

Luna gasped and looked to see him standing by the end of the couch. How long he had been there? "What does Amy think she's doing?"

Chance looked genuinely concerned as he sunk into the open seat beside her. "What do you mean?"

"She's playing some kind of game, right? I mean, what does she think she's *doing*, trying to move in with us?" she asked him.

Chance shrugged. "What's wrong with it?"

Luna stared at him open-mouthed. "Am I the only one who sees a problem?"

Chance's lip twitched, but he stayed silent.

"You want to know what's *wrong*? I *killed* her sister. How am I supposed to handle *living* with her? Every time I look at her face, I remember stabbing Michelle in the throat … I remember watching her sister *die*."

Chance blinked. "Haven't you been doing that since you killed Michelle anyways?"

Luna pursed her lips. "But this is different! Without Amy around, I could try my best to pretend Michelle's death was some horrible dream. When I have to look at her, I'm forced to remember the reason *why* she's here. As long as she's in my life, I'm never going to be able to move on from what I've done."

"Imagining it to be a dream brings you comfort with everything, you know?" Chance asked, with an incredulous eyebrow raised.

Luna gave him the stink eye.

"It doesn't have to be all doom and gloom," Chance said.

"How else should I see it?"

"Just look at it this way … Amy was always quiet when you knew her, right?"

Luna hoped he had a great tangent of ideas that hadn't already occurred to her. "Right."

"Maybe she'll still be like that. Maybe she'll stay in her room mostly, and you won't even see her much," Chance said. "She *is* still grieving, after all."

"The thought she's going to be staying in Asher's room only makes it worse."

Chance frowned. "Yeah, I didn't care for that either, but maybe it's a good thing Rose is going to make it a guest room. She had a point by saying you need to move on."

"You're just like the rest of them," Luna snapped, folding her arms across her chest.

"I'm not trying to poke the lion," he said, holding his hands up. "I'm simply saying that it's not healthy for you to hold onto that. The longer you take to grieve, the worse it's gonna be on you. You don't need any more stress, Luna."

Luna considered his words, but wouldn't say so out loud. There was something about the way he said it that made it tough to tell him he was wrong.

***

LUNA CHANGED OUT of her pajamas before riffling through the papers on her end table. She found one of the pictures of Asher's ultrasound, and clutched it tight in her hand as she sat on her bed. The thought of that day seemed like years ago, and remembering it, brought instant tears to her eyes.

It's not fair, she thought, and set it down on her dresser.

She listened to the hallway as she waited for Amy and Rose to leave Asher's room, then glanced around to see if Chance was watching her, but she didn't see him. When she noticed the room was clear, she crept inside. Her footsteps were silent as she moved through the room. She hadn't been in it since Asher's death, and the pain stabbed into her heart like never before.

She stifled a sob and looked around the room, sneezing at the noticeable layer of dust sprinkled about. A tiny lion toy in Asher's crib grinned up at her with a happy, innocent smile, but she didn't see it—the thought of the forever empty crib forced tears to run down her face. Choking as she cried, she gripped onto the crib for leverage, as her sobs rocked her body.

"Hey, hey …" Chance's voice whispered consolingly in her ear. "What are you doing in here?"

She turned to see him standing there, with a look of concern on his face.

"It's not fair," she rasped.

"I know," he replied, reaching out a hand to stroke her hair.

"Why'd he have to die?" she asked.

"I don't know, sweetheart," he replied, pulling her against his chest. "I don't know."

CHAPTER THIRTY-THREE

THAT LOOK OF betrayal in Luna's eyes … that was all Rose could see. How could she not understand Rose was trying to *help*?

After the decision with Cassandra, Rose had done everything she could to get rid of reminders. If she wasn't prompted to think about it, it seemed easier to get through the day. Downright forgetting was impossible, of course, but it had made it *manageable*. Luna was beginning to show signs of the same, and it worried her.

Maybe Luna was past the point of help.

***

LUNA REGRETTED CREEPING into Asher's old room, because it took her at least an hour to calm the tremors, and when they slowed, the effort had drained her of a lot of energy.

When Rose came into her room, it took everything she had to even lift her head off the pillow. "What is it, Mom?"

"I was wondering if you would help me and Amy pack up some of the stuff in Asher's room?"

"A-are you really asking me to do that?" Luna asked, eyes wide. "I don't want to move anything, and I shouldn't *have* to. That's *Asher's* room!"

Rose shook her head. "I'm sorry, honey, but he doesn't need it."

"So … what? You're gonna throw away his stuff, pretend he never existed?" she asked, sitting up. "Just like you did with Dad."

Rose flinched, but hid her pain, as she said, "Of course not, honey. We're taking it to storage to make some room."

"I don't believe you," Luna said, a tear streaking her cheek.

"I'm not completely heartless, you know."

Luna narrowed her eyes at Rose and stood on shaky legs. "You know what I wish, *mother*?"

"What's that, honey?"

"I wish I never would've moved back here. I should've gritted my teeth and worked things out with Amanda. It would've been fine in the end." *As fine as it could be anyway.*

"Luna! You don't mean that!" Rose gasped.

"I most certainly do," Luna said, storming past her mother as she made her way to the kitchen.

Living with Chance before his suicide had been better than what Rose was putting her through. Stomach rumbling, Luna frowned. Food was the last thing on her mind, but her body disagreed. After all the meals she had skipped, she would've assumed her body would simply stop trying. She set a hand to her forehead and thought lazily about the small amount of variety she had. Since Chance had disappeared, she was alone. Part of her was glad. After butting heads with Rose again, she didn't know how stable her mood would be for the next person to confront her.

Luna closed the cabinet she had already searched through and stood on her tip-toes to look into the next one. Light footsteps behind her caused her heart to race in anxiety, and she turned to see Amy.

"Hi," Luna offered, suddenly wishing she had stayed in her room.

"Hey, Luna," Amy replied.

"How are you today?"

Amy smiled. "Better, now that I know I'm not going to be homeless."

Luna returned the smile, though she didn't feel it. "That's always a good thing."

206

Amy's face softened after a minute of what Luna guessed was careful thought. "So, how've you been since … well, since your luck went downhill?"

Luna guessed she was referring to her miscarriage. In the slosh of terrible things that had happened to her in her lifetime, it was hard for her to keep track. Luna shrugged. "About the same really."

Amy shook her head. "You seem so brave. It's crazy to think we're both in pain from losing someone."

Luna's blood turned cold. Amy took a seat at the table, and Luna couldn't speak. Amy wanted to talk about Michelle—it was the conversation Luna had known would be inevitable the next time they bumped into each other. If Luna was in Amy's position, she would want to do the same, but Amy had no idea Luna was the worst person she could possibly choose to confide in.

"We're both pained from losing someone," Amy's voice repeated the quote in Luna's head, and she smirked sardonically. *Isn't that the truth?*

"I feel like we're in high school again," Amy piped up suddenly.

The usual rush of chills accompanied the thought of high school, and she wished Amy would stop saying that one horrifying statement. "Why say that again?"

"Just the feeling I have. Everything has changed and yet nothing has."

Luna's nostrils flared slightly. "Where did you go? After Brentwood?"

Amy sighed and propped her chin on her hand. "I was sent on a mission."

"As a Keeper?" Luna asked, raising an eyebrow.

Amy bobbed her head. "I needed to seek out the Rosebone."

"And?" Luna asked, standing still with the look on Chance's face in the back of her mind.

"I found it."

So that *was the reason behind Chance's recent interest in her.*

"So now what?"

"We need to find some way to destroy it," Amy said, tapping her fingers on the table.

"And you still don't know how?"

Amy shook her head. "I know as much as I did in high school."

Luna couldn't avoid a glare at her that time.

Amy lifted her palms. "I know I keep saying it, but I honestly can't think of another situation that has been like this."

Luna was uncomfortable with the topic, but Amy didn't seem to notice.

"So many of our classmates have died," Amy continued. "It's like this town swallows people up and never lets them go."

Luna sighed wistfully—she was too kind of a person to let Amy's sad words go without comfort. She stopped searching for food and walked over to the girl. Sitting in the empty chair beside her, she tried to decide the best thing she could say and came up blank.

In the back of her mind, she could imagine Amy's rage and anger if she decided to admit what she had done. That DreamWorld wasn't responsible for Michelle, and Chance's hands were clean. That *she* was the villain. She could imagine Amy's face turning as red as an apple, as she charged toward her to strangle the life out of her like Luna had done to Michelle. Luna had to blink to clear the scenario, but the thought continued to chill her, even after she pushed it away.

"You have to have faith that your sister will be okay," Luna said finally. It seemed like the right thing to say, but the look on Amy's face made her doubt herself.

Amy shrugged. "Why? I mean she was terminally ill. I knew she was going to die soon, but I never thought it'd be like this. If someone kidnapped her, the *stress* probably killed her before anything. Besides, I … saw the crime scene. There was so much blood, even after they took out the carpet."

Luna stared at her, surprised at the hopelessness in her words. She was right, of course—Luna knew that too well—but she wanted to argue anyway.

"You don't know is my point," Luna said quickly. "Maybe she went somewhere and forgot to tell anyone."

"It's been almost a week. If she was going to leave for that long, she would've told *someone*." Amy's eyes half-closed, leaving a dubious expression on her face. "Even if it was just work."

Luna bit her lip. She was trying her best to be a friend, but Amy was backing her into a corner without even realizing it, and Luna had already used all of her best lines. Luna had never heard Amy talk so much before, especially with so much emotion, and Luna feared if she talked, she might accidentally let something slip. A prickling feeling made the hair on the back of Luna's neck rise in anxiety. She was trekking into dangerous territory and didn't know the way out.

Luna took a deep breath to calm herself. She had to carefully remind herself that Amy had no idea she was the one who took her sister away. She was merely coping with the loss by talking to someone she considered her friend. *Why is my anxiety so high?* No one would ever suspect her of murder unless they found proof, and she had made sure to leave no evidence behind. Chance had double checked.

The thought didn't make her feel any better.

Amy sighed suddenly. "Why is it so hard to deal with losing someone you love? It literally feels like your heart has been ripped out. I-I miss her so bad. Being locked up for all that time made me think I was mad at her. I even had an entire speech prepared, if she ever decided to visit me. Now that I'm out of that place, and I know my sister is gone, I'm so *empty*. I hate myself for being mad at her. I wish I knew if she was okay. It's killing me, the not knowing."

"Have you tried … checking in DreamWorld?" she forced herself to ask like she knew a real friend would.

Amy shrugged. "What's the use? If I can't find her in this world, I won't be able to find her there either."

Luna tried not to look relieved. "I can't imagine that kind of pain."

Chance had put her through all kinds of hell, but one she had never had to experience was the pain of someone going missing. Everyone she had known was killed. Even her baby—while the pain had been immense—hadn't made her wonder as she cradled his corpse.

"What I don't understand, is why people feel the urge to kill others to begin with? What do they get out of it?" Amy asked, tilting her head. "Not a day goes by that I don't think back to the woods. What would Chance have gained if you had decided to listen to him and kill me?"

Luna tensed. Amy was leading her through more dangerous territory, oblivious to the caution signs. "People are sick," she managed.

"I understand it in some situations, war and self-defense, but to end someone's life for a thrill? They put out a bright spirit and erase a lifetime of memories in a heartbeat. Then they wash the blood off of their hands, eat dinner, and return to their own lives like they did nothing wrong."

"Eventually justice catches up to them," Luna offered. *Is that my voice still talking?*

Amy shook her head. "No, it doesn't. Most often, all they earn is life in prison. They get three free meals a day and have all day to do whatever they please. On the stand, most of them cry about getting the death penalty, even though the reality is, they'll probably die sitting on death row before they ever get the lethal injection. It's ironic. They can end someone else's life and not care, but when it's them, they turn into big babies. Like they actually believe they deserve our mercy after what they've done."

Luna instantly thought of Chance. He killed, because he felt as if some people didn't deserve to live. He didn't get a thrill from it; he had only done what he thought was right at the time.

Just like Luna had done to Michelle.

Amy forced out a laugh, and the sound caused Luna to jump. Laughter wasn't something she was used to hearing anymore. "I wish I could go back to high school and change my life. I wish I could fight off Chance, go to my graduation, and start college with my classmates, instead of being sent to a nuthouse to rot for four years. If I had lived my life the right way, I bet Michelle would still be alive today."

Luna drank in her words and emotion. Regret was something that weighed on her heart and mind every day. Many times over, she wished she could go back to high school, go back to where it all began, and save Violet, to prevent the chain of death and destruction that had plagued

210

her for years. She could think all she wanted, but it would never bring back any of her dead friends, or even herself.

All it was, was wishful thinking.

There was always a voice in her head that reminded her that things could never be changed. When she tried to ignore it, it only became louder, reminding her that her past was written in stone, the same way her friends' names were engraved in their headstones.

"You don't know that," Luna spat out, visibly struggling for words.

Amy shrugged. "Regardless of whether I'm right or wrong, it's nice to think things didn't have to be this way."

CHAPTER THIRTY-FOUR

AMY'S WORDS WEIGHED on Luna's mind, hours after their conversation ended. What would Amy think of Luna if she knew the truth? Luna scoffed to herself quietly; that was one question she could answer—Amy would hate her.

Luna stirred her pasta slowly before she sat at the table alone, staring at the curtains above the sink. Amy had retreated to her room not long after her rant, and Luna knew she wouldn't be back out for a while. Amy's crying radiated down the hall for the past forty minutes, leaving Luna in a predicament of her own. Did Amy *want* her to try and comfort her?

Water bubbled in the pot on the stove, and Luna decided maybe it would be best to give Amy her space for the time being. If Luna was in her shoes, that's what she would've wanted. Luna got up and rushed to stir her pasta again. As she went to work draining it and adding a sauce, she wondered how much of Amy's rant applied to Chance.

Luna believed in her heart that Chance got no joy from spilling blood. For sanity's sake, she *had* to believe it.

Luna didn't want to believe he had gotten *any* joy from tearing her life apart. While he seemed to regret it now, she knew that hadn't always been the case. She could almost *hear* the eerie whistle he had done while kidnapping her, *see* the smirk on his face as he stabbed her. Luna stirred the sauce slowly, sighing as she watched the marks left by the spoon. Had Chance heard Amy's rant? If he had, what had he thought of it? Had he compared Luna, the way she was comparing him?

"Are you okay, Luna?" Chance asked suddenly.

She turned to look at him, wondering if her thoughts had summoned him. "All I can think about is Amy."

"I expected that, actually," Chance said, dipping his head in acknowledgement. "She's upset. It's understandable that she's acting this way."

Luna flared her nostrils. "She's not just upset ... there's *something* different about her. She seems so *angry*, maybe even suspicious. She's not the same as she used to be."

"Are any of us?" he asked.

Luna shot him a scathing look, inspired by the fact that she couldn't dispute his statement.

Chance met her gaze. "Look, she feels guilty about being mad at her sister, but it will pass. There are five stages of grief after all."

"How can you be so sure? Some people are good at holding onto their anger ... she might not be different."

"You know as well as I do that Amy isn't an angry person," Chance said. "She's *sad*. Just the way you were sad after, well ... after everything I did."

Luna shook her head. "That's not the point. I think that time at Brentwood changed her. Being secluded from human contact for all those years completely reprogrammed her personality."

"This is what kind of person she is deep down," Chance said. "Michelle's death only brought it out of her."

"How much more upset do you think she'd be if she knew I did it?" Luna asked, running a hand through her black locks. Chance lifted his eyebrows, and Luna could nearly read his thought. *You can't be serious.* "It's too dangerous with her living here. All she wants to do is talk about her sister, and that's the one thing I want to avoid. I don't know how much of this I can take. I feel like she's going to make me crack."

Chance shook his head. "It doesn't matter if this is hard, she can't be allowed to know. It'll be the end of you."

"Don't you think I know that?"

Chance pursed his lips. "Just relax. If she pulls it out of you, that doesn't completely mean you're going to go to jail."

Luna raised an eyebrow quizzically; a feeling in the pit of her stomach made her wary of what he was going to say next. "What do you mean?"

"Doesn't she remind you of Sarah?" Chance asked, his face tightening with the effort of carefully picking his words.

The last time Luna had seen Sarah alive was the day Chance killed her. Guilt pricked at her yet again as she remembered she had chosen to run from the scene instead of helping her. *Why bring it up?* she wanted to ask, but instead, Luna looked at the floor, too ashamed.

Chance sensed her thoughts. "Emotions aside, doesn't she? Right now, the only thing she wants is to get revenge on the person who took her sister away, like Sarah did for Susan."

"What's your point?" Luna asked.

"If she finds out it was you, then you have to kill her, too," he said. "Just like I did to Sarah."

Silence.

"Did you hear me, Luna?" he asked.

She blinked once as she regained herself. "How dare you?" she whispered. Chance crinkled his forehead, and his confusion *annoyed* her. "I can't believe you would say that. After all the horrible things I've had to do already, you think the best way to handle it is to do *more* horrible things?"

"I'm not saying it's for the best. Take it from me, this cycle you're on is a terrible one. One murder can never just be *one* murder."

"It would've been … if you hadn't made me kill Michelle," Luna said darkly. "It would've been only Kylie, then the topic of killing Amy would've never had to come up, because she never would've been an issue!"

"No, you're right, she would've just wasted her life in that nut ward, waiting hopelessly for her sister to finally decide to let her out, or heaven forbid, *visit* her. That's all."

Luna glared at him. "You know as well as I do that Michelle was going to visit Amy on her own."

"Oh? You do? You psychic now or something?"

Luna's cheeks burned with her rage. "No, she said—"

"That doesn't guarantee *anything*! Even if she did remember to visit her, that doesn't mean she would've checked Amy out. Amy herself said she had a speech to yell at Michelle if she ever came to visit."

"Michelle would've understood."

Chance sighed deeply, reaching up to rub his temples, and Luna knew he was trying to keep a hold on his temper. "You probably guessed this would come up. If things go sour between you and Amy, killing her is the only way to protect yourself. It's your only out."

"No," she whispered softly. "I don't care what you say, I'm not going to kill Amy," Luna stated. "I'm tired of what I've become, Chance … I'm not you! I can't tread this cycle like it's okay! It's wrong … I *know* it's wrong. Amy has done nothing to me to deserve that."

"After everything she's put you through, why continue to stand by her?" he asked. "You have to realize at this point that she's not your friend. Even though you put her life above yours, she refused to help you when you needed her. You weren't even her first choice when she signed out of Brentwood. Now that she's got nowhere else to turn, she comes to you again."

"That's not true. She's my friend," Luna stated stubbornly. That was all she could say. If he didn't know about Amy's search for the Rosebone, she certainly wasn't going to be the one to tell him.

"Are you sure about that?" Chance questioned. "If she ever finds out it was you, she won't be. She'll become your worst enemy."

"What part of 'no' don't you get?" Luna asked him, hostility making the hair on her arms stand up.

Chance blinked and although he looked calm, Luna knew he was beginning to get frustrated as well. "Stop being ignorant, I'm only trying to help you."

"So you say!" Luna stared at him, pouring every ounce of her anger into the look, until finally it broke away. It was hard to

215

concentrate, hard for her to feel anything anymore, besides defeat. "How do I know this isn't another lie? I killed Michelle and Kylie, just because you told me to!"

"Now, *that's* not true. Kylie had it coming."

Luna laughed, though inside, she wanted to cry. "You keep saying Kylie killed our baby, but she didn't!"

"Are you in denial?" he asked, setting a hand to her shoulder with his eyebrow raised in surprise.

She smacked his hand away. "Listen to me, dammit! She didn't kill Asher, Chance. *You* killed our baby!" Her sorrow made it hard for her to speak as she stared at him, her hands curled into fists, as she pretended to be strong for reasons currently unknown to her.

He scratched at his jaw. "You have every right to get mad at me for the terrible things I've done to you, but how *dare* you accuse me of *that?*"

"You *stabbed* me, Chance. Remember that? Did you think I'd have no repercussions from it?" she asked, tears leaking from her eyes.

The anger dissolved away the instant Chance realized what she was talking about, and he stood in place, mortified with his mouth hanging open like a fish. "Luna …," was all he managed.

"You've never done what's best for me … only yourself. That's all you know how to do."

"Please listen to me, Luna. I want to help you."

"Maybe I don't need your kind of help," she said quietly, lifting her nose to avoid looking at him.

Without waiting for a reply, she turned and left the kitchen. Not caring about the food on the stove, she left the house and ran down the street as fast as she could, with the hope that for once, Chance wouldn't follow. The movement made her stomach greatly uncomfortable, but freedom was too welcome to give up.

Luna didn't know where she was going or why she felt so determined to keep moving. She was trying to escape from the hurt and surprise his words had inspired. She knew his past—the long bloody track record that was his life. Yet, she had submitted her trust to him.

Deep down, she knew it was only because she had started to

become him.

CHAPTER THIRTY-FIVE

WHEN THE PAIN in Luna's stomach finally became unbearable, she stopped her frantic running, and clenched her fingers to her stomach, desperately trying to work out the pain, cringing at the comparison of her miscarriage. Panting hard, she tried her best to regain a bit of energy for the walk ahead of her. She had made it all the way to the cemetery.

Even though she didn't feel safe from her past at home, the sensation would only be worse here. With the names of her lost friends and family engraved in stone, she would be forced to face what she would rather avoid. She wondered if she should turn around and go home instead, but her mind scarcely controlled her feet, as they decisively led the way into the cemetery.

At least they can't tell if I slip, she thought quietly.

Passing the gate didn't give her any memories, but the graves within did. She moved along, carefully reading the names of her fallen friends in the order they had died. Her eyes made sure to avoid the grave of her baby—that was a wound that was nowhere near healed. Amanda's grave was the last one Luna passed. She stood there for the longest amount of time, not knowing what to think. For all her warning, Luna hadn't been able to save her friends … any of them.

"I'm sorry," she whispered, and turned her back to the stone.

218

After all the months that had passed, it still hurt to think about Amanda's death, about how close she had come to getting away unscathed. Max's and Violet's passing hurt as well, but time had equipped her with an ability to cope with those. Amanda's death was still fresh, still raw.

A tear sliced down Luna's face as she looked at the empty spaces in the cemetery, imagining more graves filling the plots. If she took Chance's advice and ended her friend's life, Amy would most likely be buried beside Amanda, her name forever etched in a sharply polished stone to complete Chance's macabre collection.

Luna stared at the blank patch of grass, picturing the funeral procession, *seeing* the new coffin carrying her friend in death. Luna closed her eyes and turned away sharply, glad that since Michelle's body hadn't been found, there was no trace of her in the cemetery. Sarah's body was absent, too, and Luna wondered if her parents had bothered with a coffin, since she had been burned to ashes anyway.

Shivering at the thought, Luna turned to begin her journey out of the graveyard with Chance's words weighing on her mind. If Amy somehow knew Luna was responsible for Michelle's disappearance, what *would* she do? Would she panic? Or would the moment take hold of her the way it had with Kylie? Luna bit her lip. If Amy accused her, she'd deny it, of course, and try to turn the blame to someone else.

But who?

If Amy narrowed her search down to Luna, then there was no expanding it again. Amy wasn't gullible. Once that trace of doubt was present in her mind, it would stay there, and Amy would do what she could to expose her. Luna pushed the thought away. If she was good at covering her tracks, Amy wouldn't stumble upon anything that would arouse suspicion. Chance's expertise would also keep her from getting caught.

That thought only slightly comforted her, because even if Luna had done everything right, she would never truly get away with it. Her heart would always be stained with the memories of what she had done.

***

LUNA STAYED IN the cemetery for hours, sitting in the soft grass, with her eyes on Max's grave. His stone was dirty, smudged with mud and grit from a year of sitting in the elements. Grass had grown over the spot where they had placed his coffin, but Luna knew the exact edges anyways. She missed him. He had been the one thing that kept her sane through everything—her rock.

Yet, he was a stranger.

Frowning, she rubbed at her eyes and wondered what he would do if he found himself in her situation. Would he do the right thing, or the best thing for himself? A bead of water streaked down her cheek. There was never a better time to wish she could switch places with him.

Max should've lived. Since he had been the one to start it all, he should've been the one to end it, too. Max would've done the right thing by ending Chance forever … something Luna could not do, for a reason she didn't understand. As evil as he was, he was the only source of comfort she had left. She could almost *feel* Max frowning at her from his grave for that thought.

A new bout of hysterics, mixed with bitterness, overtook her. He was in no place to judge, but his opinion mattered to her more than anything. Luna cried until the sun met with the horizon line. Even if he had been a monster, she had loved him with all her heart. With an aching in her throat and stinging eyes, she looked up at the sound of footsteps.

Her heart thudded as she caught sight of Amy entering the confines of the cemetery. Neither girl spoke as they eyed one another, as Amy came to a rest beside her.

"I thought I'd find you here," the tiny Keeper said at last.

Luna didn't speak, instead letting her gaze fall to Max's tombstone.

Amy came to a rest beside her friend and read the name. "He was a good man," she said.

Luna felt cold at her words. "Is it true?" she asked, knowing she would need to give no specifics.

Amy bobbed her head. "Only if you're ready."

CHAPTER THIRTY-SIX

LUNA LET AMY take charge, the tiny Keeper leading the way to the spot in the woods where she had hidden the Rosebone. It was placed in the crevice of a dead tree and a boulder, and Luna wondered how it had escaped the attention of any curious animals.

Luna stood back and let Amy scoop it into her arms. She could remember all too well what the pain felt like, and didn't want to go anywhere close to it. Amy didn't have the same fears, as she tucked it into the crook of her arm like it was an infant she needed to care for. Once again, the Keeper was in the lead, as they traveled solemnly through the trees. Luna didn't dare to speak, didn't dare to *hope*. She just wanted it to be over. She studied the curling tendrils of Amy's dark brown hair and thought of Chance's words.

"If things go sour between you and Amy, killing her is the only way to protect yourself."

Luna curled her hands into fists, letting the tiny pinpricks of pain from her nails digging into her palm center her. At last, the grass beneath their feet turned to a rocky shoreline beside the edge of a creek, and Amy stopped, glancing around, as if she was looking for someone.

"This should be good enough," she said and set the Rosebone down on the shore.

"Now what?" Luna asked.

"Now, this is where I need you," she replied.

Luna blinked at her.

Amy reached into her back pocket to pull out a book of matches and handed them to Luna with a careful look through her lashes. Luna had no real thought on her mind as she reached out and took it into her hand, feeling the smooth surface beneath her thumb.

She held her breath as she opened it and broke one of the matches free, striking it against the box. Both girls watched the flame simmer on the tip, the heat warming the skin on Luna's fingertips, before it bit into the flesh and then went out. Luna struck another match, and her eyes darted between the new flame and the ugly contraption on the ground, before she flicked it away like an insistent mosquito.

The flame caught onto the thing with ease. Luna and Amy watched as the flower entwined to the bone, began to blacken, the petals turning to dust and the fire charring the white bone. Luna's relief soared as she watched it. Amy was stiff beside her as the minutes dragged on. At last, the fire went out and the remnants of the Rosebone sat in a destroyed heap.

"It worked," Amy whispered.

Luna was about to join in the relief of her friend, to scatter the ashes of the contraption and put the mess behind her, when she stopped. The process began to reverse, and the Rosebone *came back* from its ashes. It sat there, vibrant red petals and bone stark white, as if it hadn't been reduced to cinders seconds before.

"What happened?" Luna demanded.

"You're not strong enough to counter the magic either," Amy said, her voice barely a whisper.

Luna stared at the ugly device in the charred stones around it. "So what do we do?"

"We need to find the source of its magic," Amy said.

"Chance?" Luna asked.

Amy just shook her head.

The girls stayed in the clearing for what felt like forever, before Amy resolved to find the person they needed to talk to. She scooped the Rosebone up, vowing to hide it someplace safe until they would be able to tackle it again. Luna didn't argue, she just watched her go. She was numb, both inside and out, and she wanted to go home.

Sleep, she thought numbly, *I need to sleep.*

Luna stumbled the distance between the woods and her house, not wasting any time heading to her room once she made it home for fear that Rose would've noticed her disappearance, but no one was home. She took the opportunity to jump into bed, and drifted off. When Luna opened her eyes, her heart fell to her stomach, as she recognized the part of the forest where Max and Sarah had brought her before. Had Max seen her in the cemetery after all?

A chill ran down her spine … she was being watched. Taking a deep breath, she hoped to tap some inner strength to face them. There would be no escape without their okay. After a bit of searching, she found no one, and let the hope build inside her for a fleeting second. *Maybe they changed their minds.*

She turned to head back the way she had come, and stopped when her eyes caught sight of Amanda, accompanied with a sickening punch of surprise that took her breath away. The unexpected horror made her sick to her stomach.

"Mandy," she whispered.

Amanda said nothing, instead, glancing down into her arms. That was when Luna noticed the tiny bundle.

"I-is that …?"

Amanda smiled. The tiny baby in her arms turned at the sound of Luna's voice, looking up at her through wide blue eyes—*Chance's* eyes. He blinked and cooed at her. A tear dripped from Luna's eyes as she slowly took him from Amanda, cradling the baby to her chest.

"I love you so much," she said to the bundle in her arms. "Did you miss me?"

"He's truly beautiful, Luna," Amanda said softly.

Luna turned to look at her. "I-I'm so sorry about what Chance did to you."

Amanda stilled at the statement, and Luna had a sympathetic moment of regret, when she realized how close her line was to the kind she often received … and hated. It was hard to keep Amanda's gaze when the slash across her throat was so visible. A small trickle of blood ran from the center, reminding Luna of the wound in Michelle's throat. She looked back down at Asher again, enjoying the life within his tiny body.

"You have nothing to apologize for, Luna. You warned me, but I didn't listen," she said finally.

"You're not here to give me closure, though," Luna guessed.

"That's right."

Luna closed her eyes and ran her thumb across Asher's cheek, as she waited for her friend to speak.

"I know you're struggling inside. Facing new demons that are much harder to conquer than the monsters of your past. We all worry about you, but it's my turn to warn you."

"You think Chance is wrong about Amy, too, don't you?"

Amanda exhaled slowly. "This place is lonely, Luna. The souls who are forced to stay here, do so in constant agony. We're your *friends.* We don't blame you for our deaths …"

"But?" Luna asked.

"But … those you kill *will*," Amanda said.

"Why is Asher here … with you, instead of Chance?"

"Asher died, because of the wound Chance gave you. That makes his death Chance's fault as well, Luna. He's trapped here … like the rest of us. If you listen to Chance and take Amy's life as well, she'll be one of us, forever. She'll always remember what you've done to her, along with anyone else he convinces you to kill."

Luna stared at her old roommate, her thoughts drifting to the day of Amanda's death. She had suffered so much in her final moments of life that she carried it to her death. Luna thought of Michelle suddenly. Was she wandering through the woods, hating Luna for taking her life? Or was she still in the school with Susan and Kate?

"Mandy … do you think I'm a bad person?"

Amanda's face drew tight. "No, you've just been far too unlucky. It's easy for someone to become confused about who they are."

Luna mulled over the word "unlucky."

"I'm not confused about who I am … I'm confused about what I should do! What am I supposed to do if Amy finds out what I did? What's the right answer?"

Amanda blinked at her, her lips held tight in a pencil straight line.

"D-do you think I should go to jail?" Luna asked in a barely audible voice. "I-I don't think I could last in prison."

Amanda continued to look at her with that same absent look of sorrow, reaching out to gently pull Asher from Luna's arms. "I know you'll do the right thing."

Luna held the baby to her body, reluctant to let him go. She gritted her teeth, knowing she had to give him up, but at the same time, she couldn't do it. "What if I don't know what that is anymore?"

Amanda simpered, finally pulling Asher free, and cradled the newborn to her. "You *think* you don't know. Your mind has been so clouded with anger and hate that you forget who you are. Your heart is pure of that confusion. Deep inside, you still know what the right thing to do is."

Luna was doubtful. As she watched her old friend with her baby in her arms, Luna had already made up her mind that she didn't want to wake up. Even if it meant being stuck there forever, she would do it for Asher, despite the look on Amanda's face.

The scene around her shifted, as if she were on the verge of waking up, but instead of the walls of her bedroom, she recognized the clearing that Chance's cabin sat in. She didn't know whether to be relieved or cry.

Chance had summoned her … that couldn't be good news. Did he know what she and Amy had done? Or what she was *trying* to do? With a deep breath, she walked toward the cabin and went right inside without a knock. If she was here, it was for a reason. Chance looked up at her from his table, through wide eyes, before he kicked out the nearest chair for Luna to sit in.

"Hi," he said, looking at his knife, as he resumed polishing it.

She nodded. "Did you bring me here?"

"Yeah, I was worried you were trapped in, uh … less desirable parts of DreamWorld again," he said, glancing up at her once.

A small smile showed on her face, before she let it drop.

Chance frowned and sat down his knife. "Are you okay?"

She reached for it and he slapped his hand onto hers.

"I don't want to wake up, Chance," she admitted.

"What happened?" he asked.

"*What happened?*" she echoed, and pulled her hand away. "I saw Asher."

"You did?" he asked, friendliness dissolved from his voice.

Luna laced her hands together on the table. "He's trapped … in DreamWorld with Max and Sarah and Amanda … all my friends," she said, barely able to keep her voice steady.

"They won't let me see him," Chance said, his shoulders drooping.

Luna rounded on him. "You knew he was there? Why didn't you tell me?"

"No, I didn't know, but I *do* know how they feel about me."

"They have every right—they're stuck there, because of you."

He smiled bitterly. "They're not wrong."

"What if I were to make a dream cycle and pull them in? Then you could work your magic and get him back, right?" Luna asked, her eyes growing wide with hope.

Chance smiled, but it was that painful smile again, the one that made Luna's heart hurt to look at. "You could try, but I guarantee that it won't work."

"*Why not?*" she demanded. "If I have as much power as everyone says, I should be able to do anything I want … including getting our child back."

"For living people, maybe, but these are dead people, Luna. They have their own rulebooks."

"Roughly translated, it means I'm useless. I can't do anything to stop them, just the same as you."

Chance's lips pulled tight. "Just about."

"I think they want me to kill myself, and maybe they're right! Maybe I should stop all this insane nonsense and end it."

"You can't do that, Luna."

"Why not?" she snapped, before her gaze softened. "I miss Asher, Chance. Holding him made me feel complete … I want that."

"I miss him, too, Luna, but this isn't the answer."

"You're in no place to preach about this subject."

"I'm not trying to," he said with a frustrated sigh. "I just want you to think before you act."

"I *have* thought about it. The more I do, the more I realize I don't have much reason left to live anyway. Max, and all of them, think I should … should end this chain and break the curse you hold over everyone."

"I don't hold a curse," he said with a scoff. "They don't know a thing about DreamWorld. They're telling you information they *assume*. While it's true we're linked together, because of the Rosebone, they're stuck here, because of me. They'll stay. All of them."

Luna looked at him skeptically. "Doesn't change my mind."

Chance's nostrils flared. "You're not thinking clearly. What about Rose? She needs you!"

"She *hates* me. You see the way she's constantly talking down to me. Besides, she has Amy to make it all better."

"Luna, I hope you know better than that," he said with a frown. "She doesn't hate you, she's worried about you."

"Well, it feels the same," she said, with her hand to her face. "This is so hard, Chance. It's so hard to function, day to day, anymore."

"I understand. Believe me, I get it more than anyone, but things will get better. You have to believe that. Otherwise, you'll never make it."

Luna stared at him. *'Cuz that's what you did, right?* With effort, she managed to bite back the statement. He was only trying to help, but his words were like a fresh punch to the abdomen, one that had the power to make her hurt.

"Maybe I'm not meant to make it," she said.

Chance offered her a loose smile and set his hand on hers once more. "Only time will tell."

CHAPTER THIRTY-SEVEN

EVEN WHEN HE was awake, Reese wondered about the missing Rosebone. *He* had been responsible for keeping it safe, and he had failed Chance, but the man didn't seem to care, though Reese didn't know how he *couldn't*. That night, Reese dedicated his time to searching again, finding Chance, to come up with a plan.

"We need to seek it out," he said without so much as a greeting. "Is there anyone you know of who might have taken it? Anyone out for revenge?"

Chance didn't answer. Rather, his face was glossed with an emotion that looked somewhere between annoyed and tired.

Reese's confusion blossomed, as he tilted his head to the side. It was as if Chance didn't even know he was there. "I don't understand. Aren't you worried it'll be destroyed? That you'll be stuck?"

Chance shrugged and looked away, as if he just wanted Reese to go away.

Reese felt useless at such a lackluster response, and it almost *angered* him. "What about the revival? Wasn't that the plan?"

"That *was* the plan," Chance said finally, tilting his head back in Reese's direction. "But it has to wait now anyway. I'm not going to leave this place. Not when my son is still here and needs me."

Reese stiffened. That was news to him. "Your *son*?"

Chance's brow pulled together as his eyes lifted from the floor to meet Reese's gaze. "This comes first. *He* comes first."

Reese looked at Chance and realized that the man was staring back at him with intensity. Every bitter emotion from before was gone, and Reese knew that this was his indirect way of saying what he didn't want to actually say—he needed *help*.

"I'm here for you," Reese said at last. "Let me know what I can do."

Chance smirked. "I was hoping you'd say that. Think you can make me something that works just like the Rosebone?"

Reese arched an eyebrow, internally questioning the man's sanity. "It won't work for you."

"It's not for me," he assured his friend, and added a dazzling smile that sent a chill right down Reese's spine.

CHAPTER THIRTY-EIGHT

WHEN LUNA WOKE up, she was immediately alert to the sound of sobbing. With her mind clouded with the remains of her dream, she tried to decide who the sound came from. She patted her face, but it was dry. She sat up and realized it was Amy, and it was *loud*. Did Amy suffer from night terrors, too?

The sound drifted from the living room, leaving Luna to wonder why she would cry that loudly outside the comfort of her room. Luna's curiosity urged her to investigate. Not caring that she was in her nightgown, she followed the sound to the living room, and stopped in her tracks like a deer in the headlights, as she caught sight of two officers leaving the house, afraid that if they noticed her, they would whisk her off to jail … where she belonged. When the door closed behind them, Luna remembered the reason for her voyage, and found the courage to snap out of her trance. Amy sat in the armchair beside the door, her face buried in her hands as she sobbed.

Luna's heart pounded in her chest as she stared at the side of Amy's head. "What did they want?"

Amy looked up, her eyes wide in surprise. Her face was red, where her tears had soaked into her skin. "Did I wake you, Luna? I'm sorry," she said softly, glancing back down at her hands.

"I-It's fine. Don't worry about it," Luna said taking a cautious step closer to Amy. "What did those officers say?"

"They wanted to let me know they found Michelle today," she said, her words hard to understand, as another sob wracked her body.

Luna's heart sank in her chest at her words. Without a body, the chances of her being connected to the murder had been slim to none, but now her chances had skyrocketed. If she had messed up the smallest detail, the officers would be back in less than a day to take her away. Luna realized an entire minute passed without her speaking. Hoping Amy hadn't noticed her sudden silence, she quickly cleansed her face of shock and tried her best to look sympathetic as she approached.

"They found her body in the woods just outside of town. Her throat was cut, and it wasn't done nicely either," Amy continued before Luna said a word.

Is there such a thing?

"Amy! I'm so sorry!" Luna crouched down to drape her arm over her friend's small shoulders, partly to hug her friend, but mostly to hide her face. Amy continued to cry into her hands, and Luna stared at the side of her face, selfish questions worming their way into her mind. "Do they know who did it?" she dared herself to ask.

Amy looked at her through teary eyes, as she whispered, "No, but we know who, don't we? He kills everyone." A moment later, her face returned to its place in her hands.

Luna deadpanned and let out the breath she had been holding. Amy assumed Chance was the culprit? *It makes sense.*

Amy cried until she paused to wipe desperately at the water that had gathered on her skin. She looked up at Luna, the mix of emotions swirling in her eyes more painful with each passing second. She opened her mouth as if she would speak, but she didn't say a word.

She has no idea the person who made her feel this way is the same one who's trying to comfort her, Luna thought to herself sardonically.

"You want to know what the last thing I said to Michelle was?" Amy asked, her voice so raspy, her words were near impossible to make out.

Luna had the feeling Amy would tell her, whether she wanted to hear it or not.

"When she took me to Brentwood to sign me in, I told her that I hated her." Amy's voice grew too soft for Luna to hear. "I told my own sister—the only real family I ever had—that I *hated* her."

Luna frowned. "You shouldn't be so upset with yourself, Amy. I bet Michelle knew you didn't mean it …"

Amy shook her head. Tears stuck in the strands of brown hair that grazed over her face. "It doesn't matter … I never should've said it! The last thing she ever heard me say was that I hated her, and now I can never take that back. I spent all those years in Brentwood hating her, but now I wish more than anything that I could have one minute with her to tell her I'm sorry."

Luna found herself once again speechless as the girl cried. Regret. That was what her friend currently felt, and Luna knew all too well what it was like. A year after his death, Luna still remembered the last interaction she had had with Max. Time did nothing to make her forget the fact that she had failed him.

She doubted it ever would.

Life's funny like that.

"Okay, maybe you shouldn't have said it," Luna said uncertainly, "but can't you tell her in DreamWorld?"

As soon as she said it, she wished she would've kept her mouth shut. This was her second time suggesting it to Amy, and she might find it as suspicious. Not to mention the fact that if Amy did find her, Michelle would tell her *everything*.

Luna held her breath, and Amy shook her head. "No, I still can't find her."

Luna could've cried with relief, but somehow, she managed to keep her face steady. "Michelle probably brushed what you said right off. She *loved* you, Amy. The whole reason she checked you into Brentwood in the first place was because she was worried to death that something bad had happened to you."

"Literally," Amy sniffled.

Luna crouched beside her friend, losing momentum in her

attempts. She didn't know what else she could say to make her friend feel better. She thought briefly of mentioning Michelle's illness, but stopped herself before saying a word. Chills of anger raced down her spine, as she remembered that was the same line Chance had fed her.

Luna tried to think of something she could use to comfort her friend … hobbies, interests, games. If anything, her efforts had only made Amy worse. Luna didn't know how to comfort someone. She only knew what it was like for people to try and comfort *her*.

"I'll leave you alone to grieve," Luna said, finally pulling her arm off of Amy's shoulders. Her throat was suddenly dry with unease, and she wished she had decided to stay in bed.

Amy shook her head. "You don't have to leave, Luna. The company is nice."

Luna shrugged, guessing Amy was trying to avoid hurting her feelings. "Look, I know a lot of people will say they understand how you feel when they really don't, but I get what you're going through more than anyone. When I lost my baby, all I wanted was to be alone. It's okay."

Amy looked at her and offered her a sad, small smile, as a tear dripped from her eye. "I don't know why it's hard for me to think of the terrible things you've gone through. I guess it's because you're so nice when you have every right to hate the world."

I'm much worse of a person than you would ever believe.

Amy drew in a long shuddery breath and wiped the soaked strands of brown hair out of her face. "I guess we have no choice, but to support each other, huh, Luna?"

Luna felt as if she wandered the Earth, disconnected from the people who mattered to her, but worse, she had lost herself. As she stared at the broken girl beside her, she wondered if prison would be the one place that could make her regain herself. While talking to Amanda, the thought of being taken away for murder had horrified her.

But looking at Amy's tears, it was impossible to ignore the fact that she deserved it. If she didn't confess, Amy would spend the rest of her life wondering who took her sister away … and why they had done it. Luna could take away that burden, by speaking one single sentence.

The words burned on the tip of her tongue like acid.

Amy wiped at her face again, before she asked, "Is something wrong?"

Luna took a deep breath, her heart hammering in her chest with anticipation of the life-changing action before her. Just as she was about to speak, someone cleared their throat across the room. She looked away from her friend, only to catch Chance's gaze. His eyes were questioning, but the solemn look on his face was enough for her to know that he guessed what she was trying to do.

Luna closed her eyes, thinking of Amy's words once again. Despite the horrible things Luna had done, Amy sat beside her, willing to support her, while Chance competed to be the one she leaned on. One of the choices was right and one of them was wrong. Reality crashed down on her, and once again, her heart and mind clouded with uncertainty.

CHAPTER THIRTY-NINE

A FEW MINUTES later, Amy changed her mind and decided she wanted the alone time after all. Luna watched her go without a word, glad for her departure. Luna had been in Amy's position too many times to count. A frown etched itself on her face, as she listened to the sounds of Amy sobbing all the way down the hall.

As her crying grew softer, Luna grew more aware of the new problem she faced. Chance was still in the living room, watching her, but after their fight, she had nothing to say. Without looking at him, she turned her back to him and began to walk down the hall, when his voice stopped her.

"I regret it, you know," he said softly, his voice gruff, as if he had been crying.

Despite her feelings, she turned to face him. His pale face was pulled tight in a look of despair, as his blue eyes searched her face. He took a step toward her, and she wondered if that had been a conscious decision of his.

"Regret what?"

"Stabbing you, killing your friends, hurting you. Do I really have to list every horrible thing I've done again? I regret it all. You're so beautiful and frail; you're supposed to cherish something like that ... not break it."

Luna was silent, choosing to stare at the ground, rather than him. "Just because you regret it, doesn't mean it's okay now. Every night I have nightmares about high school. I had to see all the people I love *die*, because of me."

Chance smiled bitterly. "I know, but you realize it wasn't because of you … it was because of me."

"Why did you do it?"

Chance's sad smile fell, and now it was his turn to look at the floor.

"Every time I ask you that question, you don't have an answer …" Luna trailed off. "If you really regretted what you did, you would at least give me some peace of mind, by letting me know what the hell you were thinking when you did it."

"That's fair, I suppose." He paused to scratch his chin in thought. "I did it for the same reason I made you hate me. I'm not right in the head. Simple as that. Maybe it's because of my past, maybe it's who I am, I don't know."

Luna fell silent again. For all the years of grief she had endured, she had thought every possible horrible thing about Chance. From high school onward, she had known he was different, but hearing him state it didn't make her feel better; it didn't come close.

"Is that enough of an answer for you?" he prompted.

Luna wanted to get angry. She wanted to demand the answer she deserved, but at the same time, she had never gotten this close before. If she resorted to anger now, Chance would respond by diminishing her chances to zero. Luna took a minute to carefully compose herself before she spoke.

"What do you mean you're not right in the head?" she asked.

Chance gritted his teeth and looked away from her, as if he was suddenly ashamed. "I-I have dissociative personality disorder, okay?"

Luna didn't know why she felt surprised, but she did. She stared at him through wide eyes, temporarily out of things to say. He looked up at her through hardened sapphire eyes, and she could tell he was both angered and hurt by her reaction.

"Multiple personalities," he clarified, after a moment of silence.

"W-were you ever diagnosed with it?" she finally managed to ask.

Chance shook his head. "No, I don't need a doctor to tell me what I already know. For a long time, I thought I was schizophrenic like my mom had been; Layanna told me she suffered from it, suffered worse, because of everything my father put her through, but it turned out that I somehow created my own insanity, because people like me aren't born this way, life shapes us."

"If you knew what was wrong with you, why didn't you ever try to get help?" she asked.

"I didn't want to admit it was true. I didn't want to accept the fact that I was crazy and that I had found a way to make myself even crazier. I don't blame my mother, but my father is a different story. I *never* wanted to be like him."

"But you're not," Luna tried to say, but she didn't know either way.

"All I wanted was to be normal," he said, sinking to the couch, "but all the medicine in the world wouldn't be able to make that happen. How do you force two people to become one again? I don't care what psychiatrists say ... it can't happen."

Luna frowned and took a small step toward him, torn about how to respond. In her mind, she was still furious with Chance, to the point where she wanted to walk away and let him sit in his sorrow. On the other hand, she sympathized with him. She knew all too well what it felt like to be alone.

"How many ... personalities do you have?"

"I have two, and you've met them both: Stephen and the murderer. He ... has no name. They're as different as night and day, Yin and Yang."

"But ... what about—"

"Chance? *Fabricated* personality. There's a difference."

"So back in high school, at the restaurant, you—"

"I was being Stephen. My *true* self, because I trusted you with the knowledge that I wasn't the person everyone else thought I was."

"Oh," Luna stuttered stupidly. It was the only thing she could think to say.

"Can I ask you something?" he asked suddenly, his voice jerking Luna from her internal dilemma.

"Sure."

"Were you seriously going to tell Amy what you did?" His eyes were piqued with curiosity as he watched her.

She knew the answer to his question, but the thought of admitting it made her sick.

"I can tell by the look on your face," he said and forced a short chuckle. "Why would you do that?"

"You never considered telling anyone about what you did?"

"I didn't see the point. Telling wouldn't take it back," he replied.

Amanda was convinced telling Amy was the right thing to do, but Chance was right, too. What would confessing accomplish? Make her life more miserable than it already was?

No, thank you.

CHAPTER FORTY

LUNA WENT OUT for another walk, enjoying the way the cold air cooled her down and made her throat burn. She just wanted the day to end, for everything to be over. The terrible sounds of Amy's strangled sobs rang out in the back of her mind, and she hated it, hated herself for causing it, and hated Chance for ever convincing her that what she had done was the right thing. Her mind circled through the man who had tried to attack her and the Rosebone, to Layanna's mention of alliances. Then Luna froze, wondering how she hadn't come across the connection sooner. If Chance knew of people who would help him, wouldn't Layanna have an idea who they were?

Luna tucked her lip between her teeth. She didn't know how valuable that link could be, but it was certainly better than the dead end they had previously had. She needed to find her, but had no idea how to do so. She remembered Layanna's words, *"In this day and age, it's not hard to find anyone,"* and decided to go to the library to borrow a phonebook.

When she got there, she found the flaw in her plan—she had no idea what Layanna's last name was. While Layanna was distinctive, it wasn't distinctive enough in the hundreds of pages of names and numbers. Luna sighed dejectedly as she left the library.

Then she caught sight of something that made her heart soar—*Layanna.* Her eyes stretched wide and before Luna knew what she was doing, she jogged toward the girl. Layanna's face was horrified as she took a step back like she thought Luna would strike her.

"I promise I wasn't following you," she stuttered out quickly.

Luna waved it away. "I don't care if you were. I'm actually really glad to see you."

Layanna's eyebrows pulled together in confusion.

"You said Stephen had alliances. Who are they?" she demanded.

Layanna folded her arms across her chest. "The less you know of them, the better."

Luna stilled. That wasn't the answer she had expected. "Please, I need to know, I ..." Luna stopped, wondering just how much of the story she should stay. Did Layanna know anything of DreamWorld, or was she just as clueless as Violet had been?

"Why do you need to know?" Layanna asked, arching an eyebrow.

"I can't tell you," Luna said at last.

"Then I can't help you. Those are dangerous people, the kind you shouldn't get mixed up in unless you absolutely have to."

Chance is, too, Luna thought, but found she was stuck for words. The truth seemed to be the only thing that would work in this case, but it might be too much. "I think they know about me," she said, quickly considering one last angle.

"Oh?"

"Someone ... before I lost my baby, someone tried to attack me with a knife. I didn't see his face, but I wondered ..." She swallowed heavily. "I wondered if it had something to do with Stephen."

Layanna flared her nostrils and breathed out heavily. "Yeah, I saw him lurking around the first time I visited you."

Luna stiffened at that. "And you didn't call the police?"

"No, I confronted him and told him to back off," Layanna said.

"And that *worked?*" Luna's blood ran cold. "I thought you said they were dangerous!"

"They are, but ..." Layanna trailed off, looking truly torn. "I guess you have the right to do what you will." She reached into her pocket to pull out a tiny notebook and a pen, and scribbled something down on the page, before she ripped it out and handed it to Luna. "Here's his name and address."

Luna blinked as her eyes traveled from Layanna's face to her outstretched hand. Could it really be that simple?

"Whatever you need to talk to him for, just remember that his services always come at a price."

Before Luna could ask her what that meant, Layanna turned on her heels and walked away, even though all Luna wanted was for her to stay.

***

LUNA CALLED AMY to meet her at the library, and the entire time she waited for her friend to arrive, she stared at the tiny piece of paper Layanna had given her, reading it until she was sure it was permanently engraved in her memory. Amy looked windblown when she finally arrived, and Luna wondered if she had actually *run* all the way there.

"Luna, what's going on?" she asked, holding her hand to her side as she bent over to catch her breath.

Luna thrusted the piece of paper toward her friend. "Him. This is the guy we need to talk to about breaking the spell."

Amy's eyebrows drew together as she stood up, taking the paper gently from Luna's fingers. She read it before peering over the edge to meet Luna's eyes. "How did you get this?"

"Chance's sister," she said.

"Chance's ..." she trailed off, as if the thought was too much to process and shook her head to clear her bewilderment. "This is great."

"Do you know who he is?"

"No, but we're about to find out."

"Want to go now?"

"I do, but I need to go get the Rosebone first," Amy said, scratching at the side of her face. "Go home and get some rest. I'll meet you back there in a few hours."

Luna agreed and the girls went separate ways. The entire walk home, filled Luna with both hope and despair at the idea of their plan being successful.

***

LUNA FOUND CHANCE was waiting for her when she returned home. Her heart beat erratically in her chest with the assumption that he knew where she had been, that he would call her out on it and try to stop her before she could ever meet the "Cody," who his sister had so graciously told her about.

"Will you do me a favor?" he asked without a greeting, as soon as she walked through the door.

Luna, surprised by both his tone and sudden appearance, nodded once.

"Do you remember where I used to live?" he asked. "The old house in the woods?"

Luna bobbed her head uncertainly.

"I want you to go there."

"Now? Why?" she asked, visibly shaking. The only time she had been there, the house had already been on the verge of collapse. She could only wonder how it looked after four years of weather damage and abandonment.

"After I found out you were pregnant, I wrote my suicide note and hid it under my mattress."

"W-why did you hide your note?" Luna asked.

"It was an emotional thing," he said, reaching up to scratch the back of his neck. "It was something I didn't want just anyone reading."

"I thought your lawyer had your note?"

Chance shook his head. "That was my *will*. I wrote that a long time ago."

Luna scrunched up her face. The timeline still didn't make sense. "If that was written a long time ago, why did you leave your stuff to me?"

He chewed on his lip and stared down at his hands. "I have my reasons."

Luna frowned, knowing that was the best answer she would get. "What do you want me to do with your note?" she made herself ask.

244

"Read it."

"Th-that's it?"

He nodded, keeping his eyes locked on the floor.

His emotions were obvious in the tensed stance of his shoulders, but what thoughts ran through his head? All the years of playing cat and mouse with him had given her time to figure him out, or so she thought. Even in death, he continued to baffle her. Would she ever be able to unravel the mystery of Stephen Harris?

***

HALF AN HOUR later, Luna parked Chance's truck in the exact same place he had parked it years ago—the first, and only, time he had ever brought her there. As Luna stepped out of the truck, she felt uncomfortable being alone among the vast expanse of wilderness. A tiny breeze rattled the leaves around her, sending a chill down her spine. She was tempted to get back in the truck and drive away, but when she closed her eyes, she could see the intense look on Chance's face, and the urge to know what had been his final thoughts tugged her onward.

Pulling her coat closer to her body, her mind played memories of that day four years ago. She never would have believed that she would've traveled back willingly on Chance's request. The old building Chance used to call home was more disgusting than it had been then. The image that she had created in her mind didn't do a justice to the building that stood before her. It was leaning slightly, as if it was ready to collapse, and various plants grew along the rotting siding and through the glassless windows.

She stepped on the creaking porch, staring at the parted front door. From where she stood, she could *smell* the decay of the wooden frame. Sighing heavily, she pushed slowly on the door, and a bat shot out of the darkness, its wings close enough to her head to scatter her hair.

She screamed and swatted at her head, nearly falling backward off of the porch. Her hart hammering like a jackhammer in her chest, she peered warily into the darkness of the open door. The situation before her could expand into two possibilities: She would either come to understand the man who had torn her life apart, or walk away with the same inescapable pit of confusion that she currently carried.

The only way she would know, would be to enter the old house. She steeled her face in preparation. She had come this far, she wouldn't turn away now.

CHAPTER FORTY-ONE

WHEN LUNA WENT inside, she spotted an old candle by the door, covered in a layer of cobwebs. She swiped at it lightly and noticed the dusty matchbook beside it. Carefully, she pulled one out and lit the candle. A few of the remaining traces of web caught on fire before disappearing completely. She ignored the smell as she made her way through the house.

The tiny glow of the candle illuminated the area around her. Progress was slow and, as memories flooded through her mind, it became hard to maneuver. Where could Chance's room be? Skirting around the clothed furniture in the living room, she made her way down the nearest hallway. She passed a bathroom without slowing down and knew where she was. A chill ran down her spine as she remembered the satanic room of bones she had found. She had only been seventeen then, years before she knew that what she was seeing would ruin her life. When she had first seen the pentagram drawn in blood, it created a fear in her she never knew when she looked at Chance.

She decided to make it a priority to avoid that room.

Cautiously, she checked every other door down the hall, searching for the one that opened into Chance's room. Finally, the last door on the left swung open, to reveal a medium-sized bedroom. She stood in the doorway, letting her eyes take in the tiny details that the candlelight revealed to her. She was surprised to find the room empty, except for a large lumpy mattress pushed into the far corner. It had turned green with a myriad of fungi that had made it their home. Luna wrinkled her nose at the musty smell.

Had it been in that bad of a condition when Chance used it? Pushing the thought—and unpleasant smell—to the back of her mind, she forced herself to move closer. Her heart began to pound with another wave of anticipation, as she realized how close she was to uncovering the note Chance had sent her to find. Setting the candle on the floor, she hesitantly placed her hands underneath the grimy mattress. The worn fabric was wet, causing her to grimace at the unpleasant sensation on her hands as she lifted it.

A single envelope sat on the floor underneath. Luna grabbed it quickly, letting the decayed mattress fall back to the floor with a splat. She frantically wiped the slime that had accumulated on her hands onto her clothes, before studying the envelope. The side that had touched the mattress was damp, but other than that, it appeared to be in decent condition. Tucking the envelope into her pocket, she picked up the candle and casted one last disgusted look at the mattress, before stumbling back through the dark house. The light filtering in from the open door proved a more useful guide than the candle. When she reached the end of the hallway, she blew out the tiny flame and set it down at her feet. Her hand instinctively sunk into her pocket, searching for the envelope, as she coasted easily through the living room.

Once she stepped outside of the house, her thoughts eased. Clutching the envelope tight in her hand, she ran all the way back to Chance's truck and sat in the driver's seat, holding the envelope up to the light. It had turned yellow around the edges and smelled as bad as the mattress had.

There was no writing on the outside, no indication of what the envelope held. Luna held her breath as she opened it and pulled out Chance's suicide note. She unfolded the crinkled sheet of loose leaf paper and began to read:

To whom it may concern,

I'm very aware that the end of that statement is no one. Nobody cares about me; I've given them no reason to really. I've killed people, torn countless families apart, and looking back on all of it . . . I'm not really sure why I did it.

Misery loves company as they say, and as such, I can't believe this is what my life has become. Thinking about everything I've been through, I never would've guessed it could've ended at such a dead end. I have no one, and I am no one. I was born alone, and I will most certainly die alone. What makes it worse, is thinking, I wonder every day, if my life could have possibly turned out different.

The heavy feeling in my heart gives me my answer.

I was conditioned to be cold. From little on, I was different. I always thought not having feelings could be a good thing—it was a defense mechanism of sorts, or at least I thought it was. I got through a lot of tough spots on my own, simply because the logic in my head did not have to compete with the incompetence in my heart.

Luna, you were definitely the death of that.

You always thought I treated you differently, because I

hated you. You never realized I treated you differently, because you were the one person I **didn't** hate. Hearing about the conception of our baby was devastating. Not because I didn't want him, but because I know you don't want me. I barely survived the broken home I came from . . . I don't want to be part of another one.

I never really felt as if I was living before, but now, it seems as if my existence is superficial. I can't handle it anymore. Especially not with my child coming into this world. God knows I wouldn't be any good for him.

I know what I must do. I know it means saying goodbye to you, Luna, and never meeting my child. At least I am comforted by the knowledge that he'll be in good hands. What I'm doing will be the best for everyone. Without the threat of me alive, maybe you will finally get to move on with your life. This way, our child will never know what a monster his father was.

Promise me that, Luna.

Just know that even though you'll never feel the same for me, I'll always carry love for you.

Goodbye forever,

Identity Uncertain

The last thing he had thought about, before taking his own life, was her. The thought stung. She read the note over, four or five times, absorbing the raw grief that dripped from every word. The sadness of his thoughts was oddly beautiful to her, like some kind of dark poetry. After reading it the fifth time, she tried to convince herself to fold it up and put it away.

She couldn't win.

Very slowly, she began to read it over for the sixth time, and suddenly, she could see Chance's sorrowful sapphire eyes in the back of her mind, as he told her about the note. Remembering about it must have been as painful as writing it had been. Finally, she folded it, as delicately as possible, and placed it back inside the aged envelope, which she gingerly placed on the seat beside her. Her hand hovered above it, as if she expected it to disappear as soon as the contact was broken.

The entire way home, the dilemma over Chance blossomed in her mind. She wanted to hate him, it was the logical thing she should do, but her heart didn't agree—it seemed determined to show compassion and understanding. He had wronged her so many times, but the more she thought about it, the more she wondered if he had even meant to do it, or if it had been the true him who had. Luna bit her lip, remembering his confession. Could his mental illness be enough for her to forgive him for everything he had done?

She didn't know the answer to that.

No matter what confusion rooted itself in her mind, she was glad for the note. It shed some light on the rare side of Chance … *Stephen.* Even if she was confused, the haze would clear eventually, and she would have her answers, one way or another.

Another sparse glance at the envelope brought the final, most haunting question to her mind: Had Chance been in his right state of mind when he killed himself?

***

ROSE SAT IN the kitchen, sipping carefully at her cup of tea with the hope that it would calm her rattled nerves, but instead, she felt worse. Footsteps in the hall caused her to look up, expecting to see Luna, when

Amy's face appeared instead.

Rose sighed in disappointment, and stirred her tea with the spoon, clanking it against the side to distract herself, while Amy crept nervously into the kitchen. "How are you holding up?" she asked.

Amy frowned and pulled a chair out. "I guess you heard about Michelle."

"It's a terrible thing. I'm so sorry, dear."

Amy smiled, but the look was painful. "I knew it would end like this. It's what usually happens in Lima."

"It's still a shame. Like the suicide they showed on the news on Halloween."

"Is everything okay, Mrs. Ketz?" Amy asked, refusing to comment her thoughts on Chance's death.

Rose tipped her head to the side and stared at the amber liquid in her mug. "I'm worried about Luna," she said, setting her hand to the table.

Amy gnawed on her bottom lip. "Honestly, me, too. She's a lot different than I remember."

"Has she said anything to you about what she's feeling?"

"She's withdrawn," Amy admitted. "That's about all I can get out of her. It's hard to get her to stay in the same room as me, let alone talk."

Rose shook her head, looking down at her fingers. "She's been like this for so long, so secretive about everything. Whenever I try to get answers from her, she shuts down. A couple years ago, we put her in therapy. She only went once, but she seemed to get better afterwards. She left Lima, moved into her own place, and really got a hold of her life. I wonder if she was just pretending. She does that, you know? Always tries to seem stronger than she really is."

Rose didn't blame her daughter. After Cassandra, she had done the same, except instead of distancing herself, she dove into a marriage she hadn't even been sure she was ready for.

"Maybe she *was* getting better," Amy offered, "but she's been through a lot lately, Mrs. Ketz."

Rose twitched at the formality. It left a bad taste in her mouth.

"You can call me Rose, Amy."

The small girl nodded politely in response.

"I've seen her through her worst times. Sometimes she beats herself up so bad, she won't eat for days at a time. Worries me to death," Rose said, remembering the summer after Luna's graduation. "The world could've ended, and it wouldn't have been enough to make her leave her room. She's never been one to handle her emotions well."

Are any of us?

"If I were you, I'd give her a little more time. Maybe when she's ready, she'll want to talk."

Rose wouldn't bet money on it. "I don't know how to help her. I know she wasn't ready to be a mother, and I can't shake the feeling that Stephen hurt her more than she admits."

"He was a bad person," Amy said in agreement.

"Has she said anything to you? About what he's done?"

Amy stilled, uncertain of how to answer the question.

Rose didn't notice the reaction. "I never told Luna, but when I was her age, I gave a baby away."

Amy's eyes widened.

"I was young ... struggling to make it myself. I wasn't ready for a kid. I regretted my decision so much—still do, almost thirty years later. I was so proud of Luna when she said she was going to keep the baby. She ... gave up so much for that child—something I could never do."

"You did it for Luna though," Amy pointed out.

Rose sighed, swirling the last sip of tea around the bottom of her mug. "When I got pregnant with Luna, I had only been dating her father a month. I ... panicked and thought too much about the child I had already ... *abandoned*. I married Luna's father. He didn't even propose. *I proposed to him.*

"I just didn't want to be alone ... to make that decision again. I can't explain the pain of choosing what I did, just like I can't imagine the pain Luna's going through for simply not *having* a choice. I need to know ... everything that Stephen put her through, but I can't get her to open up. Will you do me a favor? Do you think you could try and get her to talk to you?"

Amy hesitated. Luna hadn't seemed eager to talk about much at Brentwood, and doubted it would be much different in the security of her own home. Seeing the pain in Rose's eyes made her push away her uncertainties and nod. "I'll see what I can do." She was about to stand up, when the sound of Rose's voice stopped her.

"What about you? How are you doing?"

Amy took in a deep breath, planting herself back in the chair. "I've been … better. I'm glad that at least I know for sure what happened to Michelle, and I can give her a proper burial. It's only a matter of time, before they find the monster who did this."

"Have you already started on the funeral arrangements?" Rose asked, tapping her finger on the table.

Amy shook her head. "I haven't quite gotten there yet, ma'am."

"I understand, it's hard. When my husband died, I didn't know what to do with myself," she said and counted to ten, letting only the sound of her breath fill her mind, as her counselor had once taught. "Thankfully, I had Luna to help me through it."

Amy smiled. "I'm so grateful you took me in. At the very least, I know Luna can connect with me about loss."

"If only you could get her to talk about it."

Amy tilted her head to the side. "I'm sure that in time, she'll open up."

Rose, never having smoked in her life, suddenly craved a cigarette.

"I wouldn't be so sure. Luna has always been a strange girl. She has her own way of coping with things. I've never understood it. Her therapist told me she has a tendency to hold in things and ignore them," Rose said.

"I've noticed … that's not healthy."

"That's part of my concern."

"Like I said, Rose, I'll see what I can do," Amy said with a friendly smile on her face.

In the back of her mind, she wasn't as confident. She could easily remember the horrors Chance had inflicted on her that day, three years ago. It was next to impossible for her to imagine what Luna could have gone through. Amy remembered when Luna had come to Brentwood to beg for her help a few months back.

What kind of morbid terror had actually persuaded her to try and reach out to somebody?

I shot her down, she thought, a sickening lump in her stomach growing. *She reached out to me, and I shot her down. I've been a terrible friend.*

CHAPTER FORTY-TWO

WHEN LUNA PARKED the truck back at home, she found herself staring at the envelope, once again, and picked it up gingerly, with the temptation to read it over yet again. She pursed her lips as she tucked it away into her pocket. Reading it again wouldn't give her answers to the questions it had created. Only one person would be able to explain it to her.

She needed to find Chance.

Part of her expected him to be waiting for her when she got home, but after a minute of careful observation, disappointment washed over her, when she realized he was nowhere in sight.

Was he so afraid she would judge him that he was avoiding her? *Unless he's hiding something* from *me,* she thought idly.

Soft talking drifted from the kitchen. Momentarily distracted from her thoughts of Chance, she followed the sound, to find Amy and Rose deep in conversation. They sat beside each other at the table, heads bowed closely together. When Luna stepped into the kitchen, the pair took no notice of her. What did they have to talk about? The only common ground they shared was her. The paranoid voice in her mind was beginning to grow certain, worried they were discussing what should be done with her.

The uncomfortable feeling grew in her stomach the longer the pair ignored her. After a minute of her presence going unnoticed, she finally spoke up. "What's going on?"

Rose turned to look at her daughter and stood up to greet her. She approached her slowly, as if Luna was a dangerous animal that couldn't be provoked. "Hey, Luna," she said simply.

"What're you guys talking about?" Luna asked, trying to keep her worry out of her voice, as her gaze flicked between her mother and her only remaining friend.

"I was helping Amy."

Luna scrunched up her face in confusion as she glanced around the nearly immaculate kitchen. "With what?"

"The, uh, funeral arrangements," Rose said.

From the corner of her eye, Luna noticed Amy's face drop to look at the table. Why had Amy gone to Rose to talk about her sister's death instead of Luna? Was it possible she suspected Luna of the grisly crime she had committed?

It's not possible, a tiny voice in her mind said stubbornly. Luna frowned at its confidence. *But what if it is?*

"The funeral is on Friday," Amy spoke up, her tone stiff, with her eyes firmly rooted on the table.

Luna blinked, unsure of how to respond. "So soon?"

Amy glanced up at her through glassy eyes. "Yeah, I want to get past this as soon as I can. The quicker Michelle gets put in the ground, the faster everyone can start healing."

Luna opened her mouth, disagreement ready on her tongue, when Rose set a hand on her shoulder, making her jump. Luna glanced up at her as her mother led her to the living room. With Amy still in the kitchen, Rose turned to face her daughter, but Luna was taken aback. What couldn't be said in front of Amy?

"Did you hear the news about Amy's sister?" Rose asked quietly.

"Of course, Mom. I talked to her about it this morning."

At the end of Luna's sentence, both women looked up to the shuffling sound of Amy making her way out of the kitchen. She flashed them a distressed smile before her eyes fell to the floor, and she slunk down the hallway to her room. They could whisper all they wanted, but Amy was no fool—she knew exactly what they were talking about.

"Why weren't you home?" Rose asked Luna, bringing her thoughts back to the present.

Luna drew her eyebrows together. "I-I … uh … had an errand to run, Mom. Why?"

"Well, your errand shouldn't be more important than your friends!" she scolded.

Luna recoiled from the sharpness of her tone. The anger that radiated off of her mother came to Luna by surprise. "Excuse me? For your information, I *did* try to comfort her this morning," Luna replied, lifting her chin. "She told me she wanted some alone time, so that's exactly what I gave her."

Rose frowned, and Luna knew she wouldn't accept her answer. "Luna, you've spent your entire life avoiding people. I know you've been through a lot lately, but that's no excuse to abandon the people who depend on you. This girl needs a friend, desperately, and honestly, Luna, I believe you do, too."

Luna took in a deep breath through her nose. "Mom, I told you I *tried*. She wanted to go to her room, and I didn't blame her. Take it from me; she doesn't need a friend right now, she needs time. Death is a huge change. Don't you remember how long it took you to cope with Dad's death?"

Rose looked away sharply. The glint of sorrow in her eyes was only barely concealed by the shadow that fell over her face. "Well, you should try harder in the future."

Luna didn't like the harshness of her voice. It was as if she was chastising her for something she had done wrong. Luna ground her teeth together, barely able to hold in her temper.

"Why are you doing this? This is my problem, Mom. *Amy* is *my* problem. This whole situation has nothing to do with you!"

"As long as that girl is under my roof, she is my responsibility. I'm not going to let her hurt herself, just because my daughter decides to be too standoffish to help!"

"I did what I could this morning, and when she wanted me to

back off, I listened. Believe it or not, people don't like it when others breathe down their neck all the time!"

"She just got out of a *mental* hospital, Luna! What if she had tried to hurt herself while you were gone?" Rose asked.

Luna stared at Rose without a trace of emotion, her mind focused on the two deep gashes on her right thigh. Rose invested so much energy in Amy that she had no idea what thoughts her own daughter had. Would Rose be as bitter toward her if she knew, or would she lock Luna away in the same place she had rescued Amy from?

"Amy wouldn't do something like that," Luna said, holding her chin up defiantly.

"How do you know?" Rose demanded.

She wants to see me fry for what I did.

Luna bit back the response and remembered the drawings Michelle had shown her a year ago, and the progress Amy had made since then. If Amy had dark thoughts, Luna was positive they would have surfaced years ago, toward the beginning of her trauma, but Luna couldn't tell Rose any of that.

"I know her better than that," Luna stated simply. "I'm her friend."

"You don't act like it," Rose said.

Luna felt as if she had acid on her tongue, but she didn't say another word as she turned to walk down the hallway. Life had been better when she lived in the apartment, away from her parents. She loved them, but both her mother and her father never seemed to understand what it took to be good parents, and Luna wondered what had driven them to even have her in the first place.

They should have never had a child.

Luna's blood boiled with anger, and she was glad Chance wasn't hovering. When the anger vanished, she would want someone to share her mind with—someone who could understand, but in the meantime, it seemed as if she had no one to turn to when she needed them.

That's nothing new.

***

"ANY LUCK ON the device?" Chance called to Reese, as he caught sight of him sitting in his usual place on the beach.

Reese sighed, looking at the remaining pieces scattered around him in the sand. "Somewhat, I suppose. I just don't understand what you need something like this for, if not yourself. These aren't easy to make, you know, and I'd really like to know who the hell is going to be connected to me like this, because I assume I will be the host."

Chance looked at him evenly for a rough second. "Reese, you trust me, right?"

Reese hesitated on how to answer. Chance had never asked such a direct question before. "Yes. Yes, I do."

"Then believe me when I say I have a plan. It's not for me, but it's for someone who's in a dangerous situation."

Reese watched the wave inching its way up the beach. "You're not going to tell me who, though, are you?"

Chance only smirked.

"Will I be in danger?" Chance didn't answer that question.

Reese frowned. He wanted to believe Chance, that was the initial reaction, but he couldn't let himself be sure. Chance had too much up in the air to have much in the way of a solid plan. Reese knew that. He wondered if Chance did, too, and just didn't want to believe it, or if he thought himself to be so immortal that he could ensure others could be, too.

Reese sighed, finally giving in, and dug into his pocket to reveal a small silver cylinder. He held it up for Chance to see and the metallic surface reflected the light.

"A switchblade?" Chance asked, skeptically raising an eyebrow as he plucked it from Reese's palm.

Reese nodded, though he didn't lift his eyes. "Unlike with the Rosebone, this connection won't have a direct link. If it's going to work, their blood needs to touch this, and I figured a knife would be the most practical way of going about it."

Chance sighed and reached up to touch the back of his head with his free hand. "Blood magic. Didn't know Keepers did those kind of things."

Reese smirked. Not much, just enough for the corner of his lip to turn up slightly. "They don't."

CHAPTER FORTY-THREE

IT TOOK LUNA a considerable amount of time to push away the anger that Rose had caused and the effort exhausted her, almost to the point where she forgot about her true mission—finding Chance. Luna felt as if she *was* back in high school, dealing with the nonsense and mind games of the most popular cliques in the school. *But I'm not,* she reminded herself. *This is my life.*

The thought made her sadder than she would've imagined possible.

Luna sat on her bed, staring out the window. The gentle snowfall outside put her oddly at ease, when she heard a soft knock on her door and looked up at Amy coming into her room. Her coat was bulged out on one side, and Luna guessed the Rosebone was hidden away there.

"Ready to go?" Amy asked.

The question was easy enough to answer, but Luna paused. "What were you and my mom *really* talking about?"

Amy's eyes went wide like a rabbit freezing at the sound of a predator. "The funeral arrangements. I thought I told you that."

Luna rolled her lip in her teeth and looked away. She knew a lie when she heard one, but found she had no energy to fight. Luna grabbed the keys to Chance's truck off of the table beside the door, and the girls piled into the truck. Amy shivered, wrapping her scarf tighter around herself as she settled into her seat.

"I never would've thought I'd be glad for this piece of shit," she said.

Luna wholeheartedly agreed as she turned on the engine and read over the address once again. They drove in silence, the Rosebone tucked into Amy's lap. The address that Layanna had given them dumped them from the paved roads of the city to a dirt backroad, littered with potholes.

Amy frowned, obviously unhappy for the bumpy journey, as she squinted out the window. "We have to be close. There's nothing out here."

Luna wanted to agree, but couldn't. If there was anything that Luna's experience with Chance had taught her, it was to never underestimate a potential enemy. So they continued to drive, and eventually, the road ended in a flat expanse of land, covered in knee-length grass.

"Is this the place?" Luna asked, frowning as she glanced at Amy.

The woman clutched the paper with the address on it and glanced between the windshield and Luna. "It has to be. There's a building in the distance."

"I don't feel good, being here," Luna admitted.

Amy's face turned grim. "There's dark magic at work in this place."

Luna shut off the engine, and the girls climbed out with that ominous note ringing in their mind. The trip through the frost-encrusted grass seemed as if it took forever, but eventually, they stood at the door of the building. It was giant and square-shaped, the design reminding Luna more of a mausoleum than a house.

Amy kept the Rosebone tucked just out of sight, as Luna took a breath and reached out to knock, her thumps radiating loudly on the strange metal door. After a minute, no one answered, and Amy frowned.

"Knock harder," she ordered.

Luna complied, but they got the same lack of a response. "What do we do?" she asked, glancing at the Keeper beside her in despair.

Amy's shoulders slumped. "Nothing we can do, except come back later."

It was disheartening, but Luna had no choice, but to agree. Turning back to head to Chance's truck, they froze, taking in the same surprised gasp of air, as they realized that someone was standing *behind* them. He was cloaked in a black shirt with black pants and a red cloak on top, his hood pulled to shadow his eyes.

"Who are you?" he demanded.

Luna's heart fluttered at the sound of his voice. She recognized it—it was the man who had attacked her … or tried to anyway.

"Why ask? You already know that," she snarled, forgetting Layanna's threat about how dangerous he was.

The man tipped his head to the side. "Yes, I am aware of you, *Luna*. I meant short stack here." He gestured to Amy.

"Who she is, is none of your concern," Luna said.

"Maybe, but the device in her hands *is*."

Amy tried to shield it from sight, but it was too late, the man's eyes were already on it.

"You know what it is?" Luna asked, taking half a step into his line of sight to partially conceal Amy from view.

He laughed. "Probably more than you do."

"Then you know how to destroy it."

He tilted his head to the side, and Luna couldn't tell if he was amused or annoyed. "Maybe I do."

"Then will you?" Amy spoke up, holding it out in sight. A tiny snowflake drifted down and landed on one of the vibrant petals of the rose.

He didn't speak, and the moment dragged on forever, as his eyes stayed on the object. He reached out with shaky fingers and tried to pry it from Amy. She held onto it before finally letting it go. He held up the creation and closed his eyes, before he said, "I'll help you."

Luna's body eased as the words pushed away everything else. "Will you tell me who you are?"

"Chance never told you?" he asked and scoffed. "Can't say I'm surprised."

"No, he never mentioned you, but he must've told you some shit for you to want to hurt me."

"I'll tell you who I am, if you stop talking."

Luna narrowed her eyes.

"I'm Cody. Now come the fuck on," he said and pushed past them to go into the building. He paused in the doorway, then glanced over his shoulder at both of them. "Oh, and no talking in the compound."

Amy and Luna stood by and watched Cody, following him into the bowels of the place he called a "compound," as he gathered the materials necessary for the ritual. Eventually, they moved to the basement, where he piled a table high with different vials and bones. Amy and Luna exchanged a glance, and suddenly, Luna understood why Layanna had said these people were dangerous. They were magic, but not even in the conventional sense that Luna had come to know.

"I need you to light the fire," Cody said to Luna.

She nodded and took the matchbook from him, looking at the cauldron before her.

"Ready?" Cody asked, glancing between Amy and Luna.

The women were quick to agree, and Cody went to work, murmuring words in Latin and throwing together liquids and bones in a series of poultices. At last, he set it into the cauldron and looked to Luna to give her the signal. The striking of the match was loud, and she didn't wait nearly as long to throw it, as she had in the woods. A few seconds later, the cauldron was spouting flames, crackling, as the Rosebone was steadily destroyed. Luna watched the fire eat up every ounce of the Rosebone, reducing it to mere ashes, and she didn't know if she wanted to laugh or cry.

This was it—her mission was complete. She was severed from him, *free*. *Free*. She repeated the word in her head, but it just didn't sound right, didn't *feel* right. Luna reached out, grasping Amy's hand tightly, as her heart thudded in anxiety. Amy's shining eyes turned to her, bringing home the weight of her troubles.

Cody circled the cauldron and said a few more phrases, as the fire began to die. When it went out, Luna dared herself to creep over and peer inside to the mess of ashes left behind. For all her staring, they did not materialize back into the Rosebone.

CHAPTER FORTY-FOUR

LUNA AND AMY were blissful as they drove back home. Luna was in such a good mood that she had even considered hugging Cody ... if she wasn't so sure he would hurt her if she tried.

As they left the strange expanse of nothingness behind them, Amy blurted out, "Luna, I think I owe you an answer to that question you asked me before."

The bliss drained from Luna instantly. "Which one?"

"The one about what happened to me ... that day in the woods."

"Why talk about that now? It's over," Luna said, her stomach lurching with the promise of vomit.

Amy shrugged. "Maybe, but I feel guilty."

Luna licked her lips, out of words.

"Where should I begin?" Amy asked.

"Wherever you're comfortable," Luna said, gripping tighter into the steering wheel though she'd rather Amy not say a word at all.

They had been on Cloud Nine, why couldn't it stay that way?

Amy nodded and took in a deep breath as she braced herself to divulge her memories. Luna wondered what caused her to willingly take the cap off and let them free, when Luna would give anything to keep her bad memories contained. Maybe it was the journey they had shared, or the fact that it was finally over.

"I don't remember much about the trip," Amy admitted. "Chance must've broken into my room during the night, because when I woke up, I was bound in the backseat of his truck."

Luna shivered, remembering how Chance had forced her inside by holding a gun to her head. It seemed he had different methods for everyone.

"I thought it was all a dream," she admitted.

"What changed your mind?" Luna asked.

"When Chance stopped the truck and tried to make me get out. I refused … of course. He got angry and looked me right in the face. His eyes were *green* with his anger. It was like he was morphing into some kind of monster before my eyes, and I couldn't move when I saw that."

When I didn't move, I got stabbed, Luna thought. "Then what happened?"

"I kept telling him no, and he got so mad, he hit me," Amy said, her lip jutting out. "Several times. I listened after that … it was like my survival instincts kicked in."

Or you gave up.

Luna could remember sitting in the cabin alone, bleeding profusely from the hole in her stomach, as she covered the wound with her hands, her shirt … anything she could reach, in the hopes of keeping herself from bleeding out. Death had seemed easier, it had seemed *better*.

"What did he want you to do?"

"He wanted me to go into the temple. He had already set up the candles and made me sit on the floor before he tied up my feet. He went to get a jar. I thought it was colored water at first, but then he dumped it on the ground, and I could *smell* the blood. It went everywhere," she said. "When he was done, he stuffed a rag in my mouth and *smiled* at me. He had the *audacity* to be happy after everything he had done. Can you believe that?"

Luna nodded dully, the haunting memory of his whistle in her head. "Did he leave after that?"

"Yeah, but he didn't tell me where he was going."

"He went to kill Violet," Luna stated. She had gone through the timeline that day so many times in her mind that she had Chance's movements down to the minute.

"I wish I could've stopped him," Amy said, bowing her head. "I had all the power to, but when it mattered … I just froze up. I was so *scared* … I guess that's two deaths that are on me."

Luna set her hand on Amy's shoulder, and she looked at it in surprise. "In the end, he knew he was a monster—just remember that."

"Yeah," Amy said, "but there's one thing I don't understand about that day. Why didn't you stay and get help when the EMTs came? You were *bleeding*."

Luna pulled the truck to a halt. "I was scared to go to the police. There was no way they would've believed any of the story I had to tell them, and I didn't want people to know … what he did to me. My Dad especially. I … actually tried to go to the police after Susan disappeared, but they all but laughed me out of their office. I couldn't face that again … have people not believe me. I regretted the choice later, but at the time, what the hell did I know? Chance was the bane of my existence."

"I-I'm sorry," Amy said, twining her fingers uncertainly.

"I'm sorry for a lot of things that happened, too," Luna snarled before stepping out of the truck, leaving Amy alone.

***

AMY STARED AFTER Luna, trying to catch a glimpse of the emotion on her face. It was hard to tell if the truth had made an impact or not. She got up hesitantly and moved to follow her friend into the house, when she heard Luna's bedroom door shut.

She has a lot of problems, Amy thought. She couldn't imagine being hurt the way she was and not telling anyone. She had cracked, so badly that she had been locked up.

She's stronger than I'll ever be, Amy thought as she stepped into the hallway.

"Ah, Amy, there you are," Rose's voice said from behind her.

Amy turned to look at her through wide eyes.

"Did you talk to Luna?" the woman asked.

Amy nodded. "Yeah, but she didn't say much."

Rose's shoulders drooped. "I can't say I'm surprised."

"I think she blames herself a lot for Violet's death," Amy said softly, wondering just how much Rose knew about the twisted relationship between Chance and her daughter.

"Knowing her, she probably blames herself for her roommate's death, too. Do you think she was …" Rose stopped, looking at a loss for words before she finally managed, "*raped?*"

Amy let out a long breath through her nose. "Yeah, I think so." When Rose made a squealing sound in her throat, Amy continued. "I don't know what to say to her at this point, Rose. I opened up to her, but she keeps her feelings to herself. I think she's scared of being judged for what happened."

"Why would she feel like that? Doesn't she understand that I love her?"

"I don't think it's as simple as that. I don't know what she thinks exactly, but I know one thing … she doesn't want to look weak," Amy said, glancing down the hall again. "After everything she's been through, I don't blame her."

CHAPTER FORTY-FIVE

THREE DAYS PASSED without a sign of Chance, and Luna didn't know how to feel.

Perhaps the most troubling part was the realization that she *missed* him ... so much so that she had taken the time to dig out his letter, which had been carefully hidden in her underwear drawer like some kind of paraphernalia, and reread it, haunted with questions she feared she would never receive answers for.

Tomorrow was Friday, the date of Michelle's funeral. Between that unpleasant reminder and the odd conversation she had had with Amy, she made sure to avoid her as much as possible in the days that followed. If Chance had somehow survived, did he have an idea about the dilemma she faced?

I dug my own grave this time, she thought and curled up into a ball under the safety of her covers.

Sleep was remarkably easy for her to come by with her troubled mind. When she opened her eyes, the familiar trees of DreamWorld surrounded her, and it was hard to tell what side she was on, but hopefully it would be somewhere she could find Chance. She stunned herself with the thought, but convinced herself it was because of how unsure she felt about seeing Max, Sarah and Amanda again. Gritting her

271

teeth, she pushed the problem to the back of her mind.

Chance was all that mattered.

Maybe if she couldn't find him in reality, she could find him in the land he felt the most comfortable and see if the bond was really broken. She let that thought course through her as she made her way through the trees, and when she reached the clearing with the cabin, she caught sight of his form as he crossed the grass away from her. Her heart beat with a sickeningly strong beat of anticipation, and she ran to close the gap between them.

Panting, she set a hand on his shoulder. "Chance … wait! I-I have some questions for you."

He turned to look at her with a distant look on his face, his sapphire eyes sparkling as he smiled at her sadly. "I'm not ready to talk about it."

Without another word, he turned to walk away. Stupefied, Luna stood in place with loneliness hitting her the hardest yet. Suddenly, it didn't seem like a good thing anymore.

***

WHEN LUNA WOKE that morning, her face and pillow were covered in a thin layer of tears. She blinked to try and clear away the sting that crying had caused. The pain Chance had inflicted in her dream carried into reality and she winced—never before would she have thought his disinterest in her could cause her to feel as badly as she did. It was unfair. Hadn't she wanted this? The bond to be broken, him to disappear? She lay in bed, staring at the ceiling, as if she were searching for the answer in the uncaring white paint.

I'm alone.

That one single thought haunted her as she progressed through getting dressed, in a way no other thought had. When she finished getting herself ready, she dared a glance at her reflection in the mirror. The black shirt and skirt, her proper funeral attire, delicately clung to her small frame. It was looser than it had been … the result of her sparse meals.

A knock on the door caused her to jump as it pulled her attention back to reality. "Ready, Luna?" Rose's voice called from the other side of the door.

The tension stiffened her shoulders at the sound of her voice. Despite the days that had passed, Luna was still sore at her mother for turning on her, convinced she was behind Amy's "sweet" talk.

"Yeah," she replied flatly and took a deep breath to calm herself, as she continued to look at her reflection. She didn't like the dark glint that appeared in her eyes when she was angry.

Who am I? she thought.

The sight of the evil on her own face made her feel ashamed. She pulled her gaze away from the mirror and opened the door to pass Rose without a word.

"It's good to see you're ready," she remarked.

Luna stopped, smiling in a very Chance-like attitude. "It's nice to see you still have an attitude."

"Excuse me?" Rose asked.

"You heard me," Luna said, lifting her chin.

"That mouth is unnecessary."

"I think it's warranted."

"Why? What did I do?" Rose asked, putting her hands on her hips.

Luna gaped at her. "What did you do? You have no idea what thoughts have run through *my* mind. Yet, it doesn't seem like *you* care about anything besides Amy."

Rose stared at her as if she had just told her she was secretly a dragon. "You haven't been having suicidal thoughts, have you?"

The tone swinging suddenly from anger to concern, caught Luna off guard. The silence sufficed as an answer to Rose, and she rushed toward Luna to pull up her sleeves, checking her wrists.

"Mom, what are you doing?" Luna demanded, stumbling backward. She tripped over her shoelaces and landed painfully on her tailbone, groaning at the pain that ran up her spine. She was too distracted to realize her skirt had fluttered upward when she hit the ground.

Rose noticed the cuts on her thigh instantly. "What are those?" she asked, her voice nearly hysterical.

Luna glanced at where she pointed and realized that her two gashes were exposed. "They're nothing," she said defensively, rushing to stand to her feet.

Rose grabbed her wrist. "Did you do that to yourself?"

Luna ripped her arm out of Rose's grip. "No. I'm taking Amy to the funeral. I'll see you later."

Luna rushed down the hall, momentarily pausing to grab her keys, and ran out the door before Rose could say another word. She was glad Amy was sitting outside, already prepared to go.

"Come on, I'm driving," Luna said, leading the way toward the truck without hesitation.

She caught the look on Amy's face, but said nothing. Luna climbed into the driver's seat and glanced at the seat beside her as she waited for Amy to climb in. The sight of the empty passenger's seat reminded her of the yellowed envelope that contained Chance's note.

Amy settled herself into the seat, watching Luna as she began to drive. "I thought Rose was supposed to take us. Is she okay?"

Luna pursed her lips. "She'll drive herself."

Amy looked out the window.

Luna was glad for her silence as she drove to Chance's cemetery, her mind stuck on Chance's letter and the dream where he had flat-out rejected her. It was something to see that he was still alive in DreamWorld, but he seemed … different. Did he know their bond was broken? Or was he still upset about his note?

He should never have had me look for it.

Suddenly, she placed herself in his shoes. It was hard for her to understand him, but that was because she had no idea about everything he had gone through. If she had lived his life, she wondered if she would've gone down the same path as him. Would she have handled the situation any differently?

Could she have?

Luna cleared her mind and pulled into the cemetery. Tearing her

274

mind apart would provide her none of the answers she needed. As soon as she parked, déjà vu hit her like a ton of bricks. Amy didn't seem to notice her dazed state as she climbed out of the truck, and the sound of the door closing brought Luna back to life.

She followed Amy across the field, and Luna caught the familiar sound of Rose's engine as she arrived. Luna glanced at her small friend from the corner of her eye. Amy walked with her head bowed; her long dark hair created a veil between Luna and herself. Amy didn't need any more stress today—she was already crying.

They approached other people, and Amy split away to go talk to her relatives, which was fine with Luna. The less time she had to talk, the better she felt. She stood at the edge of the group until she noticed Rose approaching from her car. Wanting to avoid a scene, Luna made her way through the group. For the time being, she was safe; Rose would never pick a fight with other people in earshot.

Worries of Rose quickly fell from Luna's mind when she caught sight of Michelle's coffin. The feelings she had managed to repress suddenly came to light. There would be no forgetting them and she stood frozen at the sight of the wooden box. One thing was for certain … she didn't want to approach it. She didn't want to see Michelle again, didn't want to see *how* she was … because of her.

Luna already found it difficult to eat and sleep; she couldn't imagine how much worse it could get to handle.

CHAPTER FORTY-SIX

MICHELLE'S FUNERAL HAD been the longest event of Luna's life. She sat beside Amy as the tiny girl sobbed, her shoulders rigid with guilt and fear, but she couldn't bring herself to cry, and wondered if Amy would find it suspicious. The thought brought back that tiny whispering paranoid voice in her head. As the Pastor spoke, Luna kept her eyes focused solely on the ground, too scared to make eye contact with anyone, in the fear that she would find judgment in their eyes, which made no sense, because, apart from Amy, they were all strangers to her.

Chance was right about one thing, I am paranoid.

When the service ended, Luna never felt more relieved. Amy hardly seemed to notice her presence as she got up and trotted a few feet closer to Michelle's freshly covered grave. Luna was hesitant to follow, instead staying a foot away from the chair she sat in like she was chained to it. After a few minutes, Luna realized Amy and her relatives were talking of planting flowers. Not wanting to draw suspicion to herself, Luna offered to help, but Amy insisted she go home and rest.

Luna didn't plan on arguing.

Going home meant facing Rose, which would be a battle on its own. Her mother had left the cemetery a few minutes before the service ended, and Luna knew she had gone home to wait on her daughter. The thought made Luna's blood boil, but her choice was easy—she would much rather feel anger than guilt. Having nowhere else to go, and the weight of her evil deed residing heavily on her subconscious, Luna finally headed home. She parked the truck out front, staring at Rose's car in the driveway. When Luna turned off the engine, she stayed in the vehicle and took a few deep breaths.

When she found her nerve, she made her way to the house and winced as she walked through the front door, expecting Rose to berate her the second she stepped inside. Instead, silence greeted her. Luna was hopeful. Maybe Rose had given up and retreated to her room.

About time.

Relieved, Luna walked down the hall toward her own room, when scuffling sounds took her focus. She opened the door to her room to find the place had been trashed. Rose stood there, in the middle of the mess, tears streaking her face. She turned to toss some papers to the floor as Luna stepped hesitantly into the room.

"Mom! What are you doing?" she demanded.

Rose turned to look at her. "What am *I* doing?" she asked, her voice hysterical. "What are *you* doing with this?"

It was then Luna realized Rose was holding Chance's dagger, swinging it as she spoke for emphasis. Luna flinched at the movement, horrified at the sight of the knife. Rose had found the weapon that connected Luna to Michelle and Kylie, and she had no idea of the weight it carried.

"Mom, you know how I got it! You were there when Chance left it to me in his will!" she snapped, surprised at how strong her voice sounded with the nervousness eating her up inside. She moved to yank the weapon away from her mother, but Rose swung it out of Luna's reach.

"There's blood on the blade!" she screeched.

Despite her anger, Luna's heart pounded with an odd sensation of fear. It was hard to distinguish what Rose thought through her hysteria, but Luna knew all too well the panic that was running through her own mind. She was positive she had cleaned the blood well after Michelle's murder, but the night was too hazy for her to remember one way or the other.

"It's mine!" she spat finally, showing her teeth. *If I get out of this, it'll be a miracle.*

"I know it is!" Rose sobbed, dropping the knife to the floor, as if she suddenly didn't want to see it anymore. The solid metal clanked loudly on the wood, pronouncing her mood swing. She took a step toward her daughter, setting her hands on both shoulders as she looked into Luna's eyes. "Why are you doing this to yourself?"

Luna could see the sorrow glittering in her eyes and her anger disappeared. Her mom wasn't turning on her, because she hated her ... she was *worried* about her. Luna was the only close family she had left.

"You would never understand if I told you," Luna replied, knowing it was the complete truth.

"If that's the case, then you need therapy," Rose said briskly. "I'll see if—"

"No, Mom," Luna said flatly, her voice sharp with her lack of emotion.

"What?" she asked, clearly baffled as she took her hands off of Luna.

"I said, no, Mom. I don't want therapy."

"B-but you need it," she stammered.

Luna shook her head. "I don't *need* it. I *need* time. Now, please, for both our sakes, let this go."

"I'm gonna find help for you," Rose said, determination surging in her voice. "You'll see it's what you need."

"Mom," Luna said, as anger came back. "I'll be fine. Besides, therapy didn't help me before, what would be different now?"

"Then talk to *me*," Rose said, blinking at her. "Maybe I can help you work through something."

Luna was silent. "I can't do that."

"Why not?"

"Talking won't help anything."

"How would you know? You never try."

"Call it intuition. Whatever the case, I need to be alone right now." Luna closed her eyes.

She heard Rose breathe in through her teeth in the same way that she did when she was irritated. "Fine, but you need help, and I'm going to find you some," she stated and left the room.

Luna's anger nearly choked her. Why was Rose so *stubborn*? Luna screamed once in frustration, but didn't feel any better for the effort. She took a step toward her bed and stepped on a notebook. With effort, she picked it up, only after processing the fact that it was the one Rose had given her on Christmas and not the original.

It seems I'll be able to get use out of it after all, Luna thought, scooping a pen up off the floor. She sat on the edge of her bed, with the chaos of her room surrounding her, and opened the cover. Writing the dark details of her life had helped her in the past. Maybe it still could. *It can't hurt to try*.

She opened the notebook on her lap and began to write:

It hasn't even been a month since poor Asher left this world, and I know I'll be changed forever for the experience. Nothing feels the same as it did when I was pregnant. Everything was simpler then ... I wish I could say the same for now. I have no hope, I have no sanity, I have no one.

I'm utterly alone.

I found myself forced to create a veneer of strength, just to benefit the people around me. Just to keep them happy. I cut myself to vent, but even that doesn't help me much. I'm not allowed to be who I am, but maybe it's for a good reason.

I stopped believing in fairy tales a long time ago, because there's no such thing as a 'happy ending.' The only real ending is death, and I don't think anyone's *happy* about it.

I hurt Kylie in the heat of the moment. Chance was right about that one. He might've destroyed my uterus, but the doctor said Asher would've had a chance to be saved if *someone* had been there. At least to me, her death is warranted.

I have no idea why I hurt Michelle.

It was the worst mistake of my life. I had no real reason to do it ... I only did what I was told. Like a child. My actions are coming back to bite me now. Life is so hard—every day seems to drag on, and I don't see much purpose in fighting anymore. Mom found out about my cutting and that didn't go well, of course. I can hear her breaking something in the kitchen as I write this.

But what am I to do?

I understand I upset her greatly, but I don't think she understands how much she hurt **me**. I still can't get over the way she turned on me about Amy. She has no idea about the dilemma that goes on inside my mind, every single day. She doesn't even know I should be buried out in that cemetery along with everyone else I know. I can't fully blame her. Of course, she can't see how fragile I am.

I have to put on that stupid happy face in public. See how my life has become irony? Before I used to know the difference between reality and insanity, right and wrong; now is a different story. Chance's words have tricked me in ways I can't explain, though honestly, I'm not really sure why.

When she was finished writing, she closed the notebook and stared at the plain cover. Somehow, it seemed too normal for the insane thoughts she had scrawled inside. It needed to look as demonic as she sounded. She took her pen and carefully carved the word "Confessions" into the cover.

CHAPTER FORTY-SEVEN

LUNA SET HER notebook and Chance's dagger on her end table so she wouldn't lose them, as she went to work, cleaning up the mess Rose had created. It wasn't long before Luna heard something else break from the kitchen, and she knew Rose was still on her rampage. Sighing, she turned to glance out into the hallway, guessing the only way to calm Rose down would be to confront her.

The remains of a few plates were scattered across the kitchen floor, and Rose was backed into the corner; tears streaked her reddened face as she hyperventilated. Luna stepped nervously into the kitchen, worried about what reaction her mother would have next. Luna was glad Amy wasn't home to see this.

"Mom! What are you doing?" she asked.

"I'm a terrible parent!" she wailed.

Luna blinked, confused. "What are you talking about, Mom? You're not a terrible parent!"

"You're my only child and look at you!" she said. "You're a disaster! I can't help you."

Luna tried to blink away the immediate hurt, and said, "Mom, it's not fair to react like this. You know what I just went through! I lost my *child*, Mom. That's not something I can get over that easily. I mean, I can't imagine you were much better than this after Dad died."

282

"I did what I was supposed to do, Luna. I went to the counseling I thought was needed, and I got better."

Luna laughed and shook her head. "Do you really believe that? You think sitting in some room with a stranger can solve your problems? Because it can't. The only one who can help you, is *you*!"

Rose frowned at her daughter.

"Don't frown, Mom. You *know* it didn't help. You haven't gotten better. Look at how much you've changed since Dad died! You used to be so in charge, you never did *this* before!" She gestured to the broken plates on the floor. "And where's your hijab? I haven't seen you wear it in too long to count."

Rose scoffed. "I went to therapy for *weeks*. You're not gonna stand here and tell me it was all for nothing."

"Whatever therapy you had obviously didn't help!" Luna pointed out. "Why are you defending something that's useless? Grief can't be talked out of you. No one can tell you how to grieve properly!"

"That may be true, but how can I get better when my only daughter hides her pain from me?" she demanded. "I don't even feel like we're family."

"I'm sorry you feel that way … really, I am, but I do what I have to do," Luna replied, sending Rose's line back at her. "If I allow my emotions to show, then it hurts you."

"More than this?"

When Luna didn't respond, Rose looked like she was either on the brink of crying or screaming. Maybe both. Her daughter watched her through uncertain eyes, as her mother suddenly passed her, stomping out of the kitchen, toward the front door. She grabbed her keys and ran outside. Luna followed her.

"Mom! Where are you going?" she called after her.

Rose didn't say anything or even pass a glance over her shoulder as she hurried into her car and sped off. Luna stayed standing in the grass as she watched her go, her lips pushed into a pencil straight line. The frustration welled even stronger in her and Luna ran to the backyard, suddenly too overwhelmed with emotion to think clearly. The

283

dam that had held in every bit of insanity and emotion vanished. She felt *crazy*. It was the only word she could think of to describe herself. She yowled out her frustrations to the sky, not caring who heard her. She was so mad at everything, but nothing more than herself. As soon as her outburst faded into silence, she collapsed to her knees in the snow. She didn't feel the cold as her mind tried to desperately uncover herself from the burden that buried her.

"Are you okay?" Chance called, with worried in his voice.

She looked up through the thick veil of her raven-colored hair and tears to see him standing there, his face creased with concern. Her eyes bulged slightly and she smiled when she caught sight of him, but it wasn't out of happiness. The sight of him hit her like an extra, un-needed pain to slice through the troubles already weighing her down.

How could she still see him? Luna closed her eyes again, wishing her tears away. Asking Amy how this was possible would mean admitting the truth—that he had been by her side the entire time, guiding her like a literal demon on her shoulder, but the only alternative would be to ask Chance himself. With that option, came the time where she would have to admit what she and Amy had done, that she had met Cody, that she had had the Rosebone *destroyed*.

Either way, she couldn't risk it.

"Finally ready to talk to me again?"

"I'm sorry if I hurt you by being short. I meant nothing against you. I think we both just needed some time," he said.

Luna kept her face guarded as she listened to his words. *Did* he know what she and Amy had done? "Sure," she replied simply.

He visibly struggled for something to say and as she stared at him, she realized just how much easier everything would be if he was *gone* from her memory. He was supposed to be her *enemy*, her worst nightmare. Yet, here she was, taking his pain for him to add to the pile. For what? She stood to her feet, brushing the snow off of her knees.

"I hate my life," she stated simply.

His face was bland, but his eyes betrayed his sorrow as he watched her. It was obvious he hadn't expected her topic choice. "What happened?"

Where to begin with that question.

"Rose found out I cut myself, and now she's freaking out. I have no idea where she went. All I know is, she found your blade with some blood on it, and I panicked she would connect it to Michelle's death," she said.

"You ... *cut,* again?"

Luna stared back at him, and inside, she kicked herself as she remembered she had been keeping that from Chance, too. "No," she said looking away.

Suddenly, Chance's ghostly fingers gently touched her under her chin as he turned her face back toward him. The contact was as real as if Chance had never jumped from that building, and deep in her gut came an unsettling whisper, a possibility she hadn't considered—what if the destruction of the Rosebone *wasn't* the end of their bond?

"Let me see," he demanded.

"Why? You already knew."

"We have more in common than you think," he said, and when Luna offered him a questioning gaze, he lifted his sleeve to reveal a myriad of scars.

Luna remembered seeing the purple marks the night of her car crash earlier that year, but had never bothered to ask how he got them.

"Your turn," he said, dropping the sleeve to cover his ghostly arm.

Luna was hesitant before she gave in. She lifted the bottom of her black skirt to show the heavy, ragged wounds that lined her leg. Chance glanced at them and back at her without a change in emotion.

"Why did you do it?" he asked.

She stared deep into his blue eyes. There was something about the way he spoke so calmly that tugged at a part of her that Rose's anger had failed to reach, and the pile of battered emotions fell apart. A sob fell suddenly from her lips. "I don't know."

He wrapped his arm around her as she began to cry, and she didn't fight. She moved closer before blurting out, "I-I can't stop thinking about your note," through her waterfall of tears.

He pulled back to look at her before his gaze darkened. "You must think I'm insane for writing that."

She scoffed. "No more than I ever did."

"What did you really think?" he asked, pulling his arm off of her as he turned away.

"It was sad," Luna said softly. "Not in a pathetic way ... but ... *heartbreaking*. I can't believe anyone could ever feel like that ... especially you."

He was silent.

"Were you depressed?"

Chance shrugged. "Most of the time, I didn't even know who I was."

"It's just ... were you ... you know ... *you* when you wrote that?"

Chance almost looked hesitant to answer.

"You don't have to answer that," Luna said.

He shook his head. "No, it's a fair question, I guess. I was perfectly coherent. It's kind of a short note, but it took me hours to write it. It was hard to decide what I wanted my final words to be, when I just wanted to rant and rant like a maniac. When I picked up a pen, I never wanted it to stop."

"Did you really kill yourself, because of me?" she asked, her voice barely audible.

"Would you hate me if I said 'yes'?" he asked, peering up at her through his lashes.

Luna's frown deepened. "No, I wouldn't hate you. I'd have another thing to hate about myself." She bowed her head as the first tear dripped from her eyes. Even after all Chance had done to her, it hurt her to know the pain she had caused. *Why am I so damn* human?

Chance wiped her tears away with shaking fingers. "Hey," he said softly. "I don't want you to blame yourself for it. It was a long time coming."

"How can you even pretend? Despite everything you went through, you held on and tried to make your life better. Because of me, you didn't even care to *try* anymore," she said.

Chance shook his head. "Not true. It was our *baby* who made me not want to try anymore."

She snorted at the callous statement. "How was it Asher's fault?"

"Babies are one of the most innocent things in the world. To think one of them would be *mine*; to think it would share my looks and personality. To think it would learn from *me*," he said. "I knew I wasn't good enough to raise a child. Just like the rest of the world, he would be better off without me."

Silence hung in the air as Luna digested his words. If even death hadn't helped him conquer his twenty years' worth of pain, frustration and loneliness, then what hope was there for her?

CHAPTER FORTY-EIGHT

LUNA STARED AT him. "I'm sorry."

"Don't be," he said, but the tick in his jaw didn't help her feel any better. "It was my own fault you hated me for all those years."

Luna blinked once, and he was gone. She sighed, her heart heavier than ever. There was so much to think about that she almost wished the world would stop for a little while to give her time to sort it all out. She was glad she had broken the bond, yet nothing had changed. He was still here, and she was still too far gone to save. With the chill of the snow finally sinking in, she made her way inside. Rose's car was *still* nowhere in sight, and Luna wondered idly how long she would be gone.

Would it really be so bad if she never came back?

Luna went to the living room to wait, thinking maybe she *had* overreacted. She and her mother had done nothing, but butt heads for too long, and she missed feeling close to the only remaining member of her family. On the night of Asher's death, they had held each other and cried. Rose was capable of support … Luna just didn't know how to pull it out of her.

She's hurting too, she reminded herself. *Your mother is a door of mercy that Allah opened for you. Don't ever close it.* The resounding thought caused her to squeeze her eyes shut even tighter.

Luna sat on the couch, waiting. She twirled her thumbs, her mind so lost in thoughts that she didn't bother to turn on the television. Was it possible that after everything she had gone through, she had become insane? *I think that ship sailed a long time ago.* She couldn't remember the last time her life had been normal. Had it *ever* been? When Rose finally returned home, Luna wasn't sure which approach she should take.

"Oh, uh, hi," she said, trying to hurry to the kitchen.

"Mom, wait," Luna said, standing to her feet. Rose turned to look at her, and she could see the uncertainty in her eyes. "Are you okay?"

Rose nodded. "Yeah, how are you feeling?"

"I … don't know anymore. I'm so sorry for everything, Mom," Luna said, wishing she could see the sincerity in her eyes. "I don't know what's wrong with me anymore. M-maybe I do need therapy."

"The choice is up to you. If you want, Miss Hannigan will see you at any time. She took good care of me after your father's death, even if you don't want to believe it."

Luna sighed at the thought of facing her old therapist again. After high school, she had agreed to only one session with Miss Hannigan and had never gone back. It had seemed easier to move, ignore the problem, and pray it would go away, but things had a way of coming back around. Max had made the same realization. The only difference was, his mistake had ruined her life. *And people are still paying for mine.*

"Can we go now?" she asked.

Rose looked at her through wide eyes. "Are you sure?"

"Maybe it'll help me this time."

"Why the change of heart?"

Luna shrugged, knowing Rose would be happy for the trip if she answered or not.

As predicted, Rose didn't push the conversation as she led her daughter to the car and to Miss Hannigan's office. Luna guessed she feared that any resistance at all would cause Luna to change her mind.

In reality, Luna chewed on her lip, hoping she would be able to keep everything inside. If she slipped even once about Chance, it could be bad. Miss Hannigan would have her committed for a seventy-two-hour psychiatric hold if she knew the truth, but it was a risk she would have to take. Luna hated the strain forming between her and her mother. The wall that she had slowly built around herself over the years finally managed to seclude her from the world immediately around her, and she didn't know how to escape from it, or if she even could. She wanted a clean slate, and making her mother happy was the only way she could picture that happening.

Rose checked her in, and Luna's anxiety grew stronger as they sat in the uncomfortably silent waiting room. She leafed through the old magazines on the table until it was her turn to go back. She bid Rose a farewell smile she hoped Rose wouldn't see was fake and followed Miss Hannigan into the small secluded room, her heart rate increasing the closer to the cozy room they got.

"Luna, it's been a while," Miss Hannigan said as she took a seat in her large chair.

Luna nodded and sat awkwardly on the edge of the chaise lounge.

"What's on your mind today?" she asked.

"I-I just … things have been strained between me and my mother," Luna said.

Miss Hannigan bobbed her head. "Why do you think that is?"

Luna crinkled her brow. "I don't know. Isn't it your job to figure it out?"

"Hmm, is there something you don't want to tell me?"

Luna barely heard her as she remembered details of her last visit. She had been nursing the stab wound in her stomach in secret, but the pain had burdened her, despite her efforts to hide it. Rose had hoped therapy would help her cope with Violet's death, but that was only one of the problems her daughter had been facing. Luna had been emotionally shot as well.

She was starting to regret her decision to come, with the memories making it much harder to focus than it should have been. The scar in her stomach felt suddenly raw, and Luna sighed, tapping her fingers against her knee with the loud ticking of the clock behind her head. Everything would unravel if she told her what was on her mind.

"I think I made a mistake coming here," Luna admitted, with no emotion on her face. "I just wanted to make my mom happy. Is it okay if I leave now?"

Miss Hannigan looked up from her notebook. "But, Luna, we just started. I don't think your mom would be happy paying for an hour you didn't use."

Luna sighed and turned to glance out the window. The breeze outside gently blew the branches of the nearby tree against the building, and the scratching sound was faintly irritating.

"How are you feeling?" Miss Hannigan asked.

"I feel fine," Luna said, keeping her eyes on the window.

The therapist frowned. "You do know Rose has talked to me about your situation, right?"

Luna nodded absently, but still couldn't find the words to talk.

Miss Hannigan sighed, twitching her nose. "All right, let me ask you a different question. Have you had any dreams recently, anything significant?"

"I have nightmares of monsters," Luna said slowly, her eyes moving from the window to the plant in the corner of the room. An image of Max's face filled her mind, and she had to blink to hold in the tears. "They come in and kill everyone around me."

"Do they kill you, too?"

"No, because I'm one of them," she said, thinking of the look in Chance's eyes as he freed her from the circle of her dead classmates.

"Why do you think that is?" Miss Hannigan asked, peering up from her notebook.

Luna shrugged. *My whole life I was surrounded by them.* "I don't know. I guess I feel guilty."

"Is it about Amy moving in?"

Guilt came from many aspects of her life, Amy was just one. "I don't want her in Asher's room. Too much is changing too fast. We set it up for him … she can't have it."

"Who is Asher?"

"My son."

"It must have been hard to go through what you did. How did it make you feel when he passed?"

"Sad, of course. What kind of question is that?"

Miss Hannigan jotted something down before she looked back up at her. "You have an understanding he's passed, and yet you don't want Rose to clean out his room. You're having trouble letting him go?"

Luna balled her hands into fists. "This is stupid. He shouldn't have had to die! After everything I've been through, it should've been me … not him."

Miss Hannigan raised her eyebrows in surprise. "Luna, what exactly have you been through?"

Luna bit her lip, extinguishing her rage and holding back her tears at the same time. "Everyone around me dies," she said softly, "and I can't save them."

"Rose told me about the fire," Miss Hannigan said. "The one who hurt your friend, Amanda. I think what you're experiencing is survivor's guilt."

Luna laughed and looked at her hands. It wasn't survivor's guilt; it was deeper than that. It had been her job to protect her friends, but she watched them all fall, one by one, because of her.

"This is pointless," she said, standing to her feet before she bolted from the room.

Rose looked up at her through wide eyes as she stormed into the waiting room. "What's the matter?"

"Nobody can help me," Luna said with tears trailing down her cheeks, as she whipped open the door and left.

***

THAT LOOK, THE one Rose had dreaded, was all she could see through Luna's tears when she busted out of Miss Hannigan's office like the place was about to explode. She glanced at her watch—not even an hour had passed. Sighing, she got up and paid the receptionist for the mostly unused session and headed outside to find Luna.

Rose had been so hopeful on the drive up, thinking maybe Luna was finally pulling herself from her pit of despair, to find the help that

Rose had been unable to after giving away Cassandra, but part of her expected it to go like this ... to end in bitter failure.

Rose thought of the unsaved number in her phone—*Cassandra's* number, which she had tried unsuccessfully for years to work up the nerve to call—and knew there were some things that could only be resolved on your own and in your own way.

She could only pray that Luna hadn't found solace somewhere she shouldn't.

***

YOU'RE HAVING TROUBLE letting him go?

As Luna was curled up in bed that night, all she could hear were Miss Hannigan's words.

It's a stupid question, she thought. *Any mother who lost her child would be in the same boat as me.*

After everything she had lost, it was only natural to try to hold onto the few things she had left. Luna knew it had been a technique to spark a reaction—which it had—but Luna still hated Miss Hannigan for it.

Luna closed her eyes, trying to block out her thoughts. She wanted to sleep, a deep dreamless sleep that would let her escape the pain for only a little while, and wondered if she would see Max. The thought that she would *never* see him again, gave her a weird feeling in the pit of her stomach, but lately, everything did.

CHAPTER FORTY-NINE

WHEN LUNA WOKE up that morning, her mind was still cluttered with thoughts of Asher, and she felt worse for going to see Miss Hannigan, not better. *Every time I make a choice, it always ends up being a mistake.*

She sighed and brushed her messy hair back, before she went to the bathroom to clean herself up. When she went out to the living room, she realized Rose was gone, and she guessed she was at work. The house was oddly silent with Amy gone as well. Luna wondered where she could've gone.

She turned to head back to her room when she noticed Chance staring at her. "So … we haven't talked about that therapy session."

Luna raised a hand and walked past him to her room. "Don't. I don't even want to think about it," she said, throwing on the nearest outfit.

"Do you feel any better?" Chance asked, raising an eyebrow.

Luna shrugged. "I don't feel anything anymore, honestly."

"Where are you going?" he asked, folding his arms over his chest.

"For a walk. I don't like how quiet it is here," she said.

Chance nodded and watched her walk down the hallway. She grabbed her jacket and wrapped it around herself as she stepped outside, and the crisp breeze blew through her hair. She let out a breath of air, watching the puff that appeared. The cold was a good distraction from her thoughts.

Everyone's happy now, that's what matters, she told herself.

"You're not happy," Chance said suddenly.

She sighed and turned and looked at him. She hadn't realized he had been following her the entire time. "Are you a mind reader now?"

"Just good at reading your face."

"I'll cope," she said.

"By freezing to death?" he asked.

Luna frowned. "I guess I should go home," she said, but when she turned, she realized Chance had already disappeared.

He lost interest, she guessed, shrugging, as she made her way back home.

The cold was enough to make her teeth chatter, and she dug her fingers deeper into the depths of her pockets, in search of any trace of warmth she could find, brainstorming things she could do at home that would keep her mind busy.

When she got home, she reveled in the warmth as she hung up her coat and slid off her shoes. She headed to her room, hoping the manual labor of cleaning would distract her for a while. Swiping her hair out of her eyes, she turned out of the hallway to see Amy sitting on her bed.

"When did you get h—" Luna started to say when she realized Amy had her notebook open on her lap. "No!" Luna uttered, lunging forward to pull it away from her.

Amy twisted away to continue reading before she looked up at Luna through wide, horrified eyes. "It was you," she said softly, the horror as clear in her voice as it was on her face.

"N-no! You read it wrong!" Luna said, desperately trying once again to snatch the book from her friend.

"You killed Michelle?" Amy asked, her voice a hushed whisper as she skimmed the page again.

"No!" Luna blurted out stupidly, too shocked to even *begin* to think of an excuse. Her heart pounded painfully against her ribs, and she could hear the blood pumping in her ears, making it difficult for her to focus on the situation at hand.

"That's what you wrote here!" Amy said, standing to her full height with the notebook dangling weakly from her hand.

"But it's not what it sounds like!"

"I don't see how I could be mistaken!" She threw the notebook to the floor. "How could you do this to me!? I thought you were my *friend*! I *trusted* you! I was ready to give my life for you."

Luna stared at her friend, desperation giving way to acceptance. All the denying in the world wouldn't save her from the words she had written. "I don't have a reason," she said simply.

"How could you *kill* her, Luna? She was your *friend*!" Tears streaked Amy's face as she drew a breath of air.

"It wasn't me, it was Chance ... he...," she swallowed roughly. "He made me do it."

Amy shook her head from side to side, slowly. "I should have known something was wrong when you didn't cry at the funeral. This whole time ... I've been looking for Michelle's killer, and I've been living with her!"

"I did what I thought was right," Luna whispered, thinking ironically of the time Chance had fed her the same line.

"And what possible reason could you have had to kill her?"

"I was trying to help you!" Luna said, tears streaking her face.

"Did you really believe killing my sister could *help* me?"

"It *did* help you!" Luna said, desperately waving at Amy. "Do you think you would be out of Brentwood, if I hadn't done what I did?"

Amy was silent. "I'd be willing to go back, if it meant Michelle would still be alive. Even if me and her hadn't had the best relationship, she was still my sister. She never would have left me in there forever."

Luna ran through the argument she had had with Chance only a week ago. She had never decided what she would do if Amy found out the truth, and now she was in hot water, sinking fast with no way out.

"Don't you have anything to say for yourself?!" Amy yelled in Luna's face, pushing her back a step, as a sob rattled her body.

"You have to do it, Luna, you're out of time," Chance said

296

suddenly from behind her. "You didn't decide, so I'm making the choice for you. Now or never."

The time when her heart had been filled with righteousness was over. She was in the cycle—the very one Chance had warned her had killed him. She smiled at Chance as tears bubbled in her eyes. He was right … he was *always* right.

Why did I ever argue?

Amy scoffed, bringing Luna's attention back to her, as Luna hurried to grab the knife off of her dresser, and Amy's eyes widened when she caught sight of the dagger.

"What are you doing?" Amy asked hysterically, taking a small step away from her.

"What needs to be done," Luna said quietly.

"You'll never get away with this!" Amy screeched, falling backwards onto Luna's bed. "Help! Please! Anyone!"

"I'm sorry," Luna whispered, letting the tears coat her face.

She hovered over her friend, blade reared back ready to strike. Amy tried to roll out of range, but Luna reached forward to grab all of Amy's dark brown hair in her fist. Amy sobbed as the raw hysteria finally claimed every bit of her. Struggling, her body wrenching painfully, as she used every last bit of energy to try and escape Luna's grip. Luna only watched her, hesitating her next move.

"Please, Luna. I'm your friend," she insisted.

"Finish it," Chance's voice overlapped.

Luna sobbed and closed her eyes as she paused for the smallest second, before stabbing the knife into Amy's neck as she had done to her sister. The resistance almost caused Luna to stop, but she forced herself to add enough pressure to pop her windpipe as the knife pierced her throat. Amy gasped, and Luna let go of her hair, knowing the fight was over.

She kept her eyes closed as any sounds of life left Amy. After all she and Amy had been through, she couldn't watch her friend die.

"It's over," Chance announced.

Luna's eyes opened to take in the macabre sight before her. Amy was sprawled on her bed, the white covers stained red. She lay face down, and Luna was glad at the small blessing—at least she couldn't see the girl's face. She had managed to remove the dagger before she died and the blade was clutched loosely in her hand.

"You made a mess," Chance whispered.

Luna laughed once, the sound rough and sarcastic as she turned to look at him. "I don't care."

"You have to clean this up!" Chance urged, taking a desperate step forward as his sapphire eyes bored into hers.

"I *have* to?" she asked with a laugh and sunk to the floor. "What's the point?"

"Oh, my God!" a voice said from the doorway suddenly, and Luna realized it wasn't Chance this time.

It was Rose. She stood in the doorway, a hand over her mouth as she stared at Amy's bloody corpse. "Luna! What did you do?!"

Luna was silent as she observed the blood that dotted her hands. No excuse could cover it up.

"I knew something was wrong with you … that you needed help! But, I was too late …" she trailed off, placing a hand to her forehead as she leaned against the wall, appearing suddenly frail.

Luna still didn't acknowledge her. She kept her eyes on the floor, wishing more than anything that she was somewhere and something else.

"I'm gonna have to call the police," Rose said finally.

That caught Luna's attention. She looked up at her mother through red and swollen eyes. The look on her face was primitive, almost animalistic. Rose flinched at the evil she caught on her daughter's face.

"No," Luna said.

Chance watched in silence as she jumped up and pulled the bloody knife from Amy's hand. She walked on shaky legs toward her mother. Rose lifted her hands in a gesture to mean no harm, her face full of panic, as she watched her daughter approach.

"Luna, honey, let's talk about this," she said.

"I told you talking doesn't help."

"Okay, we don't have to talk. We can just sit and breathe. You don't have to do this."

"But don't you see I do? It's the cycle, Mom."

"The police will see you're mentally impaired, and then we can get you help. Please, think about your future!"

"I am," Luna said, her voice hoarse, and she broke eye contact.

Rose sensed the danger and tried to run, but Luna was a lot more athletically fit. With her mind empty of her conscious, she was deadly. She ran after her mother and caught up to her in the living room, sending the first stab through her abdomen, beneath her stomach. Rose grunted and toppled forward, desperately pulling herself along the floor, trying fruitlessly to escape her impending doom. Luna watched before she decided to waste any more time. She pounced on her, driving the knife through her again and again, splattering warm blood all over herself and the room.

Luna wasn't sure which stab was the final blow, but eventually, Rose stopped moving beneath her. Luna held the bloodstained knife above her mother's devastated body, panting, prepared to slash again if Rose showed any sudden signs of life. A moment later, the dagger slipped her from her hand to land in a pool of Rose's blood.

CHAPTER FIFTY

LUNA WAS GROGGY as she stood up. Without her adrenaline, she was dead on her feet. She stared down at the bloody corpse without an ounce of emotion, then turned and walked robotically to her room, her socks trailing through Rose's freshly spilled blood. Luna crawled into bed, on top of her bloodstained sheets, and rolled Amy's body onto the floor with a thump. She was still covered in Rose's blood, and now Amy's as well, but made no move to clean it off.

It barely registered in her mind that Chance had disappeared sometime during Rose's murder. All she could think of was what she had done. A pain in her chest turned her concentration back to Chance. All the haziness disappeared, and she understood everything about him; she understood the pressure he had collapsed under.

She wiped the blood off her face onto her arm and curled up, trying her best to sleep. It was the closest thing to disappearing she could fathom, without actually dying herself. When she opened her eyes again, she wasn't in her own dark reality, but the reality of DreamWorld. She stood in the grass outside Chance's cabin, wondering why she was there.

"Luna," Chance's voice greeted her.

Luna turned to watch him approach from the other side of the field, his face glowing under his blond hair.

"Chance," she said.

"You look tense," he observed.

Luna stared at him through watery eyes. "You disappeared. I needed you, and you weren't there."

"You didn't need me, Luna," he said softly. "You never have."

Luna was unable to speak as tears bubbled in the corners of her eyes. She couldn't blink them away. Chance came up to her and set a hand gently to the side of her face.

"I'm so sorry about everything I've ever done to you," Luna said, looking him in the eyes. "Y-your life wasn't easy to understand, but I know it was the hardest of anyone I ever met."

"It was," he whispered, stepping closer to set his free hand on her waist.

"I hate myself for not listening to you," she admitted. "I-I understand why you did what you did. *Everything* you did."

"That's all I ever wanted to hear," he said, locking his blue eyes on her.

"I-I can't live with myself anymore," Luna said, giving into her grief. "This has to stop."

At one time, she would've hated herself for shedding a tear in front of him, but things had changed. He was the last person standing in a world that, at one time, had looked so bright.

"Shh," he said comfortingly, bending forward to kiss her on the lips.

She pulled back and looked at him, a stray tear brushing her cheek. "What do I do, Chance?"

"I have an idea," he said, with a hint of a smile on his face.

"What is it?" she asked, her voice echoing with the absence of emotion.

He pulled a switchblade from his pocket, flicking out the blade, and Luna wiped at her eyes as she looked at him. "What are you going to do?"

"This is only going to hurt for a minute, then we'll be together forever," he said.

Before she could respond, he pulled the blade across her throat. The pain was fierce, burning with an unfathomable chill Luna never would have imagined. She held a hand to her skin, as her blood poured from the jagged wound. Her knees buckled, and she suddenly lost the energy to stand.

Chance reached out, catching her before she hit the ground, and he crouched beside her, holding her close to his chest. He dropped the bloodstained knife into the grass as he rubbed the top of her arm comfortingly. Luna gasped for air, struggling to breathe, as her own blood drowned her.

"It's almost over," Chance said, wiping a lock of hair from her eyes.

She looked up at him, knowing she was dying, but she felt no fear; she was *relieved*. He had freed her from the one monster she couldn't escape—herself.

Right before she took her last breath, she gave him a small smile. "Thank you."

EPILOGUE

THE RED ROBES billowed in the breeze as the members danced and bowed in a fluid rhythm, moving in a continuous circle around their victim, who lie in the very heart of their dance. He was dead now, finally succumbing to the multitude of stab wounds he had endured over the past few hours.

Cody had been the one to deal the final blow, and he eyed the bloody mound of flesh that had, at one time been alive, as the dance came to a close. He watched as a handful of the newest members grabbed the corpse and carried him away, before Cody turned and went into the compound. Despite his light footsteps, the sound echoed as he pulled off his red robe, before rounding the corner to go into his room.

He opened his closet and thrust his ceremony clothes inside, catching just a glimpse of the rose entwined bone sitting on his shelf, before he closed the door to submerge it in darkness.

About the Author

Kayla Krantz is a proud author, responsible for a number of fantasy novels, and is fascinated by the dark and macabre. Stephen King is her all-time inspiration, mixed in with a little bit of Eminem and some faint remnants of the works of Edgar Allen Poe. When she began writing, she started in horror, but somehow drifted into thriller and fantasy. She loves the 1988 movie, "Heathers." Kayla was born and raised in Michigan, but traveled across the country to where she currently resides, in Texas.

http://www.facebook.com/kaylakrantzwriter/
https://twitter.com/kaylathewriter9
https://authorkaylakrantz.com/

Other Works By This Author

The Council

(The Witch's Ambitions Trilogy Book One)

The Council is the governing Coven over the Land of Five, a region entirely inhabited—and split apart—by witches with varying powers. Lilith Lace, a witch thought to be born powerless, happily resides in Ignis, the Coven of Fire, until she suddenly develops telekinesis, an ability only seen in some witches born in Mentis, the Coven of the Mind. When The Council finds out about her odd development, she's taken under their wing and is finally told the truth—everything she's learned about the Land of Five, herself included, has been nothing but lies.